RINGS ON WATER

THE MATAKANA SERIES

MADELEINE ESKEDAHL

Matheson
BAY PRESS

PRAISE FOR BLOOD ON VINES

"Littered with twists and turns, Blood On Vines is one of those novels that will have you second guessing with motive and the killers identity again and again."

AustCrime

"I couldn't put it down...The second sentence gets you in the prologue, that's how gripping the novel is."

Kapiti Beach Radio

"This isn't evil for the sake of evil, Eskedahl knows the motivation... for it to really get under your skin."

RNZ, Standing Room Only

"Readers who enjoy a more traditional crime novel will love Eskedahl's debut set in the halcyon environs of Matakana wine country...But what elevates Blood On Vines are the multi-dimensional and relatable characters, something she worked hard to achieve...As the shocking events unfolds...Eskedahl expertly ramps up the tension to an action packed finale."

New Zealand Herald Canvas Magazine

"Eskedahl has a tight grasp on writing a crime thriller, emphasised by an obvious understanding of pacing, and a strong sense of place. This is an author to watch!

Chronicles of Crime

"Madeleine's willingness to wade into murky territory makes this an assured and exciting read."*Woman Magazine*

"Eskedahl brings a descriptive literate touch to the genre that will entice crime fiction aficionados. Blood On Vines is a solid start to what promises to be an interesting and distinctive local series."

The Police News Magazine

"From the opening page, Eskedahl sets up a thrilling mystery. It's beautifully written with fabulous description throughout until the plot brings you to a satisfying conclusion. So looking forward to the second book in the series. Well done Ms Eskedahl, take a bow."

Catherine Lea, author of The Water's Dead

"Eskedahl has written an immensely enjoyable murder mystery... word pictures are drawn, the Matakana area with its vineyards and nicely drawn characters. The mounting tension is handled well and there's just enough gruesomeness to satisfy the most discerning aficionados of the crime fiction genre The attractions of a wine growing area are beautifully evoked and I felt a close connection...I look forward to the next book in the series. *Reading High Reviews*

"In conclusion, this novel is worthy of a film screenplay for Netflix. It combines all the elements one could wish for - fast paced, escalating suspense, frequent plot twists and secrets. Subtle clues, psycho-thriller, and the best of all, wait for it...a surprising end."

S Fairchild

This edition published by Matheson Bay Press 2023

ISBN 9781738594900

This book is set in New Zealand and written in British English.

A catalogue record for this book is available from The National Library of New Zealand.

Cover design: Jeroen ten Berge

To my darling Mormor, thank you for being the most incredible grandmother a child could ever have.
You always had time for me, and your love and passion for so many things have made me what I am today.
But most of all, thank you for showing me your love of books, and for passing that on to me.

I wish that you were still here....

PROLOGUE

TI POINT, NEW ZEALAND

He knew they should never have gone out in these conditions.

The two-metre-white caps washed over the Sealegs amphibious craft and tossed the boat like a toy. He'd underestimated the ferocity of the churning sea, which soaked the three men as they hunkered down in the open hull. Before leaving the small sandy beach in Ti Point, Mike had handed out their life jackets. He knew it would be a rough ride. The impenetrable darkness of the night and the stinging rain made it impossible to see more than a few metres ahead, let alone each other. The small craft and the strong wind threw the men around like bowling pins.

Mike lowered the front of the boat and powered through the waves head-on to stabilise and keep them from being chucked around more. It took them a good hour fighting the currents before they reached the shipping channel. Mike slowed the boat as they neared the pickup site. The GPS screen lit up, and he was thankful they were in the right spot for the retrieval.

"Get the gaff, Chook," Mike yelled at the top of his voice.

The hammering wind meant he couldn't hear Chook's response

but could see his thumbs-up sign. The blue plastic barrels were well camouflaged and floated all around them.

Chook leaned over the boat's edge and looked around in the churning black water.

"Can you see them, Chook?"

"Yep, bring me a bit closer to starboard."

Each barrel was packed in a precise way to make sure that the GPS not only transmitted but that the blinking red light was visible, even on a stormy night like this when the darkness closed in. According to the instructions, there were thirty barrels. It took a bit of effort, but Chook got them all. What the boy lacked in age, he more than made up for with experience, having been commercial fishing with his old man since he was fourteen. Chook was a strapping lad of twenty but had the natural ability you'd see in people born to a life at sea.

His broad shoulders and strong arms had been built up by daily back-breaking work. Some people would call him ruggedly handsome, even though his hook-nose was not in balance with his features. Chook had an air of confidence about him and had been out with Mike for the last six months at every pickup. Mike knew he could trust him.

Chook's dad usually came out with them as well, but since dislocating his shoulder last time, the old man had to stay behind. So they had roped in Fanta, a mate of Chook's, for the pickup. Fanta was in his late twenties, a heavily tattooed, small-time criminal with a list of charges as long as your arm, and recently released from Waikeria Prison. A prominent number thirteen was displayed on his right forearm for luck. The dumbass had served time after a break-in where he'd encountered the house owner and assaulted him with a baseball bat. Luckily for him, the poor man had survived; otherwise, he'd still be locked up.

Fanta's lanky figure stooped as he tried to balance some barrels, stowing them securely in crates at the back of the boat. Despite the compact size of the barrels, they were still quite heavy, and Mike wondered if they'd made the right decision as the skinny ginger was a real lightweight and seemed to struggle under the weight of the load.

The sea sprayed the cockpit, and water sloshed around it. Chook gave Fanta a helping hand as they loaded the last barrel. Fanta signalled a thumbs-up and returned to the front. Mike was relieved as he turned the boat around to head for home, they'd retrieved all the barrels.

The net secured across the precious cargo had come undone, and he yelled at Fanta to sort it out. The last thing they needed was to lose some of the packages of drugs overboard in this weather. Fanta let go of the cockpit railing as he made his way aft on unsteady legs to secure the load. Mike turned to watch him make his way to the back. The deck was wet from all the wash, and Fanta slipped and was thrown to the leeward side of the boat but managed to hold on and not get flung over the side into the black water. Mike held his breath. At least the skinny prick wore a life jacket. Fanta gave him a cheeky thumbs-up and continued to the back of the boat to pull the net across the storage crate and secure it.

Fanta's red, scraggly shoulder-length hair was sea-washed under the dewy moonlight and hung in lank sections over his pale face. Saltwater and rain dripped off his sparse moustache and beard. The inflammation of his hair follicles looked angry through the beard tufts. Fanta smiled cheekily. What a cocky bastard, Mike thought. He has the luck of the Irish.

Without warning, a massive rogue wave hit them side on. The boat squealed and jerked in torment, listing precariously to port. Mike was thrown sideways and held on to the wheel as best he could. They were all soaked as he managed to get the boat under control.

His first thought was the shipment, which was hopefully still secured to the back of the boat. "Check the shipment," Mike shouted.

Mike looked for the crew and saw Chook. Where was the skinny ginger, though? He looked around wildly but couldn't see him. He dreaded scanning the inky sea, fearing Fanta may have been thrown overboard. Mike shouted Fanta's name as Chook leaned over the side, desperately searching for any sign of the man in the water. Let's hope that he hasn't been swept too far away from the boat, Mike thought as Chook shone the spotlight into the water, turning it frantically this way and that, calling out Fanta's name. The situation was serious—they had to locate him before he lost consciousness in the chilly sea.

"Over there," Chook yelled, pointing wildly. "I can see him. About twenty metres away."

In the swirling seas, they caught a glimpse of an orange life vest tossed like a cork in the sea foam. Mike threw the boat in gear and powered over to where they'd last spotted him. The boat lurched up and down precariously, and Chook managed to get hold of the orange fabric with the boat hook he'd grabbed. But as he hauled it in, only the life vest was on the hook. There was no sign of Fanta, who must not have done it up, the stupid idiot. They searched fruitlessly for the next hour until Mike admitted defeat and said, " Chook, mate, there's no use. We need to get back to dry land."

As Mike returned to base, he was downcast and in complete disbelief that they had lost a man out there and was worried about the fallout this would bring. It appeared Fanta's luck had run out.

1

Sunday the 2nd of July

Zac wondered if he would regret tonight. Partying wasn't his thing. He hoped that he wouldn't stand out too much, but he usually did with his nearly two-metre-tall frame, inherited from his father. His mother would say that he was a carbon copy of his dad, with the same short dark hair and green eyes. He wasn't short of female attention but felt nerdy and not very confident around girls. Tonight he'd thrown on a white shirt and some tidy dark jeans, which kind of proved the point as his mates looked cool in ripped jeans and T-shirts. It was too late to get changed anyway.

He'd reluctantly agreed to go with his mates to the party in Omaha—not that he'd had much choice in the matter. Luke, Ant and Steve all thought he needed a night out. They'd all quit school a year early, in Year Twelve, to start apprenticeships. Zac was the only one in the group who had finished high school and gone on to university. He'd always loved animals and had kept an array of critters since he was young, and of course, Georgie, the beloved pony he had growing up. He was in his first year of veterinary school, and keeping up with the workload was a hard slog. They were right; he didn't go out nearly as much as he should. What could it hurt to go to this party, he thought. It might do him good to blow off some steam.

As they arrived around 10:30 p.m., the party was in full swing. Zac had never seen anything like it. The address in Omaha was in the upmarket southern end, and the house was a mansion.

"This is Jett Starr's house. You know, the old rocker. Apparently, he has platinum records everywhere," Luke said. He shut the door to the old plumber's van as Ant and Steve tumbled out. They'd already had a few beers too many.

Zac couldn't help but be a little impressed. It was a world apart from his family's modest home in Matakana. But then again, his dad was on a cop's salary.

The street was crammed with cars parked at every angle. They walked up the long driveway to the house. Zac started to regret his decision to come along as the strobe lights and loud music welcomed them. This kind of flashy party wasn't his thing. "Come on, man. Stop gawking. Let's go inside!" Zac's expression must have said it all.

"Don't worry. We'll look after you. Come on, let's get lit," Luke said.

Two beefy bouncers were at the door, their bulging muscles apparent through their jackets. Zac hesitated. There was no way he belonged here.

"Don't worry, man. We're on the guest list. Phoebe got us in," Luke said and shoved him along. Phoebe was Luke's latest girlfriend. Zac had met her once, and at first glance, she'd seemed high maintenance and nothing like the girls he knew.

Luke strode up confidently and exchanged a few words with the man on the right, who checked him off the guest list.

"Come on, lads," he said. "Let's get ready to party!"

"Enjoy," the bouncer said before he turned to the people in the group behind.

"Wow, what a cool place. This is what I'm talking about," Ant said, almost shouting because the noise was deafening.

"We have to find Gazza to see if we can score some Molly," Steve said as he looked around at the crowd of people dressed to the nines.

"He said he'd be here."

"I'm not sure about party pills, guys," Zac said.

"Don't be a fucking wimp."

"Cut loose. Live a little. It's not like it will hurt you to have some fun. Besides, everyone does it, " Ant said.

The DJ was set up in the corner of the spacious open-plan lounge and kitchen on a small stage, just like at a professional gig. Luke led the way as they pushed through the crowd and became swept up in the lights and the infectious beats. A bar had been set up on the large kitchen island at the other end, and bottles and glasses were piled neatly.

Zac couldn't believe what he saw—Jett Starr, the ageing rockstar and host, being the centre of attention and with girls hanging off him. The old geezer was hard to miss, dressed in a bright yellow glitter blazer that looked like something he'd worn back in the 1970s.

"Here, take this," Luke said, passing Zac a pink pill. All the sensible thoughts in Zac's head screamed, *Don't take it.*

Luke popped a pill and took a swig of beer to wash it down, handing Zac the open can.

Everyone looked at Zac. He held the pill in his open palm; the beer can in his other hand.

"Come on, man," Luke said.

"Swallow it and have some fun."

Zac raised the can halfway to his mouth, thinking he'd be an idiot to take it, but it was only one pill. What harm could it do? So, he stuck the tablet on his tongue and felt the cool mouthful of beer make its way down his throat as he swallowed the little pink pill.

"See? That wasn't so difficult, was it!" Luke said.

Zac knew he was past the point of no return. In his mind, he just hoped that he'd be okay.

"You might feel a bit sick initially. It will pass quickly, I promise," Ant said and dragged him across the dance floor to the bar situated on the massive kitchen island. A huge chandelier hung overhead, and Zac could see the large pool lit up in the background and he wondered how long it would take before the Molly kicked in.

"Let's go, boys! The drinks are flowing, and they are free. Now, let's find some hunnies."

Zac's last sober thought before the effects of the ecstasy kicked in was that perhaps this might not have been the best idea. There was no backing out now; he'd just have to roll with it.

2

Monday the 3rd of July

Sergeant Bill Granger leant back in his chair at Matakana police station as he put the finishing touch to the paperwork on his desk. His neck was tight, and he did a couple of stretches that released with a satisfying crack. His shoulders were the same, and he did a couple of circular movements to get some blood flow and loosen them up. They were affected by years of rugby, and his left shoulder had never come right after he took a bullet while working in Auckland city years ago. Despite a couple of operations, it had never been the same.

Part of the perks of his job was a gym membership. He could count on one hand the number of times he'd used it, though. He was fortunate that his broad, one hundred and ninety-five-centimetre frame hid a multitude of sins, but he was well aware his favourite leather belt barely stretched around his stomach. He knew he should take better care of himself, and at least he'd signed up for the local old boys' team at the rugby league club. Hopefully, he might lose a kilo or two while having some fun with the other guys more or less his age.

He had no regrets about moving back to Matakana and being forced to take the demotion from senior sergeant. The lifestyle here was so much better.

The morning sun was weak, and the ominous late June sky barely cast any light into the police station. The old converted villa was under heritage protection, making renovating and improvements a complicated matter. The damned condensation on the old single-glazed window panes annoyed him. Even though he'd squeegeed and wiped them down before, they'd only just begun to dry. It was a futile job, a bit like painting the Auckland Harbour Bridge—once you reached the end, it was time to start from the beginning again. The lack of insulation in the walls and ceiling cavities exacerbated the situation, and the damp seeped into his bones.

As it was winter, Bill was back to a sole charge position in the small village of Matakana, and thankfully, the Queen's Birthday long weekend at the beginning of June had come to an end without the need to arrest drunken youths or troublemakers.

There had been the expected influx of visitors to the area. It was the last holiday break before the colder weather set in. They'd had the normal break-ins, a couple of drunk and disorderly and two cars and one motorbike that had come off the road in the wet. Only minor injuries were sustained, and Bill was happy things had returned to normal. He liked the lull of the quiet winter months.

A distraught mother from nearby Snells Beach had called first thing in the morning to report that she'd found drugs in her son's room yesterday. She wanted Bill to arrest her son and lock him up to teach him a lesson. He smiled as he explained that it wasn't quite how things worked, but he'd be happy to come by and chat with the lad. They arranged for Bill to come by late afternoon when the boy had returned home from school.

Bill understood her concern. Hopefully, he'd be able to talk some sense into the young man.

3

It was seven in the morning, and Annika Granger rushed across the windswept gravel car park to the Matakana Gym. She was late. She preferred to get there early, so she could set up her yoga mat somewhere at the back, out of the way. As she sprinted past the car park, she noticed a black Cadillac Escalade parked in the disabled space, and as far as she could see, without a permit displayed. The windows were tinted black, which made it impossible to see through. What a selfish jerk, she thought.

She opened the front door to the gym, and warm air rushed towards her. Annika felt irritation creep in as she scanned the room. Her favourite spot at the very back was taken by a woman wearing red yoga pants, and the class was full.

"There's a spot here," a voice could be heard from the front.

Annika turned to see a leggy, curvaceous woman in her mid-twenties who looked as though she belonged on the cover of *Fitness Illustrated.* She sat up the front and wore bright pink leopard yoga pants with a matching top. She waived Annika over.

Annika couldn't remember how long it had been since she'd looked like that, if she ever had. Either this woman had just returned from a holiday on some Fijian beach, or she sported an amazing fake tan. The woman's skin glowed and seemed flawless against the perfectly pearly white teeth revealed by the warm smile she gave Annika as she made her way over to where the woman was sitting. They must be veneers, Annika thought as she returned the smile, feeling self-conscious in her dated and less-than-flattering workout clothes. She'd barely glanced in the mirror as she'd tied her long blonde tresses up in a high bun before leaving home. Then again, she was twice as old as this young woman. Annika rolled her foam mat next to the Khloe Kardashian look-alike and settled herself.

"I'm Crystal," the young woman with a high ponytail said, her long hair cascading down her back.

"Hi, I'm Annika. Thanks for making some room for me."

"No problems," she said and smiled. "Is it always this busy?"

But before Annika could answer, the class started. Maeve, the yoga teacher, entered the room and said in a soft voice, "Hello and welcome, everyone. Please lie down on your mat in Shavasana Corpse Pose, and we'll start the class slowly. Release your bodies into the mat."

The ninety-minute class went quickly, as always. Annika felt the knots in her back and neck from hours spent painting and bending over canvases on the floor melt away. Despite being in her late forties, she was still quite athletic. Though in the last year, her weight had crept up little by little, and her love of baking didn't help. Crystal had obviously done yoga before as her body easily slipped into one pose after the other, which Maeve guided them through.

"She's great," Crystal said, gesturing to the teacher at the front.

"Maeve is awesome. I always feel so much better after her class," Annika said.

"Hey, not sure if you are busy, but do you fancy a coffee next door after the class? I'm new and haven't got to know anyone yet," Crystal said, looking down at her hands.

"I guess so." Annika was a little surprised that a glamorous younger woman like Crystal would like to spend time with an older woman, a woman with a few laugh lines around her eyes. What would we have in common? Annika wondered.

When the practice finished, they packed up their gear and walked through the gravel car park towards the small café next door, avoiding the large puddles. Crystal stopped on the way and handed her mat and drink bottle to a neatly dressed man in his thirties leaning against the black Escalade. He wore smart camel chinos, tan shoes and a slim-fit Oxford stripe shirt, casually open at the neck. A heavy gold wristwatch adorned his hairy, thickset forearms.

"Your husband doesn't mind waiting around?" Annika said as Crystal turned back.

"Mike's not my husband. He works for my boyfriend, Andrei," Crystal said as she flicked her hair and laughed.

They reached the café. It was cosy and one of Annika's favourite places.

"Can I have a long black and one of those blueberry muffins, please?" Crystal said as she pointed to the cabinet stocked with various delectable cakes and sandwiches, a chunky gold bracelet dangling on her wrist.

Annika recognised the hardware and the distinct U-shaped clasp —Tiffany & Co. She had a similar piece, although thinner and definitely worth a lot less. Bill had given it to her for one of their wedding anniversaries well before the kids came along. Annika glanced at her own paint-stained hands, complete with practical shortcut nails—the opposite of Crystal's French manicure perfection—and immediately put them down by her side.

"A flat white, please, Val," Annika said as she came up behind Crystal at the counter.

"And a cheese and onion toastie."

She almost instantly regretted it. Not because of the toasted sandwich but more to do with her waistline.

It was busy inside, and no tables were available. Everyone else had the same idea of getting their morning coffee. Annika and Crystal walked out the door and sat down at a table outside. The wind had decreased, and the sun warmed their faces even though it wasn't more than ten degrees. The patio heater near them took away the worst of the chill and radiated a welcoming warmth.

A slightly awkward silence followed as they waited for their order.

Annika could think of nothing better than to state the obvious. "I haven't seen you at yoga before."

"It was my first time with Maeve. We moved up here in the summer, and you can only do so many workouts online," Crystal laughed. "It drove me crazy to stay in the house, so I decided to join the gym. I thought I'd do some classes to get a feel for the place."

Crystal glanced towards Mike, who was presumably back in the driver's seat, even though they couldn't see through the tinted windows.

The coffee arrived, and they each had a sip, which was a nice reprieve.

"My boyfriend Andrei is in construction. He has some houses being built in Point Wells. You know, that new subdivision on the right as you drive into the village?"

"Sure, that's awesome. There are some lovely homes there."

"We live in the house on the Point," Crystal said, happily chatting and sipping her coffee. "What about you? How long have you lived here?"

"My husband Bill was born and raised here. We moved back when the children were young."

"What made you move back ?"

Annika took a sip of coffee, unsure how much she wanted to share with this young woman she barely knew.

"Bill was badly injured on the job, and we decided to come back here for a slower pace of life, which was a good move for us as a family," Annika said as she held her coffee cup in both hands to warm them up.

"Oh, what happened to your husband?" Crystal asked.

Almost immediately, Annika regretted sharing personal details with a complete stranger. It had been a long time since she had talked about the harrowing event where Bill almost lost his life. It felt like a lifetime ago, but in other ways, not.

"Bill's in the police and worked in Auckland. He was in the wrong spot at the wrong time and walked in on a drug deal. He was shot in the stomach and the shoulder. We very nearly lost him," she said.

"That's awful. I'm so sorry to hear that," Crystal said.

"It was a tough time in our lives for sure," Annika said as she remembered the pain.

"Is he still in the police? Crystal said, placing her cup back on the saucer.

"He is," Annika said as she sniffed and cleared her throat. She was unsure if Crystal had noticed her emotions get to her.

"And what do you do?

"I paint. I'm a full-time artist, although it's a busy household with four children still living at home," Annika said, relieved to change the subject.

"Wow, four kids! You look amazing. What's your secret?" Crystal said, her voice full of admiration.

Annika felt the colour rise in her cheeks; it wasn't often she received a compliment.

Reece, their neighbour, pulled up in his old Ute. He climbed out of the car in his work boots and fleece jacket and gave Annika a cheery hello. Reece was a plumber and, like most tradespeople, wore shorts year-round, despite what the weather was doing. She said hello back, thankful for the reprieve.

"Andrei wants kids, but I'm not sure I'm ready yet," she said, squirming in her seat.

"There is still time, right? I'm not thirty yet."

Annika felt a little sorry for her. She sensed it was a point of contention in their relationship.

"I used to work in human resources before I met Andrei. It was a good career.

However, he is very old-fashioned and prefers that I don't work."

"What about you? What do you want?" Annika wasn't sure how to feel about such an antiquated statement.

"I guess I would like to do something, to work, to contribute and feel useful again." Annika detected an underlying sadness in Crystal's voice.

"What about Andrei? What's his background?"

"His family owned a construction company. Andrei took it over when his dad retired."

"I'm sure if you talk to Andrei and tell him how you feel," Annika said, "he'll understand. It's 2022, not 1922. Women run companies these days."

"He just likes to provide, I guess," Crystal quickly added.

Annika didn't know what to say, so she took another sip of coffee.

"He's not had it easy from the beginning. He was only five years old when a lovely Remuera couple adopted him and his sister from Russia. Andrei and Daria had a privileged life as soon as they came to Auckland. It was private schools and all that comes with that. His mother never worked. He feels the same should apply to me," she said.

Val came over and put their orders on the table. She was Annika's age and already a grandmother. Her daughter Gabby was the same age as Zac and had a three-year-old boy. Val was proud as punch and loved to show off the latest photos of the wee tyke. Even though she also looked forward to grandchildren, it gave Annika a little anxiety, and she hoped her children would wait until they were a little older before they made her a grandmother. She felt a twinge as her mind wandered to Zac and how he'd involved them less and less in the last year with what was going on in his life. Annika knew he was a young man who needed space. Yet she struggled with her firstborn no longer needing her.

"Enjoy, ladies," Val said, smiling.

The large heated berry muffin arrived with a neatly wrapped square of butter, the greaseproof paper twisted at both ends like an old-fashioned bonbon.

Annika's toasted sandwich was piping hot and smelled delicious, just how she liked it, and with lots of melted cheese. The conversation flowed, and they ordered a refill of their coffees before Annika looked at the time and an hour had flown by. "I can't believe where the time has gone. It was nice to have a coffee with you."

"Thank you for joining me. It's been so lovely to talk to another woman. I'm a little over all the testosterone at home," Crystal said.

They gathered their things, and Annika made a point to stop in the café doorway to wave goodbye to Val before they left and walked the short distance back.

"Let's catch up again soon, that is, if you want to," Crystal said as she stopped by the black car. Annika could see Mike through the windscreen, but he either ignored them or hadn't noticed that they were there. She thought the whole situation was a bit strange, to say the least.

"I'd love to. Perhaps after yoga next time, if that suits?"

"Absolutely, that's perfect," Crystal said as she got into the car.

Annika walked to her car and threw the yoga mat in the boot among an assortment of paint pails and various sporting equipment, like the twins' hockey sticks. As she drove away from the gym, she couldn't help but wonder about the young woman with the driver at her beck and call.

4

As Vivianne Harper walked along the long white dunes of Omaha Beach, she gathered her knee-length bright yellow raincoat closer around her, pulling up the collar around her ears.

She held the hood to prevent it from blowing off, the string long gone.

It was a chilly, blustery day, and Vivianne wished she'd thought to put on an extra layer of clothing underneath the raincoat. In one hand, she held two leads: one blue, the other red. The compact container of rolled-up poop bags attached to the red one swung as she walked. Bramble, the two-year-old West Highland White Terrier, scampered around in the wash ahead of her, and the rolling waves hit the beach with all the ferocity of a typical winter storm over the Pacific.

Bramble loved the water and played 'catch me if you can' with the incoming tide. He barked and chased a couple of large black gulls that dared to land on *his* beach. The stocky terrier was a little Napoleon. Despite not being large in stature, he was the bravest dog she'd ever known.

Duchess, a six-year-old girl of the same breed, trotted ahead of

Vivianne, her head held high with dignity and decorum and not interested in the least in getting her feet wet. Vivianne remembered the day she got her beautiful little girl—those big, round beautiful eyes like two shiny grapes, and the unconditional love she endlessly gave. It had been a dream to have a Westie. To have two of her own exceeded everything.

She'd got Duchess right after she gave up her nursing career. The lifting and shifting of patients had taken a huge toll on her back and shoulders. Sure, giving up her job and, ultimately, her security had been a life changing decision. It was all she'd really known. Thankfully, she'd had some success writing books in the last ten years. It was her passion and something she'd never dreamt she'd be able to pursue full-time. It had been a big step to quit nursing, but she didn't regret it for a minute because it meant she now worked her own hours from home, and as a result, she'd been able to get Duchess. Even though her back and shoulders still gave her problems, things had improved with her new career.

A couple of surfers took advantage of the morning's massive waves and rode the rolling crest into shore. The squally wind pushed Vivianne's slight frame every which way.

She could feel the jolts in her lower back and neck as she struggled to regain her balance.

Almost two years ago, she'd inherited her aunt's small cottage in the older northern end of the Omaha Beach settlement.

Aunt Beverly had left her a small nest egg as well as the house. Combined with her own savings, she was comfortable. The publisher sent her a royalty payment twice a year, but she still kept an eye on her expenses. Bramble ran back and forth, splashing in the waves rolling onto the shore. He looked like a little sand monster and was completely soaked, his white fur covered in wet sand. Vivianne groaned. She could already smell the wet dog aroma, not that she minded that, but still. The young dog was still like a puppy and demanded his two walks a day without exception. Nevertheless, in between working at her desk, it was nice to get out for regular walks and blow the cobwebs away.

Vivianne had never married. Not that there had been a lack of suitors, at least not when she was younger. In a way, she wished she'd met someone to share life with. Lately, though, she'd started feeling content with her life; perhaps she was destined to be alone.

She was only in her mid-forties but felt old today, as her back was stiff and sore from being hunched over the computer. She'd just finished the first draft of her new book. It was a locally set thriller and the second book in the series.

A rogue gust flung the hood of her rain jacket backwards off her face and head, which made her shoulder-length curly hair blow in all directions. Then, as Murphy's Law would have it, the heavens opened, and in no time at all, her hair was plastered in wet strands across her face. Water trailed down her neck before she could get a hold of the wayward hood again and regain her composure. She felt like a drowned rat. Oh well, not that it mattered; she wasn't going anywhere today.

The beach was empty. No one in their right mind would contemplate walking their dog in weather like this. Bramble, the little rascal, moved on and disappeared around the reeds in the dunes. Duchess, the alpha dog, was close by, and Vivianne kept an eye on them both.

"Bramble, come on," Vivianne yelled as she competed with the increasing howling of the wind. It was futile, she knew. The stubborn little dog had loads of 'Westietude,' and it appeared his ears were only painted on this morning. Duchess glanced at Vivianne as she waited for instructions.

"Clever girl. You go and find your brother," Vivianne said, pointing toward the dunes.

Duchess disappeared as well but came into view again. The dog barked and let out a shrill wail.

"All right, Duchess. I'm on my way. Calm down."

Duchess ran in circles around Vivianne, nearly tripping her up.

"Duchess!" Vivianne growled as the dog took off up the sand dune, which meant she had no choice but to hurry after her. Where was the naughty little boy? Clumps of grit stuck to her gumboots, and with every step, she felt sharp twinges in her lower back as she climbed the wet sand.

"Bramble!!" The stubborn little dog was still nowhere to be seen. Duchess appeared again and ran towards Vivianne, guiding her closer to what appeared to be a dip in the dune.

Vivianne could see that Bramble was investigating something next to an upturned old rowboat. She didn't have her glasses on and couldn't quite make out what the rounded shape was. It better not be a dead seal like the one they encountered a couple of weeks ago, she thought, swallowing hard to avert an anxiety attack. Being inquisitive, Bramble had rolled in the decayed seal carcass, which had taken not one but two soapy baths to get the ripe smell of rotting mammal off his little body, as it seemed the stench had permeated through his long winter coat and also into his skin. She didn't fancy giving him a bath after all this effort today.

As Vivianne came closer, both dogs ignored her attempts to get their attention and continued to sniff around and explore. A cold, prickly feeling spread inside her, and her heart beat faster and faster.

What was that beneath the boat? Bramble dug furiously at something, sand flying everywhere, and she yelled at him to stop it, but he ignored her. Then, as she approached the boat, she inched a bit closer and realised it was a human arm, the skin a greyish blue against the wet yellow sand. She screamed, and Bramble stopped momentarily, moving to the side.

He looked up at her, and that's when Vivianne saw the shocking contrast of candy-pink nail varnish on a perfectly manicured hand, making it even more difficult to comprehend. Bramble's whole head was back under the boat as he tried to get in, but the gap was too small. On the other side, Duchess dug furiously, and Vivianne felt her anxiety rise as the realisation set in over what she'd seen.

"Bramble! Duchess! Leave it!!" Vivianne shouted but to no avail.

The tough little dog whimpered as she dragged Bramble out by his hindquarters. Her hands trembled as she grasped the collar and hooked him onto the lead.

"Duchess, come here!"

Duchess did as she was told and trotted over, pressing her whole body against Vivianne's leg as if to say sorry. Both dogs seemed proud of what they'd found and looked at her for rewarding pats and some fuss. Bramble, ever the puppy, jumped up on her legs, craving praise.

"Calm down, boy. It's okay," she said as she pulled them away and hooked the leads through the rowlock of another boat a few metres away. The dogs wriggled, and she had to kneel on the wet sand to get them sorted. She stood, wiping her sand-encrusted hands on her sodden trousers, and took a deep breath before turning back to investigate.

Could it be a mannequin? It could be; they look so life-like nowadays. But deep inside, she knew it wasn't.

She walked closer to the rowboat and knelt as she lifted the riveted aluminium hull to take a peek. It took all her strength to hoist it up. Her shoulders protested; it was heavier than it looked. She took a deep breath and stretched forwards, her face parallel to the ground and only inches from the sand.

Vivianne pulled away and took another deep intake of breath as she sat back up, her shoulders aching. She inhaled once more before bending down hesitantly to take another look. There it was: the pale face of a scantily clad young girl, her shoulder-length, curly dark hair dry and draped partially across her face. The marbled blue tinge of her almost translucent face made her look cold. The mouth was open, and dried vomit was on her chin and the sand.

Vivianne's first instinct was to cover the girl up from the elements, but she knew she shouldn't do anything to disturb the body. The girl's eyes were slightly open, her lashes coated in a thin layer of fine sand, as was the rest of her body. The thought of the life that had escaped those unseeing eyes was too much, and Vivianne had to look away. Even though she had trained as a nurse and had seen her fair share of dead bodies, it was still a shock.

The hood of her rain jacket flapped in the wind, and she barely noticed the water running down the back of her neck and face. She shivered and felt sorry for the girl. What a tragic thing. What had happened to her? The girl didn't look much older than her early twenties. Despite the macabre situation, she looked peaceful in death.

Even though in her books, Vivianne wrote about murder and dead bodies, it was another matter altogether to see an actual dead body in situ, and it was not something she wanted to experience in real life.

Vivianne fumbled for her phone in her raincoat pocket, and her shaky hands immediately dropped it on the wet sand. Damn, she cussed under her breath and reached down to pick it up.

She wiped the screen as best as she could on her jumper, which was still relatively dry. Her hands were still sandy and wet, making dialling difficult. She was about to call 111 but remembered that she'd programmed her phone with the local emergency numbers when moving to the area. Vivianne pondered for a few moments before she decided to call the local number. A couple of signals went through, even if it did feel like forever before someone answered.

"Matakana police station. Sergeant Granger speaking."

"Umm, hello. This is Vivianne Harper here from Omaha. I've just found a young girl here on the beach," she said, pausing for a breath.

"Is she lost or injured?"

"She's dead," she said, putting her hand to her eyes. "I just found her under one of the old rowboats on the beach, or actually, my dogs Bramble and Duchess found her."

"I see. Any obvious injuries?"

"I don't think so, not that I could see anyway." Vivianne's mind was all over the place. She hadn't seen any blood, although there was no telling what was underneath the body—an injury or even a weapon.

"Is the boat above the high tide mark?" Bill's voice ripped her back to reality and the incessant rain.

"It's up in the dunes, well above . . ." Her voice cracked. "She might not have been found so quickly if it wasn't for my Bramble."

"I want you to stay where you are. Don't touch anything, and keep anyone else away, including the dogs. I'm on my way now. I'll be there in five minutes or so," Bill said.

Although Vivianne already knew this, the police needed to keep the crime scene as uncontaminated as possible.

"Oh, okay, of course. I'll stay with her."

"Where exactly are you on the beach?"

"Umm, I'm just north of the lifeguard tower, down from the surf club to the left as you walk onto the beach."

She hoped Sergeant Granger would get there quickly. Vivianne turned and looked at the raging sea where the surfers rode the crest of the massive waves, seemingly without a care in the world, while her heart ached for this young woman, and an overwhelming sorrow hung over her.

5

Bill swallowed the last mouthful of his strong coffee as he hung up the phone. He'd only recently switched from drinking his usual flat whites to long blacks. For some reason, the milky drinks didn't seem to agree with him anymore. He looked out the window and saw rain beading down the glass panes and bruised-looking clouds hanging low in the sky. The low clouds and inclement weather made him wish the day was over. The woman's voice on the phone sounded shaky. She was clearly rattled but had remained calm enough to keep it together and relay the facts. It wasn't every day a body was found in the small settlement.

He grabbed his raincoat and regulation hat, locked the station door, and stepped outside in the damp cold. Was this young person someone he knew? This was one of the downsides of working in a small community, as there was often a connection to the victim or their family. Regardless of the cause of death, the impact on the deceased's family would be considerable.

Bill turned left from the police station and continued driving down the village's main street. He still had the old Holden Colorado Ute. A nationwide rollout of lower-emission vehicles was underway, but being away from the metropolitan areas, they'd likely be the last to receive them. Not many people were out and about, and the street was almost empty.

He passed the cinema and turned left at the roundabout and over the river on Leigh Road towards the Omaha turn-off. Two tour buses turned into the Sculptureum, the popular outdoor gallery, and he thought those poor people had picked a terrible day to wander around the gardens filled with wonderful sculptures and beautiful trees. He was sure the fancy restaurant on site would do a roaring trade as people more than likely would want a nice hot lunch and to dry out. He turned into Omaha Flats Road and passed the fruit orchards and vegetable growers, perusing their empty road side stalls as he drove. As he continued over the concourse to Omaha, it was low tide, and the long-legged oystercatchers waddled around, pecking at crabs and small fish like they were at a buffet. As he arrived at the popular beach settlement, he turned right and headed straight for the Surf Club. A handful of people were in the café on the corner.

The beach car park was virtually empty, and he parked the Ute as close to the surf club as he could. Before setting off down the wooden walkway where the caller had directed him, he spotted Henry Long, the surf club president, striding towards him. Henry was in his late fifties but was fit and looked at least ten years younger. His bright red hair, streaked with grey, and his light complexion made Bill wonder how much sunblock the guy had to use in the harsh summer sun.

"Bill, how are you going?"

"Not too bad, Henry. I just wish this bloody rain would let up."

"Yeah, I know what you mean, but as long as the weather is fine on Saturday for the fundraiser, that's the main thing. You and Annika are still going to swing by, aren't you?"

"Yeah, of course, we'll be there. I'll see what I can bring for the silent auction, too," Bill said, feeling guilty for letting it slip his mind.

"Can I ask you for a favour, Henry? A body's been found on the beach. Could you assist me by taking the lady who called it in back to the Surf Club? She's been out in the rain for a while and will be soaked."

"A body?" Henry's face dropped. "Here on our beach? That's just awful. What happened, and is it anyone we know?"

"I don't have any answers yet, but you'd be helping a lot if you could come with me." Bill's tone was impatient.

"Of course, glad to help. Give me a few minutes to turn the heaters on in the clubrooms, and I'll grab an umbrella and meet you on the beach."

"That's great, thank you. Her name is Vivianne. Please stay on the walkway. I'll send her over to you, and you might want to make her a cup of tea while she waits for me to come back up and take her statement," Bill said and got going.

"Of course, no worries, Bill." Henry's initial shock seemed to have settled, and he looked to take his role seriously.

The wet weather and sideways rain soaked through Bill's uniform trousers, the navy wool polyester mix already chafing his shins. They were the worst part of the uniform.

Then, he spotted a woman wearing a bright yellow raincoat. She waved him over, and as he trudged through the sand, he looked at the luxurious beach homes lining the white sandy beach. This truly was another world. By the time Bill got to her, he was thoroughly drenched.

"Vivianne?"

"Yes," she said anxiously. The pale middle-aged woman shivered as the rain beat down on her. Her eyes darted back and forth to the upturned old boat. Two energetic Westies bounced around her feet, eager to sniff who the newcomer was.

"These are my two dogs, Bramble and Duchess. It was Bramble who found her." Vivianne looked over to the boat.

"Hello, you two."

Bill bent down to give them both a pat and was greeted by an excited Bramble who strained at the leash, eager to get the attention and fuss. Duchess was more uncertain and stuck close to her owner's legs.

Bramble licked him and slunk underneath the boat, which was slightly propped up. He was tethered to it in an attempt to get him out of the weather. The young dog rested his head on his paws, intrigued as he peered at the two of them. The older female was a little anxious and wouldn't budge from Vivianne's side.

"It's all right, Duchess. You be a good girl and stay here. It won't take long. She's over there," Vivianne said, pointing with her whole hand.

Bill could just make out the shape of a person, mostly covered by the old boat. He walked down the dune, careful where he put his feet, and pulled a pair of disposable gloves out of his pocket. As his hands were wet, they were difficult to get on. He moved closer to the boat, sat on his haunches, and lifted the boat up a bit. There was the body.

The young woman barely looked out of her teens, but it was hard to tell these days anyway. She looked like she'd just come from a party and laid down to rest. The skinny-fit jeans and a crop top were something his teenage daughter Katie would wear. The naked arms had a light purple tinge and were almost translucent. He knelt on the wet sand, reached in, and gently lifted the left eyelid. Her face was cold to the touch, and the cornea was cloudy, which indicated that the girl had been dead for hours.

Bill stood and pulled the gloves off, balling them up and placing them in his pocket. He brushed the sand off his knees, leaving large wet patches, grabbed his phone, and took a series of photos. He scanned the area, taking in the houses closest to the site, a couple of upturned rowboats, and the clumps of tussock grass almost horizontal because of the weather. Where had she come from, and who was she? No missing person had been reported. The windswept sand was smooth, and from what he could see, the only foot impressions looked to be Vivianne's and his own and, of course, an assorted amount of paw prints. Somewhere there would be a family or a close someone blissfully unaware that she was dead. He stood up and snapped himself out of his thoughts. The worst aspect of the job was informing parents that their child was dead.

In his professional opinion, she hadn't been out here for long; the body was still in relatively good condition. A few more days undiscovered, though, and it wouldn't have been pretty.

Had she come out here and crawled under the vessel and had an episode of some sort? Perhaps she had epilepsy, although he shouldn't speculate.

As it was a suspicious death, it had to be investigated to rule out foul play. At least she looked peaceful, with no visible signs of violence.

The good thing was that the body was fairly dry and covered. If it was natural causes or not, the area was preserved. Bill dialled headquarters in Orewa, who said they'd send someone straight away. Then he called Warkworth police station as he needed a couple of scene guards.

He felt a bit sorry for the poor dog walker, who was still exposed to the elements. She looked cold despite her raincoat and jacket. Thankfully, the rain seemed to have diminished slightly. He couldn't leave the scene until it had been cordoned off. The Warkworth officers should be there soon. As Bill walked back to where Vivianne and her two very drenched dogs were standing, he spotted Henry under an umbrella on the walkway by the clubrooms.

"All right, let's get you guys out of this weather. I've arranged for Henry Long to take you over to the Surf Club until I can come and take a statement." Bill gestured with his head in the direction of Henry.

"I understand," she said, nodding. "Poor wee girl. Do you think she died of natural causes, Sergeant Granger?"

"It's difficult to tell. I can't speculate. We'll have to wait and see what the investigators say."

Vivianne looked down at Bramble, rolling in the sand in a futile attempt to dry his coat. Duchess was still clinging to her legs, suitably unimpressed with the situation.

Bill turned his coat collar up to try to stop the rain running down his neck and wished he'd brought an umbrella.

The dogs were impatient and a bit antsy and keen to get on their way back home, Bill suspected. He bent down to give them both a little scratch under the chin.

"All right, guys. You behave now. Thank you, Vivianne. Once we get the area closed off and some officers stationed, I'll come up and take your statement."

As soon as the first officers arrived from Warkworth, Bill issued directives, the perimeter was set up, and he walked up to the Surf Club. Bill wiped his sandy boots on the grass verge before entering the clubrooms. Vivianne and Henry were sitting at one of the tables with a cup of tea each and a plate of biscuits in front of them. The conversation appeared intense, but this was not strange, considering the body discovered on the beach. A couple of towels had been put on the floor for the dogs. Henry looked up.

"Fancy a cuppa?"

"That would be great, mate, thanks," Bill said, swiping a biscuit as he sat down.

"Are you okay if I ask you a couple of questions?" Bill brushed some crumbs from his damp trousers, simply making the whole thing worse. Vivianne nodded and took another mouthful of tea as if to brace herself. Bill asked her to go through the events that led up to the young woman being found, and his phone recorded the conversation. Vivianne went through the morning chronologically.

"Did you see anyone else around the girl?

"Sorry, I'm not sure if I'm very helpful. I didn't see anyone."

"Thanks, you've done a great job, Vivianne, and I appreciate that you stayed on."

"Of course, I was happy to."

"You'd be surprised; every detail is important. Let me drop you guys home. Where do you live?"

"Umm, we're just a couple of streets over," Vivianne said as they stood up and walked towards the door. She pointed to the right.

"Thanks for the tea, Henry," Bill said as they walked outside.

"No worries at all."

Bill looked at the two drenched dogs, pulled a tarp out of the back to cover the backseat, and let them jump in.

For a split second, he wondered if he would live to regret the decision on account of the wet dog smell. Once in the car, the dogs shook and dried their fur as best as they could, and Bramble started to whine and act up.

"Stop it, Bramble. You will have to settle down, boy." The little dog slunk down on the seat with a loud huff, and Vivianne settled into the front seat. It was obvious he was not very pleased with the arrangement.

"Sorry about that. He's had enough adventures for the day," Vivianne said as she turned to the front.

"We'll be in touch if we need anything else," Bill said as he stopped by her house.

He was pleased to get the dogs out of the car, even if the smell of wet dog cologne wasn't that bad.

As he drove back to the Surf Club, the Orewa SOCO team pulled up, and Bill's heart sank.

Through the windscreen, he could see Brian Rudd stepping out of the passenger side. The old twit was still around. His colleague, Andrew Copeson, came from the driver's side and waved as he saw Bill. Of course, from the handful of Scene of Crime Officers in Orewa, they had to send the grumpy old man.

"Granger, what have you got for us this time?" Rudd said on his way over, taking big strides. The old git's surly demeanour hadn't changed one bit. He still combed the thin grey strands of hair over the bald spot on the top of his head, and his face was as weathered as the last time Bill had seen him. The wind and rain wreaked havoc with his hair, wispy strands flying this way and that. His eyes betrayed his annoyance. The older man smoothed his hair down as best as he could and pulled his cap on to keep it all in place. Bill smiled at the older man's vanity.

Copeson jogged to catch up.

"Hi, Bill. How are things, mate?" the lanky younger man with a friendly face said.

"Yeah, good, mate, and I hope it stays that way."

"Hopefully, this is straightforward, a natural cause of death, and we can put it to rest," Bill said, leading the way down the beach.

"Well, I guess we'll see about that," Rudd scowled, his voice as gruff as his furrowed face. "Just let us do our job first."

6

Zac opened his eyes. Everything was a bit blurry, including the previous night.

Was he on the couch in the basement of Luke's parents' house? He looked around and recognised the old football table and the worn old lounge suite. His mouth was dry. Is there any water in here? He shook his head a few times to clear his mind enough to feel guilty about taking the drugs last night. He couldn't believe that he'd been so easily led.

As he searched for some water, he nearly tripped over Ant, snoring on a pull-out mattress on the floor. Steve was nowhere to be seen. The tiny room had a real funk in the air and reeked from an obvious overindulgence in alcohol. He found an open bottle of water in the corner and greedily tipped the few mouthfuls left down his throat.

What the fuck had happened? He couldn't remember much and glanced at the time on his phone—it was eleven o'clock. He could hear the tread of footsteps upstairs in the kitchen.

Hopefully, it was Luke rather than his parents.

"Who's for some leftover pizza for brekkie?" Luke called down.

Zac didn't think it could make him feel any worse than he already did.

"Mate, keep it down," Ant murmured.

"I could do with something to eat," Zac said, pushing past his friend.

He'd slept in his jeans and a shirt and felt sweaty and grimy. All he wanted was to go home and take a hot shower, but he headed upstairs, the light from the kitchen too bright for his eyes.

"Mate, that was one hell of a night!" Luke said, laughing. "You were on fire. I can't believe you danced on the table with those two girls. I hope you at least got their numbers."

Zac had no memory of anything. It probably had to do with the number of beers he'd consumed on top of the pill.

"Yeah, it was a good night," he lied.

"You were a beast. I've never seen you like that."

"Help yourself to pizza. If the lazy bone's not awake, he'll miss out."

The cold pizza stuck like cardboard to the roof of Zac's mouth, and he could only eat a few mouthfuls.

"I think I'll head off home. Thanks for letting me crash here last night."

"No worries, mate. Anyway, you weren't in any shape to go home. I don't think your dad would have been very happy with you," Luke said, grinning as Zac headed out the door.

Zac didn't think so, either.

7

Vivianne ushered Bramble and Duchess up the paved path outside the 1970s weatherboard house. She fumbled with the keys and finally unlocked the door while the impatient little dogs trampled all over her feet, pushing to get inside. "Calm down, guys. Let me get the door open." All three were utterly drenched.

Bramble and Duchess rushed inside. Bramble pushed past and made Duchess fall over in the process. She gave a shrill bark and complained loudly, looking back at Vivianne indignantly. Bramble rolled on the hallway rug in an attempt to dry his fur.

"I know, sweetheart. Boys are a bit rough, aren't they?" she laughed and gave Duchess a soothing pat.

Vivianne kicked her gumboots off and put them upside down on the boot rack by the door to dry out. Her feet were stiff and cold, and she massaged them to get some blood flow going. She took her raincoat and jacket off and hung them on the hook as a small trail of water pooled on the floor.

Bramble—full of beans and the pushiest—ran backwards and forwards to the kitchen, indicating that breakfast was well and truly overdue.

"All right, let me get inside and get a towel to dry you a little, then I will get you guys something to eat."

She started walking down the hallway to the kitchen, the dogs following closely behind, when *bang*, the door slammed. She jumped, and the dogs sensed her apprehension, cuddling up to her and leaning against her legs.

"Jeez, it's okay, guys. It's only the wind."

It was typical New Zealand winter weather, especially when the prevailing wind came from the east. Today was worse, the gusts were swirly and couldn't make up its mind from which direction it came from.

She reached for the towel she'd left on the chair before they went out for their walk. It was always best to be prepared. As usual, Bramble pushed in and demanded that he'd be dried off first, and Duchess was not impressed.

"Now, let's get some breakfast sorted," she said, putting on her cheeriest voice.

She fed the dogs and then went into the bathroom to get out of her wet clothes and shower.

The old house was not on town supply water. They had to rely on rainwater or have the water tank filled by tankers. Luckily for them, it had been an extremely wet winter, and though there was plenty of water in the tank, Vivianne was still cautious and had a quick shower. She put her towelling robe on and wrapped her hair in a turban. The steam in the small bathroom fogged up the mirror, not that it mattered—she didn't particularly want to see her ageing face peering back at her. Not today; she felt fragile as it was.

She'd only just managed to hold it all together in front of that policeman. She'd felt like sobbing. He'd seemed very nice and concerned about her, but seeing the deceased young girl on the beach had brought back memories—memories she'd long suppressed and never thought would surface again. A wave of nausea washed over her. She grabbed the side of the bathroom sink and swallowed hard, forcing herself not to think of her sister. It hadn't been her fault. Not that anyone had blamed her.

She'd only been four years old, too young. Vera had been two. Vivianne tried to save her, but the swollen river rushed by too fast. Vera must have slipped and fallen. They'd been exploring on the farm, and even though their parents told them to keep away from the river that could be treacherous, they'd taken a shortcut home. Vivianne clambered down the river embankment, slipping and sliding, but she'd been unable to save her sister—there was no sign of her. The nightmares still plagued her, and she was sure that's why she'd become a nurse—to help others, even though she had failed her little sister.

Vivianne dressed in her comfortable dark stretchy jeans and a warm Merino sweater; her hair was damp, the curls requiring too much effort to pull a comb through them, so she let her hair hang loose to dry. She padded into the cosy kitchen and peeked at the grey skies outside her window and at the house next door.

The small settlement of Omaha, with its three-kilometre-long white sandy beach, was home to only a few hundred permanent residents. Many houses were empty until the busy summer season when holidaymakers flocked up the coast to escape the city. Vivianne's little house was one street back from the beach, which meant she didn't have sea views. Not that it worried her. It was a short walk to the beach, which was great for walking the dogs, and she could still smell the salty air and hear the screeching seagulls bickering over food.

She looked at the bread bag on the countertop. Could she eat anything after this morning's walk? The dead girl's pale face was like a film being played in her mind over and over again. She could not shake a great feeling of sadness for the girl's family—it reminded her of the loss of Vera forty years ago. It had been hours since she'd last eaten, so she popped a couple of bread slices in the toaster. Her throat felt dry, and she struggled to eat the toast smeared with a little butter, but a large swallow of tea helped her breakfast go down.

Vivianne pushed the images and thoughts in her head aside. Who was the poor young girl? She poured herself a large glass of water and walked into her office in the spare bedroom. A desk was pushed into the corner, which made it easy to keep tidy if someone stayed. Not that she had that many overnight guests. A large whiteboard was fixed above the desk, and next to it, the notes for the current novel in a linear diagram with multicoloured adhesive notes in an ordered pattern.

She picked up her reading glasses and sat down. The dogs had settled after their breakfast and were content in their baskets, already asleep. She smiled as Bramble snored in the corner, his tongue sticking out between a straight row of tiny teeth.

Vivianne opened the working document and read what she'd written yesterday. This was her daily routine before she started to write. Somehow it helped to know what came next in the book, but this morning, in the back of her mind, was the terrible image of the young girl on the beach, her hair against pale skin and so void of life.

8

Annika had spent most of the day in the studio completing the final touches to the last painting, ready for the upcoming exhibition in the adjacent gallery. She stepped back, hands on hips, and stretched, every vertebra along her spine audibly cracking into position. It felt good to have the pressure relief and for the tightness in her muscles to improve. She tucked a rogue strand of hair into her loosely tied-up bun. Her stomach was in knots, and she felt nervous anticipation. The familiar 'imposter syndrome' always reared its ugly head, but it wasn't as though it was the first time she'd had her work exhibited.

The painting was on a large drop cloth on the floor in front of her. It was too big to put on an easel, and she found it more creative to work like this—it freed her senses, and she could enjoy the journey from the first layer of thick paint to the last satisfying brush stroke. Although it was never complete, she thought.

Empty paint tubes and various palette knives lay scattered around her. Molly and Finn, the two standard poodles, were sprawled in the doorway, blocking the way, their long legs stretched out sideways. Finn was jet-black and bigger than his sister. He was curious and a typical boy, already having stepped through one of the dropped paint splotches. Thankfully, she used acrylics which were not considered toxic, but she'd seen the blue paw prints and washed them off immediately to be sure. Not that it really mattered out here in the studio. Molly, who had a curly chocolate coat and looked like a teddy bear, was more sensible, usually watching from afar. The floor had years of paint spills, which Annika found somewhat comforting and inspiring. Years ago, Bill had suggested they sand the old floorboards, but she'd not been keen.

Various colours covered the entire floor area, all remnants from the different stages of development she'd been through as an artist. To get rid of it would be like erasing all the memories. Not that she cared for them all. The last few months had been a blur. She'd struggled to stay on task and complete her paintings after getting caught up in a horrific altercation a few months ago with a deranged gunman hellbent on revenge and wanting to cause as much damage as possible to as many people as he could, including herself.

Some days were more difficult than others; the fear was always there under the surface. To be honest, she'd thought she was going mad with the irrational thoughts, racing heart and recurrent nightmares. To paint and focus on the exhibition was cathartic. She could work through some of the trauma she'd suffered by throwing herself into her art. She looked at the pieces on the floor and was struck by the difference in style.

Her paintings had always been vibrant, but her latest efforts showed the overwhelming darkness she felt weighing her down like a heavy blanket. Perhaps it was a combination of her creative development, too. She hoped the buyers would like what she'd come up with.

The studio was glum, and the ordinarily well-lit space mirrored her mood. It was a cavernous space to heat, and their heaters weren't the most efficient. This time of the year, she rugged up well in several layers and wore home-knitted fingerless gloves to keep the dexterity in her hands. Besides, the cold air made her think better. The only downside was that it took forever for the acrylic paint to dry. Not that it mattered too much. She had a great system worked out whereby she had three or four paintings she worked on at the same time. As they were all in the same series, the palettes matched but were in different stages of development, so she rotated one after the other until she was happy with what she'd produced. It wasn't the most efficient way, but it worked well.

Years ago, they had converted the old farm barn near their house into a gallery with a studio space at the back. Annika had been adamant they should put in the cathedral windows throughout both spaces, allowing in as much light as possible. She loved light. It reminded her of Sweden, where she'd been born. There was something special about the Nordic daylight, the shimmering northern lights, and the relationship between cloud cover and light intensity, with its unique frequency and luminescence, so translucent and soft it could make you weep as it touched your soul.

Not so much this afternoon, though, when the raindrops were falling like plump gemstones. The rhythmic sound of rain pelting against the floor-to-ceiling windows soothed her with the backdrop of heavy drumming on the corrugated roof. The noise became louder as the deluge got heavier, and it sounded like someone was standing with a bucket above them, the water gushing over the edge in large sheets. She switched the two floor-standing spotlights on and flooded the room with light. Annika knelt on the floor and put the last few brushstrokes on her latest creation before wiping her hands on her paint-stained jeans.

She stood and pulled the canvas upright against the wall, careful not to smudge the front, and stepped back to look at her handiwork. The one-and-a-half metre by two-metre acrylic painting had a layer of thick colours covering the surface. The blooms of the tactile, three-dimensional field of wildflowers literally swayed on the canvas. She was pleased with how it had turned out.

She stepped over Maggie and Finn, who both stirred. Maggie yawned but stayed put next to Finn as Annika entered the gallery. She looked at the finished pieces. They were in varying sizes and colours, leaning against the white-painted walls. The collection was ready.

Tomorrow's job would be to hang and photograph them, ready

for the catalogue to be printed. There was so much still to be done for the exhibition opening in a few days. It was her first show this year, as she exhibited in June and December. This time it hadn't come as easily as it usually did. She had felt preoccupied with other things, mainly the kids, especially Zac, who seemed to either fight his parents on every issue or not want to spend time with the rest of the family.

Of course, this was part of him being more independent, but she missed her sweet boy and hoped he would mature sooner rather than later.

9

Jett woke in the Californian king-size bed with two girls that he couldn't for the life of him remember the names of. It was a great party. Only two of the neighbours had complained about the noise, so that was a success. He'd had a lot to drink last night. He'd stopped doing drugs years ago. Perhaps he should have given up the booze as well, he thought, rubbing his aching head.

Jett pulled his arm out from under one of the girls who rested her head on his shoulder, strands of her blonde hair falling across his mouth. Gosh, they were young—barely early twenties. His already compromised bad conscience reared its ugly head, but he couldn't help it if the girls threw themselves at him, could he? He knew it wasn't his faded looks or wrinkles but rather his money and the fact that he used to be someone. It still fed his ego, which had always been oversized.

He could hear the purr of vacuum cleaners and dishes clanking in the kitchen sink—the cleaning crew was downstairs. The mess was the only downside to a good party. Thankfully, the cleaners always came in early. It probably looked a hell of a lot better already than when he'd gone to bed.

Jett was stark naked as he climbed out of bed and headed into the adjacent bathroom, grabbing his robe from the hook behind the door. An unopened bottle of water sat on the sink, which he grabbed, twisting the lid and drinking greedily. His head throbbed, and he saw his reflection as he leant against the sink. He craned his neck and scratched the stubble on his chin, which matched his spiky grey hair and stuck out in all directions. His face was more swollen than usual, and his deep wrinkles competed with each other, making his eyes look like piss holes in the snow.

The girls' scant clothing was scattered all over the floor. Jett walked barefoot on the plush carpet and opened the bedroom door to the hall to go downstairs. The regular crew had the carpet cleaner out on the stairs, and he could see red wine stains and pink RTD spills on the light carpet. With any luck, they'd be able to get the stains out.

"Morning, Pete. Are those stains shifting?"

"No worries, Jett. We're onto it."

"Thanks, man. I appreciate it as always."

Jett walked downstairs and into the open-plan kitchen. The recycling bins were outside the bifold doors by the pool area. He heard the clink of empty bottles being hurled into the bins by one of the crew while another two wiped down all the surfaces in the kitchen from untold spills.

He could see the barge board around the kitchen island had swelled because someone had spilt an entire bottle of something, the streaks visible on the cupboard door. Thankfully, the kitchen designer would be here in a few days, and the renovation wasn't far away. The next kitchen would be high spec, with no engineered wood in the form of MDF cupboard doors or barge boards that swelled with the slightest bit of dampness. The dark granite top would be replaced with a light, luscious marble. The parquet floor seemed okay, which was good.

His assistant, Sam, came around the corner; her hair tied up in a messy bun. If they were out, she always wore smart business attire. Today she wore jeans and a crisp white shirt with a jumper. Her sensible shoes coordinated with the casual look.

"Good morning, sunshine," she said, taking in her boss's bedraggled appearance and the cleaners working away. "Looks like it was a good night."

Sam was in her thirties, lived in Point Wells, and was a go-to person for everything. She was a mum of two little girls, and Jett felt fatherly towards her.

"It was pretty epic," Jett said, smiling wryly. "You sure missed a doozy. Any chance of some breakfast? My head is a bit delicate this morning."

"I thought as much. Luckily, I brought you some bacon and eggs on the way over this morning. How do you want them?"

"Did you get some fresh bread, too?"

"Of course."

"In that case, I'd kill for some poached eggs on toast with streaky bacon on the side, sweetheart."

"No worries. I'll get that started. You want some coffee while you wait?" "You are a lifesaver," he said and rubbed his forehead.

The cooking smells tempted him, so he wandered into the kitchen, where Sam gave him a couple of paracetamol. She handed him a strong black coffee to wash them down with, and he sat while he watched the hive of activity around him. The room quickly took shape, the lemony smell of clean floors and fresh surfaces comforting.

Sam set the large dining table with cutlery and a placemat and brought the warm plate over. It was laden with all the foods to soak up the alcohol, but not necessarily something his doctor would be happy about. At the last check-up, he'd been told to watch his cholesterol and reduce his alcohol intake. He'd ignored both. "You only live once," he'd said.

"Thanks. You're not eating?"

"I had my breakfast with the kids at about seven o'clock," she said, taking a crispy bacon rasher from his plate. "But don't mind if I pinch one of these."

"The flowers are beautiful. Did you bring them?" Jett asked, looking at the colourful arrangement of roses on the table.

"I thought you could do with some. Glad you like them."

As he finished his last mouthful of sourdough toast and a smear of egg, he looked at Sam.

"Erm, do you think you could help the girls upstairs to get going and put them in a taxi?"

"Girls?" she said. "There's more than one upstairs?"

"Two, and I can't help that I'm irresistible to the ladies."

"Whatever you say," Sam said, laughing as she walked away.

Jett felt exhausted and wondered if he was too old for this. There were always so many hangers-on. People he barely knew came along for the free booze and entertainment.

He'd seen Ringo supplying drugs to the younger crowd. Even though he had his security turf him out, it still annoyed Jett.

10

The wind blustered across the dunes, but at least the incessant rain had stopped, and a pale sun peeked through the mostly grey sky.

Bill looked up at the crowd of onlookers gathered on the grass verge above the beach by the wooden walkway. A few had their phones out, busy recording the scene, no doubt hoping to become the next social media sensation. Why is it that we are attracted by the morbid? So curious about other people's misfortunes. Not that those gathered could see anything because a tent had been erected to preserve the crime scene. Bill turned around to see a group approaching from the seaward side, trudging right up to the perimeter tape.

"Step away from the cordon immediately," he said in an authoritative voice as he moved towards them. The people dispersed and skulked away, most of them with embarrassed looks on their faces. A trio of two men and a woman looked out of place with the dog-walking crowd. Bill cast his eye over them, gauging the men to be in their early thirties, both dressed in tight black jeans. They didn't look like they came from the area. The man on the left had shoulder-length dark hair, a silly-looking large hat, and what appeared to be facial piercings. The other man was more clean cut, with shorter hair, his mobile phone in a tight grasp.

The woman, probably in her mid-twenties, had red puffy eyes as though she'd been crying. "Sorry, officer. We saw a post on the community social media page that a young woman's body had been found," the man with the piercings and hat said.

For Christ's sake, Bill thought. The jungle drums were already beating.

"Our friend is missing. We're worried it might be her," he said.

"When did your friend go missing?"

"Um, we're not exactly sure, but I think at some stage late last night or early this morning. We'd had a big session. As far as I know, she was there when we all went to bed. We've been looking for her, but no luck so far."

"A big session?"

"We were celebrating the release of our new record and had one too many shandies; you know what it's like," the man with the piercings said, a slight smile emerging across his face.

Well, that explained why they didn't look like they belonged, Bill thought.

"Do you have a photo of your friend?" Bill said, gesturing to the phone the other man held on to.

"Oh, of course," the clean-cut man said, scrolling through his phone until he found a candid shot.

"Here, this is April," he said.

Bill took a photo of the screen. The girl in the photo had the same dark hair colour as the dead woman under the rowboat. He took a breath to stop himself from showing any sign of recognition, instead taking out his notebook and tapping his pen on it. He needed to get more details to confirm her identity.

"What's April's last name, and how old is she?"

"It's West, and she's twenty-two, nearly twenty-three. Her birthday is next week," the clean-cut man said.

"Address?"

"Um, she lives in Cambridge normally. We are just up here for a couple of days and rented an Airbnb here in Omaha. I'll have to get back to you with her actual address. I can't recall at the moment."

"Is it her that you have found?" the younger woman said, looking over Bill's shoulder in the direction of the rowboat.

"I'm not able to say yet," Bill said, even though he was sure it was April.

"You need to wait here. I'll need to take a statement from each of you. In the meantime, what's your name and contact details?" Bill said, opening his notebook and shielding it from the damp as best as he could.

They all cooperated and gave Bill the details required and stayed put.

~

AS BILL WALKED BACK to the tent, thinking about the girl he now knew to be April West, he found Rudd and Copeson had already photographed and documented most of the scene.

"Stop, don't come any closer," Rudd grumbled as he balanced on the stepping plates they'd placed on the ground to prevent contamination of the evidence. "You did enough clomping around before we got here!"

"There was only the woman who found the body and me. Anyway, we might have an ID for the young woman," Bill said.

Rudd still glared at him.

"I've just had a conversation with three individuals." Bill gestured towards the cordon. "Their friend April West has been missing since late last night or early this morning."

"It would fit with the timeline. She's not been out here for long. I'm guessing less than twelve hours, but it's really up to the pathologist," Rudd said. "You got a photo?"

"Yes, this is the woman," Bill said, holding out his phone. "I'm pretty sure it's the same person."

Rudd and Copeson glanced at the body still in situ on the damp sand. Bill had no doubt it was April.

"Is she a local girl?"

"She's from out of town. Here for a couple of days with friends, but we've yet to establish her exact movements and what led to this," Bill said as he looked over at the body.

11

The rain had cleared, but the damp rose from the sodden ground as the three friends huddled under one of the trees just up from the beach. Bill was soaked and pulled his raincoat collar up around his ears as he came to have a chat with them.

"All right, I'll take each of your statements in turn."

"How about ladies first?" Bill gestured for the young woman to sit on a nearby seat.

"Can I have your name, please?"

"Lisa," the girl said, flicking a long strand of wet hair off her face. Whether she was a natural redhead or her hair was dyed, Bill didn't know, but it was the same colour as her red-rimmed eyes.

"What time was it when you last saw April?"

"We were together for most of the evening. The guys hooked up with some girls, and I didn't see them until this morning. I had a headache and went back to the house we'd rented around midnight. April walked back with me. As far as I knew, she went to bed as well, but this morning, her bed hadn't been slept in, and I got worried. So, I messaged the boys, who came back straight away and helped me look. We even went to Jett's house, but there were only the cleaners, no one else."

"What can you tell me about last night?"

A pesky seagull landed nearby, and Lisa looked over at it before answering. "We arrived yesterday, settled in, and then went to Jett Starr's house for a party. We couldn't believe we were in his house. It was wild," she said, temporarily forgetting the circumstances of this morning.

"Wild as in how?"

"You know, lots of people, an open bar, amazing food, all laid on. I've never seen anything like it. I'm pretty sure there were drugs there, too, although I didn't take any. It's not my thing," she hastened to say.

"All right," Bill said, continuing to take notes. "Your friend mentioned you were here to celebrate some music achievement; is that right?"

"Yes, the four of us are in a band, and we've recently signed a contract with Jett Starr's record label."

Bill knew of the old rocker but didn't know he had a music label. Then again, they didn't move in the same circles.

"I'm the singer," Lisa said. "April's on keyboard with the guys on guitar and drums." "You said you messaged the boys. Where were they? Not at the Airbnb with you?

"Oh, they stayed overnight with the girls they'd met at the party. Girls love musicians."

"I see. Do you know if April knew anyone around here? Perhaps she went to visit someone?"

"I don't think so, no."

She glanced over at the ocean for a moment as a woman with a toddler walked by. "Is it her?" Lisa asked, looking back at Bill.

"I'm sorry, but I can't tell you at this stage," Bill said. Tears started falling down the young girl's face as the reality of the situation sunk in. "We need to make a formal identification first to be sure."

Bill talked to the two men and confirmed they'd stayed overnight with some girls. The only variant was that Ziggy—the pierced one with the hat—had seen April with a young man around one in the morning. All he could say was that the man didn't look like April's type; he was grungy and seemed quite drunk. Apparently, she'd met him earlier that night, and he'd messaged her and convinced her to come back to the party.

"Why did you leave her with him?

"I did ask her if she was all right, and she said she was."

April had convinced Ziggy that she'd get this man to walk her back to the house again after they'd had a few more drinks. Bill could see on his face that he regretted his decision now.

12

Bill glanced at his watch. He'd left Rudd and Copeson and headed back to the station in Matakana. There was nothing more he could do until they'd finished. It was late afternoon now, and the strong wind had not let up.

He'd not had a chance to go home and get changed out of his wet clothes, and he felt itchy and uncomfortable in his damp trousers. Back at the station, he'd typed up the statements from the dog walker who'd found the body—Vivianne Harper—and the three musician friends of the dead girl. Based on the evidence so far, he concluded she was most likely a sad statistic, an accidental death.

Rudd had phoned. April's purse, including her phone and wallet, had been found not far from where she was discovered, and they had been able to ID the body. A call had been put through to the local Waikato police to notify the girl's parents in Cambridge of the tragic news and to get them to make a formal identification at the morgue in Auckland.

Bill felt restless and couldn't wait to head home for the day, but first, he had to make a stop at Snells Beach. The woman he'd spoken with earlier had been on the verge of losing it. To find drugs in your sixteen-year-old's room was every parent's nightmare. He could hear the devastation in her voice and understood when she said she wanted him to be talked to sternly so he would never touch the stuff again.

Bill remembered when he'd found weed in Zac's bedroom. The stupid boy had been of a similar age, perhaps even fifteen, when a few of his mates—Ant, Luke and Steve—came around and lit up a joint in his room. Bill had smelt it a mile away. How dumb could they be? Smoking pot in the house when your dad is the local cop? It could never end well.

Now it seemed he could do nothing right in his son's eyes. Zac barely wanted to spend any time at home. He'd been talking about moving out, and perhaps that would be the best solution. He'd have to get a student loan, but to take some responsibility and mature would do him good.

He turned into Sharp Road. Another deluge had set in, and the windscreen wipers were going full tilt. It was a bleak afternoon, and there wasn't much traffic. Nearing the intersection that separated the road three ways, he stopped to give way to a caravan of motorcycles. The motley crew of patched gang members, seated low on their motorcycles, saluted him as they thundered past. They were coming from Sandspit and heading to Warkworth. He'd had dealings with them before, even though their base was farther up the coast. They must be soaked to the skin in these weather conditions. He could imagine what the wet leather smelt like and screwed up his nose.

The pit in his stomach told him this had been no social call. It never was. In the last year or so, the gang's presence had increased. He kept seeing them in the street. There was no law against that, and they always had a cheeky grin, but they wanted to aggravate and cause upset. The locals crossed the road to avoid them. He'd dealt with gangs for the twenty-five years he'd been a cop and wasn't the least bit intimidated. The only way to handle them was to show no fear. In the meantime, drugs and weapons were being sold, and violence followed. It was a vicious circle with no end.

Bill drove past the ornate Snells Beach sign, and the long winding road usually offered glimpses of the coast, but not on a miserable day like today. New houses had sprung up since he'd last been there, and he continued down the long hill into the settlement, where he turned left just before the shops. The street was quiet, and the brick, tile, and weatherboard family homes looked lived in, with trampolines and bikes scattered in the front gardens. Snells Beach was a pleasant place and had lots of permanent residents.

The woman he assumed he'd spoken with earlier appeared in the living room window as he pulled up to the address he'd been given. He parked the police car in the driveway, wondering what the neighbours might think.

"Do come in out of the wet," she shouted from the doorway, beckoning him to hurry out of the rain. Bill turned his jacket collar up to stop the rain running down his back.

"I'm Elisabeth Clayton. Stanley's mum."

Bill wiped his wet hands on his trousers before shaking hands with her.

"Thank you so much for coming here to deal with the little ratbag. And here's his wee stash," she said through gritted teeth, placing a small bag in the flat of Bill's hand. Bill opened the bag to find three small tablets that looked like lollies. The bright design was a familiar one.

"Thank you. I appreciate that you called. It's a worrying time for parents and young adults," he said, reassuring her that she'd done the right thing. "Is this the first time you've noticed your son bringing this home?"

She nodded, and he sensed a dark cloud of worry wrapped around her thin frame.

"Please talk some sense into him, Sergeant. I can't bear to lose Stanley as well," she said, wiping a tear from the corner of her eye.

Something jogged in his memory. *Clayton*. It seemed familiar. Yes, this family had lost an older son a long time ago in a car accident, just before Bill came back to live in Matakana. He remembered the paperwork.

"Of course, I'll see what I can do," Bill said, wiping his boots and following her up the stairs.

The 1970s brick and tile house was cosy. The steep pine stairs were narrow, and he broke out in a sweat in the dim confined space. He was immediately transported to the old unused well he'd fallen into as a child, and claustrophobia set in. He held on to both sides of the cramped space, his palms touching the walls. The sensory feel of the smooth surface quietened his mind, and he was back in the present. The landing and hallway upstairs were also gloomy, and he followed her into the dated kitchen. On a fine day, the views from the compact room would have been lovely, being in such an elevated position.

The skinny boy slouched at the far end of the dining table was subdued, his head bowed. He gazed at Bill through a long, greasy fringe. His expression was petulant, and Bill suspected the lad was unsure of what was to come. Bill pulled a chair out and sat down, his hands on the flannel-backed oilcloth, the kind that had been common when he'd been a boy.

His mother still used one, and he disliked its slightly tacky feel. "Hi, I'm Bill. How are you going?" The boy didn't speak.

"Stanley, where are your manners?" his mother said.

"It's all right," Bill said and turned around. "Is it okay if I have a chat with Stanley on my own for a minute?" He sensed the mother's presence was not helpful.

"Yes, of course. I'll be in the living room if you need me."

"So, your mum tells me she found some drugs in your room. Is that right?"

"Yes, but they are not mine, I swear," Stanley said as he looked up, his face acne-covered and blotchy. His eyes flared with anger, and his whole being was filled with contempt and defiance. "She shouldn't have snooped around in my room. She's not respecting my privacy at all."

"Okay, hang on a moment, Stanley," Bill said, holding his hand up to stop the verbal barrage that had started.

"My name is Stan," he snapped.

"Okay, Stan. Listen up. You are a minor still living in your parents' house. Their rules apply, as does a level of respect and being civil,"

Bill said, as he leant forward in an imposing manner. "Not to mention it's illegal to be in possession of Class B drugs."

"Okay, back off, man. I'm not falling for the police handbook intimidation," Stan said.

"We can do this talk officially at the station if that works better for you," Bill said dryly. "This means it would go on your record."

The demeanour of the young man instantly changed.

"Sorry, I didn't mean to be disrespectful," he said, cheeks flushing.

"All right, let's start over. How did you end up with the bag in your possession?" Bill said. As he weighed the bag in his hand, the movement tumbled the multicoloured tablets inside the bag.

"A mate of a mate handed them out at a party."

"You mean you didn't pay for them?"

"No, they were samples for me to share with friends. Next time we'd have to pay, he said."

"Who said that?"

"Look, man. I don't know this guy's name. He's not my mate; I already told you!"

Bill's ears pricked up. It was an obvious sales tactic used by street dealers to get the kids hooked and wanting more. The second bag was never free, which was how they got sucked in.

"Stan, can you see what's going on here? This is how these dealers get young kids addicted to this kind of shit."

"I told you. I don't do drugs!" Stan said.

"That may well be, but when you mix with this kind of crowd, the outcome is never good. Trust me," Bill said, finally breaking through to the lad. "Look, you are not in trouble here if you come clean. But I'll need a name and for you to tell me everything you know. It's not okay that these guys are selling this crap to school kids, right?"

Stan nodded. "All right, but I won't tell you my mate's name. You don't nark on your mates."

Bill put the bag of tablets in his pocket and pulled his notebook out, waiting for Stan to reveal what he was willing to.

"All I know is that he got it from this dude, Ringo. I'm not sure if it's his real name or if he has a surname, but that's what they call him.

He hangs around in Warkworth. The word is that he can supply anything. My mate got weed off him once, but apparently, he sells meth as well. Not that I want to have anything to do with his lot. The gangs are bloody crazy."

Bill's ears pricked up. He knew the gang presence had increased significantly in the last year, and he'd just seen them pass through from Sandspit. He'd have to check with the Warkworth Station regarding this individual, Ringo.

He was sure the local guys probably knew him. His thoughts went again to his son Zac and his moodiness. Was he doing drugs? Was the pressure at university too much? Bill knew a whole range of drugs was easily obtainable, especially in the city where Zac went to school.

13

Crystal heard heated voices coming from Andrei's study. She walked past the office on her way from the bedroom, where she'd picked up a book. The wide hallway echoed as they hadn't yet chosen the art to go up on the walls. The study was at the end of the hall, opposite their spacious master suite. The thick timber door was slightly ajar, and she could hear Mike's deep, gravelly voice. He and Andrei were arguing.

"For fuck's sake, what were you thinking to rope in a random person?" Andrei said.

"It should have been a straightforward pickup. The guy came highly recommended," Mike said.

"Tell me you picked up all the goods." "We got it all," Mike said.

"For your sake, Mike, you'd better hope there are no more loose ends."

Andrei's tone had changed to ice cold, and she could hear how angry he was. Crystal shivered. She had seen him like this before, and it scared her. Chairs scraped against the hardwood floor, and she could hear the footfall moving towards the door. She hurried into the large kitchen and quickly perched herself on the barstool by the thick Italian Carrara marble. She reached for the half-finished berry smoothie, took a sip, and braced herself for what was about to unfold. She knew his foul mood would carry on and ultimately impact her.

Why had Andrei been so angry with Mike? They'd been friends since school and always so tight. Andrei's parents had sponsored a less fortunate boy, and that boy was Mike. He'd received a full scholarship for his high school education, including board, as his family lived out of town. As fate would have it, they became the best of mates. Andrei convinced his parents to let him board at the prestigious school as well. Mike spent school holidays travelling with the Bowen family to places he could never dream of. Their friendship resulted in Mike working for Andrei's dad after graduating from university. And now he worked for Andrei, not that she knew exactly what he did.

Crystal didn't want to be caught eavesdropping. Andrei always kept her at arm's length, away from his business dealings, and disliked her knowing anything about what went on. She quickly pulled her phone out and started to scroll her Facebook feed before sensing a presence behind her. She could feel her rapid breathing but tried to remain calm.

"Hi, darling," Andrei said, coming up behind her. His hand gripped her shoulder tighter than usual. He always used his size to his advantage. Andrei looked down at her as if to mark that she was his property and placed a firm kiss on her mouth. Crystal felt her shoulder tense as his fingers burned into her flesh, but she did her best to relax.

"Yoga took a long time today. Any reason for that? Didn't the class finish at eight thirty?" he asked as his ice-blue eyes burrowed into her soul. The square jaw and thick-set face were intense. She had fallen in love with the blond muscle-bound Adonis of a man two years ago. Now she wasn't entirely sure of her feelings. She felt suffocated.

"I had coffee with a friend after yoga today. Mike was there."

"That's great. I'm glad you have a friend," Andrei said, scanning every inch of her face as though he were evaluating the truth of what she'd said.

"Who is this friend?" he continued, tilting his head and looking at her as if she were a child. No doubt, Mike had filled him in, but he clearly wanted to hear it from her. His firm hand squeezed the nape of her neck, forcefully massaging it as if to encourage her to speak.

"Her name is Annika. She's a local artist," Crystal said, wishing she was someone just like that with the freedom to express herself and come and go as she pleased and not constantly being babysat. Andrei increased the pressure on her neck, pushing her slightly forwards and off balance. She removed his firm grip and did her best to ignore his dominance.

14

Bill leant against a goalpost, his lungs screaming as he caught his breath, but each intake of air burned his windpipe. He'd spent the last hour and a half in an interval training session at the Rodney Rams rugby league ground in Whangateau. He wasn't as fit as he should be.

He wiped his sweaty forehead and felt his pulse slow down. Was he too old for this shit? The dirt from the ground caked his legs, and his training clothes were wet through. The Old Boys' session had been intense, but mostly, he enjoyed hanging out with the lads. He was one of the older guys, but what he lacked in speed and agility, he more than made up for in strategy. The old dog still had the odd trick up his sleeve to teach these younger guys.

It was eight thirty and time for a beer at the clubrooms. He felt a bit worse for wear and decided to call it a night, limping to the car. The clubrooms were right by the car park, and he could wave to the rowdy group that had already pulled the top off their first beer. Every inch of his body ached. It would be good to lose the few extra kilos he carried around his middle. The training session had taken a toll.

The team met twice weekly for a good run around, and his fitness was slowly improving. Tonight, he'd taken a bit of a tumble and pulled his right hamstring, so he thought it best to head home. The streetlights on the main road through the small settlement cast hazy reflections, making the dismal night seem even more dense and damp. Not even keen dog walkers ventured out in this terrible weather.

As he drove away from the rugby grounds, the skies opened again, and large raindrops mixed with hail pelted the car. His thoughts returned to the young woman they'd found on the beach today. He felt for her poor parents; you shouldn't have to bury your child.

In the short five-minute drive home, his leg had seized up sufficiently for it to be a struggle to get out of the car. He limped up the garden path and was greeted by the hugely excited Maggie and Finn, who jumped on him as soon as he opened the front door. Legs, tails, and curly coats were in a jumble.

"All right, guys. Settle down. I've missed you, too," Bill said, grimacing as he hobbled through to the kitchen.

"Jeepers, you're mucky. How was training?" Annika said and laughed. His long-suffering wife was used to getting stains out of his police uniform and training clothes.

"It was a lot of fun. Great to let off some steam."

"You're limping!"

"I'm sure it's nothing. I've just pulled a muscle," he said, smiling.

"Well, you're not twenty anymore," Annika said and kissed him.

Bill melted. He knew she was right, of course. But he was in no way ready to hang up his rugby boots just yet.

The smell of the leftover spaghetti bolognese permeated the kitchen, and Bill's stomach rumbled. It was a long time since breakfast, and he'd missed lunch, only eating a banana before training. Annika usually left his dinner in the oven on a covered plate so it wouldn't dry out.

"I'll get out of these wet clothes and shower. I'll be downstairs to have dinner shortly," he said to change the subject. The last thing he needed was a lecture about what was age-appropriate. He still felt in his prime, well, just about anyway.

Bill put on a brave face and climbed the stairs. He threw his dirty training clothes on the floor next to the hamper in the bedroom before he limped into the ensuite bathroom. The slight hamstring strain wasn't serious, but he knew it would be tender for a few days. A hot shower would do the trick; then he'd pop a couple of anti-inflammatories and apply some ointment. There would be a few days of hobbling around, but nothing that he couldn't cope with. An early night was what he needed.

The conversation with Stan was still on his mind. It infuriated him that drugs were being peddled to high school kids. Without a doubt, this set some of them on a self-destructive path and ultimately destroyed any future prospects they might have.

In the dim light, he didn't see the large puddle of water on the dark Rimu floorboards outside the shower cubicle. His left foot slid out from under him like he was on a banana peel, and he fell sideways before regaining his balance. His ribcage slammed into the edge of the toilet seat. The impact winded him, and he fell to the floor with a deep groan. The ugly pain radiated across his side to the sternum, and he struggled to get more than shallow breaths into his lungs. He heard footsteps rushing up the stairs.

"Bill, are you all right?" Annika said, rushing into the bathroom.

The intense pain made him dizzy, and he couldn't respond.

"Did you hit your head, Bill?" Annika dropped to his side.

"Don't think so, but my ribs are giving me grief," he groaned through gritted teeth.

"The girls used our shower earlier. I suppose they didn't dry the floor properly," Annika said, helping Bill get up.

Bill leant against the handbasin as a cold sweat ran down his forehead.

"What the hell is wrong with them using their own bathroom?" Bill sneered.

"Well, apparently, Zac had been in there just before, and they couldn't use it because it stank. So, I said it was okay for them to use ours."

"I can't believe Zac is home. That's a rare treat," Bill said.

"He's gone again. He was only home to eat, then left to see his mates."

"Well, I guess it's good that he takes the time to see some friends and not just study," Bill said. "Come on, help me into the shower before the adrenaline wears off and the pain worsens."

Bill held on to the door handle for support as the warm water rinsed his battered body. The water pressure aggravated the nerve endings on his side, and he felt physically ill. He washed quickly because it was an effort to move his body, but at least he was clean.

"I've put your towel here. Will you be all right to get out on your own?" Annika asked through the steam.

"I'm fine, thanks," Bill groaned.

He let the warm water soothe him while Annika dried the floor to prevent him from slipping again. When he was done, he took care as he stepped on the bathmat and grabbed the towel, and dried himself as best as he could. The adrenaline still coursed through his body, numbing most of the discomfort; he knew worse was to come once it wore off. He limped into the adjacent bedroom and caught his breath as he held on to the end of the dresser.

Annika had laid some clothes on the bed for him. It was an effort to pull the T-shirt over his head as he had to lift his arms.

"Do you need to see the doctor?" Annika said as she came back upstairs to check on him. "Judging by the discomfort, you might have a couple of broken, or at the very least, bruised ribs."

"I'll be all right. Let's see what it's like tomorrow morning. I've had broken ribs before, and you can do nothing beyond putting up with it."

"Yes, but that was at least twenty years ago when you were much younger. It won't heal that quickly now," Annika said.

He sighed, hoping that she wasn't right. He'd have to be dead not to show up for work, but in his current state, there was no way he'd be able to cope at the station on his own.

~

Annika sat opposite Bill. His face was pale with a sheen of sweat on his forehead, and he kept shifting in his seat as he attempted to take in some food. It was obvious he was in discomfort. Why was it that men always pushed themselves way beyond the limit? she thought as Bill limped up the stairs after he'd eaten his dinner. She'd given him pain relief and hoped that he'd be able to get some rest.

Annika curled up on the old settee and returned her focus to the book she'd been reading. The open fire crackled and sizzled, and as Annika looked at its flames, she wondered what people would think of her latest paintings. Would they like them?

She leant back and got back into her book. It was a local thriller set in Matakana. The author was a friend, making reading even more special. Annika enjoyed the local flavour and the setting immensely, and she had toyed with the idea of writing a book herself, but perhaps not a thriller. She wasn't sure she could tie up a good murder mystery with all the necessary twists and turns required. Perhaps something historical about the area and the settlers? Maggie and Finn snuggled by her feet and snored ever so gently.

A great feeling of contentment washed over her as she pulled the blanket over her legs and continued reading. She turned the page to find out what would happen next and enjoyed the well-needed escape and being swept up in the wonderful world of fiction. Little did Annika know this was just the beginning of what would unfold.

15

Tuesday the 4th of July

It was only seven in the morning, but Andrei had already been up for a couple of hours. The workout had been great, and he'd pushed his muscles to the limit before tipping a large protein shake down his throat and then taking a quick shower.

He was in his early forties, still in good shape, and couldn't imagine not looking after his body. He wiped the fogged-up mirror with a hand towel and admired his physique before slicking a dollop of clear gel in his palms and through his short blond hair.

Crystal was still asleep in the big bed in the master bedroom. He glanced over at her and contemplated if he should head back to bed but decided that he'd best get going—he had a lot to do today. As he brushed his teeth, the phone vibrated on the marble-topped vanity.

His foreman's number bleeped up on the screen.

"Kingston, what can I do for you?"

"Sorry to call you this early, but some fuckwits have vandalised the house here at site one."

"Fuck, what are we talking about?" Andrei said as he spat out some toothpaste.

"What's the damage?"

"I've just arrived, but someone has smashed a couple of windows. There's glass everywhere inside. It doesn't look like anyone's been inside or stolen anything. There's also a fucking massive pile of cow shit on the driveway."

"What the fuck?"

"I'll get the boys to sweep up, but I'll need the digger to get rid of the shit."

"Any idea who did this?"

"No idea, boss."

Andrei was angry and hung up. He wasn't sure who was behind this, but he had his suspicions. When he did find out, he'd make them pay, the useless fucks.

He dialled Mike, who was desperately trying to sound like he was awake while Andrei told him what had happened.

"I want fucking cameras up on every site, Mike!"

"Do you think it's about Fanta?"

"What else would it be?"

"We need to keep it cool and not overreact. It sounds like someone's pissed off."

He knew Mike was right and that they needed to calm down and not go off halfcocked. The assholes would keep.

16

It had been a rough night. Bill felt like he'd pulled an all-night bender despite the pain relief. He parked the car outside the Matakana Medical Centre. He couldn't remember when he'd last been there, but it must have been years.

He walked up the wheelchair ramp that was closest to the car park. Before he'd even reached the front door, he could hear the screaming of a couple of boisterous toddlers wreaking havoc in the waiting room. He sighed as he pulled the heavy door open and was distracted momentarily by the noise before the pain radiating from his chest hit him.

He felt like he would pass out. Bill steeled himself as it would not be a good look to sag to his knees while in his police uniform and alarm the kids.

The room went quiet as he stepped through the door with a strained smile on his face.

The toddlers gazed at him in awe. He'd been the same. All he wanted to be as a kid was a police officer. The bright-eyed receptionist gave him a warm smile and waved him over.

"Good morning. What can we do for you today?" she said, her copper-red, tight curls gently bouncing as she spoke. She was in her twenties and had the fresh-faced appearance of someone who hadn't yet had kids, who got to sleep well and had 'me time.' Her name tag said 'Denise,' and Bill didn't know her. Her appearance was a stark contrast to some of the mothers in the waiting room who had dark circles under their eyes.

"I'd like to see Dr Duncan, please. I may have broken some ribs," Bill said, trying not to flinch.

"I don't think I have seen you here before," Denise said, urging him to volunteer his name.

"My name is Bill Granger."

"Unfortunately, Dr Duncan is away on leave, but we have an excellent locum. Her name is Alice."

"All right, I suppose that's fine, then," Bill said, a little annoyed. He wanted to see his doctor, not some young, fresh-faced locum barely out of medical school.

"I can see you are in pain. Unfortunately, we're booked up, but I will try to squeeze you in before the toddlers," Denise said.

"Thanks, Denise. I appreciate it," he said, looking for somewhere to sit.

The only seat left was in the corner, and he was relieved that he could lean his body against the cool surface of the brick wall for a moment. It didn't take long before the noise was in full swing again, and he regretted stepping into the clinic.

He had barely made himself as comfortable as possible when he heard his name being called from the doorway to his right.

"Bill Granger."

The mature woman who greeted him was not at all what Bill had expected. The locum looked to be in her sixties, and the wrinkles around her eyes gave him the impression that she laughed a lot, making him feel better. She wasn't a pimply-faced, recent graduate, after all.

"Hello, I'm Alice," she said and extended her right hand.

"Hi, nice to meet you," Bill said as they walked into her room.

"So, what brings you in here today?" she said as she warmed her hands by rubbing them together.

Bill gave her the whole rundown about what had happened.

"Okay, take off your shirt, and let's have a look at you," Alice said.

"Sure." Bill struggled to get his arm out of the sleeve and contorted his body without touching the right side of his torso.

"Yep, looks like you did a bit of damage," she said, examining the large purple bruise.

Bill gritted his teeth as the pain shot off the scale, and the doctor's fingers poked and prodded along the ribs.

"What happened here? she said, seeing the puckered scar on his abdomen. The remark took Bill by surprise. He hadn't even thought of it as he'd stripped off.

"It was in the line of duty. I was in the wrong place at the wrong time with some trigger-happy, drug-crazed people. They did not appreciate my presence. Hence they used me as target practice," Bill said, trying to put a humorous spin on a traumatic event.

"Oh, dear. You were lucky they weren't the best shots, then."

"I suppose I was," Bill answered as he thought about how he'd lain on the floor in the warehouse, surrounded by a large pool of blood. He'd almost lost his life. "Very lucky, for sure."

"Well, you most likely have a couple of broken ribs there, Bill. Of course, we'll need to send you for an X-ray to give you a definitive answer, but that's up to you. You'd need to go into Warkworth," she said as she washed her hands after the exam.

"I'm happy to write you a referral."

"No, I don't think that's necessary, but can you give me something for the pain? It's killing me, or at least something to help me sleep."

"Are you still working?"

Bill nodded. "I'll definitely be at work. There's no one else. I'm the sole charge here in Matakana."

"In that case, I can't give you anything stronger for the discomfort. I'm afraid you will have to put up with it," Alice said, looking up from the computer over her reading glasses.

"I can prescribe Paracetamol and some anti-inflammatory drugs. As for your sleep, how about a few days' worth of sleeping tablets, although I'd recommend not taking them every night as it can really bugger up your sleep," she said straight up.

It was refreshing to deal with an old-school doctor. She was just like Dr Duncan—someone who called a spade a spade and didn't guess or dance around.

"You can have one of these rib support belts," she said, pulling a packet out of the storage cupboard in the examination room. "It'll give you some support and make you slightly more comfortable."

Bill looked at her in disbelief.

"It's still going to take six to eight weeks to heal, and I strongly advise avoiding activities that could further injure your ribs. And absolutely no heavy lifting until then. Now, let me help you with this elastic support."

"Oh, okay, thanks," Bill said. He felt rather uncomfortable being assisted with getting the elastic around his chest. The tight garment felt like no air was going in or out of his lungs.

"You'll get used to wearing it, and if you feel it's not a help, you can remove it."

"All right, thanks."

Bill felt like he would pass out from lack of oxygen as he stumbled out to pay at reception.

"It went well then?" Denise said, her hair flopping as she spoke. Bill nodded and paid. He had to circumnavigate the room and skirt around the outsides to avoid a couple of crawling babies on the floor. He saw a vast number of toys scattered mostly in the play area in the corner and thought to himself it was a real health hazard, thankfully contained.

The crisp, cool air made him feel better. The doctor's heated surgery had made him feel a little giddy, and having his ribs squeezed in place did nothing to help. He should probably have gone to the pharmacy to get his prescription filled but went to work instead.

BILL HOBBLED out of the car and up the steps to the police station. The icy wind rushed by his ears, and the dampness inside the station did nothing to improve his mood. The pain relief he'd taken this morning barely took the edge off the discomfort and pain, but the last thing he wanted was to stay at home when there was work to do. He rummaged around in the desk drawer to find a couple of Paracetamol tablets, popped them out of the blister pack, and walked into the kitchen for a glass of water. He swallowed them in one large gulp.

Bill filled the electric jug and pressed the button for it to boil. He gagged for a coffee and hadn't had the energy to pick one up from the bakery this morning. It was one of life's silver linings and a little luxury that he allowed himself to have, but the effort had been too much this morning. He'd have to make do with the rubbish they had in the kitchen cupboard.

The jug clicked off, and he spooned the instant coffee into a chipped mug and poured in hot water. A weak coffee smell hit his nose. It would have to do today.

He knew he had to let headquarters in Orewa know he'd need some help for the next couple of weeks without letting them know the full extent of his injury. There was no way he wanted to be forced to take sick leave.

The winter had been quiet. Hopefully, it would stay that way. He was more than capable of pushing paper around and made his way to his desk, turning the computer on.

He found the remote for the heat pumps in the drawer and turned the temperature in the main office up to blast the damp chill from the air. He wished he'd brought a jumper, but it had been enough of an effort to put his shirt on.

Bill picked up the phone and rang his superiors in Orewa, explaining what had happened. They suggested he probably should be on sick leave for a few days, but he convinced his boss he was all right. Before the conversation finished, Bill suggested they could send Niko up. He'd worked well with the young Samoan constable—Falaniko Sopoaga—or Niko to his mates. The boss made no promises; the decision had to go through the proper channels. Everything was so bureaucratic, Bill thought as he hung up.

The elastic girdle contraption the doctor had given him this morning squeezed his ribs as he sat at his desk. The elastic belt might hold everything well supported, but the pressure also increased the pain. He pulled his shirt up and undid the Velcro, almost passing out in the process. “Fuck this,” he said to himself. There was no way he’d be able to put up with this for six weeks.

17

The soft tones and gentle vibrations of the harp and the kalimba soothed Annika's frazzled mind as she walked into the yoga class. She was stressed beyond her limit about the exhibition, and she'd had words with Zac this morning about helping hang the paintings for the exhibition. He'd promised to help her weeks ago but had now reneged. Apparently, he'd made other plans. To say that she was hurt and disappointed was an understatement, and to have Bill with cracked ribs topped it all off. Annika slipped her shoes off at the entrance.

The few people already there either talked quietly to their neighbour or did gentle stretches in preparation for the yoga practice. Annika found a spot at the back of the class, rolled the yoga mat out, and set herself up with her water bottle and bag next to her.

Crystal arrived a few minutes later, fresh-faced and with a big smile. She waved to Annika and put her mat down in the middle as there weren't many empty spaces left. She pointed to her wristwatch and in the direction of the cafe next door to see if Annika wanted to catch up after the class. Annika had anticipated this and nodded. Something about this woman intrigued her—she came across as confident yet very vulnerable. Regardless, it was nice to make a new friend.

The ninety-minute class went quickly, and Annika felt refreshed in body and mind as she gathered her things.

"I'm so glad to see you here today," Crystal said, her face lighting up.

They walked past the blacked-out car in the car park on their way to the cafe. Mike had his window partly down, and Annika noticed there was no expression on his face, nor did he acknowledge them.

"Does he drive you everywhere?" Annika asked.

"It's complicated. My boyfriend is very protective and feels better if Mike comes with me," Crystal said.

Annika's first thought was how controlling Andrei sounded.

The café next door was busy, and almost all the tables were occupied. A mother and toddler group were spread over most of the back of the café with more squealing two-year-olds than she'd seen in a while. At least they were happy screams of delight rather than the gorgeous little cherubs crying.

"Shall we take a seat in the corner over there?" Crystal said.

"Perfect. At least we are out of the main path of these little ones' fun and games," Annika said.

Annika never ate before yoga class, as it made her feel terrible. They ordered their food and drinks, which arrived almost immediately.

"I won't be able to go to the next class. My exhibition is the same day, and I have so much to organise," Annika said.

"You're kidding me," Crystal said, looking intrigued. "I had no idea you were getting ready for a show. That's so exciting!"

"You'd be very welcome to come along on the opening night," Annika said, a bit bemused at the reaction.

"That would be amazing. I'll see if Andrei wants to go. We could really do with some vibrant art pieces on the walls in the new house," Crystal said. "It's still a bit bare."

"Perfect, that's settled then. Now we just need some more people to turn up on the night," Annika said and laughed.

"Do you have any photos of your work on your phone?" Crystal asked.

"Of course," Annika said, pulling her phone out of her gym bag and scrolling through the photo roll before handing it to Crystal.

"Oh, wow. These are fantastic. I love your use of colour, and the tonal depths of these pieces are outstanding," Crystal said as she scrolled from one to the other, delightful murmurings escaping her lips.

"Thanks. I'm glad you like them," Annika said, inwardly thankful that someone appreciated her new painting style.

"I just love them. My gosh, you are one talented woman Annika.What's the inspiration behind this series?"

"I guess I take inspiration from the landscape and the community around me. Just look around you. The undulating valleys, dense bush, and breath-taking coastline are all there to draw on. To be able to take a walk on one of our pristine beaches, smell the salty air, walk barefoot and feel the sand between your toes, or witness the wildlife; fills up your creative well. I'm sure it wouldn't matter what I did—painting, sculpting, textile work, whatever—I would still draw on inspiration from nature."

"Wow, I think you're amazing," Crystal said, beaming. "Do you have a catalogue you can send me?"

"Sure, I can do that. Give me your email address, and I'll get it all sent to you as soon as it's done."

"I'll send it to my contacts. Who knows who might turn up on the night?" Crystal said. "Andrei knows a lot of people, too. I'm sure he'd be happy to spread the word."

Annika was surprised and a bit taken aback. She was not used to 'people who knew people' to sell her paintings. It was probably a long shot anyway, although it would be nice to have a full house and many prospective buyers.

Deep inside, Annika fretted that no one would turn up on the night. Ridiculous, really, for a woman her age to be stressed about things she had no control over.

"I so wish I could create something outstanding," Crystal said, breaking Annika's train of thought.

"You can do anything you put your mind to, Crystal," Annika said, putting her hand on the young woman's arm.

"You really think so? Crystal said.

"Of course. You only have to find what brings you joy in life. The other important factor is not to get disheartened if it doesn't fall into place straight away. To get good at something takes practice and time," Annika said.

"I suppose you're right," Crystal said, reaching for the last mouthful of the green smoothie she'd ordered. "Oh, my goodness, is that the time? " she said as she looked at her mobile phone. "I should get going. Otherwise, Andrei will wonder where I am." "Doesn't Mike let him know?" Annika asked.

"Yes, I suppose he does. I don't want to get Mike in trouble, though. He has places to be rather than to wait for me." Crystal stood up from the table and glanced toward the car Mike was waiting in.

They walked out together. Annika's car was parked nearby.

As they waved goodbye, she wondered what sort of hold Andrei had over Crystal.

18

Annika paused and looked around the large gallery space next to her studio. She finally felt all the loose ends of the exhibition were coming together. The stress she had experienced over the last few days was all but blown away. She should have known better. It was always the same. The feeling of being out of control before the last pieces of the puzzle came together.

Today they would hang the paintings. She was still upset that Zac had let her down at the last minute, but at least Andy, her friend from the gym, would be there to help.

She'd rolled a fresh coat of crisp white paint on the walls. She always did, whether she needed it or not. It was a ritual that was a part of the lead-up to every exhibition. The metallic smell of the paint clung to the air. The backdrop was perfect, and the paintings would speak for themselves. This project was six months in the making, perhaps even longer. She had poured her heart and soul into it and pushed the boundaries. It was her most provocative collection to date. She'd experimented with organic materials like crushed shells, leaves, plants and paint mediums. The effect of mixed media on the canvas was tremendously exciting.

After the trauma a couple of months ago, it felt like a fresh gust of wind had ripped through her creative mind, enabling her to be free and take her art in a different direction. Now, she just had to decide where to hang each piece.

She grabbed the canvas closest to her. Her arm muscles bulged as she lifted the heavy art piece. Annika placed each canvas where she thought they'd go best and leant them against the wall as she sorted out the optimum spots.

It was mid-morning by the time Andy walked through the door. He was one of the personal trainers, and his light blue eyes made him a firm favourite with the young ladies.

"Sorry, I'm late. The body combat class went over time," Andy said. "Then one of the yummy mummies wanted to talk about a personal program. I got away as quickly as I could."

His navy tracksuit pants and white singlet accentuated every muscle as he threw on a grey hoodie. To be honest, he could have worn a sack and looked great.

"That's all good, and congratulations on picking up a new client."

"Absolutely, but now I'm at your disposal," he said, smiling. "I thought Zac was going to be here as well?"

"Don't ask," Annika said as she shook her head.

"We'll be fine, I'm sure," he said. "Wow, you've really outdone yourself this time, Annika." He stepped close to look at one of her favourite paintings.

"Thanks, Andy. Let's hope everyone else likes them as well."

"They are absolutely wicked. I'm so proud of you," Andy said and hugged her. He carried a takeaway tray of coffee from the café across the road. The delicious aroma permeated the air with a bouquet of caramel, roasted almond and maple syrup.

"And I brought you one of these," he said as he dangled a brown paper bag with a slight grease mark on the outside. "It's a savoury scone with butter. I thought we could share."

"I suppose some sustenance won't hurt. We have a lot of work to do," Annika said.

The sweet-tasting coffee went down a treat, and she got hold of the first painting—an abstract seascape with deep blues and opaque accents of white and gold, with a luscious, effervescent sea foam that magically washed over the edge. She was pleased with it. This one piece of art reflected so many emotions.

"A little to the left. Up a bit, there. That's perfect," Annika said, standing back and admiring the large canvas Andy had hung. "That's one. Only nineteen more to go." Annika laughed.

They had done this many times before, and she knew it would take the rest of the day to get it sorted. Andy picked up the next one. It was bigger than the first, and his muscular back strained under the weight, but he was used to it.

"I reckon you have piled this lot with more paint than usual. They weigh a ton."

It was true. She had needed to put supporting crossbars on the back of the wooden frames on the paintings to support their weight. She was really pleased with a couple of paintings in this series and had called it *Ti Point, The Blue Light*.

Every collection was unique. It had taken months to build up the texture and the different layers. She loved the artistic freedom she had and that she could pursue her passion—not everyone was so lucky. Her thoughts briefly went to Crystal and her strange relationship with her demanding boyfriend. What kind of imbecilic man did not let his girlfriend work or even drive? One thing was for sure; she'd never put up with Bill if he had carried on like that. Annika knew he was incredibly proud of her and all her endeavours.

This morning, he'd been extremely grumpy and in a lot of pain before he went to work. She had suggested he'd take the day off and rest, but he wouldn't hear a word of it.

"I might be a cripple, but I can still answer the phone and push paper around," he'd said before heading out the door. Oh well, it probably did him good to have his mind occupied by something else rather than getting bored at home.

"Annika, where do you want this one?" Andy said, pointing to the next one.

They had done well time-wise. It was mid-afternoon, and there were only five paintings left to hang.

"Okay, let's take a break. I don't know about you, but I'm running out of energy. Let me go get something to eat. I made lasagne this morning. Do you fancy a piece?" Annika said.

"Go on, I'm starving," Andy asked. "Do you need a hand?"

"No, thanks, it just needs to be reheated. It shouldn't take long."

She stepped out of the gallery into the sun, which felt good on her face. The weather had improved, but a cool wind blew around a corner as she hurried up the wide wooden steps to the old house. She wiped her paint-stained gym shoes on the doormat before she stepped into the cosy entrance full of shoes and Molly and Finn's large dog beds.

The sun streamed into the dated kitchen, giving it a warmth she so loved. It needed renovation and didn't have enough storage and bench space, but it was still the heart of the house and a place she loved to spend time with her boisterous family. She heated the food and covered the two plates with foil and perched them like a waitress in her left hand, carrying a basket with a tablecloth, cutlery, and a couple of cold drinks in her right hand.

Molly and Finn woke from their slumber in the corner of the studio.

The smell of the melt-in-the-mouth, homemade lasagne wafted throughout the studio, and she realised how hungry she was. The rich Italian tomato sauce, fragranced with loads of Italian herbs from their own garden, and the rich cheese topping smelt divine. Andy just about inhaled his.

"Does it taste all right then?" Annika said and laughed.

"Oh man, this is delicious!!" he said, wiping his mouth with the back of his hand.

"Glad you like it," she said, handing him a serviette.

Molly and Finn mooched around, wanting something to eat.

"Go on, guys. There's nothing here for you," Andy said and shooed them away.

The food renewed their enthusiasm and energy, and they were all done by late afternoon.

Andy sat on the couch at the back and flung his feet on the low rattan coffee table. It had been a proper workout. He was more than happy to help; anything to take his mind off his current girlfriend issues, he'd told Annika. For all the years they had known Andy, he'd always picked the dolly birds, who seemed to come with a lot of drama.

"Thank Christ for that," Andy said and massaged the top of his shoulders. He was glad they were finished for the day.

"All set for the exhibition. I think we have outdone ourselves with the pieces this time," Annika said.

"It looks fantastic if I do say so myself," Andy said, smiling at Annika.

The natural light from the skylights above made the paintings come alive. She was more thrilled than she could have dreamt of.

19

Crystal sat in the back of the car as Mike drove her home. A whirl of thoughts swirled in her head. Even though she had everything she could ever want, she didn't have what Annika possessed.

Sure, Andrei was a generous man. He wanted her to have what made her happy, and she had it all: designer clothes, handbags and trips away. He always made things happen. It was great in the beginning. She'd got swept up in it all and enjoyed the lavish gifts and exciting experiences. Now, she felt there was more to life than the latest fashions. She wanted what Annika had—accomplishment—something of her own and genuine happiness.

Compared to that, her life seemed a bit like a veneer, and she craved more.

Mike had been quiet on the drive home. He was usually chatty, but it was obvious that something was on his mind. She wondered what was going on with Andrei and him. They were always a tight unit. Lately, though, it seemed there had been fractures in the camp. She knew there was no point asking Mike. He would never discuss what was going on.

Mike dropped her off at home. The house seemed so empty

despite its beautiful furniture and latest gadgets. Andrei preferred a minimalist look—every piece in the house had been carefully purchased and positioned in just the right spot, every colour-coordinated cushion plumped to perfection on the large sofas. They'd chosen the colour scheme with care, a few base shades with matching accents.

She couldn't imagine having little people running around with sticky hands, toys strewn everywhere, and general disruption to the Zen-like calm. Of course, she'd like to have children one day with the right person. But Crystal wasn't sure Andrei was the right one. He already had two daughters from his previous marriage; he was a doting father and loved them unconditionally, but she doubted he'd ever changed a nappy or taken the 'night shift.' She was sure it had all been Joanne, his ex-wife's job. She'd only spoken to Jo on a handful of occasions, but she seemed nice.

On one weekend a month, Andrei's girls came to stay with them. He performed the perfect Dad duties, taking them to movies and showing them a good time. He was there wholeheartedly. Like he'd been there for her. He'd wooed her, taken her out, and put her on a pedestal in the beginning. Now, he was hardly ever around. She was lonely. She missed her old life, her messy flat, and her friends in Auckland. It felt like a lifetime ago.

Perhaps she could convince Andrei to let her get a job. It truly drove her crazy to stay at home. She needed air, people around her, something interesting to do, and a purpose to her existence. There was no way in the world she would give in to Andrei's desire to have a family. Not yet, anyway. She wasn't ready to take that leap, but Crystal wasn't sure how long she could hold it off. Her excuses were flimsy, which made Andrei even more determined.

20

Bill was looking forward to his first takeaway coffee of the day. He had asked Laura from the bakery to deliver it as he could not stomach another instant brew. She had also kindly picked up his prescription, which had been emailed directly to the pharmacy.

He took the first sip and savoured the nutty taste, feeling some joy returning. Then, the phone on his desk rang.

"What the bloody heck have you done to yourself, Sarge?" Niko said, letting out a deep-throated laugh.

"You don't want to know," Bill said as he held his ribs, trying desperately not to laugh.

"The Senior said I could leave tomorrow, but I'll be up after work today. I have to go home and gather up a few things first," Niko said.

"It'll be good to see you," Bill said, and he meant it. He enjoyed the young South Auckland constable working alongside him.

He took another sip; the caffeine hit the spot, and he felt marginally better—as long as he didn't breathe or move.

He made a few phone calls and finished some emails needing a response. The air temperature had dropped like a stone despite the sun peeking out. The weather forecast was for the cold weather to get worse, with a couple of days of polar blasts and south-westerlies coming straight up from Antarctica. It was rarely this chilly, but he liked it when it was because the hoodlums stayed inside and didn't cause too much havoc. Not that there was much trouble in the area, and certainly a lot fewer shenanigans in winter than in summer, with the thousands of visitors who poured in. Of course, there were always the bored teenage ratbags, but they only did what kids usually do.

He could see his breath hanging in front of his face.

The station was as cold as outside. He got on with his work, but it was a struggle because it didn't matter if he sat, stood or walked. The pain was ugly. He put up with it until just after lunchtime. Then, exhaustion overtook him, and he needed to rest if he was to make it through the day. He closed up shop around one, diverted the phone, and with great effort, contorted himself into the Ute to drive home. A cold sweat beaded down his forehead despite the chill in the air.

He didn't have the energy to walk into the studio to check on Annika's exhibition set- up; instead, he pulled himself gently up the front steps and into the house. He leant on the kitchen counter and groaned as he reached into the paper bag from the pharmacy for the pain relief. He popped some tablets out of the blister pack and gulped them down with tap water. The pain radiated along his side as he struggled up the stairs. He only bothered to kick his shoes off before gently easing himself down on the bed. The pain made him tired, and lying down was a relief. He was out within minutes.

21

Niko's Holden Commodore hummed along the Northern Motorway. He was glad he'd left Auckland before the worst of the rush hour traffic. It was mid-afternoon, and no traffic to speak of on the Orewa side of the motorway. It was such a contrast to the crazy Southern Motorway that was always so busy, no matter the time of day.

Niko put the cruise control on and enjoyed the scenic drive up the coast. Andrea Bocelli's soft tenor voice reverberated through the stereo. Niko turned up the volume and sang along. If his mates could hear him now, they'd surely give him a ribbing. Just because he was built like the proverbial brick shit-house, it didn't mean he wasn't sensitive. Due to his likeness to Dwayne Johnson, the actor, they called him The Rock. Sure, they were both of Samoan heritage, were built similarly, and had tribal tattoos. Niko's were on his chest and arms; he wasn't too sure about the actor's. Niko also had a full head of jet-black hair that was slicked back. He was in his mid-twenties, half the age of Dwayne Johnson.

People often judge a book by its cover. He was a young Samoan man who took pride in his appearance, worked hard and played hard, especially in the gym. There were no shortcuts. He ate well and looked after himself. He owed it to his girlfriend, Katarina. She'd brought him down to earth and helped him mature. His family loved her, too, and there was immense pressure for them to get married. They had talked about it, but neither of them was quite ready.

He stretched the legs of the car, and the growl of the V8 roared, which sent vibrations along his spine. The car was his pride and joy. When his Senior Sergeant had called him into his office earlier and asked if he'd be keen to go to Matakana to help for a few weeks, he hadn't hesitated for a moment. Niko finished his shift just after lunch and went straight home to pack his bags—not that he needed much. The timing was perfect, as Katarina had returned to the United States last month.

He was happy to have the distraction. It wasn't as if he had any plans for the next little while. Katarina was a forensic scientist and was in the United States for her PhD studies, and they planned to have a holiday together when she was back in a couple of months. He missed her a lot. They Face Timed each other every night, and he couldn't wait to tell her that he'd been sent back to Matakana when they spoke later tonight.

They didn't live together in a conventional way. Both their Samoan families were devoutly christian and would never have been happy with them 'shacking up.' There were standards to uphold.

Her dad was a community elder and a chief, and Niko would never bring shame on their families by going against their wishes. He and Katarina had been together for just over two years, and it was probably time for Niko to ask for her hand in marriage. To be honest, he was a bit intimidated by her father. He missed her a lot; it had been difficult to stay apart.

Niko smiled. It was a lucky break to be asked to return to Matakana so soon again. He liked the village atmosphere and working with Bill. The old cop could be a bit on the grumpy side sometimes and definitely carried some baggage from a long career in the service. But there was no ambiguity, just straight talk. You knew what to expect from Bill, and it was just how he liked it. Niko's parents were God-fearing people, where respect and duty to family and community came first. There was no grey area.

He still felt bad for the trouble and shame he'd brought his mum and dad during his teenage years. Thankfully, he'd straightened himself out and enjoyed his work in South Auckland—one of the toughest police districts in the country. He felt a sense of purpose and could relate to the troubled youth he dealt with. He'd been one of them not so long ago. But by the grace of God, he'd slipped through and survived the drugs and the gangs. It was his turn to repay and make good.

It didn't take long to reach the tunnels at Puhoi, and Niko slowed down. It was a couple of months since he'd left his summer secondment in the holiday town. Even though not many people knew he could sing, Niko's boyhood years in the local church choir had paid off as he belted out the notes along with the Italian tenor. He was happy to be on his way.

The clouds looked dark and angry on the horizon as he neared Warkworth, and in an instant, the heavens opened to a torrential downpour, and visibility was reduced to almost non-existent.

He could see a couple of brake lights in the distance. Large sheets of rain blanketed the car, and the wipers worked hard to disperse the water across the windscreen. The deluge of water on the road made it hazardous, and he slowed down.

Despite the terrible weather, it didn't take long until he cruised into Warkworth and turned right at the infamous Hill Street intersection towards the coast. As soon as he was on Matakana Road, the familiar undulating valleys and scattered vineyards bought a sense of calm, and he felt as if he'd arrived home. There was something serene and peaceful about it. He could definitely live and work here as he got older. But, for now, he quite enjoyed the action in the city.

It was late afternoon as Niko drove to the Matakana police station. Bill was nowhere in sight, which was unusual, but he still had the lock code, parked the car, and let himself in. It was like he had never been away. Nothing had changed; even his desk was just as he had left it. A key and a note were on his desk: *Welcome back! I've gone home for the day. See you tomorrow. Bill.*

As Niko sat on the office chair, it creaked from his weight, and he traced his fingers across the pockmarked wooden desk. There was a faint smell of bitter instant coffee, and he noticed that even with coffee, nothing had changed—there was still no coffee machine.

Despite this, it felt good to be back.

22

Wednesday the 5th of July

Niko was already at the station when Bill hobbled in.

"Morning, Boss," Niko said.

"Niko, I'm glad to see you, mate."

Bill shook Niko's hand to welcome the young constable as Niko rose from the more solid chair he'd found, swapping the old, rickety one.

"You don't look too good there, Sarge."

"I'll be all right. I'm sure it will settle in a few days. I've had worse," Bill said, making light of the situation.

"You sure you shouldn't take a few days' sick leave? I can hold the fort."

"Christ, no. I can't just sit and be idle. Besides, it's normally quiet here over much of the winter months. I appreciate having you here for the next week or so, though."

Although he'd taken some of the sleeping pills the locum doctor had prescribed, Bill felt rough. His eyes hung out of his skull, and dark circles were under his eyes. A lack of restful sleep had caught up with him.

"It's only a couple of ribs. They'll heal," Bill said as he sat down.

"I know how you feel. I did my ribs in when I played rugby. It's a hell of an uncomfortable predicament," Niko said.

"Yeah, and the God-awful damp weather does nothing to help the situation, either."

"Nah, it's not very tropical, is it? I think I prefer summer up here."

The air was still raw; the windows had the usual morning condensation on the inside that ran down the windowsill, slowly pooling on the floor.

At least Niko had been there early, and the heater tried to pump out warm air.

They really needed to do something about the work conditions of this old building. Bill had complained before, but as always, there was no budget. He imagined if this was in town, there was no way the city boys would put up with these conditions. Squeaky wheel and all that, but he was on his own. No one cared.

Niko plonked a cup of instant coffee in front of Bill.

"Thanks, mate. I could do with something stronger, that's for sure." "Have you been to the doctor?" Niko asked.

"I saw the doc yesterday. There's not much she could do. It just needs to heal by itself. I'll be all right. The first week is always the worst if I remember correctly," Bill grumbled.

"So, what's been going on since I left?" Niko asked.

It's been pretty quiet, but—"

Before Bill could fill Niko in on the young girl's body found on the beach, the phone rang.

"Matakana police station, Granger speaking." Bill listened intently. "All right. So, someone's kicked your letterbox over? I see." Bill rolled his eyes as he looked at Niko, who was doing his best not to laugh.

"Yes, all right. No worries at all. Come by the station and make a formal complaint.

Thank you, yes, we'll see you later."

As Bill hung up, he chuckled to himself. "See, this is what I have to deal with on a regular basis."

23

It was well after lunch, and the man from Omaha had been in to make his complaint. He'd been adamant the damage was connected to the party at Jett Starr's mansion. Apparently, this was a regular occurrence. Every time the old rocker held a party, his rowdy guests turned vandalising nearby property into a sport. After the disgruntled man left the station, satisfied that Bill had taken his complaint seriously, Bill picked up April West's file. He'd already filled Niko in on the case details and how April and her friends had been to Jett Starr's latest party.

"Let's have a look at the Facebook profiles of April and her three friends. People of their age always post from these parties," Niko suggested.

Bill hadn't thought to check social media out; he wasn't really into it.

"Hey, Sarge. Come and have a look at this, will you? April's friend, Lisa, is a prolific poster, and what do you know? There are at least twenty photos from the night in question."

"Can you print the photos from there?"

"Of course. Give me a minute, and I'll get it done."

The other three accounts only had a handful of photos; the only one showing April with a man was her and Jett Starr.

"I think we should go and pay a visit to the rockstar. What do you say, Niko?"

"I think that would be a good start," he said, picking up his uniform jacket from the back of the chair.

"I'd better drive since you're a bit of a cripple," Niko said, stifling a laugh.

"Hey, careful. There's still life in the old dog yet." Bill said, slapping Niko on the back.

~

A HIGH MASONRY fence and solid gate surrounded Starr's house. Bill pulled up close to the intercom and pressed the button.

"Yes?" A man's voice with an American accent came over the static.

"Hi, this is Sergeant Bill Granger from the Matakana Police. We'd like to ask you some questions. Can we come in?"

A short delay followed before Bill and Niko heard, "Sure, I'll buzz you in."

Jett Starr's house on the beachfront in Omaha was more impressive than Bill remembered. He'd attended a call-out many years ago and been first on the scene when a fight had broken out between guests.

"Man, this is kind of impressive," Niko said as they parked out the front.

The door to the large garage was open, and they could see a red Ferrari and a black Bentley parked side by side. Out the front was a casually parked late-model white Range Rover. The house was an architectural build that consisted of masonry, cedar and massive glass windows.

Jett Starr was waiting for them by the front door. He hadn't aged all that much since Bill had last seen him. He looked good for a man well into his sixties, but the tattoos on his arms were a new thing.

Starr reminded him of Keith Richards, particularly because he wore a headband tied around his scraggly grey hair.

"Hi, fellows. Come on through," he said as introductions were made. Starr led the way through the large atrium to the living areas. Large pieces of art accented the rather stark white interior. The tasteful nude theme of the photographs was something ethereal, a celebration of the aesthetic of body and beauty. It wasn't perhaps what he would have chosen, but quite extraordinary for a living room wall, Bill thought. A grand piano had pride of place on one side of the room and had an impressive wall of framed platinum records behind it.

Jett invited them to sit on the oversized leather couch in front of the large glass sliding doors. Bill thought it must be a custom design as he settled into its luxury.

"Coffee?"

"We're good, but thank you."

"So, officers. What's this all about?" Jett said as he sat down in a chair opposite Bill. The aged rocker fiddled with his large silver rings. There seemed to be one on every finger, and from what Bill could see, skulls and bones were the predominant design.

"We'd like to ask you about the party you hosted the other night."

"Sure, what about it?" Starr said, letting a slight smile past his lips. His American accent had marginally toned down after years of living in New Zealand.

"Did you know everyone who attended?

"Well, most of them, although there are always extras. It's difficult to keep track of."

"What can you tell us about the evening?"

"Why do you ask? What's the problem?"

"The body of one of your guests was found on the beach early the next morning," Bill said, pulling out a photo of the young girl. "Do you remember seeing her at your party?

"Yep, April West was here," Starr said, his eyes slightly downcast. Bill wasn't sure if this meant the old rocker felt sadness at the young woman's tragic death or just annoyance at being drawn in.

"Any trouble breaking out at the party?"

"I don't think so. The DJ worked all night and kept everyone entertained. I had a couple of guys on the door, and we had the bar set up over there," Jett said, pointing over to the kitchen. "My guys had strict instructions to send people home if they'd over-indulged. There comes a time in even the most gracious host's life when you get sick of having to clean up the damage and wiping up the vomit of people who can't hold their drink."

"I suppose so," Bill said, nodding. "What was your relationship with April?"

"I didn't know her very well. She was the keyboardist in Pandemonium, the band I'd just signed."

"How many guests were here, and do you remember what time April might have left the party, and if so, with whom?"

"I couldn't really tell you to be sure. I had my hands full elsewhere, if you know what I mean," Starr sniggered. Any concern the old rocker had shown two seconds ago had evaporated.

"If you could kindly answer the question, please." Bill was in no mood to explain himself.

"All I recall is seeing April with a red-haired female friend earlier in the evening. I can't recall the redhead's name . . ." Jett Starr said. It was most likely Lisa, Bill thought.

"Well, anyway, it looked like everyone had a good time. Put it this way, no one's complained," Jett said. Bill raised an eyebrow, unable to hide his annoyance. He wasn't in the mood for smart comments. Jett picked up on the joke falling flat and straightened up in his chair.

"If I had to make a guess, I'd say there would have been around eighty people here, but I could be wrong."

Bill scribbled in his notebook as he knew they'd have to pass the information on to headquarters in Orewa if anything came of the post-mortem.

"Well, if that's all, I guess we can wrap this up. I've got a meeting shortly," Jett Starr said and stood up. The abruptness surprised Bill. "Regardless, it's very tragic when a young person is found dead."

"Is Jett Starr a stage name or your actual name?" Bill asked as they were ushered out the door.

"It's a name my management suggested. It sounded better than Adam Wazinski when I first started out."

"Last question, what about drugs? Let's be honest; people would have been taking them."

"As far as drugs go, I have no idea. Maybe April took some, maybe she didn't," Jett Starr said, obviously wanting them out of his house.

Bill wasn't sure how truthful the man was. He didn't come down in the last rain shower. Of course, there would have been drugs here, and Bill was sure Jett Starr knew more than he let on.

24

Annika put the final touches on her long blonde hair, her face framed by loose curls. She perched the hot hair straighteners on the edge of the narrow porcelain sink, balancing it precariously next to the toothbrush holder. She'd done her makeup: a touch of black mascara and a soft pink lip.

Her daughter, Katie, had given her a stick highlighter and had shown her how to put a little to the top of her cheekbones, the centre of her forehead, and on her Cupid's bow. The application gave her a slightly more youthful shimmer. She didn't look too bad; a few emerging lines here and there, not that it bothered her too much. She ran her fingers through her hair, gently separating the curls, and reached for the hair spray. The mist ensured her fine Scandinavian hair held her locks for longer than five minutes, especially in this damp weather. Annika smoothed the fabric of her black and gold dress that fell softly over her hips. Not too bad, she thought as she twirled in front of the bathroom mirror.

Bill lay on the bed, propped up with an assortment of pillows to get comfortable, the bathrobe pulled tight to keep him warm after the shower. The pained expression on his face was clear as he eased himself off the bed.

"Are you sure you're all right to do this tonight?" Annika said.

"Of course, darling. This is your big night. I wouldn't miss it for the world." Bill strained as he steadied himself against the dresser and let the pain subside a little before he moved again with difficulty.

"Come on, I'll help you get into your glad rags," Annika said, reaching for the button-down shirt hanging on the front of the wardrobe door. "Did you ask Niko along?" She undid the top button of the freshly ironed shirt.

"He'll be there," Bill said, groaning as he put his arm through the shirtsleeve, his robe crumpled at his feet.

"I'm glad, especially since he's been dragged up here in the middle of winter," Annika said, buttoning the front of his shirt.

Finn and Maggie lounged at their feet, feeling the excitement in the air and desperately wanting to be part of it.

"Come on, you two. Settle down," Bill said, bending to scratch Finn behind the ear.

"That's the catering van from Smiths," Annika said as she glanced out the window.

"I'd better help with the setup. Can you manage on your own, Bill?"

"I'll be all right. You get on with what you need to do," he said and smiled. "I'll catch up with you in the gallery as soon as I'm dressed."

"Take your time; no rush. There's not that much left to do."

Annika stepped over the dogs, went downstairs, and walked through the kitchen, where the girls chatted noisily while eating their dinner. Maggie and Finn were close behind her with their tails in the air. Textbooks from this afternoon's homework were piled at the end of the table.

"How's the dinner, girls?"

"It's awesome. We love meatballs and mash. It's the best," the twins shouted at the same time. Being a little older, Katie looked mildly amused at her sisters' outbursts.

"Are you still okay to take the photos tonight, Katie?"

"Of course, Mamma. I'll take heaps and will edit the best ones."

"You don't have to stay the whole time, perhaps the first hour if that's okay," Annika said. "I have no idea what time it will wrap up, but normally these events go quite late."

"Just enjoy yourself. You have worked so hard for this, and don't worry; it will be a great success!"

Annika's heart swelled. How on earth had her eldest daughter become so grown up all of a sudden?

"Mum!! Can we be there for a little while as well?" Anna asked, her twin sister Veronica nodding enthusiastically.

"Of course, you can, but only until Katie has finished taking photos, then it's straight to bed."

"Yay!! Thank you. We promise to be good," the ten-year-old twins shouted at the same time.

"I'll make sure they get to bed at a decent hour. Besides, Zac should be home soon. He can help," Katie said.

Annika wondered if her son would be home in time—he hadn't been the most reliable person lately.

"Thanks, darlings. Wish me luck!!"

"Luck!!" all three yelled in unison, which soon turned to giggles.

She had no idea why she was so worried. It wasn't as if it was the first time she'd exhibited. She'd done her best, and at the end of the day, that was all she could do.

Maggie and Finn waited by the door, their tails wagging enthusiastically, ready to go with her as always.

"Sorry, guys. You have to stay here tonight," Annika said, turning to the disappointed dogs, their tails and ears dropping as they sulked and slunk away to their beds.

The weather was atrocious. Even though it was only a fifteen-second sprint across gravel, Annika decided to leave her coat behind and grabbed the umbrella by the door. She had to hold her dress up to avoid getting the hem soaked as she zigzagged between the puddles.

The warm gallery space was well-lit, and as she ran through the double doors, she felt the nervous tension dissipate and excitement build. This was her night. She deserved it. She said hello to the catering staff from Smiths, who were busy setting up the finger food.

Annika walked through the gallery. It had only just gone quarter past six. A pile of catalogues detailing each work was neatly stacked at the entrance for people to pick up as they would start to arrive between seven and seven-thirty. She wanted to make sure everything looked perfect and paused for a moment to take a mental snapshot.

From experience, she knew the evening would go fast. People would be here to see her, of course, but the paintings were the real stars of the night.

She set the stemmed glasses on the white tablecloth and hoped they'd ordered enough wine. As always, with these events, you never really knew how many guests would turn up. Annika glanced out over the treetops at the edge of the property in the distance. The sky was dark and ominous. No stargazing tonight, she thought to herself. She turned her attention to the table at the entrance. The food looked delicious; the kitchen staff had really outdone themselves.

Annika went through to the cool store next door, where they kept potatoes and preserves, and carried the wine boxes that her best friend Lexi had dropped off. It was a selection of award-winning bottles from Matakana Valley Wines.

She returned to the food and drinks table and set up rows of Pinot Gris, Chardonnay, Merlot, and Cabernet Sauvignon—plenty there for every discerning taste and the reason the region was called Auckland's answer to Tuscany.

Annika took a moment and glanced around the room a final time. She was happy; it looked amazing. The paintings spoke for themselves. Her artistic flair had developed over the years. She had matured and felt they represented the concept she had come up with. The collection was dramatic and deep-rooted in her adopted culture. Although darkness and death could be interpreted in some of the current works, the mood reflected the turbulence and stress she and Bill had experienced not so long ago. On reflection, it had been the best therapy to work through the trauma.

There was a slight smell of freshly dried paint in the air. Annika took a deep breath, which immediately grounded her and settled her nerves. Her hands smoothed out the crisp white tablecloth, starched to within an inch of its life. She was ready.

~

PEOPLE STARTED TO ARRIVE, and Annika became swept up in a wave of friends and acquaintances there to support her. To her surprise, there were many faces she didn't recognise. The gallery space was soon packed.

Lexi made a beeline for her as soon as she arrived and gave Annika a big hug. Her shoulder-length brown hair had been straightened, and she looked amazing in a flowing dress and boots.

"Wow, you're a knockout tonight," Annika said.

"So are you. I love that dress. The colours really suit you," Lexi said, putting her arm around Annika. "Nervous?"

"A little. I definitely feel the 'Imposter Syndrome' tonight," Annika said as she fidgeted with her hands.

"You know what?" Lexi said, grabbing both of Annika's hands and steadying them. "You've poured your heart and soul into this evening, and I know it will be a tremendous success, my friend. Just relax and enjoy it. It's your moment."

Lexi was Annika's best friend and she felt great having her there as support. "Thank you. I needed to hear that tonight," Annika said, hugging her friend again.

It was nearing seven o'clock. Annika made her way to the front entrance. She could see Crystal and a man with short blond hair, who must be her boyfriend, Andrei Bowen. Crystal smiled and waved at Annika. Bill arrived with the girls, and Katie made them pose for a photo, just the two of them.

"Annika, wow. I've not seen all the paintings together. I'm blown away. You've really outdone yourself," Bill said and gave her a tender kiss.

"Thanks, darling, it means a lot," Annika smiled and disappeared into his arms for a moment until Katie tugged at her sleeve.

"Come on, guys. Do you have to be so cringy?"

Annika laughed at her fifteen-year-old daughter and let Bill go, saying, “See you guys a little later. I’d better do some mingling.”

The energy in the room was fabulous. There was an air of expectation and an effervescent buzz unlike anything else that she’d ever experienced.

25

The vast gallery space was full of people. Bill had never seen this many people attend one of Annika's exhibitions. Among the dressed-up punters, the drinks flowed, and he was sure Annika would do well tonight. He walked past the table with the food and piled some nibbles on a plate—this would be dinner.

Niko walked through the doors and wandered over. The Samoan was a good head taller than most and turned heads as he arrived. He was dressed in black dress jeans and a white shirt, open at the neck and with a hint of his tattoos showing. Most of the women in the gallery looked at Niko rather than the paintings, which made Bill smile. Niko was oblivious to female attention wherever he went. Oh, to be young again, Bill thought.

"Hi, mate," Bill said. "Good to see you."

"All good, Sarge. Sure beats an evening on my own in front of the telly," Niko said.

Bill looked at him with one eyebrow slightly raised.

"I'm kidding, Sarge. I wouldn't have missed Annika's exhibition, really."

"Well, you'd better get yourself some food then," Bill said, gesturing towards the table groaning under the weight of Korean fried chicken, pork belly bao buns, vegan gyoza, and a massive cheese board.

Annika clinked one of the wine glasses and the murmuring in the room fell silent. She walked towards the front of the crowd and smiled. "Welcome. I can't tell you how thrilled and humbled I am to see you all here. This exhibition has been six months in the making, and I'm so very proud to show it all to you this evening." Annika radiated accomplishment and pride. "Thank you to my family and everyone who has helped make this evening come off the ground. I couldn't have done it without you."

Annika blew a kiss to the twins, who stood by the food and hoovered as much cheese and crackers as they could. Katie stood not far away as she photographed her mum. Bill gave her a thumbs up from where he stood, and Annika raised her glass at him.

"But tonight is not about me. It's about the art. So, please enjoy," she continued, the relief in her face clear to see. "Let's all raise a glass to the *Ti Point* collection."

Cheers of congratulations could be heard before the room erupted in spontaneous applause. A flurry of well-wishers swept Annika away. Bill knew he would not get to talk to her until the night's end. This was her moment, and she deserved to shine.

Lexi and a few friends helped with the sales. Sold stickers went up left, right and centre.

Niko filled up his plate again and shovelled the food into his mouth as Bill's phone vibrated in his pocket. He retrieved it and the display said, 'Matakana police station.' It was rare to get an after-hours call out in the winter.

"Granger," Bill said, turning on his heels and hurrying towards a quiet corner of the room. He could feel Niko's eyes following him. Bill turned, caught his gaze, and gestured for Niko to come over. The noise in the room was loud.

"The Department of Conservation Ranger has found a body washed up on Anchor Bay beach on Tāwharanui Peninsula," Bill said in a hushed voice.

"Do we have anyone missing?" Niko said.

"Not that we've had reported."

"I guess we'd better get going then," Niko said.

Annika was in demand—everyone wanted to talk to her, praise her and celebrate. Bill spotted Lexi piling cheese and crackers onto her plate.

"Can you let Annika know that we've had a call out?" he said, eager to get away.

"Of course. Everything all right?" Lexi asked.

"Is it ever at this time of the night?" Bill said, placing a hand on her shoulder.

Bill and Niko skirted around the sides of the crowded room to the door. The festive atmosphere had kicked in, and people were enjoying a great time. The rain pelted them as soon as they stepped outside.

"Of course, it had to be a bloody awful night like tonight," Bill grumbled.

"Well, I guess the poor person didn't choose to get washed up tonight," Niko said.

"Nah, I suppose you're right on that account."

Bill grabbed a pair of gumboots off the rack on the front porch on his way to the car.

"You got something else to get changed into?" he asked, looking at Niko's polished boots that looked more suitable for horse riding than trudging along a wet beach.

"I'll be all right."

The earlier drizzly rain had turned to a torrential downpour, and the car's window wipers struggled to cope with the deluge. It was a miserable winter's night. The excess water had nowhere to go and pooled hazardously on the road. The twenty metres of visibility they had was barely enough, and the car protested around the tight corners.

"Jeez, Sarge. It's a wild one tonight," Niko said, his knuckles tight around the Jesus handle above his head.

Bill slowed the car and turned down the long winding road towards the Tāwharanui Regional Park. They went past the ranger's office and headed through the electric gate and into the car park closest to the beach. The ferocity of the rain had increased and was heavier by the minute. Bill sighed—they would get soaked to the bone. For a split second, the vision of a bloated corpse given up by the turbulent sea flickered through his head. He'd seen it before. Drowning victims were not the most pleasant to recover— the bloating and loose skin wasn't pretty, not to mention if sharks or other marine creatures had had a nibble at it.

The car park at Anchor Bay was empty and dark, apart from a Department of Conservation vehicle at the far end. Tom Ihaka, the DOC Ranger, waited for them in the car, his face illuminated by his phone screen. Tom got out of the car as Bill parked next to him. As Bill stepped out, he dodged the worst of the puddles and pulled the hood of his raincoat up to try and avoid water going down the back of his neck.

Bill got on well with the ranger, a passionate wildlife warrior whose main goal was to see that all animals thrived and the peninsula was kept pest free. They'd talked at length about the elusive brown kiwi and the nocturnal morepork the last time Bill had seen him.

"Evening, Bill. Great night to bring you out, eh?" Tom said, his sun-weathered hand stretched out. He was a nuggety man, not much shorter than Bill's own one hundred and ninety-five-centimetre frame.

Bill shook his hand and introduced Niko.

"The weather isn't getting any better. Let's go," Tom said, pulling his oilskin jacket across his chest and adjusting his collar, which funnelled trickles of water down his back. Tom was still young, probably in his early thirties, and looked like the ultimate surfer with his tousled blond hair. It wasn't unusual to see a couple of surfboards on the roof rack of his work vehicle. He wore shorts no matter the time of the year or the weather. His muscly legs would have made any rugby player jealous. Thick woolly socks came up over the heavy work boots. They looked watertight, unlike Bill's gumboots, which had a steady amount of water running into them.

"Come with me," he said and shone his torch onto the uneven, well-trodden path underneath massive trees. They headed towards the ocean, and the salt from the nearby sea was accentuated as the moisture in the air hung heavy.

"I went for my usual evening patrol. We have a couple of particularly curious sea lion pups, and I wanted to check that they were okay. That's when I found the body," Tom said, his voice a little unsteady. "It's a young bloke, and I have to confess, I spewed my guts out. It wasn't pretty."

Bill knew what he meant. To live in a coastal community meant they had to deal with their fair share of unfortunate deaths at sea every year. Whether it was a visitor with an inflated belief in their own ability in the water or fishermen without life jackets, it was equally tragic to recover the remains. They could hear the angry sea churning and the wild waves crashing well before they reached the long stretch of sandy beach.

"He's down the far end," Tom hollered over the noise and pointed to the left.

The sodden, mostly hard-packed sand put up no resistance as the icy southwesterly came off the ocean. The biting wind slapped their faces and plastered their clothes to their bodies. Bill bent his head to avoid the wind's chill and walked in the direction Tom pointed. Niko lugged the kit containing the protective gear and stepping plates. The kit acted like a windbreak, but despite Niko's strength, Bill could see it was a struggle.

Getting closer, they could see a definite outline of what appeared to be a body.

Niko set the kit down on the ground as Bill shone his torch and moved closer still. The waterlogged body of a male on his back lay before them.

"I had to pull him up to ensure the sea wouldn't take him back. The body was face down initially. I managed to roll him on his back, and that's when I saw it," Tom said, avoiding looking at the corpse.

Judging by the bloated features and loose skin, the body had been in the water for several days.

The sea temperature was only around 12-13° C in winter, which meant the body was preserved longer. The male victim wore a checked shirt and jeans. The distorted limbs were swollen like balloons, which gave him a scarecrow look. He had no shoes, and one leg was missing below the knee. Bill couldn't quite see as the denim jeans edge was ragged. The victim's long red hair was plastered over the grotesquely swollen face. It was hard to tell, but it looked like the man was in his late twenties or early thirties.

"Jesus," Niko said as he leaned over, realising that where the eyes had been, there were deep hollows. Out of the half-open mouth, a crab crawled out. "Fuck's sake. That's just nasty."

"The tide is on our side. It's on its way out," Tom said, still avoiding casting his eyes over the corpse.

Bill bent over and peered closer at the body. He spotted a distinctive tattoo on the right forearm—it was the number thirteen. He'd seen it before. "I know who this person is," Bill said, his tone sombre.

The last time Fanta had sat in the chair opposite Bill at the station would have been about five years ago. He'd been brought in for questioning over some stolen property. In the end, there hadn't been sufficient evidence to charge him. Bill knew he was guilty, though. Fanta knew that he knew, and in the end, Bill had tried his best to talk to him, to get him on the straight and narrow. A life of crime was no way to live. Over the years, his name had come up, mainly featured in investigations by the CIB in Orewa, until he was caught and sent to jail a couple of years ago. Bill didn't know that Fanta was out. It must have been recent; otherwise, he would have heard about it. Once a criminal, always a criminal.

"That's Patrick Morris, better known among his associates as Fanta," Bill said. "Last time I heard, he was in prison. So, the question is, what has he been doing to end up in the water?" Bill scratched his head. "Okay, Niko, we have to rig the tarps up and preserve the body as best we can."

Bill sent Niko back to the car to get the rest of the gear. Niko was in his leather boots and probably soaked right through to his feet. Bill was on the phone and speaking to the duty sergeant in Orewa when Niko returned. He carried the crime scene tent on his shoulder like it weighed nothing. He was sure the burly constable rolled tractor tyres at the gym.

"The SOCOs are on their way," Bill said, wiping the wet phone screen before he tucked it back in his pocket. Between them, the three men rigged the tent-like structure over the body, the wind proving to be a pain. They rolled the tent sides down and attached them with pegs in the wet ground. Bill's gumboots slipped off the thin plastic as he secured the last one, and he winced as the jarring hurt his bruised ribs. Bill couldn't help but think about what extraordinary circumstances might be next.

26

The wine still flowed, and people seemed to have enjoyed the event. The evening was a great success. The vivid abstract canvases were striking against the crisp white gallery walls and had sold like hotcakes. Annika was pleased and couldn't believe she'd sold half of her work. Her ego had received a much-needed boost.

She stood back and looked around the room. The laughter and chatter echoed in the slightly cavernous space. The only dampener of the night was that Bill had received a call out and hadn't seen her paintings snapped up by eager buyers. Of course, she was disappointed, but she also understood. When you live in a small community, and your husband is the sole policeman, he has to attend if something happens.

She swallowed the last mouthful of wine, the velvety Merlot caressing her taste buds.

Her stomach growled. She'd not had time to eat anything and made her way over to the grazing table, where she picked up a couple of pieces of cheese rolled in salami.

"Congratulations on a successful opening night, Annika," Crystal said, giving her friend a warm hug.

"Hi, Crystal. I'm so glad you could make it." Annika took in the bulky frame of the man standing with Crystal. His intense gaze seemed to burrow right through her, and she shivered as if someone had walked over her grave. It unsettled her, but perhaps she was just tired after the intense day.

"I just love your work. You're one talented woman."

"Thank you, Crystal. I'm glad you like it," Annika said, smiling at her friend.

"This is Andrei," Crystal said, leaning into Annika.

"So pleased to meet you. I've heard great things about you, and seeing your extraordinary art tonight, I can say I'm completely sold," Andrei said as he held Annika's gaze for a moment too long. His confidence and presence dominated the moment. She had the feeling Andrei was someone you wouldn't want to cross.

"Thank you. You are very kind," Annika said, feeling awkward at the praise.

"You must come by the house. We really need some art on the walls. You have perfectly captured the mood and raw emotions in your paintings, and I am thrilled to have purchased three this evening. I am, however, still looking for a special piece. Something bespoke, but on a much larger scale to hang in the lounge," Andrei said, still locking eyes with her and enunciating every word with his posh accent.

"Wow, I can't believe that you bought three! Thank you very much," Annika said. "Of course, I could do a commission for you." Her cheeks flushed as she felt a tad overwhelmed at the prospect.

"Have you got any more darkness in you?" he said, looking at her intently.

She was a bit taken aback. Had she heard Andrei correctly? Darkness? What did he mean? She wasn't sure, but it unsettled her even more. Perhaps the wine had gone straight to her head. Or maybe it was due to a lack of food. Either way, she regained her composure.

"If you mean inspiration, yes, I do," Annika said, doing her best to steady her voice. What a weird thing to say, she thought. Andrei seemed the type of man who knew exactly what he wanted and how to get it.

"Great, that's settled them. Come by during the week, and we'll sort the details out," he said, turning to Crystal, who reached for another glass of wine.

"Don't you think you've had enough?" he said through perfectly even clenched teeth. In an instant, his charming demeanour had changed. Crystal pulled her hand back as if she'd been burnt. Embarrassed, she smoothed her dress as Andrei switched to a big smile. Crystal wobbled on her sky-high designer heels as Andrei pulled her close. It was clear he considered her his property and was claiming her back. "Thank you very much for a lovely evening," he said to Annika before turning on his heels and dragging Crystal along.

"See you at yoga," Crystal said over her shoulder.

"Yes, see you then," Annika said, wondering what the hell she had witnessed. Who told their girlfriend what she could and could not do, for goodness' sake? Crystal didn't seem like she had a problem with alcohol, but who knew? They had only recently met.

Annika grabbed some more nibbles and tossed them into her mouth as Lexi approached with two glasses of wine.

"Well done. What a splendid night," Lexi said as she sidled up and handed her a glass.

"I'm blown away and can't quite believe so many pieces have sold tonight," Annika said, sipping her wine and savouring the taste. For the first time this evening, she felt like she could relax.

"Of course you did. I knew you would. You always do. By the way, who was the hunk in the expensive suit with the blonde hanging off his arm that you were talking to?"

"His name is Andrei and he's a developer. I do yoga with Crystal, his girlfriend," Annika said to her friend.

"He sure looks like a smooth operator. I bet women swoon at his feet with those movie star looks," Lexi said and laughed.

"Oh, I wouldn't know," Annika said. He certainly was smooth, but he also seemed manipulative, she thought.

27

The late-night drive from Orewa had been uneventful. Scene of Crime Officer Andrew Copeson drove, as usual; in fact, he preferred it. His senior colleague Brian Rudd rested his head on the headrest in the front passenger seat and snoozed until they reached Matakana Road. The roadworks were still going on, and Copeson slowed the vehicle, but not before he had to break hard, which woke Rudd up.

"Sorry, I misjudged the corner, boss."

Rudd grumbled, folded his arms across his chest, and closed his eyes again. It felt like the old man had already checked out. His retirement was imminent, and dreams of unlimited golf with his buddies, time spent with grandchildren, and projects around home beckoned. Not that Copeson blamed him; he'd had a long career and it was time. Many of their colleagues probably think he should have given up work a long time ago, but deep inside, he was sure that Rudd loved his work.

They continued through Matakana and turned right at the Omaha turn-off on Leigh Road. He could just make out the manicured vines at the famous Providence Vineyards on the left as he turned into Takatu Road. According to the GPS, they would reach their destination of Tāwharanui in twenty minutes.

Copeson had been to the stunningly white sandy beach last summer. It was a bit of a trek to get to, but totally worth it because it was like being in Fiji. Unfortunately, it was an ill kept secret, and hordes of people descended on the area in the summer. The beach was a particularly popular spot for surfers all year round.

Copeson drove faster than he should have on the wet, winding road. In hindsight, as there was a lot of water on the road and the tyres were worn, it probably wasn't smart. He aquaplaned, lost control for a few seconds, and they fishtailed as the surface ahead was awash with runoff from the steep hillside.

His grip around the steering wheel tightened, and he eased off the power to keep them on the road. His foot gently squeezed the brake pedal until it forced him to take evasive action and swerve to avoid slamming into a boulder protruding on a corner. Thankfully, he managed to get control of the vehicle and the tyres with some grip.

Rudd's head banged onto the passenger side window before he got hold of the Jesus handle above his head.

"For fuck's sake, Copeson. Did you get your licence out of a cereal packet?" Rudd shouted, rubbing the side of his head.

"Sorry, I didn't realise it was so slippery," Copeson said.

"Just keep your eyes on the road, and get us there safely and in one piece. That's all you have to do," Rudd grumbled.

28

Rudd felt the swollen bump on the side of his head. As if it wasn't bad enough to go out in this shitty weather, now he would probably have a headache to boot. Not only was the weather atrocious, but the incessant winter rains he hated had also set in, and he was missing his weekly bridge night with the guys—a real pity as he was on form and would have cleaned up tonight. He was sure of it. To console himself, he took a deep breath and thought about his upcoming retirement and holiday to the Sunshine Coast in Australia with his wife and grandkids in a few weeks. He couldn't wait to escape this miserable hell hole of New Zealand's wet winter. The continuous rain was enough to drive anyone batty and was only conducive to mushrooms.

"Jeez, this place is really in the back of beyond," Rudd said as they pulled into the deserted beach car park. Rudd swore as he stepped into a deep puddle outside the passenger door. Thankfully, his sturdy winter boots came up well over his ankles and kept the sodden ground out. A gust of wind swirled, and the heavy precipitation soaked him. He quickly pulled the hood of his waterproof jacket up as the rain and wind beat down.

He hated getting his hair wet and took the utmost care in the morning as he carefully secured his comb-over with just the right amount of hair spray so it would not move even in the stiffest breeze. Sideways rain, however, was a different kettle of fish, and he could feel his locks being slicked to his scalp in the most unflattering fashion, something that didn't help brighten his mood in the slightest.

"Hurry along, Copeson. We don't have all night."

Copeson didn't answer, instead getting the kit they needed out of the boot and slamming it shut.

"According to the message sent through, the deceased is located about two hundred metres on the western side of the beach," Rudd said.

They followed the path and stepped onto the wet sand. As Rudd and Copeson headed to the western side, they could see torches in the distance. The rain abated a little as they neared where Granger was standing, but the wind remained gusty.

"Granger, what do we have here?" Rudd said, ignoring the pleasantries as they reached the rigged-up tent structure.

"Evening, Rudd. This is the DOC Ranger, Tom Ihaka. He found the body."

Tom extended his hand and Rudd grabbed it with a curt nod. "Yes, yes, continue," Rudd said impatiently.

"Male in his late twenties to early thirties. Presumed drowned," Bill said, looking like a drowned rat.

"Any ID on him?" Rudd said while he inspected the bloated corpse from a few metres away. Clumps of seaweed adhered to the body, the long strands resembling fingers. It was like the ocean had already reclaimed him.

It's said that drowning was the most peaceful way to go. After the initial oxygen deprivation, the brain switches off, and you drift away before the organs finally shut down.

"No wallet, but the victim is known to us," Bill said.

"All right, let us get on with our job," Rudd said, rudely cutting Bill off.

"I'll notify the undertaker. Woods will need to come and pick up the body as soon as we have completed the preliminary investigation," Bill said.

"Copeson, you will have to photograph as Jono is elsewhere tonight," Rudd said.

29

Annika said goodbye to the last of the stragglers. It had been a great evening. Thankfully, a few friends helped tidy up. The recycling bin was full to the brim, and she'd sent everyone home with plates of leftover food. Annika took a last look around the gallery before she turned the lights out and locked up for the night.

She still buzzed from the evening; it had been a tremendous success. She'd sold a lot more than she'd expected. She couldn't believe Crystal's boyfriend Andrei had bought several pieces for their new house. It surprised her a little, especially because of the price tag attached to each painting. Money didn't seem to be an issue for him, though, and she'd even landed a commission piece. It didn't get better than this. She was glad to pursue her passion, but it could be a lonely profession, and from time to time, it was nice to receive validation that she did a good job and put quality pieces out there.

She wondered how Bill was getting on, what the call had been about. Hopefully, he wasn't too cold or wet, and she couldn't wait for him to get home so she could tell him about the evening he'd missed. He was her biggest fan and always so supportive. She'd arranged a few bits of cheese and some savouries for Bill, as no doubt he'd be starving when he arrived home, goodness knows when.

The night was pitch black, and the rain drove across the yard in large opaque sheets. The cold, damp evening air seeped through her flimsy dress, chilling her skin. She wished she'd brought a coat with her.

Annika sheltered under the eaves for a second and opened the umbrella while she balanced the plate. She dashed across the gravel, doing her best to avoid the massive puddles that had formed from the downpour. A wind gust swirled and tugged on the umbrella, which made her lose her balance and stumble straight into a deep hollow. The cold, dirty water covered her ankle, but not even that could dampen her spirits after tonight.

Her right shoe was soaked through and squelched as she climbed the stairs in a few quick strides to get inside, glad to leave the wet and miserable night behind. She looked for Zac's car, but he still wasn't home.

The lights were on in the kitchen. Two white porcelain mugs and a plate of freshly made ginger cake covered in glad wrap had been left for her to enjoy. A polaroid of her and Bill, from earlier in the evening, leant against the wrought iron candle holder that her dad had made years ago. Annika picked up the photo and turned it over, smiling as she read it.

Hope your exhibition went well. We are so proud of you. Love from us all.

Tears welled up in her eyes; the girls were so awesome. They were all going through different stages of life. Katie was a typical teenager with lots of eye rolling and often thinking she knew everything. Anna and Veronika—the twins—were only ten years old and still in their tween years and were more compliant. But more and more, she could see their individuality coming through. Zac was a different story, and she automatically checked her phone to see if there was a message from him, but there wasn't.

She boiled the jug and went into the laundry, where she stepped out of her damp clothes and grabbed a pair of leggings and a sweatshirt from the clean, folded washing pile. The warmth slowly returned to her body.

The jug clicked off, and she filled the teapot with her special tea that her sister had sent from Gotland. The Limestone Mix tea blend was her favourite. As she poured the boiling water over the black tea leaves, the sweet rose fragrance tickled her nose, and childhood memories washed over her. A pang of homesickness hit her right in the chest, and she forced herself to take a couple of deep breaths to avoid crying. It was three years since she had seen her sister Josephine and the rest of the family, which felt like an eternity.

She blew on the hot beverage, sat at the kitchen table, and picked up a slice of the still-warm ginger cake. It was her grandmother's recipe and heavy on the mix of ginger, cinnamon and cloves with the rich, dark flavour of golden syrup. Katie had probably quickly made it after taking the photos at the start of the evening. She was a great little baker.

She sipped the tea and felt a huge relief as the day was finally over. Annika pulled her phone out and scrolled aimlessly through the social media news feed she'd neglected for days. Not that she was that great with social media, but it served a purpose as she needed to promote her art.

Crystal had tagged her in a Facebook post, and a selection of photos from tonight's event flashed across her screen.

She'd posted a few photos of herself and Andrei, some artworks, and the obligatory food photos. Crystal had sung her praises. Annika smiled. She would get the photos that Katie took tomorrow. Annika glanced at the phone screen and clicked on the glamorous head and shoulder profile photo of Crystal to enlarge it. Her blonde hair cascaded in long locks to one side, and her flawless skin and perfect makeup were highlighted. It wasn't a candid shot, that's for sure.

Annika didn't usually snoop around on Facebook, but she was curious about Andrei and clicked on his photo. According to his personal information, he was a former King's College pupil with connections to a range of businesses.

He also seemed to be a frequent visitor to glitzy media events. She scrolled further down; a lot of the photos featured him and Crystal with celebrities. His words echoed in her head, and the uncomfortable feeling from earlier returned. Annika couldn't help thinking: who were these people?

30

Bill and Niko walked back to the car park with Tom Ihaka. It was nearly two in the morning, and they were all sand-blasted, soaked to the skin and exhausted. The rain was now a light drizzle, and an owl hooted in the distance. If it had been a clear night, they would have perhaps sighted the odd foraging kiwi, as the resident population was healthy due to dogs and other pets being prohibited in the sanctuary. Bill's ribs ached, and there was nothing more he wanted than to get home to bed and rest. They'd left Rudd and Copeson to wait for Woods, the undertaker, and trudged through to the dark car park with the wind still howling. Tom Ihaka yawned. It had been a long night and he looked exhausted.

"Jeez, a hot shower would be great about now," Niko said, looking decidedly drenched.

"I'm not sure if I'll get any sleep tonight," Tom said. "I keep seeing the poor bloke's face."

"Water retrieval can be nasty business, but on the other hand, we have to be grateful the sea gave him up. More often than not, the person is at the mercy of a multitude of factors. It all depends on what the currents do and how long it takes to find a body. There's a lot of rugged coastline around here. He could have equally washed up somewhere remote. I take comfort that the deceased will be returned to his family," Bill said.

I guess you're right," Tom said before he got into his car.

"You're going to have to drive," Bill said to Niko, holding his side to minimise the vibrations as he walked across the uneven ground.

"Sarge, I forgot about your ribs," Niko said.

"All good, mate. I'll live," Bill said, groaning as he stepped into the car.

"Not too many drownings in South Auckland. The gangs tend to kill each other in the streets instead, which isn't that great, either," Niko said philosophically. "Did you say you knew the man?"

"I've dealt with Fanta over the years. Last time he was in trouble, he was locked up for a few years, home invasion and serious assault. He was lucky the victim survived; otherwise, he would still be in the big house."

"Any family that you know of?" Niko asked.

"Not that I'm aware of, but I guess we'll find out when we follow up later."

"Strange there hasn't been a reported person missing at sea, don't you think?" Niko said, thinking out loud.

"It's certainly unusual. Unless he was out on his own, but you'd think the daft bugger would have at least worn a life jacket. I don't get these guys."

The outside light at the Granger house was on, illuminating the path up the wooden stairs to the verandah. Zac's car was parked next to Annika's.

"Can you pick me up at eight?" Bill asked before he got out of the car.

"Sure thing, boss. See you then."

~

BILL HELD on to the railing as he walked gingerly up the steps, kicking his boots off at the front door. He didn't bother to put them upside down on the boot rack. If he bent down, he wasn't sure he'd be able to get up again. Annika had left the front door unlocked, which bothered him. He'd mention it to her later. Life in the country was quiet, and they'd only recently started to lock the doors. Maggie and Finn, the standard poodles, stirred. Maggie made a halfhearted attempt at a tail wag, yawning loudly. Finn, who was not the best guard dog, it seemed, snored his head off, his long legs spilling over his basket in the entrance.

Annika had left a plate of cheese and some savouries for him in the kitchen. Bill hadn't eaten much before the call out and realised how hungry he was. He lifted a corner of the clear cover and grabbed two sausage rolls. He could have heated them but was too tired to bother and just shoved them into his mouth. He reached for the pain relief, too, and popped a couple of tablets in his mouth, sticking his face under the cold water tap. The bitter taste and grainy texture lingered in his mouth. To get the taste out, he shoved a piece of camembert in.

His wet clothes had started to itch his skin, so he stripped down to his underwear and dumped everything on the floor in the laundry. He rifled through the piles of clean washing and was pleased he found a pair of old track pants, some woolly socks and a sweatshirt on the folding table. He padded into the lounge in his underwear and sat down to get dressed. After the effort, he didn't have the energy to walk upstairs. Besides, he didn't want to wake Annika. The fire was just about out and he could feel the temperature drop. In a last-ditch effort, he put a few logs on and stoked the fire. It didn't take long until the living room heated up, and a warm glow spread. He reached for the patchwork quilt folded on the back of the couch and draped it over himself to get warm and comfortable.

The last thought that passed through his mind before he let sleep overtake him was: why was Fanta out on the water?

31

Thursday the 6th of July

Bill woke as the sun came through the blinds in the living room. He shivered in the cool morning air, his body stiff and aching from a night on the lumpy couch. Surprisingly, he'd slept better than he thought he would. He'd woken a few times as Maggie and Finn had snuggled up to him during the night and moved around.

As soon as he was awake, so were the dogs. They crawled over him and bounced around with tails that wagged nonstop. Maggie whined and hopped down to the floor, indicating that she wanted to go outside for a comfort stop.

"Guys, come on. Give me a break, will you?" he said as he tried to lift his head from the couch. Finn joined his sister and was equally persistent, nudging his big black nose into Bill's face and giving him big sloppy kisses.

"All right. You win. I'm awake," Bill said to the pair's delight as he turned to roll off the couch. He just about passed out from the effort and found himself kneeling on the cold floor while Finn, who had no spatial awareness, kept circling him and bouncing off his battered body.

Annika came down the stairs as Bill got up, her robe billowing behind her. She looked a lot more rested than he felt.

"So, you're home. I didn't hear you come in last night." Annika cosied up to him, leaning in for a light kiss. The stubble on his chin scratched her as she moved her face away.

"I got home late and thought it might be best if I slept downstairs. I didn't want to wake you, " Bill said.

"Fancy a coffee before you have a shower?" Annika headed to the kitchen, Maggie and Finn trailing behind her.

"Sure, that would be nice. I'm so sorry I missed last night," Bill said, opening the kitchen door and letting the dogs out. "How was it?"

"It was a wonderful night. I sold more than I expected," Annika said, her face beaming.

"I just wish that you had been there."

"Me, too," Bill said, wincing as he adjusted his position.

"You need pain relief, and are you really up to going to work today?" Annika said.

"I'll be fine as long as I don't breathe or move," he said, trying not to laugh. "Just give me the concoction of drugs." He held his hand out, and Annika handed him a glass of water and the tablets.

"Okay, I'd better get upstairs and in the shower," Bill said and reached for the cup of coffee on the bench, he felt grimy from last night.

"Go and clean up. I'll have some breakfast ready for you when you come back down again," Annika said, caressing the back of his neck.

Bill stepped into the shower and turned the temperature up, enjoying the soothing feeling on his aching bones. He wasn't pleased to see the multicoloured bruising down his side, though, as he reached for a towel, but he grabbed a clean shirt and trousers and dressed. The socks were a challenge; no matter how he contorted his body, nothing worked, and he swore out loud. To hobble seemed a little less painful, and he padded into the kitchen barefoot, carrying his socks.

"I can't get these bastards on."

"Come on, let me help you," Annika said, smiling. She knew how much her proud husband was suffering.

He realised how starved he was as he could smell the bacon and eggs. It seemed to be Annika's favourite pastime to insist he had a hearty breakfast which, as she said, set him up for the day.

A small salad and a few pieces of broccoli and sauerkraut were on his plate. The smell of bacon was tantalising, but he had to smile at the rabbit food on the plate and the paleo bread. Annika insisted he needed more green vegetables and took every opportunity she could to cram more down his throat. He knew she meant well and smiled and just ate it. Not that it wasn't good; it was just that he didn't see the need for vegetables first thing in the morning.

"What are you up to today?" Bill asked.

"Andy from the gym will be over this morning to help me clean up. We also need to package up the sold pieces and organise for deliveries," she said. "And I got a commission as well."

"That's great. Anyone I know?" Bill asked.

"You know, my new friend Crystal. Her boyfriend Andrei wants me to come over and look at their new house to create a large bespoke piece."

"That's very cool, darling," Bill said between mouthfuls of the slightly cardboardy piece of toast, which he washed down with his second strong cup of coffee.

"It certainly doesn't seem like money is a problem, especially since they have just built that large house on the point. Crystal also has a driver or a minder or whatever you want to call the guy," Annika said.

"She has a driver?" Bill asked, looking at her sideways, one eyebrow raised.

"Yes, didn't I mention that before?"

"Why is that? Can't she drive?" Bill asked.

"I'm sure she can. It's due to Andrei being a bit controlling, from what I can gather."

Bill didn't know what to say. He'd always had strong females around him and could imagine his mother or sister, Ata, or Annika for that matter, would tell him where to go if he suggested anything of the sort. He'd definitely get a clip around the ear from his mother.

"Don't you go and get any ideas," she said.

"For some reason, I don't think that kind of old-fashioned thinking would go down well here. Besides, Katie is such a staunch young woman; she'd have my guts for garters. Ah, that'll be Niko," Bill said as he heard a car pull up outside. He mopped the last bit of bread in the runny yolk on his plate and downed the last of his now lukewarm coffee.

"Thanks for breakfast," he said, kissing his wife goodbye and grabbing his jacket off the hook in the entrance.

As he left the house, the question still weighed heavily on his mind: why hadn't Fanta been reported missing? What the hell was going on for someone to be lost at sea, missing for days? What had he been up to? One thing was certain, though: if Bill knew the type, Fanta would have been up to no good. Perhaps he'd been pushed overboard because Fanta didn't seem the sort of person who would deliberately take his own life.

32

Andrei left for work earlier than usual; Crystal knew he was still angry. It was early. She'd stayed in bed until she heard the front door shut. She couldn't face his accusations and his disappointed look this morning. There was no way she wanted to talk to him.

Crystal sat at the edge of the kitchen island. The marble and stainless steel kitchen seemed like a foreign place today. It was all to Andrei's taste—minimalist, clean surfaces, polished to within an inch of its life, and clutter-free. If she had a choice, she'd like to have more things around her that mirrored her personality. She missed the apartment she had rented before she met Andrei, but there was no way she could hold on to it without her own income. Now she knew why he didn't want to spend time there; he hadn't been able to stand her relaxed style. He obviously thought he could mould her into his ideal woman. Now, she wasn't so sure.

The wind howled outside, and she could see white caps on the ocean through the kitchen window from where she was sitting. It was like the sea was angry with the world, its temper boiling over. She pulled her robe close. If she weren't quite so tired, perhaps she could relate.

She'd hardly touched the buttered toast; her appetite failed her this morning. Her stomach churned, and the few mouthfuls she'd tried to get down threatened to make their way up again. She sipped on the fresh orange juice, which she usually adored, but the acid irritated her stomach today. They'd had words last night when they arrived home. Yet again, Andrei had brought up the subject of children—a sore point in their relationship. To be honest, it was the last thing she wanted at the moment, but Andrei could be very persuasive, and she'd run out of excuses.

"Why are you lying to me?" He'd accused her of not being truthful and still on contraception, something she had vehemently denied. It was as if he could see right through her. She'd deliberately not removed the IUD at her last visit to her gynaecologist. The doctor had been sympathetic to Crystal's plight but encouraged her to be honest with her partner and start a dialogue about the subject.

"I want you to be honest with me. What is it that makes you unsure?" Andrei had said.

"I just don't think that I'm ready yet. Please, can you respect how I feel?"

In reality, she had no intention of involving Andrei in the decision. It was her body, after all. He was like a human lie detector and sensed if she lied. Last night, she'd stuck to her guns, being in so deep that there was nothing else she could do.

Andrei punished her by sleeping in the spare room. So, who was the big baby?

She'd heard when he left and hoped he had it in him to say he was sorry for his harsh words, but it was not to be. He was not in the habit of easily forgetting. How would she make it up to him? She had nowhere else to go.

Slowly but surely, she had lost touch with friends and family, people he didn't want her to have contact with. It was like he wished to isolate her, have her all to himself. What else did they need, he always said. She tossed most of her breakfast in the bin.

Crystal had made up her mind: she was her own person, not just Andrei's girlfriend. She was someone of worth.

33

Andrei was angry and couldn't understand why Crystal was so against having a family with him. It was the greatest gift anyone could give. Why wasn't she ready? He'd made sure she had everything—security and a lovely lifestyle. She didn't have to go to work. Wasn't this enough? He'd slept badly but still managed his workout, which he'd fuelled with frustration and anger.

The foreman would be at the site by now, so he might as well call in to see what progress they'd made. He liked to drop in on his builders to ensure they were always on their toes. He expected a lot from them and was a hard taskmaster; there was no room for shoddy workmanship. Andrei enjoyed the power. Survival of the fittest was all that mattered and it was ingrained in his psyche. He still remembered as a young boy being adopted from the rundown house of horror the Russian orphanage had been. They barely had enough food, were not well cared for, and lived in squalor. When his adoptive parents brought him and his sister, Daria, as far away as they could possibly get to Auckland, he'd found it difficult to trust. He'd vowed never to end up in a place like an orphanage again.

Andrei had squirrelled away food in his pockets for the first few months. His new mum knew he was doing this but let him continue.

Only later did she tell him. He had fended for himself and his sister for so long that it had become a routine part of his life. But they had certainly landed on their feet in the home of Mary and Angus Bowen, where they were loved and treated like their own children.

Mary was a homemaker and made them feel secure. She was always there to comfort them. His dad was the provider and owned a large construction company, and it was there that Andrei got his first break as a young man. He wanted to do everything in his power to show his dad that he could also provide. They'd been sent to the best schools. He'd completed all his schooling at King's, and Daria had attended St Cuthbert's, both Auckland private schools with a long history and pedigree.

Ten days after their arrival in Auckland, the decision had been made that he was to start school. He was a skinny, undernourished boy who barely spoke more than a few words in English, and his classmates thought he was odd. The class bully, Colin—a tall and confident boy—convinced everyone that Andrei was less than them. Colin and two friends took him into the woods by the soccer field and force-fed him worms they'd dug up. The rest of the boys watched on and laughed. Andrei threw up, and the abuse worsened until he came home with a black eye and a split lip at the end of the week. His mum had tears in her eyes, but his dad had little sympathy.

Instead, his father put boxing gloves on him, taught Andrei how to hit where it hurt, and gave him tactical advice on how Bowen men handled themselves. When the next week came around, and Colin and his henchmen grabbed him to hurt and humiliate him, Andrei swung hard and hit Colin on the nose. The boy dropped like a ton of bricks and his friends scarpered.

"If you hurt me again, I will crush you," Andrei whispered as he leant over Colin.

When the teacher asked Colin what had happened as the school bell rang, he convinced him that he'd fallen over. That was the end of that, and from that day onwards, no one ever picked on Andrei, and he was never the underdog again.

"HEY, Kingston, I'm not paying you to sit around to drink coffee," Andrei said, enjoying the power trip as he watched the grown man jump, spilling the contents of his mug. Andrei had arrived at site one in Point Wells.

"Sorry, Andrei. I didn't see you there. I was just about to call you. There's been vandalism here again overnight," he said, gesturing to the windows at the back. "A couple of the large windows in the lounge have been smashed this time, and there are glass shards on the floor."

"What again? For Christ's sake, we just had them fixed. I hope you had the cameras installed like I asked you to."

"Umm, the cameras have been ordered," Kingston said. "Should be here any day now." He couldn't help but feel he'd let Andrei down.

"Probably kids. Who else would do this kind of shit?" Andrei muttered. "I'm a bit sick of it, though. That's twice in one week at the same house."

"I haven't called the cops yet. I wanted to check with you first."

"The cops won't do anything. Just call the glazier and get the panes replaced. And I want those cameras up ASAP!"

"Sure thing. I'll chase it this morning."

"Everything still on track to be finished in August?" Andrei said, walking around the front of the house.

"So far, we're doing well, and things are on schedule."

"That's good; just keep me up to date." "Sure thing," the foreman said.

Andrei knew he wasn't liked. He was never one of the boys, but why should he be? He was the boss, he thought and smirked. The power trip made him feel good, especially after last night's carry-on with Crystal. He didn't like her newfound strength and assertiveness. Did it have anything to do with her new friend, that artist Annika Granger? He would not tolerate it. Crystal belonged to him; she would toe the line if she had any loyalty and sense.

He loved to have his little girls around—Emma was eight and

Emilia six, and they adored their father. He craved affection and adoration, something the psychiatrists put down to early childhood deprivation of the necessities of life. He didn't really care; they could label it any way they wanted.

His thoughts returned to the argument last night. He didn't want Crystal to drink at all; he needed her to be in optimum health to have a child, and he couldn't understand why she was so reluctant to get started. The child would be well-provided for, as would she. He needed her as the little wife at home, something pretty to hang on his arm and, of course, hand down her good genes to their offspring.

He climbed back in the car. The weather didn't look great today, and he put the heater on. He had three more houses on the go, all in various stages of the building process. It was time to stop by house number two and crack the whip.

34

Bill eased himself into the front seat. His side hurt as he sat down. Although there was a slight improvement every day, he was sick to death of feeling miserable.

"Rough night, Sarge?" Niko said.

"I've had better, that's for sure," Bill said, settling into his seat.

"I stopped and got you a coffee. Thought you might need it." Niko handed Bill a steaming hot takeaway cup.

"Thanks, mate, that really hit the spot," he said as he savoured the first mouthful. "I could get used to the service."

"You know, I would stay up here in a heartbeat if the powers that be required another full-time role in Matakana," Niko said.

"Yes, I know, mate," Bill said, letting the slightly bitter coffee with its tinge of salty aroma wash over him. He could feel the calm the caffeine brought him and breathed in.

When they arrived at the station, Bill picked up the file of Patrick 'Fanta' Morris, as he was commonly known, the body from the beach last night. At this early stage, they had no idea if they were dealing with an accidental or deliberate drowning; hence, Orewa hadn't taken over the case. However, as soon as the autopsy was done, they might want to conduct the investigation.

"Right, we know he didn't have any family in the area, but the priority this morning is to get hold of any relative who might be around anywhere else. We also have to check out his address," Bill said to Niko. "He might have had a flatmate; who knows? If you could search for a living relative, I'll drive out to Pakiri to his house." "I'll get on to it now, boss," Niko said.

BILL DROVE through Leigh and turned left at Hauraki Road by the fire station, the New Zealand flag flapping in the breeze. Then he took a left turn at the Leigh Fisheries on Pakiri Road—Bill remembered fondly working there as a teenager during the holidays. Within twenty minutes, he'd arrived and parked in front of a small weatherboard house in desperate need of a repaint. A seemingly clapped-out old mower was parked in the middle of the knee-high lawn as if it had just died and been abandoned when the petrol ran out.

A scrawny cat slunk through a trellis archway up the path towards the house, its tail trailing behind it. With the rain over the last few days and the thin layer of gravel, the ground was pitted with puddles. As the gravel crushed underfoot, the cat turned around and wove between Bill's legs, obviously starving for food and affection. The little cat ran his face against Bill's trousers and purred contentedly as he bent down to give it a scratch. A vehicle was parked in the driveway, probably not registered, but that wasn't today's priority.

The bottom windowpane in the front door was missing and had been rudimentarily fixed with a piece of plywood. Bill knocked on the door, and the skinny cat took off through one of the loose corners, and into the house.

The heavy curtains were drawn, and the house looked dank even from the outside. Bill could imagine the damp seeping from every corner. It was midmorning; perhaps the house's inhabitants were still asleep for some reason. Bill knocked on the door again, harder this time. Footsteps could be heard from the inside. A curtain swayed momentarily in one of the upstairs windows, and he caught a glimpse of someone.

A scruffy male in his late twenties opened the door. It looked as if he'd just woken up. His face was puffy, and as he ran his hands through the unruly hair, Bill caught a whiff of the man's armpits. Musty air and stale sweat prickled Bill's nose. The man reeked. It was obvious that showers and cleanliness were not a priority. Bill guessed the flannel shirt, which had just been thrown on, had not been near a washing machine for a while, either.

"Hello, I'm Sergeant Granger from the Matakana station."

"Um, okay. What can I do for you, Sergeant?" the scraggly man said, rubbing his chin.

Bill had to take a step back to not dry retch. "I'm here about Fanta."

"I've no idea where that son of a bitch is. I haven't seen him for days, and he owes me for rent," the man vented.

"And who are you?" Bill asked as he pulled the notebook out of his pocket.

"I'm Walter."

"Walter, who?"

"Walter Smith," the man said somewhat reluctantly.

"I'm sorry to tell you that Fanta is dead."

"What?" The man huffed as the air visibly went out of him. He sagged to one side of the doorframe.

"I can't believe it. I thought the bastard had done a runner down country. It's not the first time he's skipped out on what he owes."

"You said you saw him a few days ago? Where was he heading then?"

"I have no idea. I'm not his parole officer," the man said. He'd regained some of his grouchiness and defiance. Bill knew exactly why he wasn't welcome inside the house, and to be honest, he was sure he'd find assorted drug paraphernalia and, more than likely, stolen goods. But all that could wait for another day. Pick your battles, Bill thought to himself. The stupid imbeciles weren't going to change their patterns from one day to the next.

If the housemate knew anything, there was no way he'd help with the inquiries. Bill had come across people like this many times. There was no way they'd break the code for any reason, good, bad or indifferent, unless it served them personally or was a monetary incentive —neither of which Bill offered.

"I also need to get hold of next of kin. Any idea where his parents are?"

"All right, hang on a moment. I'll get it for you," he said with a look of contempt. He appeared a few moments later, handing Bill a torn corner from a piece of paper. "These are his old lady's details."

"Thanks."

The door slammed shut in Bill's face, and he could hear the sound of the lock. He stepped off the front step, ignoring a barely audible 'pig.'

35

It was lunchtime, and still no sign of Andrei. It was obvious he was in one of his moods, which sometimes lasted for days. Crystal hated it when he sulked like a toddler. Did he really think this would convince her to have a child? To make the most out of the situation, she would have to play the long game, appeal to his ego and sweet-talk him when he came home. She couldn't stand several days like this, that was for sure. She wished she had a car of her own to drive. She didn't dare drive one of Andrei's prized possessions.

She texted Mike and told him she planned to go into Matakana to buy something for dinner, something Andrei would really like. Mike agreed to pick her up in an hour.

In the meantime, she decided to tidy up. Andrei was a neat freak, and even though the housekeeper came in three times a week, he liked her to pick up the slack and make sure their home was perfect.

By the time Mike arrived, she had thrown on a pair of skinny jeans and a cashmere sweater and also put on her makeup. She grabbed her coat from the hook in the entrance, strode outside, and jumped in the front passenger seat.

"Thanks," Crystal said, giving Mike a warm smile.

"No worries at all," Mike said. "You know I'm always around."

She'd never reflected on it before, but Mike was always around, even at Christmas time and other holidays. He never went home to family, and she realised she didn't know much about him other than he came from Hamilton. She was sure there had been women on the scene now and then, and the last time Andrei's sister Daria had visited, she'd seen her sneak out of Mike's cottage in the wee hours. There was obviously some history there, and she knew he had a good heart.

"Hey, Mike. You can tell me to mind my own business, and I don't mean to pry. But don't you want to go home and spend some time with your own family?" Crystal glanced at Mike, who was smiling. He didn't seem to mind the question but took his time to answer.

"I guess it's been a while since I went to see my folks. Perhaps I ought to make more of an effort," he said.

Crystal could sympathise. Glamorous lifestyle aside, she missed her own mum and dad and the family farm down New Plymouth way. Andrei had met them several times when they'd flown down for the weekend. Andrei disliked muddy gumboots and country life and couldn't wait to get out of there. His aversion made the atmosphere uncomfortable at the best of times. It wasn't helped by her parents' more down-to-earth approach to life, either. You could say there was no love lost between them. Andrei loved the city, the parties and the glamour, canapés and champagne, nice clothes and his Botox-injected so-called friends and associates. Most of them were as shallow as a puddle. The only saving grace was that she got to live in this beautiful semi-rural setting which made her feel more at home.

Crystal was happy she'd met Annika. Although she was a bit older, it was lovely to enjoy the company of someone who was not obsessed with the latest plastic surgery trend or when the next fabulous party was.

Mike parked right outside the butcher's shop down the main street in Matakana.

"You need me to come in with you?" Mike asked.

"God, no. I won't be long, " Crystal said, already halfway out of the car.

She browsed the little butcher shop and settled on a nice piece of lamb, a perfect roast for the two of them. Next stop was the well-stocked Four Square supermarket, where she picked up some seasonal vegetables and a sprig of rosemary. She reached for a small jar of mint jelly and ingredients for a chocolate brownie, which she knew Andrei would love. After dropping the shopping in the car, she popped across the road. The village was quiet, and she walked down the stairs next to the cinema to the chocolate shop. The rich, decadent smell of cocoa greeted her, and she perused the handmade treats before settling on a gift-wrapped box with an assortment of six pieces.

Crystal checked her phone and decided she had enough time to pop into the village bookstore. Despite what people might think of her, she'd graduated from the University of Otago with an honours degree in English Literature. As she walked into the welcoming little shop, she inhaled the woody pulp of new books and felt a calm come over her. This was truly her happy place. The shelves and tables were crowded, with a wonderfully curated selection of books. She let her fingers wander over the spines as she devoured what was on offer and decided on the latest Lucinda Riley book. Before she went to the counter to pay, she looked at the children's section. Andrei's daughters were due to visit in a couple of weeks. Last time they were here, she'd read them *The Philosopher's Stone*, the first in the Harry Potter series, and she'd promised the girls that they would read *The Chamber of Secrets*, the second book in the series, next time they visited.

She picked the books up and took them to the counter, paying while she chatted to the lovely ladies behind the counter about what new releases were due to arrive.

As she hurried to the car, Mike sat back, listening to some music and tapping the steering wheel rhythmically.

"Did you get everything you needed?"

"Yes, I just need to go to the wine shop. I want to pick a special bottle for tonight's meal, something that Andrei will like," she said, closing the front passenger seat door.

"Of course, that's not a problem."

Mike turned the car and headed around the corner.

She searched the shelves of the wine shop and found the distinctive red and white label of a locally produced Malbec to go with the roast meat. She read the description on the back, which sealed the deal: '. . . *natural elegance and finesse-fragrance of black cherry and wild raspberry, fresh palate with a smooth texture and vibrant soul . . .*'

36

After Mike dropped Crystal back home, there was one more point of business to deal with before the day was over.

He checked in with his boss as he drove back towards Warkworth to let him know of his movements. Andrei wanted the loose threads tied up, and what Andrei wanted, he always got, one way or the other. Mike was used to doing the dirty work. He didn't mind. It was just that lately, he wanted more out of life. He was on call twenty-four hours a day, which was all well and good for someone in their twenties, but he was in his mid-thirties now and was a bit sick of it. He wanted more. He needed to build his own legacy, make some real money and perhaps have someone to go through life with. His mind wandered to Daria. Their casual connection was immensely passionate and spanned years but lacked stability. Mike knew it wouldn't work in real life, nor could it be a permanent solution.

He stood on the brakes at the last corner before the notorious Hill Street intersection. Cars were at a standstill from the barbershop onwards. He figured it was school traffic and people on their way home from work. He thought of Daria again and his future. When he finally reached the intersection, he shot across as the light turned green and turned right on the main highway. He steeled himself for what was to come and arrived at the semi-rural, heavily fortified property. A solid timber fence with corrugated iron panels was all one could see from the road. The gate was set back from the road. He drove into the driveway, nodded to the inconspicuously placed security camera on the side of the fence and leant across to the speaker box. Before he even had time to say a word, the automatic gate slid open.

They'd obviously seen him on the CCTV. As he drove into the compound, it looked the same as last time—gnarly old fruit trees lined the driveway, reminding him of brittle bones and skeletons, which gave him the willies.

A tired red brick house appeared, grey lichen covering most of its black roof. Two tattered sofas and a cut-off old oil barrel used as a fire pit dominated the front. Bits of garden furniture, old toys and other junk were strewn in the vastly overgrown jungle that had once been the garden. He had no idea how many of them lived here. Big Ed ran a tight ship.

Further on, three large garages stood side by side; the roller doors pulled up. Several large motorbikes were parked outside, and a scrawny-looking boy barely out of his teens did his best to polish the beasts. He glanced at Mike as he drove by and continued with the task at hand. Mike wondered who the poor sod was.

Prison-style prefabricated barracks were visible down the back, their weathered exterior peeling and desperately needing a lick of paint. Rags hung in front of the tiny windows, making the place look decidedly depressing. Mike assumed it was dorm-style accommodation. He thought you'd have to be pretty down on your luck to stay in a place like that. The barracks didn't look like they were insulated either, no doubt making for cold and damp living arrangements.

The faded red barn was equally as neglected from the outside—it was a front, though. The inside was as low key, which was kind of the point, but behind the far wall, there was an elaborate set-up where they sorted shipments of meth coming from the area, mainly via boats coming secretly into port.

He'd been taken inside once in the early days, much to the dismay of Big Ed. These days he rarely came to the house, just made the drop to one of the lieutenants at any of their pre-arranged meeting spots. This meeting was necessary because Mike needed to ensure the business relationship was okay, despite Fanta still missing. He knew they blamed him; after all, he'd been the skipper and ultimately responsible, but the truth was the dumb fuck had fallen overboard. It wasn't like they'd pushed him into the water.

Mike saw Big Ed standing in front of the barn and parked the car. As Mike climbed out of his car, he was reminded how Big Ed's weathered skin made him look a lot older than he was.

"What the fuck?" Big Ed called out. "How dare you show your face here. Have you no shame? Fanta was my blood, and he's missing. My blood is missing. What the fuck do you suggest I say to his poor mother!!"

Big Ed was a big man, not exactly tall, but definitely wide. Mike had heard he was only forty, but he looked well into his fifties, as he'd most likely had a hard life. Besides, there were no old presidents of gangs.

Despite being a few metres away, Mike could smell the dirt from his dreadlocks and unwashed clothes.

"I'm really sorry about Fanta, but it was a tragic accident," Mike said, trying to appear cool as he leant against the bonnet of the car. "No one's to blame. These things happen."

"You'd better make it up to us with your next little venture. I want a bigger shipment of Molly and a better price, or I'm going to have to let your boss know what you are doing behind his back."

Mike felt cold sweat trickle down his back. The last thing he needed was for Andrei to find out he supplied the tablets on the side and he was stretched to the limit with the ecstasy supply from Auckland. It would be hard to get a larger quantity at such late notice.

"All right, I'll see what I can do." He had no choice but to agree to the terms.

"When's the next meth drop anyway? We're running low on that as well. The demand through our distribution network can't be satisfied as it is." "I'll keep you posted," Mike said.

Perhaps he ought to have this roach extinguished, he thought. He had his own contacts in Auckland. For a couple of grand, his problem could be dealt with, and Big Ed exterminated like a cockroach.

37

When Bill walked through the door at home and into the kitchen, Maggie and Finn were ecstatic, dancing on their hind legs. He was exhausted. It had been a long day, and his ribs ached.

"All right, guys. Settle down," he said, giving the two boisterous dogs all the attention and as many pats as he could without having to bend down.

"Something smells delicious," Bill said and groaned as he sat on the dining chair.

"Long day, darling?" Annika said, wiping her hands on her apron as she prepared dinner.

"It sure has been," Bill said, his face ashen.

"What's been going on today?"

"Mainly the paperwork for the drowning victim found last night. I spoke to the officer who notified the man's mother this afternoon; she's in a nursing home with dementia. I'm not sure she could take it all in. It's all very tragic."

"That's terrible," Annika said. "Did he live on his own?"

"No, he was living with others in an old house in Pakiri. The housemate I spoke to didn't seem overly fond of him, either. But let's talk about you. How was your day, sweetheart?"

"Andy and I had a bit to do. We packed up from last night. Thankfully, we got lots done today, which is great," Annika said. "I'm really looking forward to going over to Crystal and Andrei's place tomorrow to deliver their new pieces. And, of course, to see the space where they want to have something large commissioned."

"Well, I think that's worth celebrating, don't you? Is that the leftover wine from last night?" Bill said, eyeing the three bottles on the bench. "Let's have a glass before dinner; what do you think ?"

"Why not?" Annika said, reaching for the stemless glasses on the shelf and pouring them each a taste.

"Cheers and all the best for the upcoming commission. I know you will knock them all dead, darling." Bill raised his glass.

"Skål," Annika said, clinking her glass to his as Zac sauntered into the kitchen, large headphones draped around his neck, heading straight for the fridge.

"What's for dinner tonight?" Zac asked as he peered into the fridge.

"The roast chicken is ready now," Annika said, pulling the golden brown bird out of the oven.

"I'm starving," Zac said, turning from the fridge to take in the roast dinner.

"By the time you help set the table, it will be ready to eat," Bill said.

"Can't the twins do that? I'm in the middle of a game with some of my mates."

"How about you pause the game, sit down, and have some family time with the rest of us?" Bill said, locking eyes with his son.

"Nah, I'll pass." Zac grabbed a plate from the cupboard and piled it with potatoes and sliced meat.

Annika gestured for Bill to leave it, to let him go.

"At least bring your plate and any other dishes down later. We're getting short on cutlery," Annika said. "Oh, and you can tell your sisters to come down for dinner on your way to your room?"

Zac grunted and left.

"I know what you're thinking, Bill, but we have to pick our battles. Tonight is not the time."

"I know you're right, but it's not too much to ask to have all of us sit down and have dinner together, is it?"

38

Andrei deliberately dragged his feet. Mike had told him that Crystal had organised a nice meal for him tonight. He thought about the harsh exchange of words last night and still felt very much aggrieved. He couldn't understand what the problem was—why she didn't want to have his child? He provided for her. What more could she want? She needed nothing, yet she'd told him she wasn't ready for this step. He knew she wasn't on the contraceptive pill, so perhaps it was just a matter of time before she fell pregnant. He already had two girls, but he needed a boy to take over the family name and, ultimately, the business.

It was nearly six-thirty and pitch black outside by the time he arrived home. He'd called into the local pub for a beer with Mike.

The house was lit like a Christmas tree, every damn light on it seemed. He knew Crystal was scared of the dark. He flicked the remote and drove into the spacious garage; the dark grey carpet softened his arrival. The garage was as neat and tidy as the main house, nothing out of place, and his gym equipment was the only other object there. He was a creature of habit. He rose at five thirty sharp and meditated for twenty minutes exactly before doing an hour's gym work and then having something to eat.

Andrei wiped his shoes on a mat and put them on the shoe rack by the internal door before entering the main house.

The smell of roast lamb filled the house, and the soft music of Michael Bublé played in the background. She'd put on his favourite playlist, but Crystal was much younger, so he wasn't sure if she really liked the Canadian crooner. It was obvious she'd gone to a lot of effort for the evening to be special. As he stepped into the kitchen, there she was; her natural and unassured beauty took his breath away. He forgot he was still annoyed with her. He embraced her, his nose burrowing into her hair. The intoxication of being so close to her made his head spin. Crystal seemed unsure and a little surprised by his action. She smiled cautiously and returned his affection before she turned to the kitchen.

"Dinner is ready if you're hungry," Crystal said as she opened the oven door and pulled out the perfectly cooked lamb roast, infused with rosemary. A mountain of roasted potatoes, kumara and butternut was already placed in a dish. "The meat needs to rest for a moment, but if you take these to the table, by the time I've dished up the green vegetables and poured the gravy, you should be able to carve it," she said. Andrei smiled and did as he was told.

The table was beautifully set with the best plates, glassware, linen napkins, and a trio of lit candles as the centrepiece. Crystal had poured a bottle of wine into the Riedel Amadeo decanter, his favourite one. Two wine glasses were next to it.

He could see the bottle in the corner. It wasn't one from their cellar; he knew the inventory intimately. She must have picked this one up today.

"I'm starved. It smells delicious," he said, pouring them a large glass of wine from the decanter. Andrei handed Crystal a glass and inhaled the fruity notes. He gazed into her eyes as he put the glass to his lips, tasting the wine.

"I hope you like it. The man in the shop highly recommended it as something very special."

Andrei didn't answer as he let the wine swirl, gently aerating the full-bodied, silky mouthful on the back of his tongue.

"Mmm, it's a fabulous wine indeed. It will be perfectly paired with the roast," he said.

"Come and sit down. You have outdone yourself, darling. I'll carve the meat and we can eat."

"Look, I'm sorry about last night, Andrei. I don't want us to fight," she said, reaching for the glass and taking another mouthful. The pause that followed felt like an eternity. Andrei sharpened the carving knife on the steel before he cut into the meat and served up.

"I just don't understand," Andrei said as he sat in his chair, his face solemn. "Don't you want children?"

"I'm not ready. It's a big commitment," Crystal said quietly, averting her eyes from his intense gaze. Her voice cracked; she was close to tears.

"Let's revisit the subject in a couple of months. What do you say? Andrei said, his eyes and whole demeanour softening.

Crystal was visibly relieved; he knew she didn't want the uncomfortable air between them to continue.

"Now, let's enjoy this beautiful meal you've prepared. I feel very spoilt indeed," Andrei said as Crystal relaxed.

~

CRYSTAL WAS MORE relieved than she'd thought. She'd expected him still to be angry with her. The outburst last night had upset her more than she wanted to admit. A decision about having children was not something you made lightly. Above all, he needed to give her time. As for tonight, she'd gone all out to make a special meal, and Andrei seemed to appreciate her effort.

Crystal couldn't take her eyes off the way he sharpened the carving knife with slow, deliberate strokes. Even though Andrei's mood had lightened and he seemed back to normal, she shivered at the thought that he was like Dr Jekyll and Mr Hyde— a split personality.

39

Friday the 7th of July

Annika arrived early and set her mat and blocks at her preferred spot at the back of the yoga studio. She rolled her mat out, slipped off her shoes, rested her cloth bag against the back wall, and started gentle warm-up stretches. Her neck and shoulders were stiff from the hard work to get the exhibition ready, not to mention the stress that came with the whole event. Yoga truly was her religion, as it nourished both her body and soul.

Crystal arrived just before the class was about to start. She wasn't her usual calm self and seemed a little jittery, but she waved at Annika. The full body workout did a world of good, and Annika felt herself relax into her mat as the yoga practice finished up with a long, restful relaxation. It was the best part. Maeve put calm background music on. Annika pulled her socks and jacket on and settled into the mat. She let the soothing voice of the yoga teacher lull her into a place of serenity, let her breath guide her to a state of relaxation, and let go. Afterwards, as the class came to an end, she gathered her things and waited for Crystal outside.

"Hi, how are you? We loved the exhibition's opening night,"

Crystal said as they walked to the car park together. "Andrei was very impressed with your art."

"I'm so happy you guys enjoyed the night, and I'm so excited to come over this afternoon to deliver the pieces you bought," Annika said.

"Me, too.

"Are you still good for 2:00 p.m.? I'll make sure Andrei's there. He really wants to talk to you about the commission piece for the living room," Crystal said.

Annika could see Mike sitting in the car, waiting with the engine running.

"Sorry, I have to go," Crystal said as she opened the car door. "We'll see you this afternoon!"

"Yes, I'll be there." Annika watched Mike and Crystal drive off and wondered what she might be walking into.

40

As Mike pulled up to Andrei's house, three large black motorbikes blocked the driveway in front of the garage. The riders had an unkempt, scraggly appearance with dirty jeans and leather jackets with gang insignia. It made them look menacing and out of place in this well-to-do neighbourhood.

The fairly new concrete now had tyre marks of burnt rubber in a figure eight pattern—Andrei would be livid.

Mike parked further down the driveway. Crystal could feel the tension in the air. She didn't know if Mike was scared or angry. He reached across and dug around in the glove compartment, pulling a handgun out. Crystal felt every muscle in her body tense: why on earth did Mike have a weapon in the car?

"Don't move until I come back and get you," he said curtly. Crystal didn't question what he said and sat a little lower in the front seat.

"Lock the door and keep your head down," he said. Crystal was scared. She swallowed hard; she had to get a grip. In her mind, she wondered what on earth was going on. She raised her head slightly and breathed a sigh of relief, knowing the windows were tinted. She craned her neck to get a better look.

Mike strode towards the men and she could see them talking.

One of the younger men stepped forward and waved his arms around like he wanted to take a swing at Mike, but Mike stood his ground. He had his back to her, and she could see the handgun tucked in the waistband of his jeans. The conversation seemed heated, and Crystal was impressed with how Mike handled the situation.

But why were the bikers here, and what business did they have with Andrei and Mike?

After several minutes, the men turned and walked towards their bikes. One of them shouted at Mike, but Crystal couldn't hear what he said. The apparent leader was in his fifties, and his younger deputies looked to be in their thirties. It was difficult to tell as she was sure they'd lived a tough life. Finally, the one who seemed to be the leader climbed on his bike and pointed directly at Mike while he shouted some departing words, which Crystal heard.

"You'll pay for this." His stern, tattooed face left no room for misunderstanding that the message he delivered carried a threat; something was very serious. Mike didn't move; he stood with his hands on his hips like an impenetrable shield.

Crystal crouched down again and flinched when the bikes fired up. The loud, deep throated roar vibrated through the car and into her bones.

As she peeked out, she could see the tattooed face of the leader. The bikers took off in a cloud of exhaust and with a screech, leaving more burnt rubber behind.

Crystal, who'd now slid down to the floor, jumped as Mike knocked on the window.

"You can open the door now," he said in his normal voice.

"Thanks," she said. "What was all that about?"

"It's nothing. It's a minor misunderstanding. Nothing to worry about," he said. "You can get out of the car. Everything's fine. They won't be back."

Crystal quickly walked up to the front door and unlocked it. The lemony smell of cleaning products greeted her as she stepped through the entrance. She checked the time on her phone: it was nearing eleven. Her stomach rumbled; she hadn't eaten yet today. Not that she usually ate before yoga because it was impossible to do the asanas or the poses with a belly full of food. Crystal boiled the jug and grabbed one of the tea canisters off the shelf in the walk-in butler's pantry. Magda, the housekeeper, had been there since early morning, and the thick stone bench gleamed in the warm glow of the light. The flavour of pomegranate and raspberry greeted her as she poured the boiled water over the tea bag. The sweet, tangy berries provided an uplifting aroma and satiated the worst of her hunger as she took the mug into the bathroom and turned the shower on.

The warm water washed away the unpleasant memory of what had happened outside the house. Perhaps she had overreacted? But who were those bikers? What did they want?

And why did Mike take his handgun to go talk to them?

Crystal heard Andrei calling her name.

"I'm in here. Won't be long," she answered, quickly towelling herself off. She walked into the dressing room, letting her towel drop onto the floor, even though she knew it was Andrei's pet hate. She let her hair out of the scrunchie; the moisture of the shower had made her hair curl in long twists down her back. She ran her hands down the pile of neatly folded jumpers. She pulled a warm top out and put it on, along with a pair of freshly washed jeans. The weather had turned to custard as the wind and rain had both picked up, and it was now blowing a gale. Would this wet and dreary winter ever end? She pulled a pair of woolly socks out of the drawer as she walked out to the living room.

"There you are," Andrei said as he pulled her close, burying his face in her hair. "Fancy some lunch?" He pulled away from her and stared intensely into her eyes. "Magda left a baked quiche in the oven."

"Sure, I'm starving," Crystal said, reaching for the plates on the shelf in the cupboard. She wondered if she asked Andrei whether he might tell her about the bikers. "Did Mike tell you we had a visit from some bikers?"

Andrei looked at her, nodding.

"Why were they here?" Crystal asked as she loaded her plate with quiche.

"Nothing you need to worry about, darling. Mike dealt with it. They won't be back here again." His face was a closed book, and Crystal knew better than to ask any more questions.

"Annika is coming at two. Does that still work for you?" she said, changing the subject.

"Of course," Andrei said. His brooding eyes had a faraway look, and she thought it best not to push the point in fear of what she might discover. Did she really want to know and be drawn into whatever the situation was about?

41

The station wagon was loaded, and she was all set to go.

Maggie and Finn were unimpressed at not being allowed to come along in the car and complained loudly to show their displeasure.

"It's all right, you two. I'm not going out for long. You'll be perfectly fine," she said, taking her coat from the hook in the entrance before shutting the front door.

The rain and wind had picked up again, and she grabbed the blue and white umbrella from the stand by the bench seat on the verandah. She was glad she'd put boots on as the puddles formed mini lakes along the gravel driveway.

Annika managed to avoid most of them as she dashed to the car and jumped into the driver's side, throwing the wet umbrella onto the passenger seat. Despite her windswept and slightly damp hair, she didn't look too bad as she checked her reflection in the rearview mirror. She was glad she'd taken time to curl her hair, and the soft waves around her face were holding, despite the weather. There was nothing she could do about her appearance now anyway.

Annika turned right on Leigh Road, then left and left again until she was on Omaha Flats Road. She drove by Providence Vineyards on the corner before passing the Sculptureum, a place she could wander around for hours, getting lost in the magnificent art.

She drove past the Omaha turn-off and continued into the charming settlement of Point Wells. It had been a few months since she'd seen the new subdivision's development. Things had progressed further and more houses had been finished.

She followed Crystal's instructions and continued down to the point where she pulled up in front of a pair of impressive black wrought iron gates.

A magnificent Italian-inspired double-storey house towered ahead of her. As if on cue, the rain stopped, and a glimmer of sun peeked through. The lustre of the grey masonry structure gleamed, and the rain-soaked cypress trees that framed both sides of the house sparkled in the emerging sunlight. The newly established lawn and raised flower beds appeared to be a work in progress.

The robust fence was higher than the norm. She estimated it to be at least three metres. It was the same solid masonry construction and colour as the house. To the left was what looked like a guest-house. On the other side, and in keeping with the design of the rest of the property, was another wider building, perhaps extra garaging. Annika wound the window down and leant towards the speaker box. A camera was fixed to the right gate post.

Before she'd even pressed the button, the gates swung open, and the camera's motion sensor followed her in. She couldn't help but think it was a little weird. She had envisaged a large house, but this was impressive and made her slightly nervous. Unsure where to park, she pulled up in front of the double garage.

Someone with a great eye had designed the house with its impressive front doors and topiary trees that framed them. The doors opened, and Crystal appeared. She looked like a celebrity in a *House and Garden* magazine and greeted Annika warmly. How on earth could a woman look that gorgeous at all times? Annika thought, looking at Crystal. It seemed effortless. The long-toned legs and jeans with a perfect fit, casually teamed with a divine jumper, no doubt with a hefty price tag attached.

Annika brushed her hair away from her face and hoped she didn't look like something the cat dragged in.

"I love that top," Crystal said. "It's such a beautiful colour!"

Annika blushed; she wasn't used to receiving compliments. Nevertheless, it made her feel warm inside, and she relaxed and smiled.

"Come on inside out of this weather."

"It's been a shocker today. Even with an umbrella, I managed to get rained on," Annika said as she walked up the steps and into the grand atrium. The entrance took her breath away. The light and airy space was two storeys high and complemented by large windows and a massive skylight. Her eyes were drawn to the built-in custom shelves on both sides. The wide recessed shelves with built-in lighting showcased each piece of art. A life size feathered Korowai cloak hung on the wall across from the front door. The Māori garment was proudly displayed, and she wondered what the significance was for Andrei and Crystal. Annika had wanted one for years. To get hold of an authentic, traditional cloak was difficult, not to mention expensive, as they were handmade entirely with flax, even the thread they were sewn with, and adorned with thousands of feathers. You had to know an artist who made them. Even so, a garment like this was only ever produced for something very special. Such a garment would be a family heirloom, passed down from generation to generation. The spotlight above the intricate piece shone on the copper-red and black feathers, intermittently mixed with pheasant and some other indistinguishable bird; the brown hue and texture could even be from a kiwi. If it was, it made it a special garment indeed.

"Come through. You can hang your jacket here," Crystal said, opening an almost invisible door panel to the side. There was no handle, just a press-and-release mechanism. Annika glimpsed what looked like the garage down the corridor to the left. A similar layout on the other side seemed to lead to the ground-floor bedrooms. Straight ahead, the wide hallway unfolded into a spacious kitchen and dining area. The pièce de résistance was the floor-to-ceiling double-height glass frontage that took in the ultimate view, which opened up to a waterfront vista, the sea lapping at the bottom of the garden. Despite the Tuscan villa exterior, the inside was an ultra-modern, smart house.

Annika had never seen anything like it and was almost afraid of sitting on the white leather couch in case she inadvertently marked it. At home, all their furniture was old and lived in, full of dog hairs and stains she hadn't been able to remove since the kids were young, not that it mattered in the slightest. It was home, and she liked it just the way it was.

"Wow, what an amazing view you have," Annika said.

"Isn't it beautiful?" Crystal said, gazing out to the waterfront. "I never get tired of the ever-changing moods of the ocean or the colours, force, and sound of the waves."

Annika could see it as well. She was in awe of the location. "You know Ti Point, which inspired me, is just over there?" Annika pointed to the left.

"I know," Crystal said. "I think that's why we loved your work. It's simply perfect for this house, and it's why your paintings resonate so well with me. I love Ti Point so much. But let's have a seat. I've made some lemon muffins."

Annika perched on the stool at the end of the bench while Crystal got the afternoon tea sorted. A striking collection of lights hung above the bench. The glass baubles looked hand blown and like they were made out of delicate ice. She estimated there were at least two dozen orange-sized orbs hanging above her head. Crystal touched the smart panel on the wall and turned the warm LED lights on.

"Wow, they're amazing!"

"Thanks, we were lucky to get hold of them. The artist managed to squeeze us in between his other commissions. Andrei can be pretty persuasive at times," Crystal said and laughed.

Annika could imagine he would be and wondered when the man himself would make an appearance.

"Coffee or tea?" Crystal asked, interrupting Annika's thoughts.

"Coffee, please," Annika said.

She heard Andrei before he appeared in the doorway, his confident footsteps signalling he was the man of the house. As soon as he entered the room, his body language was as imposing as his cologne, and he immediately demanded to be the centre of attention. He crossed over to Annika, greeting her warmly like an old friend. He gently held her arms as he leaned in with a kiss on both cheeks, first the right, then the left in a very southern European way.

Then, he gave Crystal a warm kiss on the lips. Annika was somewhat taken aback by his friendliness and the intimate gesture, as she hardly knew him and had only met him once.

"You have a beautiful home," Annika said, filling the awkward silence.

"Thank you. I'm glad you like it."

"I have your art pieces in the back of my car," she rambled on. She had no idea why she felt so nervous.

"That's great. I'll get Mike to give me a hand with them," Andrei said, looking intently at her. His eyes seemed to be evaluating and burrowing straight through her, making her feel like she was an insect under a microscope.

"It's unlocked," Annika said as her throat closed up.

Andrei nodded as he headed out of the kitchen.

Just like that, the air was sucked out, and she felt her heart beat faster than normal.

She could see what a profound effect he had on women. He was incredibly charismatic. Annika took a deep breath to recover her composure.

"Come and have a seat, Annika," Crystal said, gesturing for her to sit at the dining table set with delicate white bone-china cups and saucers and a small posy of cut flowers that spilt from a Japanese-inspired ceramic vase.

The smell of strong coffee permeated the air, its rich aroma beckoning as a small cup filled to the brim was set in front of her.

"You must try one of these," Crystal said, offering Annika a lemon muffin. "They are to die for. Not exactly low calorie, but you must have your treats sometimes, right?"

Annika reached for the tiny milk jug, poured a few drops into the coffee to temper the strength, and reached for the lemon muffin.

The first bite was heavenly. The muffin was soft in the middle, and the crunchy sugar topping was divine—a perfect balance of zingy citrus to make her taste buds sing.

"These are absolutely amazing."

"Thanks, an old friend, Kim gave me the recipe. I'm happy to give it to you. It's such a handy one to have. They're super quick to make and everyone loves them."

"Yes, please. The kids would love them," Annika said, taking another bite.

Mike and Andrei carried the first painting inside and leant it carefully against the far wall before getting the rest. This was the first time Annika had seen Mike properly, and he gave her a smile of recognition in passing. Andrei stepped back, admiring the colourful pieces. The glossy surface, its smooth lustre, and the shimmering hues took on a life of their own against the backdrop of the blank wall. Annika was pleased. She was never tired of the collective breath held when a piece was revealed to a customer.

"They are even more wonderful than I remember," Andrei said, a wide grin spreading across his face.

Annika was pleased. It was always nerve-wracking to see if the customer still loved the pieces.

"I adore the colours," Crystal said as she leant into Annika's shoulder and hugged her.

"Let me show you where the commission piece would go," Andrei said. The blank wall in the lounge faced the ocean vista, and her immediate thoughts were that it had to be a strong piece to hold its own against the white interior and complement the external environment.

They sat at the table again. Annika had brought along her catalogue of previously made works and colour swatches, and they threw concepts and ideas around. Andrei knew exactly what he wanted, with Crystal chipping in now and then. He was definitely the driving force in the matter, and Annika could tell he was used to getting his way.

"Well, that's given me plenty of scope to work with," Annika said as she gathered her things from the table and put them into her bag.

"As I look at these, I can't wait to see what you come up with for the larger piece. We definitely want something reflecting the ocean and coastal environment, something wild and vibrant," Andrei said, looking her straight in the eye.

"I think I have a good idea of what you want."

"Thank you for coming over," Crystal said, touching her arm and smiling at her.

"My pleasure entirely. I'm excited to embark on this next project. And thank you for the lovely afternoon tea," Annika said as she made her way to the front door.

"If you and your husband don't have any plans, you should come over for dinner tomorrow night," Andrei said as they walked her to the car.

As she was about to leave, Zac's car came up the driveway, and she wondered what her son was doing there. He waved to his mum as he parked the car next to hers and got out.

"Hi, darling. What are you doing here?" Annika said.

"I'm here for the interview. Remember I told you about the part-time landscaping job?" Zac said, his attitude a little defensive.

"Oh, of course, but I didn't realise it was here," she said. An unsettled feeling came over her. She hoped that her intuition was wrong.

42

It was Friday afternoon. The wintery landscape was bleak, and the strong south westerly breeze coming straight up from Antarctica had ice in the air. It was going to be a cold night. The windows in the police station were full of condensation despite the old heat pump being turned up high—not that it made much of a difference. Bill could feel the draught from around the window frames and doors where he sat. The whole building needed a refit and modernisation, but there was no money in the budget, as he'd been told last time he had raised the issue to the powers that be. It was quieter than usual, and Bill wondered if he should send Niko back to Auckland.

He was still a little sore but could manage. They couldn't very well just sit there and twiddle their thumbs.

"So, this is what it's like in the winter, Sarge," Niko said, rubbing his hands to warm up. "You weren't kidding when you said nothing much happens here in the off-season, were you? And what's with the heating? It's a real ice box in here."

"It's not great, is it? But you get used to it," Bill said. "Thick socks help."

The phone ringing cut through the small open-plan office. Bill answered it after a swallow of coffee and three signals.

"Matakana police station. Sergeant Granger speaking." Bill balanced the phone receiver on his shoulder as he listened and took another sip of coffee.

"All right, that's fantastic," he said and hung up.

"You know the community fundraising for the Surf Club? Well, that was the chief. He's made a call to the Eagle Helicopter crew and sweet-talked them into donating a fifteen minute chopper ride as an auction item. On top of that, we, along with colleagues at the Warkworth station, have helped raise enough funds to buy a bike, which will be in the silent auction tomorrow. Henry Long, who's running the event, will be pleased."

"That's great, Sarge, and here is a twenty from me," Niko said, pulling a note from his wallet.

"Thanks, mate. That's excellent. I guess I'd better go and purchase this bike," Bill said as he stood up and pushed the chair into his desk.

"But first, we have to collect some drug paraphernalia from a house in Point Wells. Come on, let's get going." Bill snatched his jacket from the coat rack. "It shouldn't take long, and I'll drop you back home on the way."

"All right, I'll drive," Niko said as he got in the front seat.

"Ah, that's Henry," Bill said and waved as he spotted the man's bright red hair across the road.

"Is that Henry? I see this guy sometimes when I pick up a coffee in the morning. He doesn't really look like a surfer."

"I guess not. I'm sure he did in his youth. He works at the building supply shop next door," Bill said as they continued towards Point Wells.

"Who found the drug-related items, and did they say what they wanted us to collect?" Niko asked.

"It was a concerned parent. Their seventeen-year-old son and a friend were taken to hospital late last night. Apparently, they'd both taken ecstasy. These kids never learn."

43

Saturday the 8th of July

It was Saturday morning, and the parking lot of the Surf Club in Omaha was busy. The damp rose from the dew-covered ground as the cool morning air from Omaha Bay washed over the dunes. Sand crushed underfoot, and Bill was always amazed at how much of it was carried back to the car park. He could taste the salty smell of seaweed and various creatures washed up on the beach just over the dunes. A flock of noisy seagulls soared above and zeroed in on the gathering, lured by the smell of food. The communication and collective wail of the birds was like a bunch of screaming kleptomaniacs about to swoop.

The club was the heart of the community. It was ten in the morning, and the volunteers had arrived early to set everything up. Excitement was in the air. The Eagle police helicopter had landed on the grassed area a stone's throw away, and he could see the crew talking to people and handing out stickers to the kids. It was a terrific auction item, and he hoped the punters would dig deep and make a large donation. There was also a display of the RIB boat and various lifesaving equipment. Bill remembered the patrol his children did at the Surf Club every summer. Zac had qualified as patrol captain last season, Katie and the twins had also gone through the different levels of surf lifesaving. It was a great life skill and an invaluable experience for them. Apart from the obvious fitness, it made them goal-focused and, of course, water safety conscious. Not to mention the many times he'd been on the BBQ and managed the sausage sizzles.

The car park was lined with various food trucks with tantalising cuisines. The smell of pizza, pasta and hotdogs filled the air, and Bill realised how hungry he was; he'd not yet had breakfast. A little farther along were the Italian and Vietnamese food trucks; this was more along the lines of what he fancied. People were already lining up, ready to purchase. Many were up for the weekend from the city. Kids ran around everywhere and enjoyed the occasion. The soft-serve ice cream van was parked to the side with a long line of families with toddlers and school-aged children who waited patiently for their turn. Bill had seen this before—ice cream could be eaten year-round and at any time of the day.

Should the weather take a turn for the worse, a small stage had been created under the shelter of the upstairs balcony. So far, the sun had shone from a winter blue sky. The bite in the air from the stiff sea breeze made the flags flap ferociously, and anything unsecured threatened to take off.

Country music was belted out by the live band of mature, long-haired men all dressed in well-worn denim, western boots and cowboy hats. Bill recognised some songs and enjoyed the atmosphere.

The local community had turned out in droves to raise money and services from local tradespeople to repair and renovate the damage from vandalism to the clubrooms a couple of months ago. Pizza boxes and RTDs had been strewn amongst the carnage, which pointed to youths being involved. No one had been caught in relation to the destruction. There were rumours, but that's all they were.

The usual raffles and silent auctions had been set up in the clubrooms. Bill spotted Annika, who chatted to someone she knew before joining him. "Do you fancy something to eat?" "Sure, why not?" Annika said.

The menu by the Vietnamese food truck looked great. She went over to order, and the flavours of coriander and lemongrass with a touch of Vietnamese mint drifted towards them. They ordered food as Henry Long, the Surf Club president, stood and tapped the microphone before he welcomed everyone over the PA system. He encouraged people to buy raffle tickets and bid in the silent auction inside the clubrooms. The shiny new bike that Bill had organised was front and centre. They were all a pretty community-minded lot, and he was pleased it had come together.

"That pork bun was bloody good," he said, wiping his mouth with the serviette before throwing the paper plate and utensils in the recycling bin. "Fancy a coffee?"

"That would be lovely. I'll wait here," she said. The sun peeked through the clouds, and the wind finally dropped, making it rather pleasant to sit in the warmth.

"Okay, won't be long."

On the way, Bill was stopped several times by people who wanted to say hello and chat. When he finally made it back to Annika, she was in deep conversation with a middle-aged woman. Bill spotted the two dogs and recognised the woman from the beach. She was the person who had found April West's body by the boat. The two West Highland White Terriers lay by her feet and observed everything around them with a keen eye. He raked over his memory before remembering the cheeky little characters' names.

"Hi, Bramble and Duchess," he said, bending to give both dogs tandem scratches, neither of the dogs missing out on the fuss.

"I can't believe you remember their names," Vivianne Harper said.

"Of course, who can forget these characters?" Bill laughed.

Annika looked confused. "Do you two know each other?"

"We met the other day on the beach. Vivianne found the young woman."

"Oh, I had no idea that woman was you," Annika said. "Vivianne is my friend from the book club. She's an author. She writes murder mysteries." Now it was Bill's turn to be surprised.

"Did you find out if it was natural causes, or are you still waiting for the pathologist's report?" Vivianne said.

"I can't discuss the details, I'm afraid. Regardless, it's tragic when a young person loses their life," Bill said, a bit taken aback by the line of questioning. He could understand that as a crime writer, she'd be curious, but this wasn't a TV show—it was real life, and a real person had passed away.

"I heard there was a big party at one of the fancy beachfront mansions the night before. Could there be a connection?"

"We're following up on the leads we have, and I can't discuss the details," Bill said, a bit annoyed at her persistence.

"Well, it was nice to catch up with you," Annika said, picking up on Bill's irritation and nudging his arm.

"Absolutely, I look forward to book club. Come on, Bramble and Duchess."

Bill watched the trio walk off. Nothing irritated him more than when an amateur sleuth wanted to wade in on a police investigation.

"Did you see the big book bundle on the silent auction table?" Annika said. "They are all her books. She has a couple of series going. She's one of my favourite authors, and we are lucky to have her in our book club. I just hope we get to read her books first."

Bill was lost in thought; he must chase up the report. His train of thought was disrupted by Annika trying to get his attention.

"Are you even listening, Bill?"

"Well, she certainly is nosy. I suppose it's all in aid of her research," he said, doing air quotes.

"Actually, Vivianne is lovely. There's Andrei and Crystal over there. Let's go and say hello," Annika said.

Bill looked up and saw the couple. His immediate reaction was how out of place they looked among the crowd. Crystal was a glamorous young woman, and Andrei looked a bit like an arrogant ass in his bomber jacket and tight black jeans—a desperate attempt to look younger, which didn't help one bit.

It was an occupational hazard. Bill usually summed people up within the first few moments of seeing them. He'd been wrong before, but not very often.

Annika made the introductions, and they exchanged a few pleasantries as Henry Long made an announcement and called Andrei up to the microphone.

"Here he is. The man who has generously donated not only his workmen for this project but also some of the materials to help us get the clubrooms in order. Can we have a big hand for Andrei Bowen?"

Andrei took the microphone, grinning confidently.

"It's my absolute pleasure to have Bowen Construction lend a hand. I'm proud to say that we are very happy to give something back to this amazing community. Let's have the Surf Club all sorted for the summer season," Andrei said as the crowd cheered. Bill watched the charismatic man soak up the attention. The people in the crowd wanted to shake his hand, and many patted him on the back as he made his way through the crowd. He was a PR machine to behold.

As Annika and Bill walked back to the car, he couldn't help but draw parallels with some of the most popular politicians. This guy certainly had the X factor.

"I'll drop you home. I have to pop into the station for a bit. There's some paperwork I need to get sorted.

"Don't forget that we are invited to Crystal and Andrei's for dinner tonight," Annika said.

"I haven't forgotten. I'll be home well before that.

44

Bill would rather have stayed home if he'd had a choice, watching the rugby and enjoying a couple of beers tonight. The All Blacks were due to play Australia and no doubt it would've been a great game. He didn't understand his wife's ability to make plans when the rugby was on. So, begrudgingly he would spend the evening with people he didn't really know. Terrific, he thought and sighed.

"Oh, come on. It's not that bad. It's not like you're being led off to the gallows," Annika said.

"Sorry, darling, but you know how much I dislike this kind of thing," Bill said as he was getting dressed.

"I know, but you will like them when you get to know them. Besides, Crystal is my friend."

"Andrei did seem like a bit of a narcissistic prat, don't you think?"

Annika couldn't deny that Andrei was in the alpha male category. He liked the attention and all that came with it.

"It's probably just the rough exterior. I'm sure he's lovely once we get to know him." "Perhaps, I guess we'll see," Bill said, not entirely convinced.

BILL DROVE through the open gates of the Point Wells estate and parked the car on the driveway in front of Crystal and Andrei's home. He'd noticed the CCTV on the gate. Spotlights on the ground illuminated the Italian-inspired villa and cast long shadows. No expense had been spared, and although it didn't surprise him entirely, he was still taken aback.

"You said it was big, but not how grand."

"It's like it should be in a magazine, don't you think? Just wait until you go inside," Annika said, shoving him gently towards the entrance as they stepped out of their car.

The ornate front door opened, and Crystal and Andrei stepped out. Andrei had his arm around Crystal's waist. They must have seen them on the security system.

"Welcome, you two. So lovely to see you," Crystal said as Andrei extended his right hand to say hello.

"G'day, mate," Andrei said, reaching for Bill's hand. He firmly placed his hand on Bill's and pulled his guest towards him, rolling his wrist to dominate the handshake. Bill automatically flipped it over and thought, what an odd thing to do. He'd met this type before—someone who had to be on top at all times and couldn't bear to be defeated. After an awkward moment, Andrei let go, surprised by Bill's reaction.

The perfectly curated entrance was like an art gallery, with sculptures and pottery pieces in the recessed spaces on the walls. Bill had never seen anything like it in someone's home. A large piece of pounamu, next to a traditional cloak, was displayed on a recessed shelf. The top third was polished, showing the deep green gemstone; the remainder of the stone was in its raw form with yellow and orange flecks and a solid green vein down the front. At a rough guess, the precious piece of greenstone must weigh five or six kilos. Bill wondered how the large stone had ended up in the house. Pounamu was sacred and only found in the rivers of the South Island, with sales regulated by the local iwi.

"Amazing piece of greenstone," Bill said.

"Ah, yes, this piece has been in the family for generations. I should probably donate it to the Warkworth Museum, but I don't seem to be able to part with it," Andrei said. "Now, let me take your coats."

Andrei seemed keen to change the subject as he welcomed them through to the kitchen and living area. The ultra-modern house's interior was the opposite of its traditional exterior. The minimalist look didn't float Bill's boat, and he could see why they wanted Annika's explosion of colour on the wall. The dull monochrome décor wasn't at all homely.

Each to their own. Their house was full of life, kids, and dog hair and was perhaps a little cluttered, but he loved it and wouldn't trade it for the world. Andrei took a bottle of champagne out of the full-sized glass-fronted wine fridge.

"Can I offer you a pre-dinner drink? I thought we'd have some bubbles?"

"That would be lovely, thank you," Annika said while Andrei popped the cork and poured the sparkling wine for the ladies.

"I'd prefer a beer. What about you, Bill?" Andrei said.

Bill thought his facial expression might have betrayed him.

"Yes, mate. A beer sounds great."

Andrei ripped the lid off a lager and squished a slice of lemon down the bottle's neck.

Oh, that's fancy, Bill thought as he accepted the drink.

"Come and have a seat. Dinner is still half an hour away," Andrei said.

They sat on the plush leather couch. Bill fidgeted, pushing some of the decorative cushions to the side so he could sit comfortably and propping a large one under his arm for more support.

"Don't squish them. Look at the delicate beadwork on the front," Annika whispered. Bill thought, why the heck have cushions if you couldn't use them for comfort?

Crystal came over with a large platter of antipasti and sat down next to them. Andrei perched casually on the armrest of the other couch opposite Bill.

"Cheers and welcome," Andrei said, leaning over to clink the beer bottles with Bill.

Despite the warm welcome, a slightly awkward atmosphere settled in the room. Bill wondered what they had in common, what they could talk about.

Annika's artwork was positioned against the wall in different areas, like beacons of colour. Although Bill didn't really like the 'beige' décor, he appreciated the house's grandeur. Annika's artwork added the much needed vibrancy and texture. Bill took a large swig of his beer while Annika sipped on her wine.

"We haven't quite decided where the paintings will be hung," Crystal said almost apologetically after noticing Bill glancing around. "It gives me comfort just to have them there. As soon as we have decided where each piece will go, Andrei will put them up, won't you, darling?

"Of course."

"I know exactly what you mean. It takes time to decide where the right art is best suited," Annika said.

"I understand you have a couple of new builds going on at the moment," Bill said.

"That's right. We are working on a couple of sites here in Point Wells."

"Did I hear right that there was vandalism on the site the other day?"

Andrei had his beer bottle halfway to his mouth and stopped. Obviously, he'd not expected to hear about this from Bill, but news spreads rapidly in a small settlement.

"I'm sure it was nothing, just bored kids, I would imagine," Andrei said.

It was clear from his expression that Andrei didn't want to talk about his business, so Bill left it.

"You have a very clever wife," Crystal said. "I wish I had talent like that."

"I'm sure you could do anything creative if you wanted to. Of course, it takes a little practice, but if the passion is there, it will come," Annika said, her voice full of warmth and encouragement.

"Do you really think so?"

"Absolutely. Just follow your passion. Try something new. I know you'd be great."

"The only thing Crystal is good at is shopping, believe me," Andrei said, chugging some beer.

Crystal shrunk into the sofa, her eyes downcast and lips pressed together. Annika glanced at Andrei with a look of surprise.

"That kind of comment is hardly helpful," Annika said. "You should encourage Crystal to pursue something that she enjoys, not pour cold water on it."

Andrei looked at Bill for male support, but Bill shook his head. Crystal shot Annika a look of gratitude.

"You're on your own, mate."

He knew Annika was right. He'd never put her down when it came to any endeavour she embarked on, and there had been a few over the years. Besides, never mess with a strong woman; life wasn't worth the misery.

"I'm sorry, Crystal. I didn't mean anything by it," Andrei said, putting his hand on her thigh.

"It's all right. It's fine, really," Crystal said, subdued. Her eyes were a little red, and Bill could see that she was hurt.

"How about you come over to the studio one day soon, and you can have a go at a canvas and some paints?" Annika said, trying to cheer her up.

"Thank you, that is very kind," Crystal said, and a slight smile spread across her face.

After the initial awkward situation, Andrei took on the role of the ultimate host and attentive partner to redeem himself. Bill felt a bit sickened. It was going to be a long evening, he thought.

"You into cars? Andrei asked.

"Yes, mate. I am."

"Come, let me show you the Maserati."

Bill followed Andrei's lead through the house into the adjoining garage.

"Mike mainly uses the Escalade that's parked outside, but this is my pride and joy. Come on and start the beast up," he said, handing Bill an ornate leather key fob.

The midnight blue sports car was iridescent under the garage lights. Bill ran his hand across the shiny bonnet. Neptune, the god of the seas, complete with his signature trident, emblazoned the gaudy logo at the front. He'd read somewhere that the Maserati emblem was inspired by this powerful icon and symbolised mastery of water's raw power.

"Well, go on, hop in the driver's seat, mate."

Bill didn't have to be asked twice and carefully eased himself into the high-powered Italian sports coupe. A sensory overload hit him as the supple cream leather, with its smell of tar and damp tobacco, entered his nostrils. He ran his fingers along the armrest, taking it all in. The lightweight sports seat hugged his body in all the right places, which would have provided superb comfort if he wasn't so bruised. Andrei opened the passenger door and sat in the passenger seat. The dashboard was like a space shuttle—buttons and dials for everything with a large touch screen in the centre. Bill put his foot on the brake, turned the ignition on, and fired her up. The roar of the engine reverberated in the garage. Bill pressed the gas pedal and the car roared eagerly. He could tell she was a temperamental beast and eager to stretch her legs, the race-bred power and tightness of the engine aching to be released.

"She's graceful and elegant, isn't she?"

"She's a stunner! How long have you had her?"

"Just under a year. She was factory new when I got her. Hey, I'm sorry if I was a bit short before. I don't really involve Crystal in the day-to-day running of the business. I don't even think she's that interested, anyway. You know what I mean, right? I'm sure you don't tell Annika what's going on at work, do you?" he said and laughed.

Bill thought it odd that such admiration was shown for a car, and he had a fair idea where Crystal was in the pecking order. All the gains Andrei had just made disappeared. Bill valued Annika as his wife and partner. On more occasions than he could remember, she'd been the one to come up with great suggestions and solutions.

"I guess we ought to join the ladies," Andrei said.

"Yes, that might be a good idea," Bill said, wondering what else this evening would bring.

When they returned, the atmosphere was a bit more relaxed. Soft music was playing, and Annika and Crystal had refilled their glasses and were chatting.

"Good timing because dinner is ready," Crystal said as she carried the food to the table. If Crystal was still upset, it didn't show. Bill thought she might be used to putting on a brave face.

"Please have a seat, guys."

"Another?" Andrei held up his empty beer bottle.

"Thanks, mate. I will, but that's my last one, as I'm driving tonight.

Annika smiled. She usually always drove, but he knew she might want to have a couple of glasses of wine tonight. Crystal was her friend, after all.

"Bon appétit."

"Wow, that looks amazing!" Annika said as the golden pastry dish was brought to the table.

"Beef Wellington," Bill exclaimed. "My favourite."

Crystal served the perfect rounds of pastry-covered beef at the table, the earthy aroma of mushrooms mingling with the smell of rich red wine jus. Bill couldn't wait to taste the smooth potato mash and the thinly cut beans accompanying the Beef Wellington.

"A touch of red, ladies?" Andrei said.

"Perhaps just a small glass," Annika said, her cheeks rosy from the champagne.

The conversation flowed, and surprisingly Bill quite enjoyed himself, despite the awkward earlier moments. "So what made you choose Point Wells to develop your properties?"

Andrei wiped his mouth with the corner of the cloth napkin before answering.

"The last development we did was in Orewa. I really like

Matakana wine country and coast, not to mention its proximity to Auckland. You can live the dream up here and work in the city as the drive isn't too far. We found Point Wells by chance. Crystal and I had been in Omaha for a wedding and stayed for a few extra days. We fell in love with the area. When I found out about land for sale here, I guess we jumped at the chance."

"So lovely to be able to do a sea-change and get away from the rat race of the city.

We never regretted our move to Matakana and a better lifestyle," Annika said.

"I'm so pleased I've met you," Crystal said.

"Me, too," Annika said.

"The Beef Wellington was outstanding, and the garlic mash, well, that was to die for," Bill said, leaning back in the chair.

"I'm so glad you enjoyed it," Crystal said, beaming.

"We plan to get married next summer. Hopefully, the landscaping will have been done and the place completed," Andrei said as he put his hand on Crystal's. Bill noticed the large diamond on her left hand, which was more the size of a pigeon egg and very different from what he could afford when he and Annika became engaged.

As the evening came to a close and dessert was to be served, Crystal took out the already prepared dish from the warm oven.

Expertly and with ease, she put a large, round plate over the aluminium frying pan. She tipped the dessert out in one fluid movement—the glossy apple pieces, covered in luscious golden caramel, perched perfectly on the pie base and smelled heavenly. The warm, nutty flavour of roasted fruit smothered in sweetness with a touch of Calvados filled the room.

"Tarte Tatin. It's my grandmother's recipe and one of my favourites," she said proudly.

"Wow, you do spoil us!"

Crystal had just started to serve when Andrei's mobile phone rang.

"Sorry, folks. I have to take this," he said, taking the phone from his back pocket and glancing at the screen.

As he left the room, Bill excused himself to use the bathroom and was directed to it down the hallway.

The beer had gone straight through him, and he wandered past what must be Andrei's office as he headed to the bathroom. The door was ajar and Bill could hear Andrei speaking.

"Daria, I told you I could handle it. There's no need for you to be here. For fuck's sake, just give me some space to sort this out. I've got it under control!"

Got what under control? What was Andrei referring to? The last thing Bill wanted was to be caught eavesdropping, so he continued down the hallway. Bill waited a minute or two to give Andrei time to return to the table first. His curiosity was piqued as the conversation played over and over in his mind.

On his way back, Bill jiggled the office door handle, but it was locked. Who on earth locked internal doors in the house? What did he not want anyone else to see?

"There you are. We thought you'd got lost!" Andrei said and smiled with everything but his eyes. Something had upset him.

"Did you guys leave any apple pie for me?" Bill joked.

As Bill and Annika thanked their hosts for a lovely evening, Bill was still pondering what Andrei needed to get control of and what he needed to sort out.

45

Sydney, Australia

The Sydney skyline shimmered in the evening sky. Daria twirled her glass of scotch, the ice cubes in the delicate crystal tinkling hypnotically.

Andrei had insisted he was the man to run the New Zealand operation. She'd not been convinced from the start, but somehow she'd agreed. Her brother drove her absolutely fucking nuts! He was stroppy and overconfident, but when it came to the business end of the transaction, it was as if he couldn't operate logically. She was sick of cleaning up his mess. She'd always been the one who stayed calm in the face of adversity and had bailed him out on more than one occasion. The latest clusterfuck of events was more than she could accept. It was one thing to have lost one of the guys, but to now have a personal vendetta against them made her really annoyed.

It was Murphy's Law that the man who had fallen overboard was the nephew of Big Ed. It wouldn't have been an issue if it had been anyone else. Instead, they were in the firing line for the vendetta and had Big Ed stomping around like a wounded bull. Andrei gave her no confidence in how he'd handled the current situation. There was only one thing to do—fly back to New Zealand and sort out the sordid mess.

She reached forward for the phone on the coffee table and opened the Air New Zealand app. Her personal details flashed up on the screen, along with a question about where she'd like to book her travel. Daria keyed in Auckland on a one-way trip and scrolled down to the travel dates field. Her finger lingered over tomorrow morning's departure, but she thought the better of it and booked the one-fifteen flight in the afternoon, which would get her into Auckland just after six in the evening.

Mother and father would be thrilled to see her; she hadn't been home since Easter. Work kept her busy. She'd built her legitimate business from the ground up, and she was now Australia's biggest coffee importer. Not only did she personally oversee every aspect, from the quality to the distribution, but she was also priced very competitively.

She looked around her penthouse apartment, which she'd paid for in cash. She was immensely proud of the fact that she had built her business without help from her father, unlike Andrei, who'd simply taken over the family business when their father had retired.

He had never needed to fight for things the way she had to as a woman and completely on her own. She knew her father respected her for her hard work and resilience.

Not long after she'd started out, an opportunity arose to diversify the business during one of her early trips to South America. It had been suggested by people whom she'd crossed paths with that adding a few more strings to her budding empire might be mutually beneficial. She thought about it and took the opportunity, fully aware of the conditions and the strings attached. But they'd underestimated her from the beginning, thinking she was young and naïve. Little did they know she was in complete control at all times. Her distribution network was perfectly set up to bring in lucrative and high-commodity items, with the drugs disguised in the regular business shipments of imported goods.

She had played by the rules, learnt quickly, and gained the

supplier's confidence. The hard work had been worth it, and it was her job to ensure that the distribution network ran like clockwork. The last thing she wanted was a couple of crazed Mexican drug dealers to come Down Under and cause havoc.

She was in South America on business every other month to make sure all aspects of her business worked smoothly. The red carpet was always rolled out, and she was wined and dined. She was the Queen of Meth.

Daria finished the booking and paid for her flight. She messaged her assistant, Paul, saying she would be going home to visit family for a few days.

It was eight p.m. in Sydney, which meant a couple of hours later in the evening in New Zealand—far too late to call her parents. She'd call them tomorrow before her flight; they would be delighted and insist she stays with them. Her old room in the original Herne Bay villa looked the same as it had when she was a teenager.

She had no idea why her mother liked to hold on to the past but would, of course, be the ever-obliging and accommodating daughter, despite preferring to stay in one of the upmarket hotels in the city centre. Oh well, it was only for a couple of days. She could put up with the smothering décor of her old room and her mother's inquiring questions about when she would settle down and get married. She had to find a man first. Not that she had looked very hard. The men she came across generally came with ex-wives and a brood of children, which was not something she was interested in. She picked up her phone again, opened Tinder, and scrolled through several completely unsuitable men. Her eye caught the profile of a muscle-bound, blond, true-blue Aussie with interests listed as water sports and outdoor pursuits. His pearly whites enticed her. That was more like it, she thought and swiped right. It was an instant match.

A message bleeped on the screen almost immediately, and Jack was keen to meet for a drink. She quickly replied with a rendezvous at a nearby upmarket bar in an hour—that would give her enough time.

She refilled her scotch and lingered in the open-plan lounge before walking through the primary bedroom and into the vast walk-in wardrobe. Her assistant always made sure she was travel-ready and had picked up this week's dry-cleaning, which hung neatly on the rack.

Daria grabbed the medium-sized suitcase and packed enough clothes for the trip, mostly trousers and jumpers. Auckland winters were cold and wet, and she had no intention of being cold. She threw in a suit and a couple of business tops, in case she'd have a meeting to attend as well, before closing the lid—the toiletries she'd put in tomorrow. In a way, she looked forward to the short, three-hour trip across the Tasman Sea.

Daria tied her long blonde hair up and flicked through her wardrobe before finding a dress that would suit the purpose of tonight. Then she showered. Her slender body was in good shape due to the time she spent in the gym most days.

The low-cut ruby red dress was one of her favourites and left little to the imagination. She applied a touch of makeup, chose a matching red lipstick, and took her hair out of the elastic. Her thick blonde hair only needed a brush. She dabbed perfume behind her ears and in her cleavage and took one last look in the mirror before grabbing her handbag and walking out the door. As she stepped into the lift and pressed the button for the ground floor, she felt a surge of anticipation. She could always sleep on the plane tomorrow.

46

Sunday the 9th of July

It was Sunday morning, and Bill had woken early. He'd had a terrible night's sleep and had been restless. At five a.m., he'd finally given up and got out of bed. The two deaths last week, the increased gang presence, and the drugs that seemed to pop up everywhere unsettled him. His eyes felt like they had grains of sand in them, and he stumbled around the bedroom while trying to be quiet and not wake Annika. He rummaged around the wardrobe for his uniform. He could move more freely even though his ribs reminded him they weren't fully healed.

The stairs creaked as he crept downstairs and into the kitchen. Maggie and Finn slept soundly in their baskets and barely moved a muscle as Bill popped two pieces of sliced bread in the toaster and flicked the jug on. He had to look for the canister of black tea, which hid behind an array of fancy fruit teas. The smell of the toast stirred Finn, and he stretched his long legs, yawning loudly. He wagged his tail and came over to sit at Bill's feet with eyes that begged for a taste.

"Okay, boy, but don't tell your mother," Bill said as he broke off a piece of toast, smeared a bit of butter and jam over it, and gave it to the dog. "That will have to do, mate." Finn looked at him disappointedly, turned, and slumped back into his bed.

Bill felt a bit better by the second sip of tea and after a few mouthfuls of toast. He tidied the dishes but couldn't shake the feeling that had reared its head last night, refusing to go away. He always trusted his gut. It had got him out of trouble on more than one occasion. His mind wandered to last night and their dinner with Crystal and Andrei. The bravado and inflated ego of the property developer were staggering. Bill was long in the tooth and didn't buy the fake veneer of Andrei's self-assured cockiness. Half the night had been like a pissing contest. He knew the type—indulged, privileged, and used to people being impressed. There was more to this character, that was for sure, and he aimed to find out.

He put the reluctant dogs out for their early morning ablutions and almost had to push them out the door. Their unwillingness was not helped by the ungodly hour or the cold and wet weather. Both Maggie and Finn protested before they got on with their business and quickly scampered inside again. He locked the door behind him and walked down the paved path. The car coughed slightly as the engine fired up. Bill made a mental note to book it in for a service. The water-filled potholes on the gravel driveway and the grass verge glistened as the headlights illuminated them.

Leigh Road was quiet, and he turned right towards Matakana. He loved his short commute and was on the village's main street within minutes. The lights were on at the village bakery as he drove past. He'd walk down and buy a coffee as soon as they were open.

After turning off the alarm, he fired up the computer and signed in. The logo of the National Intelligence Application, or NIA, appeared on the screen.

Bill cast his mind back to the conversation last night; something niggled in his subconscious, but what?

Bill flexed his fingers and typed in 'Andrei Bowen.' It wasn't strictly by the book, but Bill wondered where Andrei's wealth came from, which warranted further investigation.

As Bill waited for the results, he poured some water on the instant coffee he'd made and took a sip. A list of offences popped up. Here we go, thought Bill. The majority were speeding fines. He scrolled down and straightened in his chair as a couple of assault charges came into view. One dated back, listing altercations with known associates, but the charges were dropped due to lack of evidence. My ass, Bill thought. He'd come across people like this before. Intimidation did the trick if you wanted the complainant to withdraw the charges. More recently, within the last five years and before Crystal, three domestic incidents had occurred. Bowen had been charged, but his ex-wife dropped the charges the next day. It was so typical. Bill boiled inside when he thought about the female victims involved. So often, it wasn't only the woman but the children who had to bear the psychological scars.

This guy could obviously talk the talk and get out of tight spots.

His gut feeling was right—there was more to Andrei Bowen than what he wanted you to see. Bill trawled through his emails and the usual in-house correspondence sent through. There was no email yet from the pathologist with the cause of death for April West.

Bill leant back in his chair and pondered for a moment before he scrolled through the contacts in his phone. He found the name he was looking for and started typing a short message to his friend at the local real estate firm. He'd gone to school with Joanne. She was an astute businesswoman and more capable than most. Her style wasn't aggressive, and her clients appreciated her knowledgeable but soft approach. She always topped the sales for the district. He glanced at the clock. It was six thirty. He knew she was an early riser and he fired off a text:

Morning, sorry to bug you this early. What can you tell me about Andrei Bowen?

47

Monday the 10th of July

When Niko arrived at work the following day, Bill had already been in for hours.

"Morning, Sarge," Niko said as he walked in. His hair was wet, slicked back, and he moved in a cloud of cologne. "I'm glad to see the gym is still there."

"This just came in," Bill said, ignoring the pleasantries and pointing to a report on his desk. "April West's death has been classed as suspicious. Large amounts of Molly mixed with LSD have been found in her system."

"We've seen a bit of the so-called candy flipping and mixing of the two drugs making a comeback. Apparently, it was really big in the 90s and early 2000s in the rave scene," Niko said as he hung his jacket on the back of his chair.

Bill remembered it well. Niko had still been in short pants.

"Cause of death appears to have been that she choked on her own vomit, ultimately leading to asphyxiation," Bill said, still reading from the report.

"Poor girl. I don't know why they get mixed up with all the drugs."

It wouldn't be long before Katie would get invited to parties and go out. She was pretty, taking after her mother in looks. The low-lifes preyed on youth and innocence. The gangs supplied the drugs seemingly with no strings attached until suddenly, one day, there were conditions. By then, they were often hooked and would do just about anything for their next fix. The things these young girls were exposed to didn't even bear thinking about, Bill thought, unable to shake the unpleasant feeling that sunk into his core.

Being male made things marginally better for Zac. At least it was less exploitation, but peer pressure increased a lot among young men, which made them do stupid things. Egged on by their peers, no one wanted to be a wuss and not give it a go when stuff was passed around. Things had been so much simpler when he was young; they only smoked the odd joints. Marijuana never agreed with him anyway. While some of his friends experienced the sensation of highs, it had been the opposite for him—weed made him go to sleep. After he'd tried it a handful of times, he decided to give it up as it was a complete waste on him, and he stuck to beer. Thankfully, his palate was now a bit more refined, and he enjoyed a wide variety of wines and the odd single malt whiskey.

Bill stood and grabbed his jacket. "I need a coffee. Do you want one?" Before Niko could reply, the phone rang.

"Matakana police station," Niko answered. "You need to slow down, take a breath, and start again." Niko reached for a pen, listening intently. "You're sure he's dead?" Niko tried his best to calm the caller down. "Wait for us outside, don't touch anything. We're on our way now."

Bill looked at Niko. "What was that all about?"

"You know the old rocker in Omaha? He's been found dead in the bath. Looks like suicide."

"You mean Jett Starr? Has the ambulance been called?" "Yep, Starr," and no to the latter" Niko said.

***

Bill and Niko jumped in the car. Suicide scenes were one of the worst to attend. Generally, they were messy, unpleasant, and tinged with sadness and regret. They drove along Omaha Flats Road, past the pizza place and fruit stalls. They'd only spoken to Jett Starr a few days ago when they took his statement regarding April West, whose body had been found on the beach. He'd seemed absolutely fine; then again, you could never tell who hid their inner demons from the outside world.

He'd seemed typically American—upbeat and larger than life—although Bill suspected it was more the official persona, perhaps not a true reflection of the private person. It was ridiculous, really, a man of his age strutting around in tight leather pants and torn t-shirts, attempting to hang onto his youth. *But you shouldn't talk bad about the dead*, Bill could hear his mother's voice in his head. The last funeral or 'tangi' he'd attended was when a great aunt on his mother's side had passed away last year. The body had been transported to the marae, where it had lain in state. People had travelled from near and far to pay their respects, and it had been a beautiful celebration of her life. According to custom, the body had not been left alone before the burial. It was a healing goodbye. Bill thought of the body they would see, someone who'd been on their own in life and now in death.

Within minutes, they pulled up outside the beachfront address, where a pale and slightly shaken man nervously wandered along the front of the house.

"Hi, are you Michael Watson?" Niko said.

"Yes, I was the one who called. Thanks for coming so quickly," the man said, his voice reduced to a quiver. "I came here to measure up for his new kitchen. The door was ajar, and I knocked before I stepped inside. It was odd because he'd been eager for me to come and sort it out. I could hear music playing and kept calling out, eventually going upstairs to locate him. And that's when I found him." The man's ashen face said it all.

"Are you okay to wait out here while we go and take a look?" Bill said. "Take a perch over there. The fresh air will do you good."

"I could do with sitting down," he said, wobbling over to the low stone wall.

Bill handed Niko the disposable shoe covers and gloves. The house looked exactly the same—tidy, except for a few pairs of scattered shoes and a coat crumpled on the floor in the corner of the entrance.

As he stood on the Persian rug inside the door, he could smell the familiar sickly sweet odour of death. Even though he had not yet seen the body, it was obvious it had been undiscovered for a few days. The curved staircase swept elegantly to the next level. Bill glanced up. The overcast dim light of day seemed oppressive, despite the impressive cathedral windows that faced outwards.

The classic rock songs could be heard as they climbed the plush carpeted stairs, the strong notes foreboding what they were about to encounter. Bill recoiled as the smell increased, and he steeled himself. Niko looked a bit green around the gills.

"I can deal with victims who've been shot or stabbed and violent deaths, but a ripe corpse really turns my stomach inside out," Niko said.

"I know what you mean," Bill said, flinching.

~

BILL STRUGGLED to reconcile the image of the wild rocker with the extraordinary formality displayed in the house. Bill remembered the framed platinum records from his last visit. Everyone grows up eventually, he thought.

The wide hallway led to what he assumed were more bedrooms. The door to the bathroom was wide open. Bill had seen suicides before, but generally, the person was found within the first few hours. If left for whatever reason, it was never pretty.

"Jesus!" Niko said, covering his nose. Despite being in the middle of winter, flies buzzed around. Bill's eyes were drawn to the panoramic view of the beach along the wall of the room. The wide window sill beneath was covered in dead flies.

He stood in the doorway for a moment. The air seemed to have escaped, and he tried not to inhale the putrid smell.

"What do you think, Sarge? Niko said, a handkerchief over his mouth. "Reckon he's been here a few days?

"I'd say so." Bill pulled his phone out and took a series of wide-angle photos. The sickening smell, combined with the scene in front of him, made him feel a bit unwell. He forced himself to get a grip and stepped inside the bathroom.

White tiles covered the room from floor to ceiling. It was a stark contrast to what had happened in the room. The ornate antique bath was elevated and placed on a recessed platform. Bill assumed it was to maximise the view while enjoying a bath. Not that it was doing much good for Jett Starr. Bill took a few steps forward along the bathroom wall. He avoided the so-called heavy traffic areas and snapped some more photos.

"We probably should get the stepping plates from the car, but by the looks of it, it's a suicide,' Bill said.

"Jeez, the water hasn't done him any favours," Niko said.

The body of the deceased floated on its side in the dark red bathwater, the left half of the body above the surface. It looked like the wrists had been slit. There was no visible blade, but then again it could have slipped into the bath. A heavily tattooed arm rested across Starr's stomach, and his chin was tucked into his chest as if he were resting. His legs were pulled up, which at least provided some modesty. Not that Bill thought Jett would have minded, really.

The partially submerged corpse had a marked venous vascular pattern, like a marbled effect on the visible part of the torso, neck and face. Bill noticed the inside of the bathtub showed clear perimeter watermarks, indicating levels reached at different times of decomposition. Bill moved in and took some more close-up shots. He leaned in and could clearly see small groups of bubbles in and around the nose and mouth, where bodily fluid had left the orifices. Bill was no pathologist, but he knew the body was in the putrefactive phase. The metallic smell of blood and decay that reminded him of rotting meat was overwhelming. The music started to annoy Bill. His senses were overwhelmed, and the familiar claustrophobia narrowed his vision. There was nothing serene about this scene.

"All right, I think we've seen enough. Let's call this in," he said as he exited the cloying atmosphere of the room. "It should be pretty straightforward. Looks like suicide, but still . . ." Bill attempted to get his breathing under control.

"He seemed so together when we spoke to him last, but you never know the inner workings of another human being," Niko said.

"That's true," Bill said as he reached across, pressing the off button of the plugged-in portable speaker just inside the door. The silence was a nice reprieve. There was nothing more they could do here, and they backtracked downstairs the same way they came in. Bill took a deep breath as they stepped through the front door. The fresh cool air was exactly what he needed, and he took deep breaths.

While Niko phoned Orewa, Bill picked up his notebook from the car and went over to Michael, who still sat outside. Even though he wore jeans and a parka, the man was pale and appeared to be shivering. As Bill approached, he jumped off his perch and started to move his feet and arms to warm up.

"Thanks for staying."

"No worries. Terrible way to go, poor man. Seems strange, though. Jett was so full of life. Our house is not far from here; we live a few streets back from the beach. We didn't socialise or know him well, but his parties were notorious. It seemed he loved to have people over. I heard he was also quite a good cook, hence the planned kitchen upgrade. It was a big project, all top-of-the-range appliances, of course. We're a small kitchen company, and it was going to be a real feather in our cap to do Jett Starr's house," he said and sighed. He was visibly embarrassed when he realised what he had said was inappropriate under the circumstances. "But, of course, it's very tragic."

Shock did funny things to people. Bill could see that Michael only just held it together.

"I need to ask you a few questions."

"That's all good. But I'm not sure I can help with much," Michael said.

"What time did you arrive at the house this morning?

"Well, we had an appointment for 9.00 a.m. I was probably a few minutes early, say ten to nine. Jett was a stickler for punctuality, and I was not going to blow this on account of being late."

"Did you see anyone else here when you arrived?"

"No, it was quiet. The other houses around are holiday homes and vacant most of the time. I called him yesterday to confirm our appointment but got no reply. Now I know why."

"When did you last speak?"

"Let me see," he said, scrolling through the diary on his phone.

"We spoke a week ago. He called me and said he was ready to go ahead with plans and for me to come around and measure up."

"Walk me through what happened when you got here this morning."

"I arrived, spent a few minutes going through the paperwork, and then knocked on the door. After a few minutes, I pressed the handle, and the door opened. I called out, but no one answered, which was strange as I could hear music playing. I walked in, but there was no one on the ground level, so I proceeded up the stairs, all while I called out. I thought there was a foul smell, but I must say I did not expect to find him dead in the bath. That's the most shocking thing I have seen in my life."

"What happened then?"

"I ran outside. I couldn't stand to be in the house a moment longer. I got into my car and called you."

"Did you hear any noises in the house? Anything to suggest that someone else might be there?"

"No, nothing."

"Right, well, we may get in touch again should the inquiry dictate it," Bill said. He felt sorry for Michael. It was always difficult when a member of the public came upon something traumatic like this.

Bill walked back to the patrol car and joined Niko out of the cold wind.

"The SOCOs are on their way. Should be another half hour or so," Niko said while changing the radio station to another piece of music. At this stage, it was a welcome distraction.

"How about I stay here while you go and get us some takeaway coffees?" Bill said.

"All right, Sarge. Point me in the right direction," Niko said as he opened the car door and stepped outside, pulling his collar up.

While Bill waited, he googled Jett Starr and was quietly blown away by the hundreds of pages that came up. He knew he'd been big, but the man had been an icon. There were a couple of Grammys and some BRIT Awards and many more. Bill had no idea his back catalogue was so extensive. No wonder he'd lived a comfortable life here in New Zealand.

Not happy enough, though, for things to end like this.

Niko arrived with two coffees and a cheese and salami sandwich each, in separate brown paper bags. "I thought it best to get us something to eat. Who knows how long this is going to take."

Bill took a bite of the sandwich when a text came in on his phone:

Sorry for the late reply. I've met Andrei Bowen a couple of times. He's a charmer. I don't usually listen to rumours, but the word is that he's a ruthless developer and drives a hard bargain. Success at any cost. Joanne.

48

The drive from Orewa had been relatively uneventful and had taken just over forty minutes. Rudd was in an exceptional mood, something that Copeson was relieved about. The reason for the upbeat demeanour was that he'd gotten wind of his surprise retirement party from the force. A colleague had accidentally let it slip while in the briefing room and had not noticed that Rudd had walked in. Copeson smiled. The big celebration was planned for the week after next.

Despite the regular bad tempers, he'd quite liked working with Rudd. He was serious, intolerant and without humour, but despite this, he was one hell of an investigator. You'd have to respect a work ethic like that. Sure, they'd had their moments. Days that he'd wanted to get reassigned when Rudd had been an asshole, but on the whole, he'd learnt all he knew from the man. Rudd was a little like Marmite—a small smear went a long way. Some people would even say retirement wasn't a day too soon.

The area assigned to them was large, and here they were up north for the third time in a week. Copeson didn't mind, and for Rudd to be cheery was a bonus. He could see the boys from Matakana as he pulled up beside their car.

"Fancy," Rudd said in a slightly condescending tone.

"Yup. I think I've seen this one in a magazine. They did a feature on Jett Starr a couple of months ago," Copeson said. Rudd grumbled something about poncey magazines, but he couldn't hear the response. As he was about to make a smart retort, Rudd was out of the passenger door and on his way to grab the equipment from the boot.

Oh well, who cared, anyway? So what if he liked architecture and design?

Bill and Niko stepped out of their vehicle and chatted to Rudd as he organised himself and joined them.

"Right, what do we have here?" Rudd said.

"As mentioned on the phone, a local kitchen contractor found the victim this morning. The front door was unlocked, with no sign of a break-in or anything obviously untoward. We've been on the scene. The guy has been there for a couple of days, at least. It's not pretty," Bill summarised. "Looks like suicide."

"Let's not jump to any conclusions before we've done what we need to do," Rudd said.

Copeson saw the surprise on Bill's face. He'd not expected the old man would speak to them in a civil voice.

"All right, I guess we'll leave it to you guys then," Bill said. "Let us know if you need anything."

"Will do," Rudd said and walked towards the house.

Bill looked perplexed.

"He's excited about his upcoming retirement surprise party," Copeson whispered as he walked past, following Rudd into the house.

"Not much of a surprise if he knows about it," Bill said. Copeson nodded and smiled.

He knew Bill would be one of the happy ones to see the back of Rudd.

"Come along, Copeson. We don't have all day!"

"I'm right behind you," Copeson sighed. The good mood seemed to have run out.

THE TILED ROOM was bathed in light from the extra rigs that Copeson had put up. They always carried all sorts of equipment because they never knew what they might need.

"Ah, I see," Rudd grunted as he leant across the murky water of the bathtub. He continued to the end, where the head was partially submerged.

"Copeson, come and have a look at this. It appears there is blunt force trauma to the head which doesn't make this as clear cut as our dear Sergeant Granger thinks." Rudd sniggered to himself; he always liked to have 'one up' on people.

"I'll call CIB and get the scene guards organised, and I guess we need ESR to come out?"

"It certainly appears that way. You'd better get on to it then." Rudd was back to his normal abrasive self. In fact, Copeson preferred it that way. At least then, you knew what to expect, he thought.

The 'death by own hand' had been upgraded to a suspicious death, as it transpired that the back of the skull had been fractured. Of course, it was possible the victim had fallen and hit his head, even though both wrists were cut and there was a lot of blood in the bathtub. The lack of arterial spray was also curious and a possible indication the victim was already dead when the cuts were made.

"It's up to the pathologist to determine the cause of death, but my guess would be that someone hit him on the back of the head, which subsequently killed him. An easy and convenient cover would be to place the body in the bath and make it look like suicide. It's not the first time I have seen it, either. People think they are clever, but science always wins in the end," Rudd said.

"How's it going in there? Can we call Woods to come and collect the body?" Bill shouted from the hallway.

"No one is touching anything in my crime scene until we are completely done, and that's that," Rudd called back. Scene guards and Ds are on their way, and ESR has been called. This was more like the grumpy old man he knew, Copeson thought.

“Why don’t you and your colleague make yourself useful and go through the house? Look for any signs of a struggle where the victim might have hit his head. There may be a primary crime scene in the house or a murder weapon. So get going.”

49

Bill sent Niko downstairs while he stayed on the upper level as they went from room to room, searching the house methodically. There was no indication that a crime had occurred. There had been cases where people had sustained a head injury, gone to bed and not woken up. In Starr's case, though, his wrists had been slashed. The question was: did he do it to himself, or had someone done it to him?

"Seems a bit strange, don't you think? Who'd want to off this guy? He was an old rocker. What harm could he have caused anyone?" Niko said as they met up in the entrance, having finished the search of the property.

Jono, the police photographer, strolled through the door. "Hi, guys. I hear the scene has been upgraded, so they called me in," he said, lugging the photography equipment.

"Apparently so," Bill said. "Rudd and Copeson are upstairs."

"Thanks, mate. I best get up there then."

"I'd better have a word with old Ruddy before we go," Bill said to Niko as he climbed back up the stairs.

"All right, guys. We've been through everywhere, and there's no indication that an accident or foul play has occurred anywhere else in the house. At least not as far as we can tell," Bill said from the hallway as Rudd appeared at the door.

"That's strange as it's not in keeping with the injuries on the victim. ESR will go through the place with a fine-tooth comb. If there's anything, they'll find it," Rudd said as he pulled off his gloves.

The Environmental, Science and Research team was meticulous and would be able to detect the smallest drop of blood, even if the scene had been thoroughly cleaned.

"I guess we'll leave it to you guys then," Bill said.

"We'll keep you in the loop if there are any major developments," Rudd said without looking up.

"All right. Let us know if you need anything." Rudd didn't answer, not that he'd expected it.

Bill and Niko returned to the car and drove to the station.

"Peculiar, don't you think?" Niko said, thinking out loud.

"What is?"

"I guess the autopsy will show whether it was suicide or murder."

"Seems clear to me. Starr was probably in a fragile state of mind, cut his wrists, and slipped in the bath, but I guess we'll soon know, depending on what they find," Bill said as they turned into the police station.

~

IT WAS late into the afternoon when Rudd called to let them know the ESR team was there and the body had been transported to the morgue. All they could do was wait for the post-mortem to determine what had happened.

Bill checked the time; it was nearly six. "I think we should call it a day, Niko. How about a quick beer and something to eat at the pub on our way home?"

"Sure, but don't you have dinner waiting for you at home?"

"Annika's got the book club over, something about a potluck

dinner. I think I would be surplus to requirement among all the ladies. Besides, I haven't read this month's book," Bill said and laughed.

"Fair enough. Let's go then."

50

Tonight was Annika's turn to host the monthly book club. Somehow the wine and cheese get-togethers had morphed into full-blown dinners. Not that Annika minded; she enjoyed spending time with her bookish friends. The book club had six members. Annika and a couple of them were the original members who had met up regularly for seven or eight years.

The group consisted of her best friend Lexi, owner of Matakana Valley Wines, who had pursued her dreams of becoming a cheese-maker extraordinaire. Then there was Tyra, who was only in her late twenties, the youngest member of the group, a mum of preschoolers, and the most voracious reader she knew. Annika didn't know how she had the time to read as much as she did; her children were still so young. Florence and Deb were best friends and retired school teachers, just like herself, and an absolute hoot to be around.

Flo and Deb loved cooking and took turns bringing their creations along.

The latest addition to their group was Vivianne. Annika had met her at the village bookshop one day, where they'd struck up a conversation, and she'd invited her to the book club to give a talk about her own books. The evening was a great success, and they'd all made a great friend. It was only natural to extend the invitation for Vivianne to join the book club. The ladies were an eclectic mix; perhaps that's why they got on so well.

The laughter and noise echoed around the dinner table in the kitchen. The kids had scarpered early. By the looks on their faces, a book club was too cringeworthy for them.

The laughter was infectious, and the smell of the homemade dishes was tantalising. Annika had fed the girls early. They were thrilled to have pizza from Smith's across the road.

"Pass the wine, Vivianne," Deb said. "I must say I'm enjoying the lovely pinot gris." Every time they met, Deb and Flo's husbands took turns to drop off and pick up, so the ladies could enjoy a glass or two of wine.

The food on these nights was as diverse as the attendees themselves. Lexi was the dessert queen and always brought something sweet along. Deb and Flo liked exotic cuisine and coordinated their dishes. For tonight, they'd made a smorgasbord of Moroccan flavours.

The chatter increased as the night went on and a few more glasses of wine were consumed. When it was time for dessert, and the plates had been stacked in the dishwasher, everyone was relaxed and happy, and it was finally time to talk about the book they'd read.

Lexi took her famous cherry pie out of the oven. She'd made it before, and it had quickly become a favourite.

Annika set the table with dessert plates, spoons, and a large tub of French vanilla ice cream.

"Please start," Lexi said, smiling.

Everyone tucked in, and the conversation focused on the characters of the book they'd read. Deb and Tyra didn't think the book's ending had been what they'd expected, but apart from that, everyone had enjoyed it.

"Oh, my goodness. I think I've died and gone to heaven," Vivianne said. She was the only one who hadn't sampled the cherry pie before. "I love the almond cherry flavour and the pastry is scrumptious."

"Thanks. It's a recipe from my dear friend Julia."

"You are now a fully-fledged member of the book club since you've tasted Lexi's special pie," Tyra said and smiled.

The conversation and laughs continued, and they discussed everything from the local news to the holidays they planned.

"What about that poor young girl who was found on the beach in Omaha?" Tyra said.

"I heard she was up here on holiday with friends."

"It was Bramble and Duchess that found her," Vivianne said quietly. The room fell silent, and everyone looked at her in disbelief. Annika, of course, knew that Vivianne had been the dog walker who had found her but never discussed any of Bill's police business publicly.

"You're kidding!" Lexi said.

"I wish I was. It was awful and so very tragic." "Who are Bramble and Duchess?" Deb said.

"Oh, they are my dogs," Vivianne said. "Westies."

"I heard from my cousin in Omaha that the American rock star Jett Starr was found dead in the bath," Lexi said.

"What!" Deb said. "That's so sad. I used to see him around Matakana on occasion. He seemed very nice and always said hello when I saw him."

"Oh, you would have loved to have been invited to one of his house parties, I'm sure," Flo said, elbowing her in the side. "Apparently, his parties were wild."

"I guess so," Deb said, which made everyone laugh nervously. It wasn't funny, but rather a way to cope. Annika knew the emotion well. Bill and his colleagues had to joke about some of the terrible situations they were thrust into and had to deal with. It was a release valve to make sure they looked after their own mental health.

As the evening drew to a close, Zac arrived home.

"Hi, darling," Annika said. "Vivianne, this is my son, Zac." The rest of the group had known him since he was young.

"Hi, Zac. Nice to meet you."

Zac nodded and disappeared upstairs to his room. No one else said anything, but Annika was a little embarrassed at her son's lack of manners. He'd always been the conscientious one who worked hard at school and sometimes forgot to have a little fun. Perhaps it was good that he could relax, blow off some steam, and hang out with his friends, Luke, Steve and Ant. Still, basic manners didn't cost anything, and she'd have a talk to him tomorrow.

Everyone helped clean up and plates were stacked in the dishwasher. She loved this group of ladies.

"We'll see you all on Wednesday for Deb's birthday," Lexi said.

"I've booked a table at The Farmers Daughter. It will be so lovely, and the food is great," Annika said as she waved her friends goodbye from the verandah.

"Thank you so much. You guys are truly the best," Deb said, walking down the path towards her car.

As soon as everyone had left, Annika called Maggie and Finn out to the garden for a last comfort stop before bed. Maggie only took a few seconds, as she disliked getting her paws wet, and bounded up the wooden steps in a few leaps. As Finn took his time, sniffing every hydrangea bush in front of the house, she reflected and thought there had been so many tragic deaths it dredged up her own previous trauma.

51

Mike drove slowly down the wharf at Sandspit to the regular meeting spot. It was just before six: dusk and only a few people were around. They deliberately met in a public place. No one would pay any attention to a couple of blokes shooting the breeze on the wharf.

The message from Gazza had come in earlier in the day and seemed urgent. Their next lot of tablets wasn't due for another week. The demand for Molly had increased a lot in the last year. Mike bought as much as he could get his hands on, but still, it didn't seem to be enough. There was massive drug consumption up north. Big Ed's gang facilitated the distribution channels, just like with Andrei's meth.

Mike was building his own little nest egg. In a year or two, he'd branch off on his own. He was sick of working for Andrei. Already the bank balance had grown considerably, and he was only a year into his little side business. Andrei didn't suspect a thing. He was so preoccupied with his own stuff. Besides, he never gave him any inkling.

Andrei knew the gang dealt in ecstasy but assumed their source was someone in Auckland, not right under his nose. To tell the truth, he'd lost all respect for Andrei. The way he treated Crystal, or anyone in his life, for that matter, including himself, was disgusting. Andrei had changed so much over the years and was not only a narcissist but definitely a sadist as well. Or perhaps he hadn't changed, and it was Mike who had finally seen what the guy was.

Mike pulled up in the deserted car park. He watched a couple of young guys on bikes ride by and an older man and a woman walking back from the pier. Gazza was late. He'd give him ten minutes, that's all. He had a nicely marbled Scotch fillet steak in the fridge that was calling his name. Mike's stomach grumbled. He was hungry, and to think about it made it worse. He'd already peeled the potatoes and chopped them into cubes, ready for the barbecue, along with the zucchini, sliced lengthways, and some crisp broccolini. Perhaps he should add a couple of lovely field mushrooms.

A car pulled up next to the Escalade. He could see Gazza, his mate Iggy, and another bloke he didn't know the name of, who looked like the hired muscle.

He never quite understood how these gangs worked. He guessed it was a bit like the army with layers of hierarchy, just less organised.

Gazza waved and indicated they'd go for a walk along the waterfront.

Mike stepped out of the car. The clear, dark night sky was lit up with stars, and the temperature had dropped considerably. It was going to be a chilly night.

Iggy and the muscle-bound man stayed in the warmth of the car. Mike was happy about that, as he didn't trust them entirely. At least Gazza and Iggy were druggies; he didn't know about the third man.

"Listen, man, you're going to have to double your next supply," Gazza said as they walked to keep warm.

"I know. Big Ed's told me, but I'm already at the upper end of what I can get hold of. I could message my contact to see if I could get a larger shipment delivered, as it depends on the manufacturer in Auckland. It would cost you, of course," Mike said. It had been a real pinch last time to get more.

"You do what you have to do," Gazza said, "and so do we."

"What are you talking about?"

"We know your little secret and might have to let it out. I'm sure Andrei Bowen would love to know."

Mike couldn't believe that Gazza threatened him as well.

"What the fuck, man? I've supplied you with Molly for a year, and always on time.

How dare you pull this fucking stunt on me, you asshole."

"Sorry, man. The directives are from Big Ed. We need more, and we need it quick. If you can't deliver, we'll destroy you, and we'll get a new supplier. That's as simple as it is."

Mike wanted to punch Gazza in the head. His anger distracted him from the other two men who came up from behind. Mike could feel the cold steel gun barrel in his back.

"Now, you listen here, fella. We're going to walk back to the car nice and easy. You're going to get into our car and come with us. I don't want to hear a word from you in the meantime," Gazza said, his voice icy.

Mike's mind was in overdrive. Why were they doing this to him? Despite the cold, he felt sweat patches forming on his shirt.

There was no one else around. He had no choice but to follow their lead. At the car, the muscly guy tied his hands with cable ties.

"Really, man? Is this necessary?"

Gazza drove to the main road, and they turned off towards Sharp Road, then right to Matakana. Did they want to rough him up? Teach him a lesson? As they went through Matakana village and continued onto Omaha Flats Road, his insides turned cold.

Were they taking him to Andrei to force him to confess? To make him sign his own death warrant? Andrei was ruthless and would not be so gracious as to let him off the hook.

He'd be finished.

"Hey, listen, guys. I'm sure we can talk about this. How can we resolve this? I thought you were happy with our arrangement," Mike said.

Gazza stared at the road ahead and didn't respond.

"Come on, man. What is it that I have done to upset you?"

"Less talking, dude," the muscle-bound guy hissed and pressed the gun into his side.

Mike recognised the building site as they pulled up and parked on the concrete driveway.

"What are we doing here, guys?"

"Shut the fuck up," the man with the gun said as he opened the car's rear door.

A few dimly lit streetlights speckled the darkness of the new subdivision. The house next door was completely black; no one was home. The rest of the subdivision only had a few completed new builds, but mainly there were empty lots or houses still under construction. No one was going to see him.

"Walk around the back of the house," Gazza instructed. Mike did as he was told, desperately searching for a way out of the situation. They were obviously going to give him a good bash, hence the muscle-bound dude.

Once around the back, the heavy-set guy taped Mike's mouth up, and he steeled himself for the first hit. They were three against one. He could do nothing but try to protect himself as best as he could. The whack from behind with the four-by-two came out of nowhere, and mercifully his world went black.

~

When he came to, Mike was disoriented. It was pitch black. His head ached like he'd been hit by a truck, and there was an inordinate amount of pressure on his chest and lungs. He struggled for breath. He couldn't move his arms, and there was a heavy, cold feeling all over him that he couldn't place.

He forced himself to calm down and worked his conscious mind over his body. His head and shoulders were above whatever he was stuck in. An earthy smell of cement and dust was in his nostrils. God, was he immersed in concrete? The panic started to rise again. The deep void of the black night sky contributed to his escalating panic. In a glimmer of hope, he realised he could move his fingers marginally. He rocked his body from side to side, but not much gave way. He tried to scream, but his mouth was still taped shut.

As it dawned on him that he was, in fact, encased in concrete, he coughed and choked on his own saliva. The inside of his mouth was gritty. He had no memory of ingesting anything. His saliva glands were working overtime, and he desperately wanted to spit and clear whatever he had in his mouth but couldn't. A slight trickle of drool made it out on one side of his mouth where the adhesive didn't stick so well. Gravity made the saliva stream run down, which resulted in a cold sensation on his neck. Astonishment and despair overtook him. Could he get out? Would this be his fate? He wondered if Andrei had found out about his little side hustle. Was he behind this? Mike realised the situation was hopeless, and regrets flashed through his mind. The cold, rigid concrete slowly warmed up, and no matter how he fought, it squeezed tighter. Would anyone miss him?

The chemical process started gradually, and that's when Mike knew the caustic burning had set in. He felt an odd tingling sensation on his legs. He was wearing jeans and knew the lime component of the cement would be no match for what he's got on. There was more feeling in his upper body, where an obvious heat radiated. Fragments of memories and conversation flitted through his mind. He was in the present but also not. Perhaps it was the body's way of coping with increasing discomfort and pain. An image of his dad appeared. Many years ago, when Mike was just a boy, his dad received cement burns on his feet. He remembered the severe reaction and the skin peeling off in sheets when his dad removed his boots. The vice-like squeeze on Mike's chest worsened by the minute, and he struggled for breath. Saliva continued to fill his mouth, and he was forced to swallow again and again. His stomach was like a washing machine, agitating and pounding whatever was left from his lunch, making him cramp. The nausea was inevitable, and a torrent of partly digested food exploded into his mouth. He managed to swallow, and his throat burned with acid all the way back down.

What was worse: to suffocate or be cooked alive? Mike drifted in and out of consciousness and had no idea how much time had passed when a figure emerged from the shadows. He wasn't sure if he was hallucinating or awake. He looked at the figure. It couldn't be. *Was it?* A flash of long hair. Was it Fanta? Then he realised, no, it was only Gazza. *Bastard.*

His body was consumed by the increasing burn. A muffled primeval scream came from deep inside him; he couldn't bear any more of this. Mike's last conscious thought was: would there be anything left of him? Another wave of nausea overwhelmed him, and this time, he coughed and choked, which made him inhale the stomach contents, despite every fibre in his being trying to stop it from happening. He was a mere passenger and could feel the vomit going into his lungs, and between coughing and not being able to breathe, he knew this was how it ended. His eyes bulged as he slowly suffocated to death, and the one person he could see suddenly turned into ten. This was judgement day, and his head slumped forward.

52

Tuesday the 11th of July

The steam was thick as Andrei stepped out of the bathroom. The long hot shower had done wonders for his muscles, not to mention his frustration levels after Daria's phone. The conversation was still playing in his mind.

Daria knew how to push his buttons. Why did she need to stick her nose in? He had everything under control. Ever since they were young, she'd always liked to get the last word in, and she had their parents wound around her little finger. Lately, he had struggled with the power play between them. Who did she think she was? He did all the heavy lifting and provided the network. She was nothing without him. He'd taken his frustration out on his training session this morning and probably pushed himself further than he should. Not that he cared.

At least now, he felt a lot better after he'd belted the shit out of the gym equipment in the garage. Andrei towelled off before throwing his used towel in the laundry basket with one swift motion. He had a shave, slapped some aftershave on his face, and admired himself in the mirror. He flexed his broad chest and liked what he saw before he padded into the dressing room.

Crystal was still asleep, and he shut the door to the bedroom. She liked to get eight hours of rest, while he survived on an average of five to six hours.

He was in no mood to talk to her this morning, anyway. He had his own thoughts to sort out without the distraction. The morning was his favourite time; it was when he made a head start on whatever was happening. Being organised and a step ahead of the people around him was essential.

He'd messaged Mike earlier but had no response, which was peculiar. Mike was always available, no matter the time of day or night. That was how it had always been since their school days. Mike had always had his back.

Andrei perused his side of the vast walk-in wardrobe, where the built-in lights illuminated the neatly organised garments—shirts on the top row and trousers on the bottom, flanked by shelves on each side of the room. Magda, the housekeeper, colour-coordinated his shirts just the way he liked, which made it easier to choose. With only his underwear and socks on, he picked a crisp, light blue shirt with French cuffs and a pair of navy trousers and added a navy belt. He opened the top drawer, where an assortment of timepieces was displayed, and opted for the Omega Seamaster. The matt blue dial and rotating ceramic bezel matched not only his clothes but also his mood. He tidied his shirt, pulled the cuffs down, and reached for the titanium Aston Martin cufflinks. He'd always fancied himself as a bit of a James Bond, and this completed the look.

He went to the kitchen to make himself a protein smoothie.

As the blender whizzed, he tried to get hold of Mike again, but to no avail. Where was he, for goodness' sake?

He decided to go and check on Mike, walking over to the guesthouse and knocking on the door. No answer. The door was locked. Andrei went back into the main house, grabbed the spare key, and opened the door to the annexe.

"Mike, are you there?"

Andrei stood in the compact entrance and looked upstairs.

"Mike?"

Still no answer. He went up the narrow stairs to the bedroom, where the light was on. The bed hadn't been slept in. Chopped vegetables sat in a bowl of water on the bench. It looked like he'd been in the middle of dinner preparations when he'd suddenly left the house. Andrei opened the door to the single garage, but the car wasn't there.

Perhaps he didn't come home last night? As far as he knew, Mike didn't have a girlfriend. On the other hand, perhaps he did, and he'd received a better offer. Andrei shut the door behind him and returned to his office inside the main house. He dealt with the usual barrage of emails and completed more paperwork before he glanced at his watch and realised it was almost seven o'clock. He needed a coffee.

Crystal appeared as he walked into the kitchen. Despite the underfloor heating, she wore thick woolly socks and a robe over her pyjamas. She looked half asleep as she perched on the barstool by the bench. "Coffee?"

"Yes, please, that would be lovely," she said, stifling a yawn.

Andrei made hers first, just the way she liked it. The imported Gaggia machine spluttered, and the strong, velvety brew dripped into the cup. It always surprised him how good he felt after the first cup of the day. He handed her a small cup and gently touched her shoulder before he made one for himself.

"What do you have planned for today?"

"Mike is supposed to take me into Warkworth for a few errands this morning. That's all," Crystal said.

"Talking about Mike, I can't seem to get hold of him. He's not at home. Any idea where he could be?"

"I'm sure he'll be here soon to pick me up."

"I need to go. See you tonight," he said, kissing her on the cheek as he balanced the KeepCup of coffee. He could feel Crystal's gaze on him as he walked away.

Andrei felt a deep-seated annoyance in the pit of his stomach, a feeling only slightly mitigated by the first sips of coffee. He liked to control his life and those around him. Years ago, his ex-wife had suggested he should see a psychiatrist. He'd completely rejected the idea. More recently, the school had made contact, and there had been murmurings that his eldest daughter might be on the autistic spectrum and would benefit from being tested. As a father, he initially didn't care for the teacher's findings and rubbished the notion. He didn't want her labelled and investigated by some bearded, spectacled shrink. Nothing was wrong with her; sure, she was a little quirky, but so what? Why be run-of-the-mill, vanilla and boring? Again, his ex-wife had convinced him otherwise, and the girl was about to be assessed. As he'd read about the subject and reflected on the matter, perhaps he, too, had his own issues. Not that it changed anything; he liked how he was. It was an advantage in business for him because he was super focused, and nothing got past him.

He'd struggled at school as well. His father had been a hard man. There were no shortcuts. In his mind, Bowen men didn't fail at anything. Because of this, he was forced to work twice as hard as the other students. He'd developed Learn and Survive strategies in the school environment, making him resilient and tough.

He got into the car and took another sip of coffee before he pressed the garage door remote. Still no sign of Mike. Andrei tried calling again, but it went straight to voicemail. As he hung up, Kingston, the foreman, called.

"Boss, you need to come over to site one straight away! Something terrible has happened. I don't know what the fuck to do!"

"What do you mean?" Andrei was alarmed, and his mind was in a flurry with the many different scenarios of vandalism playing out in his head.

"I think he's dead," Kingston said, on the verge of losing it. Andrei could hear the man struggling to convey the message.

"What are you saying? Who's dead?"

"Found . . . Mike . . . out the back. I . . . "

"What? Get a hold of yourself, man. I can't understand what you are saying!"

Had he heard correctly? Was Mike there, and did he say *dead*? He didn't bother with more questions and hung up. He needed to get there—fast. He fired up the engine, and reversed so fast he nearly took out the row of newly planted hydrangea bushes.

Andrei's thoughts raced: what the hell had happened?

Mike couldn't be dead, surely. Acting on instinct, he drove up to the gate and hit the gate remote with such force that it split in two, which made the batteries scatter across the front seat passenger footwell.

"For fuck's sake. Come on already!"

Andrei was losing his cool as he threw the car into park and flung the door open. He raced around to the passenger side, his mind working at warp speed. It wasn't possible that Mike could be dead! He fumbled and managed to put the remote together, pressing the button as he ran back to the driver's seat.

He didn't bother with the seatbelt, just threw the car into gear and raced off. He didn't care. Within moments he pulled up to the building site, the car screeching to a halt. The foreman sat on the front steps of the house with his head in his hands, seemingly unaware that Andrei had arrived.

"Kingston!! What's happened?" Andrei said, grabbing the man's shoulders and shaking him, trying to make sense of the situation. The man blinked and looked at him, disoriented. The foreman shook his head and pointed to his left, to the paved path around the house. Andrei let go of him and ran around the back, his shirt clinging to his body. It was as if the whole world was in slow-motion. He could feel his heart and the stress that increased with every breath. As he made it around the back, he looked over the section, scanning left to right but saw nothing. The ground was covered in topsoil; the planting was due to start this week, right after the deck had been built.

The deck!

Slowly, he turned his head towards the house and the large pile of decking timber stacked and covered with a tarpaulin. He looked towards where the holes for the deck had been dug out last week and stopped in his tracks. His heartbeat increased, and he was sweating profusely. He wiped his forehead.

Andrei could see Mike's head and shoulders just above the edge of one of the holes. He struggled to process what was in front of his eyes. Due to the angle and weight of the proposed deck, a dozen or so holes had been dug a couple of days ago.

Andrei stepped forward and felt the rain-drenched soil rise above his shoes. The wet soil squelched and made its way through his impractical footwear and splattered his trousers as he ran the last few metres. Around the body and all the way up to the shoulders was hardened concrete.

Andrei struggled to comprehend what he was seeing.

"What the fuck?" He dropped to his knees. It was a shocking sight.

Mike's head tilted forwards, which made it impossible to see his face. Despite this and the mottled, blue-tinged colour to the back of his neck, Andrei pulled himself together and placed his middle fingers on his friend's neck, feeling for a pulse. Mike's neck flopped to the side, and his skin was cold and clammy to the touch. Andrei pulled his hand away as if he'd been burnt. There was no question Mike was dead. The bile rose in Andrei's stomach, and he got up, staggering a few steps before vomiting. As though he were in a parallel universe, Andrei looked up to see the morning sun had risen just above the roof line and shone gently on the few bits of grass sticking up here and there on the patchy lawn. He glanced over to where the body was and willed the whole image to go away—but it didn't.

A paralysing numbness spread through his body. His legs grew heavy, and his feet seemed glued to the ground. He felt like he, too, was encased in cement. The thumping heartbeat in his chest blurred his vision. He averted his eyes and shook his head like a dog emerging from the water. He tried to swallow, but his tongue was stuck to the roof of his dry mouth, making him cough. At last, Andrei managed to get some air into his lungs, which made him regain some control of his extremities. He took more deep breaths before he could look up again.

How the hell had Mike ended up in one of the holes? Who had done this to him?

It was a bloody nightmare—his best friend had been murdered. Andrei straightened his back and walked around to the front of the house, desperate to get away from the macabre staging of his friend. All he could think about was how much Mike must have suffered. He also knew there was no other option than to call the police.

"How the fuck could Mike end up in one of those holes? And where did the concrete come from?" he said to Kingston.

"I have no idea. We weren't scheduled to pour until next week."

Fuck! If it weren't bad enough that Mike was dead, now the police would snoop around, which wasn't ideal. But the big question remained: what had Mike gotten himself into that had ultimately seen him killed? One thing was for sure: when he found out who the fucker responsible was, they'd regret the very day they'd been born.

53

It was early morning, and Niko had been awake since five. He'd tried to get back to sleep for another hour before giving up and heading to the gym. The damp air in the small apartment wasn't helped by the fact that he'd hung his washing on the clothes rack last night. A faint musty smell permeated the room. He screwed his nose up, realising that he would have to rewash everything and hang the clothes outside on the small balcony if they were to dry and smell half-decent. He pulled everything down from the drying frame and put the clothes in the basket in the bathroom.

The main street was deserted, apart from some activity in the bakery. He took the narrow steps between the buildings to the empty car park at the back. The black silhouette of an alley cat stopped in its tracks as Niko reached his car. The annoyance at being disturbed was evident as the cat sauntered purposefully between the empty stands of the Matakana Market, its tail sashaying back and forth.

The barren car park was as sad as his personal life. He missed his girlfriend Katarina and felt a bit lost in his personal life since she'd left for the United States. It was lonely being up here, as all his mates were back in Auckland. His evenings in Matakana were spent on his own or going to the pub for a quiet beer after work. So, not a lot going on. The gym was the only place apart from work where he felt he belonged. Thankfully, they opened early, and he was there at six when it opened. The girl on reception gave him a friendly wave and got on with some admin.

Niko went straight to the lighter weights and warmed up before progressing to what he usually lifted. He was the only person there until just before six-thirty when a rowdy group of teenage lads full of testosterone and bravado arrived. Immediately, the noise level went up tenfold. The peace was shattered, but he carried on and finished his set.

The young receptionist was alert suddenly, and with it, the volume of the upbeat music was turned up. He could tell the boys recognised him, even though he was out of uniform.

They were loud, obviously eager to impress the pretty girl and show off in front of their mates. Niko had been the same at that age, invincible and pimply-faced. The only difference was that he had thrown weights in a rudimentary warehouse, using second-hand gear while the cold wind whistled around his ears in the winter—a sharp contrast to this well-equipped, temperature-controlled space he trained in now.

It was just after seven. Niko had worked through his program and packed his gear up. He gave the young lads a big smile as he left. Better to burn their energy here than get into all sorts of trouble on the streets. Even though it had been a quick workout, he'd gone hard, and his shoulders and chest muscles ached. But he felt invigorated.

The traffic on Leigh Road was light. As he pulled in behind the shops, there was a car parked in his car spot. Irritation rose, and the great feeling from the gym evaporated in seconds.

"For fuck's sake. You've got to be kidding me." There's a whole car park available, and they have to park in his reserved space, he thought. He pulled into the next row and slung his bag over his shoulder as he walked past the old Ford Explorer. The car was covered in mud and looked like it had been off-road. He glanced at the registration to have any excuse to pursue the matter further. He'd like nothing more than to slap a hefty fine on the filthy windscreen.

But it was all in order, and he continued walking. He couldn't very well issue an infringement notice because someone had parked in his spot.

The annoyance was still there as he jogged up the narrow steps between the buildings and turned left past the bakery to get to his flat. Eager to be home, he ran up the stairs, his leg muscles protesting as he arrived at the front door, fumbling around in his bag to find the keys. The sweaty workout clothes stuck to his body, and he couldn't wait to get them off. He unlocked the door, kicking his trainers to the side in the small entrance and opening the door to the bathroom. The warm shower water took away the last of his foul mood and relaxed his muscles.

As usual, he finished off with a rinse of cold water. After the initial shock to the system and the icy prickle, his skin felt invigorated, and he was ready to face the day. He towelled off, found a clean pair of trousers and a shirt, and checked his phone—he still had time for a decent breakfast. He rummaged around in the fridge and found an open packet of bacon, which he sniffed to make sure it hadn't gone off. Once it was sizzling in the frying pan, he cracked two eggs and seasoned them with a good pinch of salt and pepper.

His stomach grumbled, and the smell of the food made him ravenous, almost on the verge of 'hangry.' The sourdough loaf he'd bought yesterday was still good, and he sliced a couple of thick pieces off, slotting them in the toaster. The food hardly touched the sides as he wolfed it down. There was no dishwasher, so he rinsed the dishes in the kitchen sink to avoid scrubbing the dried egg off when he got home. He slammed the front door and stopped at the bakery to pick up his coffee. They knew him now and would make his flat white as soon as they saw him walking in. He exchanged a few words with the friendly barista before walking down the road to the police station.

Niko was happy to be in Matakana. It was a nice break from everyday duties, but he suspected his days were numbered and that he'd be on his way back to South Auckland sometime soon. Niko walked into work just before eight and had barely sat down when the phone rang.

"Matakana police station."

"Hello, it's Andrei Bowen. I'm calling from one of my building sites here in Point Wells. I'm going to need you to come over. My mate's dead," he said, his voice dipping as he struggled to stay calm. "We just found him at work. Fucking hell, I can't believe it. He's stuck in one of the holes—"

"Are you sure that he is deceased? Do you need an ambulance to be dispatched?" "I'm quite sure," Andrei said, his voice now terse.

"Give me the address where you are calling from." Andrei gave him the address in

Point Wells. "We are on our way. Wait for us out the front, and don't touch anything."

As Niko hung up, Bill walked into the station. "Don't hang your jacket up. We just got a call. Deceased male in Point Wells."

"Who called it in?"

"Let me see," Niko said, looking at his notes. "Andrei Bowen. Apparently, it was his friend that he found."

"Great start to the day!" Bill said with a hint of facetiousness as he grabbed the patrol car keys off the desk.

Niko downed the last of his coffee in the car.

"You could have got me one of those," Bill said.

"Sorry, Sarge, I'll pick one up for you tomorrow."

"It makes you wonder about these recent deaths. First, the young girl, then Fanta and Jett Starr, and now there's someone possibly connected to Andrei Bowen, who's been found dead. Is there a common denominator?" Bill said as they drove off.

~

THE DRIVE to Point Wells didn't take long. Bill knew where in the new subdivision the address was and parked out the front.

Andrei's Maserati was in the driveway, and so was another work vehicle with a Bowen Construction sign on the side.

Two men leant against a couple of shrink-wrapped pallets of grey bricks, heads down. Andrei's arms were folded tightly across his chest. Both men were pale and obviously shaken. Andrei took a few steps forward and shook Bill's hand.

"Thank you for coming so quickly," Andrei said. His face was ashen as he processed the shock. "This is Kingston, my foreman. He was the one who found Mike."

Kingston was subdued and remained silent. Bill glanced towards the house. It looked weather-tight, but it was far from being finished. "Where did you find the body?"

"Come around the back. I'll show you where he is," Andrei said, gesturing to the temporarily paved path around the side of the house.

"You stay here," Bill said. "We don't need more people trampling around than we already have. No offence."

Bill took care where he put his feet, narrowly avoiding stepping into the shoe prints on the damp ground. The impressions went in both directions. They probably belonged to Andrei and his site foreman, and Bill wasn't about to add any more—the crime scene techs at ESR would go berserk.

"Jesus Christ," Niko said as he walked into the back of Bill, who'd stopped in his tracks, taking in the scene in front of them.

The back of the house was unfinished. At the back door, holes had been dug for the piles to be driven in. Because of the gradient angle of the section, it looked like more retaining would need to be done. The holes for what was to become the deck had been covered over with orange netting, apart from the one the victim protruded from. All that was visible from where Bill and Niko stood was the very top of the shoulders, neck and head of the victim.

"My God," Bill sputtered as he stepped closer. He was shocked by the grotesqueness of the scene. He pulled his phone from his pocket and took a deep breath before snapping some photos. The victim wore a striped shirt. Judging by the slightly pulled-back shoulders, the deceased's hands were tied behind his back. Concrete had been poured around the body. On closer inspection, a red ombre tinge rose from where the body was in contact with the concrete. It looked like blood. Bill thought of the horror this man would have suffered. It certainly didn't look like a peaceful death.

"What kind of sick bastard would do this to a person?" Niko said from behind. "It's like something out of a mafia movie, for Christ's sake!"

No doubt about it: the man was dead. Bill moved to the side, taking more photos—there was no need to step any closer until the crime scene techs had been and done their job.

"Let's call it in. Orewa will most likely send Rudd and Copeson, who will want to see this one as soon as possible. Being what it is, it is likely ESR will be called in as well." Bill spoke to Orewa Headquarters, and he and Niko carefully stepped back the same way they had come.

As Bill and Niko rounded the corner, Andrei and the foreman waited anxiously.

"Was he one of your workers?" Bill said.

"Yes, Mike Fenton," Andrei said, his voice a little unsteady. "What will happen now?"

"The first thing we need to do is put a cordon up. No one comes in. We need to preserve the scene. I'd like you to be patient and stay put for the time being. Thankfully, no one can see into the back of the property, but we may still need to erect a tent to protect it from the weather."

A handful of people were about, looking curiously at the police car and probably wondering what was going on.

"While my colleague puts up the cordon, I'd like to ask you two a couple of questions," Bill said, signalling that he wanted to start with the foreman. They walked over to sit down on the front step. Kingston looked like he was about to be sick.

"Are you all right, mate?" Bill said.

"I guess so. I just can't quite fathom that Mike is dead," he said. "I don't know what he was doing here at the site. Though, he is . . . I mean, was Andrei's right-hand man." Kingston coughed, but a bit of colour returned to his cheeks.

"Tell me about this morning from when you arrived here on site," Bill said, pulling his notebook out of his pocket.

"I arrived at seven fifteen or thereabouts, got my tools off the back of the truck, and unlocked the front door. We still had a few days of work inside the house before the concrete was due to be poured for the deck."

"Did you see anyone else around or any unfamiliar cars on the street when you arrived?"

"Not a soul. I had some things to do inside the house," he said, his voice so low Bill had to lean towards him. "That's when I saw him through the back windows. At first glance, it looked like someone had bundled something in one of the holes, and then I saw it was a person. I dropped what I was doing and ran outside."

Kingston went quiet as though the dreadful scene was replaying in his mind. Bill encouraged him to continue. "What did you do next?"

Kingston looked down at his hands, flexing his fingers before answering. "I know I probably shouldn't have . . . but I grabbed the top of his shoulders. His upper body flopped as the rest of him was set in rock-solid concrete. That's when I realised it was Mike. I saw his face. . ."

Bill didn't want to interrupt him. He felt for the man.

"It's the first time I've seen a dead person," he said, swallowing audibly. "How on earth could this happen?"

"That's exactly what we are going to try to find out. I'll have to ask you to wait here for the detectives from Orewa; they shouldn't be long. I'll have a talk to your boss in the meantime."

Bill called Andrei over, and the foreman remained seated on the front step. Andrei started pacing.

"I understand Mike was your friend and that this is a terrible shock"

"Well, that's the understatement of the century! Who the fuck could have done this?" Andrei said. Saliva sprayed from his mouth, and his body shook with uncontrolled rage.

"Why don't you calm down, and we'll start from the beginning. Take your time."

"I don't need any bloody time! Besides, shouldn't you and your colleague be out there now finding out who did this?" Andrei sneered.

Bill knew shock often made people frustrated and angry, and finding a close friend dead was certainly right up there as one of the worst things to experience. Before Bill could react, though, Andrei took a step towards the brick pile and smashed it with his fist.

"Come on, mate, you really need to calm down!"

This time it was Bill who was forceful. Andrei held his right hand, his knuckles raw, blood trickling down his wrist. As he calmed down, the air went out of him like a deflated balloon, and he sat on a pile of timber with his head in his hands.

"I can't believe Mike is gone. I've known him since we were at school. We grew up together."

"It's terrible, but it would be helpful if you could answer some of our questions," Bill said before shouting at Niko. "Grab the first aid kit!"

Niko dashed over, gloved up, and started to clean the wounds on Andrei's knuckles, wrapping the hand in a wad of gauze.

"You'll have to get that seen to," Niko told Andrei and left Bill to it. Bill wondered whether Andrei's violent flash of rage and smashing of the brick pile had more to it. Was he capable of harming someone? How might his anger spill over into his relationships?

"I understand Mike was your right-hand man. Any idea why he came to the building site last night or early this morning? Was he part of the construction crew?"

Andrei covered his eyes and hunched his shoulders before looking up at Bill to answer his question.

"No, he wasn't. Mike did things like liaising with the foreman daily. We have a couple of building sites close by. There's a lot to organise. There shouldn't have been anyone here after hours, though."

"Any cameras on site?"

"Unfortunately not." Annoyance flashed across Andrei's face.

"When did you last see him?"

Andrei thought for a moment. "That would have been last night, early evening. He must have arrived home as the lights were on, perhaps just before six. Mike lived in a cottage on the property. I went to find him this morning, but he wasn't there, and his bed didn't look like it had been slept in, which was strange." Bill's ears pricked up.

"Did you hear when he drove off last night?"

"No, but then again, the house is almost soundproof with its double-glazed windows," Andrei said.

"Was Mike mixed up in things that he shouldn't be?"

"Like what?" Andrei said as his eyes narrowed and seemed to bore into Bill.

"Are you aware if he had dealings with people who might want to hurt him?" Bill said.

"Not that I'm aware. No, I don't think so. Mike was a hard-working bloke. I doubt he'd have any time or interest in that kind of thing."

"Is there a rival in the industry, anyone he might have upset, or who might even want to get to you?"

Andrei seemed to be getting irritated by the line of questioning. "I doubt it. There is fierce competition for contracts, but to go to this extent, no, I don't think so."

Bill wasn't sure what to believe. Mike's violent death was definitely a message.

Either Andrei was completely straight with him, or he was lying through his teeth.

"The question of where his car is located remains. What did he drive?"

"Mike used to drive the Escalade, a black one," Andrei said and gave Bill the registration.

"We'll put an alert out immediately and see what we can find out, and as one of the first people on the scene, you'll be questioned again. Please stay here until the detectives arrive," Bill said as he quietly evaluated the man in front of him.

Andrei had calmed down and went back to his car to wait. But the bullshit meter flickered in Bill's head. He struggled to read the guy: one minute, he was stroppy as ever; the next stand-offish. Bill was sure there was more to Andrei Bowen—what was he hiding?

54

Copeson and Rudd parked behind Bill at the edge of the driveway. The air temperature was still cool, but thankfully, the rain had held off. July was normally the wettest month, with an average rainfall of one hundred and forty-four millimetres. Bill knew this because the twins had recently completed a meteorological project at school. The last thing they needed was a deluge destroying the crime scene or washing leads away. He could see Rudd's already grumpy face and sighed.

"Good morning," Bill said, bracing himself for the vitriol no doubt coming his way.

"Is it?" Rudd said as he navigated the uneven path in front of what would become the front lawn. "I see you've already trampled the area like a herd of buffalo!" Copeson trailed behind him as usual with the crime kit.

"Don't worry about him. He's in a bad mood today. I'd stay in the background if I were you. Everyone is in the firing line today, it seems. He's already chewed out Jono on the phone this morning," Copeson said as he hurried by Bill.

"COPESON!" Rudd yelled. "Get a move on, will you!"

"Another day in paradise," Copeson said, taking a deep breath before trudging around the back of the house.

Bill followed behind but kept to the outside of the perimeter while Niko kept an eye on Kingston and Andrei.

Rudd and Copeson set their equipment up by the back door and suited up. Bill watched as they set out the stepping plates and sorted themselves.

"Jesus Christ," Rudd said as he moved closer to the deceased. The look on Rudd's face said it all.

"Copeson, we're going to need ESR for this one. Hurry up and call them," Rudd said as he backtracked over the stepping plates.

"What do you reckon, Rudd? It's one of the most bizarre things I've ever seen," Bill said from the side.

"From my first impressions, there are similarities to a case we had in Silverdale last year," Rudd said, not taking his eyes off the victim in front of him.

"In what way?"

Rudd moved around Mike, inspecting how deeply encased he was in the concrete. "There was a chap who went the same way as this guy last year, and there were links to gang activity."

Bill remembered the case but hadn't seen the crime scene photos. As with this case, the violent death had been kept out of the media. In Bill's view, this was like something out of the 1930s mafia retribution in Chicago—concrete boots and all. Although it was obvious that whoever had committed this heinous crime wanted the body to be out in the open and a message sent. In most gangland murders, the body would be disposed of, and the person would quickly become a statistic in the missing person register. Without a doubt, this was an execution.

The poor man would have suffered terribly before eventually succumbing to his injuries. It was a shame the place would soon be overrun with detectives from Orewa, and he wouldn't have anything further to do with the case. That's how it worked in small community policing. Headquarters were happy for him to take care of the everyday incidents; there wasn't the staffing here in Matakana for a serious investigation like this. It was something he struggled to agree with. He was the local cop, the eyes and ears of the community. Still, the big boys thought they knew best.

"ESR are on their way. We're going to need some earth-moving equipment. I'm sure they'll want to remove the body and transport it as is, concrete and all. So, the case last year is still unsolved?" Bill said.

"Frustratingly, no one was ever charged, but the file remains open," Rudd said.

"We'll have to wait for the pathologist's report, of course, but these look to be caustic burns," Rudd said, pointing to the bleed on the victim's shirt and torso. "Although the victim would have certainly suffocated before his body started to cook due to the rise in temperature as the concrete set. That would have caused his skin to peel off, hence the bleeding around the top of the concrete. Poor bugger. I remember the case notes for the young lad in Orewa. It was a hell of a mess when they chipped into the concrete with a jackhammer."

"I didn't know that a Kango hammer was part of the equipment at the morgue," Bill said with a straight face, attempting to lighten the sombre mood.

Rudd frowned and gave him a disapproving look. "I'm sure they will manage," he said before turning on his heels. Apparently, it was only Rudd who was allowed to deliver one-liners.

"Hey, Sarge. Do you want to come over here for a sec?" Niko called out from the corner of the house behind the tape. Even though Bill had seen many victims and ways of dying in his career, the fact that this victim had been cooked alive deeply disturbed him.

Niko was a welcome distraction.

"The cavalry's here; the two Ds have just pulled up."

Bill went around the front. He recognised one of the men as Detective Sergeant Gladstone. As he stepped out of the car with his younger colleague, his tall skinny frame towered over the other detective.

"Hi, Granger," Gladstone said. "Long time no see."

The last time they'd had anything to do with each other must have been at least two years ago when they'd worked together regarding a theft at a local art gallery. However, this was something quite different.

"This is Detective Constable Tibbs," he said, introducing his colleague. Tibbs' hunched-over smaller frame, combined with a face a mother could only love, reminded Bill of a rodent.

He extended his hand and shook it. Niko did the same.

"The body was found this morning?" Gladstone said, getting down to business.

"That's correct. The foreman over there made the discovery," Bill said, gesturing to the deflated figure sitting on the front step.

"The SOCOs are at the back. They're waiting for the team from ESR to turn up."

"We'll have a chat with the foreman first," Gladstone said. "I'd hate to disturb old Ruddy."

Bill smiled. He wasn't the only one to bear the brunt of the old guy's temper.

"I can't wait for the old git to retire," Gladstone said with a grin.

Despite the new subdivision being barely inhabited, a small crowd of nosy bystanders had gathered on the pavement outside the cordon, the police tape flickering in the wind. A couple of schoolchildren sat idly on their bikes, watching the goings-on with fascination. Thankfully, there was no view into the back from the street. It was certainly not something that he wanted to get out in the small community. Bill was used to dealing with break-ins and general disorder, but this was a first. What was this anyway? Was it a warning or some kind of bizarre statement? The body had been left in plain sight on purpose. One thing was for sure; it would have taken more than one person to orchestrate something like this. Either the crims were very sure they'd left no trace materials behind, or they were stupid. In Bill's experience, it was most likely the latter.

Gladstone tapped him on the shoulder.

"Do you think you and your colleague could do some canvassing around the neighbourhood? All the available uniforms are allocated elsewhere."

"No worries. We'll get on to that now," Bill said, glad to be of use.

The crowd had dispersed, and Bill took one side of the street and Niko the other.

The street wasn't very long, and most houses were done within the hour. The people who were at home hadn't seen or heard anything worth reporting. There was a vacant lot on one side of the crime scene and no answer from the house on the other side. Bill stuck his business card in the letterbox with a message scribbled on the back to give him a call. Perhaps the people were away or had gone to work early. Still, it was important to turn over every stone.

Niko had no luck, either. It seemed no one had seen anything suspicious.

"Did you speak to everyone?" Bill said.

"The only house that didn't open the door was the one directly opposite, and the house next door, it seems like the owners are away. Their letter box is jam-packed with circulars, but I left a note for them each to contact the station."

"Let's hope they do. If not, we have to follow up."

"You'd think someone would have walked their dog and seen or heard something," Niko said.

Bill and Niko walked around the house and updated Gladstone. Jono, the photographer, had also arrived and was busy documenting the scene. Rudd lifted the tape of the inner cordon and came out.

"If the victim were alive when the concrete was poured, he would have suffered greatly. This has the mark of last year's crime scene, for sure," Rudd said, pulling his gloves off and wiping his brow.

"Bloody animals to let him suffer in that way. Terrible," Bill said.

"Obviously, the case will be run from Orewa, as well as the case of the American rocker, Jett Starr," Gladstone said.

"But I thought that was classified as a suicide?" Bill said, surprised.

"I haven't had a chance to tell you. The preliminary report from pathology concluded that the blunt force trauma on the back of the head was the cause of Starr's death. His wrists were cut post-mortem, hence the lack of arterial spray," Rudd said.

"Well, that changes things, doesn't it?" Bill said.

"You could say that," Gladstone said. "I have uniforms in Omaha canvassing the neighbourhood; hence, we are a bit short-staffed."

That explained things, Bill thought. "Happy to help where we can," he said.

55

Big Ed looked up from his breakfast. His two pieces of toast were topped with a thick smear of butter and apricot jam. The young girl poured black tea into a large mug, her hand trembling as she added the right amount of milk. His eyes were on her, and he knew she felt the stare. That was the whole point. He demanded absolute respect from everyone around him, even her. She was there to serve him. Everyone knew their place. The crew knew better than to talk to him before he'd made his way through at least two cups of tea and eaten something.

Through the streaky kitchen window, he could see Gazza and Iggy outside as they leant against the bikes, waiting for him to come out. He'd received word last night that the job had been done. They wouldn't have dared show their faces around here this morning if it hadn't. Still, he wasn't in the habit of leaving any aspect of their operation to chance, including the 'taxing.' Although he usually let the young guys beat the crap out of the morons who either didn't toe the line or pay their debts on time.

Mike had wronged them. Simple as that. His poor nephew didn't deserve to die the way he had. He'd promised his sister that he would take him under his wing, protect him. The only saving grace was that her mind was pretty much lost. Fanta had been a grown man, but he was an addict and increasingly difficult to control. Still, he'd been family. Hopefully, the fucking asshole responsible for his death suffered until the very end. If there was something important to Big Ed, it was integrity and loyalty. If Fanta had still been alive, he might have turned a blind eye. It was a lucrative business for them as well. Nevertheless, you never shit in your own nest as that fucker had done. Andrei was still none the wiser that Mike had pulled a swift one on him. So really, he'd done the arrogant prick a favour, getting rid of his second in command. He'd do it again in a heartbeat.

The car's boot had been full of premix cement bags; all they had to do was add water, and the rest was child's play. Big Ed never got his hands dirty; that's why he had lieutenants. They were loyal to a fault and would do anything he asked. If not, they were well aware of the consequences. No one ever questioned his orders. They'd seen disobedience before, and it wasn't pretty when he dealt with it. Keep them on a short leash; that's the only way.

The missus quickly cleared up in the kitchen as he finished his breakfast. He grabbed his leather jacket from the back of the chair and went outside without a word to her. She didn't expect thanks, so why start now?

"Morning, Cap," Gazza said, averting his eyes. Iggy looked up briefly and nodded.

"You get my text last night?"

Big Ed looked at his two lieutenants before answering.

"What the fuck did I tell you about using comms?"

"But, Cap. It was a burner. It's untraceable."

"I don't give a fuck if you used your grandma's phone. Next time, don't."

"Okay, sorry, Cap," Gazza said. His face flushed red at being reprimanded in front of Iggy. Big Ed enjoyed nailing him to a cross.

"I take it everything went to plan?"

"It did. We took Grunter with us. It wasn't a problem. Your idea about the concrete and cementing him in was pure genius," Gazza sniggered.

"What about the neighbours? You'd better hope no one saw you."

"Nah, it was cool. We only saw one guy who must have come home from work a couple of houses away. I don't think he paid much attention," Gazza said as he looked at his feet.

"The fucker didn't squeal? Concrete burns like a motherfucker," Big Ed said, hoping the bastard had suffered immensely.

"I left Iggy with him and Grunter, and I drove away so no one would notice the car," Gazza said, passing the buck. Big Ed looked at Iggy, who shrivelled at the look from the boss.

"He tried to yell in the beginning, Cap, but we had him gagged. It was nasty, man.

Took hours before he finally carked it," Iggy said, shuddering.

"No one saw you?"

"Nah, Cap. It was just me. I stayed until about 4:00 a.m., then legged it through the empty sections to the main road where Gazza and Grunter were parked."

"Good job," Big Ed said, turning on his heels and walking away.

56

By the time Bill and Niko left Point Wells, it was nearly two o'clock. They'd stopped at The Point Wells General Store to pick up a late lunch. The takeaway menu was extensive. Bill chose The General Beef Burger, which was the special of the day, with a generous helping of well-seasoned fries. Niko went for the healthier Fish Burger—no bun—wrapped in large iceberg lettuce leaves.

"You know it's not a real hamburger if it doesn't come with a bun?" Bill said, sinking his teeth into the pillowy soft bun and the homemade beef patty wrapped in lettuce and oozing with cheese. The sharp and slightly tangy Dijon mustard cut through, making it a marriage in heaven.

"I can't afford to look like a lard ass when I get back. The boys will give me heaps,"

Niko said and laughed. "Besides, Katarina is home in a couple of months." "Oh, the joys of youth," Bill said.

"So, what do we know about this character Mike?" Niko said between mouthfuls.

"Not very much. All I know is that he was Andrei's right-hand man. You know, the whole thing is a bit weird. Annika is friends with

Crystal, Andrei's girlfriend, and we were invited for dinner there the other night," Bill said, pausing. "My gut tells me there's something not quite right there. I'm not sure exactly what it is, but I will figure it out." He shoved a handful of fries in his mouth. "The really weird thing is that according to Annika, Mike was Crystal's minder."

"What? That's a bit strange. Why would she need a minder?"

"I don't know, but I think there's more to come out about these characters."

"Didn't you say nothing much happens here during the winter months, Sarge?" Niko said with a huge smile on his face.

"Perhaps you tempted fate because it all seems to be happening now."

57

Daria was on her way to Point Wells to catch up with Andrei and Mike. She'd picked up a car at Auckland airport when she arrived and stayed with her parents on Sunday and last night. Two nights was more than enough. They'd been overjoyed to see her back in Auckland and had celebrated with a hearty home-cooked roast dinner when she arrived, then insisted that she stay a second night. Even though she'd been back at Easter, they'd both aged and seemed to have shrivelled. She knew she ought to be a good daughter and get back more regularly. It was just that lately, it hadn't been possible.

Her brother still annoyed her, but she always looked forward to seeing Mike. They'd had a casual relationship since their teens and been discreet. No one knew, but they had a strong bond that only the very first love creates. Mike would always have a special place in her heart, and over the years, it had been convenient to rekindle their romance on occasion. If Andrei had known, he would have hit the roof. They were good at sneaking around and had kept it a secret all this time.

The Northern Motorway was clear, and she floored the accelerator. The green, rolling hills she drove by reminded her of Europe. In no time at all, she'd reached the Puhoi tunnels, and the motorway ended. She'd forgotten how winding the rest of the road was and slowed down. She passed through Warkworth, where she turned off State Highway 1, through Hill Street junction, and onto Matakana Road. Perhaps she should call Andrei and let him know she was on the way. She dialled his number, which went straight to voicemail. She hated speaking to voicemail, so she hung up and dialled again.

"Yes," Andrei said abruptly from the other end.

"It's Daria, you idiot, and what kind of greeting is that?!" she said as she felt the annoyance increase.

"Sorry, who?" the voice on the now crackly line said. Bloody intermittent reception; that was all she needed.

"It's DARIA," she shouted, as if the coverage would magically improve when she raised her voice.

"Daria . . . it's . . . Mike . . . dead . . . can't talk," he said as the line cut out again.

"Wait, what did you say?"

Jesus, these dead spots drove her crazy. As her mind replayed the last sentence, surely she had misheard. Slowly the anxiety she normally kept at bay reared its ugly head and gained momentum like a torrent. Her mouth went dry, and her heartbeat increased. It couldn't be, could it?

She dialled Andrei again, but couldn't get through, so she threw her phone on the passenger seat in frustration. The dark heavy lump in the pit of her stomach grew, and by the time she drove into Point Wells, she was beside herself with worry.

Mike was dead? Had she heard correctly? She turned right from Omaha Flats Road and headed for Andrei's house. A stone's throw from Andrei's house and on a side street, she saw the police and emergency services. A crowd had gathered. She could see it was a building site, and then she knew.

She parked the car and hurried the last twenty metres. She saw Andrei just outside the police cordon. He looked angry and distraught. Daria walked up to him, her suede loafers already covered in mud.

The look on her brother's face was one of surprise at seeing her, but at the same time, relief. The bond they had from the rough start in their lives would be there forever. For her, it brought back distant memories of the orphanage, where it was just the two of them, and they'd been overlooked for the longest time. No one wanted a set of siblings. It had always been the two of them against the world. She was sure similar feelings flashed through her brother's mind.

Daria went straight up to Andrei and hugged him.

"Eh, this is my sister, Daria," Andrei said to the detective, looking on. "Hang on one second." He pushed Daria away, holding her at arm's length like a scolded child, while pushing her backwards, away from the detectives. "What are you doing here?"

Daria shook her shoulders and he lost his grip. "Care to explain? I'm all ears. What the fuck is this circus. Are you completely deranged?" Daria said as she glared at her brother, hands on hips.

In an instant, the air went out of her big burly brother, and they felt like children again.

"Mike's dead," he said, the pain on his face blatantly clear. As the words sunk in and the devastation of what had happened hit home, the world around her started to spin.

Disbelief and shock over took her. She had not wanted to believe it.

"How did he die?" Her voice was a mere whisper.

"Some sick fuck put him feet first in a hole and then poured cement on him."

Andrei took a step forward and embraced her. She stiffened and held the emotional turmoil at bay, balling her fists along her side, barely able to control herself. The anger that rose from her being was ugly and vengeful, and whoever was responsible for Mike's death would suffer. Daria's mind worked overtime. Mike had been Andrei's best friend since school and her first true love.

Andrei held her tighter, perhaps trying to control his feelings. She could hear their father in her head, 'Bowen men didn't lose their composure.' Daria felt Andrei's heartbeat as he tried to hold it together. She'd always been the stronger one. They eventually let go, and Andrei regained his cool, but the anger was there, and she let her brother vent his frustrations.

This was not the time or the place for her to break down. She would grieve in private for her lost love.

"These assholes," Andrei said, looking over his shoulder at the two detectives busy writing notes, "have already insinuated that I might have something to do with my best friend's death."

"That's ridiculous. Why on earth would they think that?"

"They haven't said as much, but I can feel that's where this is going. I guess I better finish up with these morons. Why don't you head home to ours and wait? I shouldn't be long."

"I'll wait. I'm not going to leave you here."

Andrei nodded and walked back to the edge of the cordon. Daria knew that despite their differences, blood was thicker than water when it came down to it.

She walked back towards her car. The small crowd seemed to have dispersed a little. She struggled to comprehend why people's morbid curiosity drove them to gawk at other people's misfortune. Although, to be fair, they probably didn't know what was behind the police tape, just had an inkling that it wasn't good.

She wanted to talk to Andrei and find out what had happened and how the hell Mike had ended up in concrete. The thunder ball of anxiety in the pit of her stomach grew, and the ground swayed as reality overtook her. She cussed under her breath as she fumbled in her seemingly bottomless bag for the keys before she fished them out and unlocked the door. She flung the door open, leaning against it to catch her breath. This wasn't like her at all. She was always in control, no matter what. Ever since she was very young, she'd learnt to control her emotions. It had taken years with a therapist to understand why she was so cold emotionally. She'd had no choice. But Mike was dead. He'd been her weak spot, and she could not control her emotions when it came to him.

Her toughness served her well when she dealt with the ruthless cartel. She'd been forced to witness swift justice served on more than one occasion. She'd literally had to take a concrete pill to harden up and get through it.

The drug business was unpredictable and volatile, but she never gave an inch and made sure there was no doubt of her ability. They'd underestimated her in the beginning, but she had proved her worth, and so far, she'd delivered for them.

She got in the car and sat down. The detectives talked to Andrei. His shoulders weren't so tight, and he looked the detectives in the eye. Hopefully, he'd calmed down. The last thing they needed was to be scrutinised by the local police. The next shipment was due soon, which meant they'd have to be extra careful as they now had some heat to deal with.

Worst case scenario, they'd have to arrange a different drop-off point.

58

Andrei's anger and frustration that he'd felt since this morning came to a head as he climbed into his car, slamming the steering wheel as hard as he could with his palms. He'd kept his cool long enough for the detectives to have a word with him before heading home. His right hand ached from before. It was nearly midday, and he'd cooperated fully with the police. It still didn't change the fact that Mike was dead.

"FUUUCK!!" he yelled, pounding the steering wheel again. This time the horn went off, which startled him enough to calm down a little. The cops glanced over at him, and he waved apologetically.

What the fuck did he have to apologise for? Nothing. He hadn't caused this mess.

In his mind, he wondered who the culprit was and why they had gone this far. Surely this couldn't have been a random attack. What the hell had Mike gotten himself into?

His mind was a mess of thoughts and possible scenarios, and the more he thought about it, the worse it became and there was only one person with balls big enough to cross him.

Daria had waited for Andrei to finish speaking to the detectives, and then she'd followed him the short distance to his house. He grabbed her suitcase from the boot and heaved it inside the entrance. A large Italian ceramic plate wobbled precariously on the wall as he shut the door behind them with more force than he'd intended. Crystal was in the kitchen and turned as he stomped up the hallway.

Daria left the bag where it was and followed closely behind. Crystal emerged from the kitchen, smiling and wiping her hands on an apron. When she spotted Daria, Crystal dropped the smile and stopped wiping her hands. "I didn't know that you were in the country, Daria. And Andrei, you're home early."

Andrei went straight to the booze cupboard and grabbed the bottle of single malt whiskey, pouring himself a double. He took a large swig and then another before refilling his glass. The warmth of the amber liquid tingled the tip of his lips. He usually enjoyed the warm burn that followed as it slid down his throat, but today there was no contentment. Daria said nothing.

"What's happened?" Crystal said, looking from Andrei to Daria.

"Mike's dead."

"What?"

Crystal sagged onto the living room couch.

"It's all right. I know it's a huge shock," Daria said, making no attempt at physical contact.

"How did it happen?" Crystal said between sobs as she blew her nose. Andrei gave Daria a look.

"He was found at site one. Someone had done a real number on him," Andrei said.

"Poor Mike." The more Crystal cried, the more Daria hardened up.

"Do you have any more of that?" Daria said, gesturing towards the scotch Andrei held.

"You know where the bottle is."

Crystal was ashen-faced and came over to where Andrei sat, curling up next to him. He put his arm around her, and she leant in, pressing her cheek against his chest.

"I'm so sorry, Andrei," Crystal said. "I know Mike and you were very close. Do we know what happened to him? Was it an accident? Did he suffer?" Crystal's words tumbled out.

Andrei's jaw was clenched shut, and he said nothing. It was as if he had no words left, but after a few moments, he said, "Kingston found him. It certainly was no accident." Andrei's lips tightened and curled inwards. "Someone must have grabbed him last night, subdued him, and stuck him down a post hole when he was unconscious, pouring cement over him."

Crystal's mouth was wide open. "Jesus, why would someone do that to him?" "I don't know, but I aim to find out," Andrei said, his voice terse.

Crystal blew her nose loudly. "I'll boil the kettle. Anyone want a cup of tea?"

Andrei shook his head and stared into the space in front of him while Daria held up her glass, getting momentarily lost in the golden brown hue of the whiskey.

A shrill ring cut through the air as Andrei's phone vibrated on the coffee table. It was enough to snap him out of his trance. He picked it up, seeing the name on the screen. "Bowen."

"I heard Mike's had an unfortunate passing," Big Ed said.

"You fucking bastard. I'll have you strung up if you've had anything to do with this." Daria and Crystal looked up.

"Calm down. I've no idea what you're talking about. I have enough trouble with my own men. What would I want with one of yours? Perhaps you should have kept a better eye on him."

Andrei's blood boiled. How dare he point the finger at him! He clenched his fists and wanted to punch something. "What the fuck would you know?"

"I know plenty. My ear is always to the ground. I have informants everywhere.

Besides, now you know what it feels like to lose someone close."

The veiled threat echoed in his mind, and Andrei knew that he was talking about his nephew, Fanta.

"You pull your fucking head in, you hear me?"

"No need to get worked up, Andy," he said, his voice dripping with sarcasm.

It took all Andrei's willpower not to hang up on the guy.

"Although, if I were you, perhaps you should take a bit more care. We wouldn't want something like this to happen to your beautiful girlfriend, would we?" "You leave my family out of this, you mother fucker!" No one threatened his family and got away with it.

59

The day had been a blur of emotions and tears. Daria's head pounded from exhaustion and the stress of the day. Her eyes were swollen and ached. She couldn't believe Mike was gone. She was in bed, and her thoughts were racing, which made it impossible to get to sleep.

Andrei had told her it was Big Ed who had called before. The conversation they had on the phone had set off alarm bells. It had pissed him off to no end, and he'd spent the rest of the afternoon shut in his office.

Daria had retreated to the guest room. There was no way she would cry in front of Crystal, the Barbie girl. Perhaps she was a bit unfair to the woman. Even though she was a bit annoying at times, it wasn't like she'd done anything specific to upset Daria. Perhaps that was the whole point. The whole aesthetics of the slightly pathetic woman rubbed her up the wrong way. Today was not the day she had the patience or the bandwidth to deal with her potential sister-in-law. Hopefully, Andrei would get tired of the bimbo and dump her for someone with a bit more substance.

There was something off about the conversation Andrei had had with Big Ed. It popped up again and again in her mind. Why would he ring and taunt Andrei on a day like today?

Daria had met him in the early days of their business relationship. There had always been a disconnect, and she didn't trust him entirely. Even though Big Ed wasn't a user, there were too many meth heads and loose cannons in his organisation.

She went to the bathroom and stuck her face under the cold water tap. She cupped her hands and drank greedily. Her face was a mess, all blotchy and swollen. It felt like she'd been out on the drink all night. A mild headache radiated behind her right eye, and she reached into her makeup bag and found some paracetamol. The gritty, bitter residue lingered and made her cough before she swallowed another big mouthful of water to get rid of the nasty taste.

Back in bed, she tried her best to relax and did some breathing exercises, but nothing worked. She checked the time on her phone; it was just after midnight. She scrolled the news feed on her phone for the next hour before sleep finally overtook her. There was nothing in the news about Mike yet.

When she woke at dawn after a restless sleep, she felt like she'd been through the washing machine. Her thoughts went straight to Mike, and she could feel her throat closing up, and she swallowed hard to get rid of the lump. *Mike was dead.*

The early morning light came through the window, and she stretched her back before wandering into the ensuite and fumbling for the light switch. She splashed some cold water on her face, brushed her teeth and tied her hair up. Her eyes still felt as though she had sand in them. She got dressed and rummaged in the makeup bag and found the eye drops, tilting her head back and squirting a couple of drops in each eye. Daria blinked and wiped the residue from the corner of her eye, but at least she felt marginally better. She grabbed the flat cross-body bag she'd brought with her as it held a lot. The bedroom door creaked ever so slightly as she peeked out into the hallway. Dull, thumping music came from the garage, and she knew Andrei was busy with his workout. Hopefully, he'd keep training until she was well gone.

Daria hoped his office wouldn't be locked. She crept down the deserted hallway and pressed the office door handle—to her surprise, it opened. She squeezed through, then closed it carefully.

In a corner was the gun cupboard. She knew Andrei kept the key in the top desk drawer. She hoped the sawn-off shotgun was still in there. Mike had told her about it to reassure her that they could take care of themselves when she was here last. Sadly, that wasn't the case.

Daria went behind the heavy wooden desk and pulled the middle drawer out. In the early morning light, she could just make out neatly stacked notepads, pens and various things. She was thankful for Andrei's OCD—everything in its rightful place and nothing where it shouldn't be. She couldn't see the key she needed and stuck her hand inside the drawer, feeling around the back. Her fingers brushed over a key ring, and she grabbed it, pulling it out.

Her hand trembled as she went over to the steel cabinet, trying the similar-looking keys until she found the right one and could open the cabinet. The heavy door opened as she pulled.

Ammunition cartons were stacked on the top shelf, and in the large compartment below, a selection of guns were slotted into brackets. The sawn-off shotgun was there. She grabbed the weapon—it was heavier than she'd anticipated—and a box of buck shot. In her rush, they spilt onto the floor.

A cold sweat broke out down her back as she dropped on her hands and knees, scrambling to collect them all. She had an ear in the direction of the door as she half-expected Andrei to burst through at any moment. She quickly gathered the shells and put them back into the box and into her bag. Her heart was in her throat. The last thing she wanted was for Andrei to stop her. This was something she needed to do before she chickened out. She trembled as she locked the cabinet and carefully put the keys back where she'd found them.

She didn't sense any movement in the hallway as she listened by the door before gently opening it. Her rapid breathing made her sweat even more, and she could feel the itch as her woollen shirt clung to her body. She needed fresh air and to get out of there without her brother noticing. He was like a human lie detector and would push her until she told him her plan.

Daria pressed the shotgun against her body as she hurried down the hallway. Before unlocking the front door, she remembered to press the button for the gate lock on the side of the wall. The rental car was parked nearby, and she held her breath as she pressed the key to unlock it. The faint beep echoed in between the buildings: so much noise for a supposedly quiet car. She held her breath for a few seconds, hoping Andrei hadn't heard anything over the music in the garage.

Her plan wasn't fully formed, and she acted on emotion and impulse today, which was unlike her. The pain was all-consuming; she knew that she had to do something. This was it. She wanted answers, and she would get them one way or the other. The shotgun was as much for show as for protection if things went awry.

The late model Toyota EV made no noise as she turned the key and rolled slowly down the drive and through the gate. Driving past the building site where Mike had been found, she shuddered. A police car was parked in the driveway. When this was over, she had no intention of ever returning to this place. Andrei could meet her in Auckland or Sydney in the future. The morning traffic was sparse, with only a few early commuters.

Did Mike's death have anything to do with Fanta going overboard? Andrei had told her Big Ed was his uncle. It was just their luck to piss off the local gang.

She glanced across at the sawn-off shotgun on the passenger seat.

Would she be able to use it if she had to? Kill another human being? It wasn't as if she couldn't handle firearms. The moral dilemma, however, was completely different. If it came down to life or death, there was no question. She belonged to the local gun club where she lived in Sydney and had done so for years, ever since becoming involved in South American business dealings. The question remained, though: could she aim at another human and squeeze the trigger? As she drove through to Warkworth, the traffic had increased, and she turned right at the Hill Street intersection towards Wellsford.

Another ten minutes on, she turned onto a side road to the left towards the gang headquarters. Her memory was pretty good even though it was almost a year since she'd been there. The discreet road frontage with its old gate and overgrown hedge hadn't changed, and she almost overshot it. Daria slowed the car down and crept past. She'd noticed the cameras on the gate and in various places on the property last time. As she moved forward, the road dipped, and a paddock with an old barn that bordered the gang pad came into view. She quickly pulled off the road, parking beneath an old elm to give her some cover. Daria took a deep breath to gather herself. Doubts and nerves plagued her. She didn't even have a proper plan. What on earth was she doing?

Her aim was to get in front of Big Ed. The least he could do was explain himself. There was no way she'd be able to approach from the front. No doubt they monitored the cameras. A wooden fence was topped with barbed wire that ran along the length of the paddock.

The next door neighbours wooden fence was easy to climb, and she jumped onto the soggy ground, wishing she'd worn gumboots. An old grey-flecked mare lumbered around, nibbling on grass and completely ignored her presence.

Daria crept along the fence line, carrying the shotgun. There were no cameras on this side that she could see. She peeked through a crack in the wood and saw no movement.

She'd expected there to be lots of security. But compared to the cartel, these guys were amateurs.

60

Wednesday the 12th of July

Bill had barely slept a wink last night and had been plagued with one nightmare after nightmare.

The images of yesterday's murder victim encased up to his shoulders played over and over like a bad B-grade movie. He could still smell the cement in his nostrils. He'd seen some gruesome things in his life, but he would never forget the macabre scene. It was a terrible way to go. As Rudd had said, the lime in the mixture would literally cook the victim before his airways were constricted, and if he were still alive, suffocation would soon follow.

He'd stared at the ceiling for hours before he gave up around four o'clock and went downstairs to make himself a cup of tea. Maggie and Finn didn't even notice as they continued snoozing soundly in their beds. Great guard dogs they are, he thought, shaking his head. It didn't help that Annika spoilt them rotten.

He flicked the jug on and looked in the fridge for something to eat. There was a plate with leftover beef sausages and some creamy potato gratin, so he grabbed some cutlery from the drawer. He didn't bother reheating the food. It didn't matter that it was cold because it still tasted great. Finn woke up, sniffing the air with its whiff of sausage.

"Come here then, boy," he said, holding a piece of sausage for the dog. As soon as Maggie heard Finn eating, she got up and demanded the same treatment.

"Here you go, girl."

Maggie and Finn knew better than to hang around and beg from him, so instead, they both went back onto their beds, watching Bill's every move.

The jug flicked off, and he poured the hot water over a teabag in his mug as he continued to eat. He let the teabag steep for a minute, putting a splash of milk in his mug and giving it a stir before returning to the table. Bill picked his phone up and flicked to the news on the *New Zealand Herald* app. There was an item about a person in the music industry who'd been found dead, but no details or name. Well, that was just a matter of time. Once they discovered who it was, the tabloids would pick up the story and run with it. This type of clickbait always got lots of exposure. Vultures. Bill scrolled on.

Nothing mentioned the deceased found on the building site. Give it a few days, and there would be, he thought as he read the rest of the headline news. It was five o'clock and still dark outside. He was wide awake and might as well have a shower and get to work. He grabbed a uniform shirt from the laundry and walked upstairs as quietly as he could through the bedroom and into the ensuite. The warm shower felt good on his skin, and at last, his ribs seemed a little better. As the small room misted up, he could hear Annika's voice in his mind, that he should have opened a window, or at least put the fan on. Never mind, nothing he could do about it now.

He gathered his clothes and dressed without disturbing Annika and went downstairs again. He scribbled a note to let her know he'd gone to work early and picked up the car keys from the hook. The morning air was raw and cold. There hadn't been an overnight frost, but he was sure it was damn near it. He could still see the stars in the inky sky.

There'd been a guard overnight at the building site. He didn't envy the young Warkworth constable who had the honour. He'd had to do his fair share of shit jobs early on in his own career; they all did. It was expected, but also a rite of passage.

The removal of the body would happen early this morning. Orewa had organised earth-moving equipment as they'd have to dig the entire concrete block out with Mike Fenton still encased in it—such a horrid way to go. The pathology assistants who'd be tasked with removing the concrete around the body before a proper post-mortem could take place had a major challenge ahead of them.

61

Bill decided to go past the scene in Point Wells to check on progress before he went to the station. He pulled up behind the police car parked in the driveway. The young constable, who barely looked out of his teens, hastily pulled a vape from his mouth as he saw Bill pull up.

"Constable, that's hardly a good look!"

"Um, sorry, sir. It's been a long night. I thought it wouldn't matter since no one was around."

"I don't care what you get up to in your personal time, but on duty and certainly while in uniform, you will refrain from such behaviour."

"Sorry, I didn't think," the constable said, looking at his feet. "It won't happen again."

"I should hope not, and you are damn lucky I'm not reporting your gross lack of judgement to your senior, for that matter. Anyhow, how's the night gone? Have they picked up the body yet?"

"You just missed them, sir. The digger turned up with the ESR team at around four thirty. It took a good hour to get sorted, remove the body and put into the back of the transporter. Most of it was prep work, as it always is. They had to make sure the back of the van was sterile. You know the drill," the constable said, obviously relieved to have changed the subject.

"That's good news. Thankfully, it's a brand new subdivision, and not many people live here yet. When do you go off duty?"

"Um, my shift ends at eight. Bredesen will relieve me."

"All right, so you're all sorted then?"

"Yes, sir, all good, thank you."

"I take it the scene is protected by tarps?" Bill looked up at the gloomy grey sky.

"Yes, they did all that. The forecast is for more rain."

Bill left the young constable and headed to his car, smiling to himself. He hadn't meant to sound so gruff. It was just that he couldn't stand the vape nonsense. It always got his back up when he saw young people suck on them like a bloody lollipop.

~

IT WAS six-thirty by the time he arrived at the station. He fired up his computer and checked his email.

He'd been copied in on the pathologist's report on Jett Starr. As Rudd had mentioned yesterday, the knock to the back of the head had been fatal, and the cuts on the wrist were post-mortem, hence the lack of arterial spray at the scene in Omaha. This, of course, made sense now when he could read it in black and white.

Bill knew what it meant—Orewa would also get involved in this case.

62

The morning sky lightened as she crept around the perimeter of the rural property. It was a clear, crisp morning and chillier than she was used to in Sydney. She could see her breath in front of her as she exhaled. In hindsight, she should have worn a jacket, but it was too late now. The only thing was to keep moving to stay warm. The wooden fence was fortified and too high to look over, so she continued down the back towards a pile of recently felled large logs.

She climbed up, and from her vantage point, she could see the outbuildings and some pre-fabricated barracks that had seen better days. She was surprised at the mess. There were old car wrecks, pieces of dilapidated garden furniture and a couple of rotten couches —all left to the elements. In the middle of all this was a large fire pit with some bench seats positioned around it. Why it was so messy, she couldn't understand. She surveyed the back of the property and spotted a large door in the fence. Perhaps it was worth a check to see if she could get through. She climbed down the log pile, careful not to get her bag caught on the way down, and made her way around the back. She pressed up against the fence, and as far as she could see, there were no cameras.

She took a few deep breaths and looked around before sticking her hand through the opening to undo the latch, half-expecting someone to grab it. The old warped door wouldn't budge as she pushed on it. Daria had to put her shoulder and hip into it before it would relent, the door creaking loudly as she pushed it open just enough to slip through. The overgrown section of the property was even more of a mess—it was like a graveyard for old items no longer needed. You'd think with all the money coming in, they'd make some effort, and for Christ's sake, why not take all this crap to the dump?

There were no cameras here, either. What a bunch of amateurs. The front of the property was like Fort Knox, yet anyone could walk in through the back. She suspected not many people did, though.

From where she was standing, the old barracks were twenty metres away. There were no windows on this side, and she kept low, running as fast as she could and pressing her body into the worn façade. She peeked around the corner and stopped in her tracks when she saw two large dogs—Rottweilers. Both dogs stood in the middle of the drive with their eyes and ears fixed in her direction. Their noses were in the air, sniffing the breeze. She swore under her breath; they'd picked up her scent. Her only choice was to beat a hasty retreat before these beasts were on top of her and her cover blown. She sprinted as fast as she could and reached the gate just as the dogs picked up their pace and were at her heels. Daria only just managed to get through and slammed the gate shut as the dogs threw themselves against it, their deep growls and the snapping of jaws leaving nothing to the imagination. She was annoyed with herself. Of course, they would have guard dogs patrolling the perimeter. If there were to be a next time, she would have to bring some meat and slip some sedatives in.

She hurried back around the opposite side of the paddock in case her cover was blown. It was a relief to be back at her car and she took a few deep breaths. It was only seven in the morning, and she turned the ignition on, heading for Andrei's place. The nervous energy made her hungry, and she turned into Ravish on Sharp Road, where she picked up a large flat white and a savoury mince pie. The drizzly rain had set in, and she sat in the car, eating her breakfast. She didn't even care that the crumbly pastry went everywhere. It wasn't her problem as it was a rental.

She took a large sip of the milky coffee and reflected on the morning. The excursion hadn't been a total waste of time; at least now, she had a way in.

63

Despite his best efforts to take his frustration out on the gym equipment, Andrei was still angry and slammed the weights on the floor. The rubber mat absorbed most of the impact, but he still felt the vibrations through the sole of his trainers. He put on the gloves and moved to the boxing bag, where his blows landed one hard punch after the other, ignoring the pain in his injured right hand. He imagined it was Big Ed's face as he pummelled the crap out of it.

Andrei was sure he was the asshole responsible for Mike's death. Of course, he'd never admit it, but something in Big Ed's tone yesterday had made Andrei's blood boil. What the fuck was the guy's problem? It wasn't as if Mike had deliberately lost Fanta overboard—the dumb fuck only had himself to blame.

As he vented his frustration, his arm muscles burned, and he continued to punch until he couldn't lift his hands anymore. His right hand was aching and bleeding as he pulled the gloves off. But he didn't care. The sweat poured off him, and he grabbed a towel, wrapping it around his neck. He pressed the remote on the wall to open the garage door. The fresh air helped calm his breath while he walked around to cool down. That's when he realised Daria's car was gone.

Where could she have gone at this time of the day? He closed the garage door, tossed the used towel in the laundry, wrapped his hand up and went to the guest room to check on Daria. He knocked impatiently. Andrei was in no mood for games today. He called her name before he opened the door and looked in.

Although the bed was made, there were signs it had been slept in. The question was: what was his sister doing out so early? Had she gone for a run or to a café for an early morning coffee? He closed the door and went to the kitchen, where he reached for the protein powder from a top shelf in the pantry, added two scoops to the water in the blender, and mixed it well before getting the bag of frozen berries from the freezer. He ripped the top of the bag to open it but managed to tear a large hole in the packaging, which sprayed most of the contents on the kitchen floor.

"You can't be serious!!" he shouted, slamming the remnants of the bag into the sink as his frustration levels spilt over. All he wanted was to put a fist through the pantry door. He placed his palms on the marble bench and breathed deeply. As calm slowly returned, he grabbed a banana and finished the smoothie. Crystal would call him 'hangry' as it did nothing for his mood if he was starving. Today was off the charts; he was livid. Andrei tipped the fruity drink down his throat, satisfying his worst hunger. He could only deal with one thing at a time.

Andrei then made himself a strong black coffee and walked down the hall to his office. He needed to make sure the guys were on for tonight. They couldn't afford another screw-up. Too much money was at stake. With Mike gone, he'd have to oversee the pick-up. He'd done it before, so it shouldn't be a problem. The forecast was for no swell and favourable conditions; it would be piss easy.

As he reached for the light switch and flicked it on, his eye immediately went to the chair by his desk. It was on a slightly different angle from how he usually left it. Someone had been in his office.

The hairs on the back of his neck went up. There were only two people who could have been in there.

~

Daria took the last sip of her takeaway coffee as she pulled into Point Wells. The coffee had settled her nerves after the encounter with the Rottweilers. The overwhelming relief she felt after this morning's escapade was massive. She realised how stupid she'd been, going off half-cocked. Now all she felt was fatigue. If she'd been at home in Sydney, she'd be tempted to go back to bed and sleep it off. A warm shower would have to suffice instead. She got out of the car and slammed the door shut. She locked the car, thinking it best to leave her bag with the shotgun under the seat. She hoped Andrei hadn't noticed she'd taken it from his office. Then again, how often did he open the gun locker?

She'd have to devise a plan and was certain an opportunity would present itself. The morning sun shining through the treetops in the corner of the property helped her breathe a bit better. The grief of losing Mike came in waves, the regret over what could have been, but it was never more than brief moments. The guilty parties would get what they deserved and swiftly. But first, they had another shipment drop tonight that had to be organised.

64

Crystal cleaned up the mess Andrei left behind and made her own smoothie before sitting down at the counter. She scrolled through her social media feed. Yesterday was surreal. She couldn't believe Mike was dead. She'd taken a sleeping tablet to try and get some rest. She heard footsteps behind her and turned around.

"Morning, darling. How did you sleep?" Andrei's cold expression took her by surprise.

"What's happened? Are you all right?" she asked.

"No, I'm not bloody all right, far from it actually," he said, spit spraying with every syllable. "Have you been in my office, been through my things?"

Crystal had no idea what he was talking about. She never went into his office. Why would she?

"Calm down, my love," Crystal said, reaching out to touch his arm. Andrei swatted it away like she was some sort of pest.

"You know I told you never to go in my office," he said. His voice reverberated in the kitchen, and she couldn't understand what he was on about. Andrei's face was centimetres from hers as he stood over her. She'd never seen him like this. He put his hands on her shoulders as she sat on the stool and pressed her into the seat.

"Why are you lying to me?" His fingers dug into her shoulders and neck.

"Andrei, stop. You're hurting me."

She got her arms on the inside of his, palms together, and pushed up, which made him lose his grip just as Mike had taught her.

"I haven't been in your office. What are you talking about? I've been nothing but supportive, and you treat me like this," she said, standing up and, in the process, kicking the stool over. He'd never put his hands on her before, and she was determined that this would not happen again. There was no way she'd become a domestic violence statistic. Not if she could help it.

Andrei took a step back, realising what he'd done. His face softened. "I'm sorry. I didn't mean to hurt you, Crystal."

"Don't you dare touch me!" Now it was Crystal's turn to be angry. She hadn't asked for this. How bloody dare he accuse her of snooping through his office.

"Come, let's talk about this. I'm sorry. The whole thing about Mike has made me a bit crazy."

"That's understandable, but I have always been on your side. I need some space, don't try to stop me," she said, stomping off down the hall. Crystal grabbed her jacket from the coat rack and stuck her feet in her gym shoes. On her way out, she almost collided with Daria, who was on her way in.

"Are you okay?" Daria said. She noted that Crystal's eyes were red-rimmed.

"I'm fine, but your psycho brother is not," she said as she hurried towards the gate. She wished she'd taken the car keys to one of the vehicles on the way out. Never mind, she had no idea where to go, anyway. But a walk might do her good. She'd seen the anger on Andrei's face, felt his strong grip on her shoulders, and realised just what he was capable of. She wasn't sure they had a future anymore.

The cold morning air made her throat ache as she rapidly breathed in and out, trying to calm herself. She didn't slow her pace until she reached the main road. What was she to do? Her family wasn't close, and she had no friends left to speak of. Andrei had made sure she didn't keep in touch with the few who had stuck around. She wished she'd taken her handbag with her. Her decision to leave had been a spur-of-the-moment thing; all she had was her phone—no wallet, no clothes, nothing. She had no idea where her strength had come from to push him away and stand up to him.

Crystal couldn't believe what Andrei had accused her of. In all their time together, she had never once looked through his things. She respected his privacy, even though, at times, she had wondered about all the secrecy.

She thanked her lucky stars she'd followed her gut and not agreed to bring a baby into this world. Then she'd really be trapped. She thought of Annika. Perhaps she could go and stay at her house for a bit to regroup and sort her head out.

Thank God she'd brought her phone with her. She dialled Annika's number.

65

Annika rolled over and felt Bill's side of the bed. She nuzzled into his pillow, where she could still smell his scent. She knew he had a lot to deal with at the moment—the drowning victim in Tāwharanui, then the young girl on the beach, followed by the tragic death of Jett Starr, and now the brutal killing on Andrei Bowen's building site. He'd been under pressure at work, which took a toll on his sleep. She'd heard him tossing and turning through the night. Although Orewa handled some of it, he was still the local cop, and they needed his connections and knowledge. Country policing was very different from city policing—here, it was all about relationships, and they knew it. From what she understood, it was a big part of why Orewa headquarters kept him in the loop.

Usually, nothing much happened here, and that's what she liked. Bill, too. He didn't hanker for the action as he'd done in his twenties and thirties. Annika was pleased Niko was here as it took a little of the pressure off.

The shrill noise of her phone ringing on the bedside table cut through Annika's thoughts.

"Hi, Annika. It's Crystal."

"Hi, how are you?"

"I'm not that great, actually. Are you home? If so, could I come over for a bit?"

"Of course, you can." Annika heard the noise of a car driving by. "Are you out for a walk?"

"I had to leave the house. Andrei and I had a fight."

"Are you safe?"

"I think so. I grabbed my jacket and phone. Everything else is at the house."

"Where are you?" Annika said. "Stay put and I'll come and get you."

"Thanks, I really appreciate it. I've just reached Omaha Flats Road, Point Wells end.

I'll wait here."

"I'm on my way. I won't be long."

Annika threw on a pair of jeans and a warm top before heading downstairs for the car. On her way, she woke the children.

"Make sure you're out of bed, dressed and eating breakfast by the time I'm back. I shouldn't be long. Fifteen, twenty minutes at the max." Grunts and muffled protests could be heard.

"I'm serious, guys. Otherwise, we'll be late for school," she shouted from downstairs.

They'd have to order lunch today; there was no time to make school lunches.

She stuck her feet in an old pair of trainers and ran to the car. The engine protested ever so slightly. It didn't like to be parked outside in the winter. They had no choice, though, as the garage was full of storage boxes. She turned the wipers on to clear the windscreen, and thankfully, by the time she'd reached Point Wells, it had warmed up and was less like a fridge. Annika looked for Crystal and spotted her perched on a wooden fence by the roadside. The young, normally confident woman looked shrivelled and vulnerable.

Annika pulled over and waited for Crystal to jump in.

"Are you all right?"

"I'm not sure," Crystal said, her voice betraying her. "I just walked out." "What's happened?" Annika said.

Crystal's dazed face said it all.

"I'm not sure exactly. Andrei was furious. He ranted on about someone having been in his office, messing with his stuff. I really have no idea what he was on about. I certainly didn't go in there. He's so particular and doesn't want anyone in there, not even the cleaner.

Besides, it's locked most of the time."

Annika didn't know what to say to that. She wondered what he kept in there that had to be kept secret.

"Okay, that seems like he might have overreacted a bit. Are you sure you don't want me to take you home?"

"Andrei grabbed my shoulders. He's never been physical with me before."

"Did he hit you?" Annika's blood boiled. There was nothing more cowardly than domestic abuse, and men in particular who thought this kind of behaviour was okay.

"No, no, nothing like that. He just grabbed me and held on. Perhaps I'm overreacting a little. He would never hit me."

"All right, but do you want to make a complaint? We can go to the station right now."

"If it's okay, I'd like to go home with you," Crystal said, on the verge of tears. Annika felt sorry for the young woman. She sounded so lost.

"Of course, you can. I've got a few things to get done at home and need to take the kids to school and to the bus, but if you don't mind that, it's all good." Crystal smiled. The relief on her face was obvious. "Thank you. I really appreciate it."

~

AT HOME, the twins were in the kitchen and had just finished their breakfast.

"Morning, everyone. This is my friend Crystal," Annika said as they walked in.

The girls looked up and smiled.

"Kids, we have exactly five minutes before we have to be in the car. If Katie doesn't hurry up, she'll miss the Warkworth bus," Annika said, glancing at the clock on the kitchen wall. "Gosh, guys. It's already seven forty-five. Katie's bus leaves at eight. Come on, get a wriggle on, or we'll be late."

"We're all sorted, apart from school lunches," Veronica said.

"Don't worry about it today. You can have a lunch order. I'll get some change sorted," Annika said, reaching for her wallet.

Crystal sat on one of the chairs and seemed happy to be part of the crazy morning routine.

"Do you have everything you need, girls? We have to go."

"Hang on, I need my sports gear," Katie said as she arrived downstairs, rushing to the laundry.

"Okay, Anna and Veronica. You go to the car, and here's your lunch money. Please put it in your pocket and zip it up so you don't lose it like last time," she said, looking at the twins.

"All right, Mamma, we won't," they said, giving Annika a cheeky grin.

"Make yourself at home, Crystal. I shouldn't be long."

"Don't worry about me. See you soon."

"Katie, hurry up. We have to go."

As the kids piled into the car, Annika wondered what had gone on in the house between Andrei and Crystal. Spats and arguments were a normal thing in a relationship, but theirs seemed so imbalanced. To physically grab her was a short step away from shoving her into a wall or hitting her. There was no excuse whatsoever for this kind of behaviour. And on top of that, to issue a decree that certain parts of the house were off-limits to your partner seemed stranger than anything she'd heard before. As far as her and Bill's relationship, they were equals, and if Bill told her she couldn't enter a specific space, she'd tell him to take a hike. But who knew what went on with Crystal and Andrei? Perhaps there was more to their story than met the proverbial eye.

66

Bill looked at the large wall clock. It had just gone eight o'clock. He'd squared away a heap of paperwork and was glad he'd gone into the station early. Niko would no doubt walk through the door any minute. He usually arrived straight from the gym with a big grin on his face and doused in cologne. The dappled light from the mild winter sun danced through the Venetian blinds in the office. Bill glanced outside; it looked like the forecasted rain was not imminent—they'd been wrong before.

He decided to go for a walk and locked up. The soggy leaves on the pavement stuck to his boots as he wandered down to the bakery for a coffee. Henry Long from the Surf Club waved as he passed the Four Square supermarket. He was the manager at ITM, the building supply firm across the road.

Bill wondered how the fundraiser had gone at the Surf Club and thought he must ask him next time he bumped into him on the street.

As he walked past the pharmacy, he could see Harry, the pharmacist, was about to open. Strange to think that just a couple of months ago, he and Niko had investigated a burglary that sparked a major hunt for a serial killer. The community had suffered, but he was pleased to see that security measures had been stepped up, and there were now both reinforced doors and cameras inside and outside the pharmacy. If nothing else, they would serve as a deterrent for the criminal element, who might get ideas about breaking in or ram raiding the premises. He wished other businesses would take the same precautions. Perhaps he ought to meet with the business association and get everyone on the same page. The challenge would be convincing smaller business owners to spend money on these things. Money was tight everywhere, especially in a village that depended on holidaymakers and weekenders spending money. Still, he would make a note in his diary and talk to the manager of the business association.

The bakery already had a queue out the door—regular customers who wanted to pick up fresh bread and their obligatory morning coffees. Bill exchanged a few smiles and hellos and joined the back of the line. The strong coffee smell and the freshly baked bread were a marriage made in heaven. Bill tossed up whether he should order a toasted sandwich when it was his turn or if he could hold off until lunch. He'd eaten leftovers before he left home, after all.

"Morning. How are things at the station?" Henry Long said from behind Bill.

"Morning, Henry. I've been meaning to ask you how the fundraiser went for the club."

"Oh, man. It exceeded our expectations, that's for sure. Not only did we receive a couple of large cash donations, but also time and materials kindly donated by local tradespeople, not the least that developer in Point Wells, Andrei Bowen. He's been very generous indeed. Did I hear there was a death at one of his building sites? His good mate, wasn't it?" Henry's face was animated, and he eagerly awaited any bit of juicy gossip. Henry Long was a gossip and liked to talk about other people and their business.

Bill wasn't surprised. The rumour mill worked overtime in a small community.

"You know I can't divulge anything that pertains to a current investigation, mate," Bill said, somewhat amused. Why did people always try it on, keen to extract some little snippet of information they could share with friends and neighbours to impress them?

"I thought as much," Henry said.

It was Bill's turn at the bakery counter. "Can I have a long black, please, Laura?"

"Sure thing. Anything to eat?"

Bill hesitated for a second, eyeing the delectable cabinet food.

"I'll have an almond croissant to go, please."

"No worries at all. Coming right up."

While Bill waited for his coffee, Henry ordered his. The barista was quick, and they picked up their orders and walked out together.

"So tell me about Andrei Bowen. What's the deal with this guy?" Bill asked as they headed back to work.

"I'm not really sure. I don't know the guy that well. I've only met him a few times, but his reputation precedes him. We're elated at the club to have this calibre of support to rebuild in time for summer."

"Doesn't it surprise you a bit? People being overly generous like this?" Bill said.

"Not really. We have some very influential donors in Omaha. It's nothing unusual.

The Surf Club is very important and a central hub in our beach community." "Does the construction industry pay that well?

"It's a goldmine at the moment."

"Well, I guess you're very lucky."

"We sure are. It would be even better if we could just eliminate the drugs the young people have access to. The vandals who destroyed the clubrooms were definitely on something. It's a pity they haven't been caught and been made to answer for their actions." "Just make sure you install cameras," Bill said to Henry. "That kind of measure will certainly be a massive deterrent and make anyone think twice before they break into the club again."

"That's the plan. Cameras will be installed inside and out. Don't you worry."

67

As Niko arrived at the station, the lights were on. He looked at his watch—he was late, so he raced up the steps. It was already after eight. He keyed in the code to the door and entered. Bill wasn't there, and he dumped his gym bag by his desk and stuck his head into the lunch room, but there was no sign of his colleague. He switched the computer on and went to get a coffee when the phone rang.

"Matakana police station."

"Morning, it's Phil here from the boatyard in Sandspit. I'd like to report a stolen or possibly abandoned car close to the boat ramp."

"What makes you say it's stolen or abandoned?"

"Well, first of all, it's a black Cadillac Escalade. We don't see too many of those around here. The other odd thing is that the car was unlocked, with no sign of the driver. I found the key on the ground next to the car. I've asked around, but no one knows anything about it. Apparently, it's been there since at least the day before yesterday."

"All right, can you give me the registration as well as your details, and we'll come over this morning to take a look," Niko said.

Could this be the missing car they'd been looking for? As he hung up, Niko ran the registration plate in the system and got an immediate hit. The car was registered to an Andrei Bowen in Point Wells.

"Morning," Bill said as he walked through the door.

"Morning, Sarge. We've just had a hit on the victim's car. A member of the public just reported it," Niko said, relaying the information from the man at the boatyard.

"Bingo! Let's take a look before we call Orewa. But if that's the registration, then that's the victim's car. I'll drive." Bill tipped the last of his coffee down his throat and grabbed the car keys off his desk.

"Oh, Christ," Bill said as they came to a complete stop by the pedestrian crossing just before the primary school. Both sides of the road were congested with caregivers dropping off their offspring, which made the school traffic come to a grinding halt. On both sides of the road, two young traffic monitors, wearing orange hi-vis vests, stood by the pedestrian crossing. Teachers on both sides of the road supervised them. It was obvious that the students took their role seriously. As the younger pupils saw the police car, excited cries could be heard from the children, and Niko gave them a friendly wave. He'd so enjoyed it when they'd visited the school the last time he was here. The kids had loved it. Bill put the lights on for a few seconds to excited cheers. The unscheduled stop didn't last long. Within seconds vehicles and parents were gone, and they could carry on. The traffic on Matakana Road flowed well, and within a few minutes, they turned left on Sharp Road, cutting across the valley. Niko was deep in thought as he was thinking of Laura, the constable who had tragically lost her life here a few months ago.

"It seems like a long time ago, doesn't it?" Bill said, cutting into Niko's memories.

At the end of Sharp Road, they turned hard left towards Sandspit. Where the road narrowed, an old van was speeding and veered across the centre line, which forced Bill to stand on the brakes.

"What the fuck?" he yelled as the vehicle scraped by, a gnat's whisker away from the side mirror. As expected, the van didn't stop.

"Jesus Christ. If there was somewhere I could turn around quickly, I would go after him," Bill exclaimed, his face full of anger.

"It looked like an old geezer. I've got part of the registration, so we can do a search. He'll keep. I'll run a check and track thc bastard down," Niko continued.

The road snaked around another sharp bend, and they went by the boat builders and the yacht club a little further on the left. Bill slowed down for the first speed bump and drove by the small campground on the right. Niko was surprised to see so many houses scattered on the gently sloping headland above. It looked like an idyllic place to live, and with an amazing view to boot. A row of cabins sat back from the road, and surprisingly, a couple of campervans, complete with colourful awnings out the front. Did people really live in these all year round?

Niko's thoughts took him back to his childhood summers up north and the smell of their old Campomatic, where they all slept under the canvas canopy. Those were the best memories of carefree days by deserted beaches, where they swam, fished, sat around campfires and ate the seafood they'd caught. It was all his mother and father could afford, and it reminded them of life at home in the islands. He felt a little guilty. He should go home when he next had some time off and see how his parents were.

The tide was in, and the morning sun glittered on both sides of the calm sea, lapping gently. He could imagine what a slice of paradise this was in the summer.

"So, is this reclaimed land?" Niko asked as they drove onto the long coastal strip consisting of the dual carriageway, a small reserve and a car park on the left.

"No, mate. This is a sandbar, hence the name Sandspit. It's all natural. The seawall has been reinforced to stop erosion. The boat ramp is just past the car park. I've launched the old man's fizz boat there more times than I can remember."

"You should take me out sometimes. It would be great to get a feed of fresh snapper, Sarge."

"Perhaps, if the conditions stay fine."

They drove by the ticket office, which by the looks of the large sign on the door, opened at nine-thirty. The café opposite was equally quiet. Maybe it wasn't even open in the off-season. The inconspicuous black Escalade was parked furthest away at the end of the pier.

A beaten-up Hilux drove up and parked parallel to their patrol car opposite the Escalade. A grey-haired man with a full beard jumped out and made Niko think of Santa, although he didn't have a generous figure. Rather, he was on the slim side, which clashed with his facial hair appearance.

"Hi, fellas. I'm Phil. I appreciate that you've come out to have a look. I work at the boatyard a little further up the harbour. In fact, if it hadn't been for my morning walk, I don't think I would have noticed the car," he said.

"Thanks for calling us," Bill said, introducing himself and Niko.

"Being winter, it's not very busy and it's not like it's an old crappy Mazda or something," he continued, laughing nervously. "Oh, and as I mentioned, here's the key I found next to the car."

He handed Niko a bright blue dog poop bag, the key a dark geometrical shape against the opaque plastic.

"I made sure I didn't touch it and contaminate things, just in case it's got to do with something untoward. I hope the owner hasn't gone and drowned himself."

"Let's hope that's not the case," Bill said, looking down at his notebook, giving Niko a nod. This was definitely the victim's car.

"I locked it, as I thought it might be the best. Hope that's okay."

"You did great. Thank you for being observant," Bill said. "We appreciate your help."

"Well, that's good enough for me," Phil said, obviously pleased to have been of assistance.

Bill went for a closer look, Niko ushered the man away to the nearest bench. "You did the right thing calling us. Thank you again."

68

Who knew how long the car would have been undiscovered without the public being alert?

It was great that Phil had the foresight not to touch the key. However, it remained to be seen if Rudd would have a conniption as it appeared the dog waste bag had a bit of condensation in it. He'd undone the double knot and let some air in. Bill pushed the button to test if the batteries still worked, opening the car.

Bill pulled a new pair of gloves from his jacket pocket and opened the driver's side. The interior of the car was incredibly tidy—no empty takeaway coffee cups in the console or takeaway bags on the inside of the door. It looked like it had just been valeted; the panels had a dark sheen, and there was a faint floral fragrance. It was obvious that Mike had been lured to his death, and he had more than likely not been attacked inside the car. Forensics would determine that for sure. With the lack of blood stains and the appearance of the pristine looking car, his gut told him it would come up clean. But stranger things had happened.

He closed the door and dialled Orewa.

"Granger here. I need you to send the SOCOs up to Sandspit. We've located the victim's car, the one that was buried in cement. Yes, that's correct. All right, we'll remain at the scene and see the team soon."

Niko had taken Phil's statement, and the man had jumped back into his Hilux and returned to work.

"Nice guy," Niko said. "Helpful to have people do the right thing for a change." "Did he mention anything else?" Bill asked.

"Only that he's noticed regular visits by gang members on motorbikes. He often works late. The boat builder is near the main road by the water. The roar of the engines can be heard as they drive by. He reckons the rumours are that drug deals go down here in the evenings."

"Yes, no surprise there. We've all heard those rumours. It's pretty much abandoned here after dark. The ferry and the water taxi don't work late, either. So no one's around. An ideal location for drug deals," Bill said. "All right, I've spoken to Orewa. They are sending their guys up. Let's cordon off the area before it gets trampled by more people. Why don't you check at the ticket office when the next ferry is due?"

"Sure thing. I think I saw a woman arrive just before," Niko said, wandering off.

As it was a clear day, a couple of fishermen arrived at the ramp and were in the process of launching their boats on the incoming tide. According to Google, it was almost high water. Bill got the tape out of the boot and cordoned off the immediate area.

Niko returned a few minutes later, carrying two mugs of steaming hot coffee.

"I see you charmed the lady at the ticket counter," Bill said, smiling. It never failed, the ladies swooned over Niko's olive skin and handsome features wherever they went.

"I guess. Either that or she felt sorry for us," Niko laughed, handing Bill the ceramic mug.

"The early ferry to Kawau Island departs at eight every morning. The next one is at ten-thirty and is the mail run."

"All right. We've got some time to get sorted, although I doubt many people will be departing," Bill said. "Wonder why the ticket office wasn't open for the eight o'clock departure?"

"Apparently, Lana's alarm didn't go off, and she overslept," Niko said.

"Lana, is it?" Bill teased. Niko looked at him, confused.

"Just let her down gently if she asks you out, eh, mate?" Bill said, shaking his head.

"I wouldn't dream of it, Sarge, but I can't help it if the ladies like my impeccable manners," he said and winked.

"If I had a guess, I think it's probably more than just your manners. Anyway, let's get sorted here before Orewa turns up and tears us a new one for botching the scene."

69

Andrei was still angry that Crystal had walked out. Perhaps he'd been too hasty to judge and accuse her of snooping in his office. As far as he knew, she'd never been through his stuff before. He'd even left things out to see if she'd been curious to glance at them. But she had never shown any interest in his business dealings. Maybe it was Daria?

He was sure Crystal would be back once she'd cooled off.

He knew she'd been very fond of Mike, and his death had shocked them all. He would deal with her, but first, he'd need to sort out the logistics for tonight's pick-up. He checked to see if Crystal had texted him—nothing. He was careful with his phone and only used it for legit business.

As Andrei returned to his office, picked up a new burner from the bottom drawer, and dialled the crew.

"Hi, are you all set for tonight?"

"Yes, mate. The lad and I are, but we really need another pair of hands. I'm at the helm, but we need at least one more crew to do the pick-up. Can you spare someone?"

"Leave it with me. I'll sort it out. Usual time?" Andrei said, wracking his brain as to whom he could rope in to help. It was probably doable as they were, but it would be a lot better with an extra crew member.

"Yeah, no worries. Who will be there to collect the goods?"

"I'll be there this time."

"All right, that's good to know."

He heard the front door open and went to see if it was Crystal. His body filled with warmth and anticipation as he walked towards the hallway. He would apologise and make it up to her because he didn't want to lose her. But it wasn't Crystal returning home.

"Hi, Mr Bowen. I'm sorry, I knocked, but I don't think anyone heard me," Zac said.

"All right, but what are you doing here today, Zac?" Andrei couldn't be bothered with the annoying kid today.

"Um, you said to come back on the first fine day to mow the lawns," Zac said, gesturing outside to the clear sky.

"So I did. The ride-on mover is in the garage. Make sure you clean the tyres before you put it back in there. I don't want wet grass all over the floor." "No worries," he said cheerily. "I'll do my best."

The boy annoyed him more than usual. He seemed like a good worker, but the whole boy scout act wore thin, especially today.

Daria sauntered in from the kitchen, finishing off a piece of toast.

"Do you mind? I'd appreciate it if you didn't drop crumbs everywhere. For Christ's sake, get a plate!"

"Don't worry. I'll bring the vacuum out and make sure I haven't left anything on your precious floors."

Andrei felt like slapping her. She was the only woman, apart from his mother, who could speak to him like that. "Another thing, did you go into my office earlier?"

"Yep, I was using your desk to get some work done on my laptop. Is that a problem?" She crossed her arms in front of her chest, looking at him with annoyance.

Andrei evaluated her mood and decided against picking a fight. "Where were you this morning anyway?"

"Not that it's any of your business, but I thought I'd take a drive to suss the gang's headquarters out," she said defiantly.

"What the hell did you do that for?"

"I just wanted to check it out," she said, shrugging her shoulders.

One thing was for sure, she might be small in stature, but she had a lot of guts. Those guys were hard-core and unpredictable, to say the very least. If there was something they disliked, it was someone who stuck their nose into their business.

"What a shithole it was. It was even more run down than I remember. I suppose the mud marsh, decrepit buildings and unkempt, overgrown surroundings didn't help. Not to mention the two menacing guard dogs."

"Did you enter the compound?"

"I had a quick peek around the back. The gate wasn't very secure."

"You moron. There are cameras everywhere. They would have seen you. Why would you do something so fucking stupid?" Andrei had to clench his fists to stop himself from punching something. He was furious. "You have risked our whole distribution network by going off half-cocked. What the fuck were you thinking, Daria!"

"I think you've done a sterling job fucking the business up on your own before I arrived. I just wanted to have a chat with Big Ed; get some answers regarding Mike's death. I know he had something to do with it."

"Dear God, did you really think you could waltz into their sanctum and get them to admit that they'd offed Mike? Jesus, you are so naïve sometimes. I've got enough to deal with today without having Big Ed and his cronies breathing down my neck. We're a man short on tonight's pick-up at sea."

"If you don't want to get your hands dirty, I'll go," Daria said.

"No way in fucking hell. Mum would never forgive me if we lost you overboard. I'd planned to ask Big Ed if he could spare a man, but I guess that's off the table after your stunt this morning. I'd rather go myself."

"Suit yourself, but the offer is there."

A loud screech was heard from the garage. Andrei immediately knew what had happened and ran the few steps towards the door. It better not be the car. Daria followed closely behind.

"What the fuck, man!"

Zac's face was pale as he straddled the ride-on mower he'd just reversed into the car.

A long scratch covered the length of the two passenger door panels of Andrei's beloved Maserati.

"I'm so sorry," the young man stammered, his face now flushed with fear and embarrassment as the realisation of what he'd done set in. "Jesus, I didn't mean to reverse into your car, Mr. Bowen. The gears stuck, and I flung it in reverse by mistake. I'll pay it off.

Just don't tell my parents. They'll go mental."

Andrei took a deep breath. The damage on the two panels would require extensive work; the scratches were dented and deep. His blood boiled. How the fuck could the guy be so incompetent?

"I'm really sorry. Tell me what I can do to make it up to you. I'll work for free for as long as it takes to pay the damages off," Zac said, downcast.

Daria elbowed her brother and whispered, "Didn't you say you needed someone to crew tonight?"

"Zac, the damage will be thousands of dollars. The whole side has to be redone."

"I'll do anything to make it up to you, Mr Bowen."

"Very well, it's going to take a while to pay off, but I guess if you are okay with working it off, you could start tonight. I've got a job for you."

70

Zac felt like his world had imploded. The enormity of what he'd done sunk in as he climbed into his beaten-up Mazda, slamming the door.

On top of his student loan, he was now indebted to Andrei Bowen. The man scared him. After all, there were rumours. His mate Ant worked in the industry, and he'd alluded to Andrei being a real hard ass and that he was involved in something dodgy. He should have listened to him. Now he'd have to spend the foreseeable future doing God knows what to make good on the damage he'd done to the Maserati. Couldn't it have been an old Ford or something parked in the garage that would cost a fraction to have repaired?

He put his head in his hands—the fury of how he could have been so careless permeated every cell in his body.

Andrei had given him a prepaid phone, a burner like they used in the movies, for Christ's sake. The strict instructions were that he was only to receive messages and the odd call on it, not to use it for anything else. What the fuck had he gotten himself into? They owned his ass now. He could never tell his parents, especially his father, who'd have a fit. Bill might be a cop, but Zac didn't want his father to be in danger, thanks to his stupidity with the ride-on. He'd have to handlc this on his own.

Zac drove out onto Omaha Flats Road. It had been a shitty start to the day. He was on a mid-year semester break from university, and the last thing he wanted to do was study. He had an assessment due as soon as the term started, which meant he had to get it done. He could feel the hangover from last night. They'd had way too much to drink, and Luke had brought a bag of rollies out. For the first time in his life, he felt like he belonged. He was having fun with the guys and not focusing only on his studies. It was the holidays, for fuck's sake. He deserved to kick back a bit. His stomach rumbled; he needed to eat something.

There was no way he could face going home. His mum had an inbuilt radar and would know immediately that something was up. So, he drove into Matakana and found a park on the side of the road across from the Tramcar Diner, next to the cinema. As he crossed the road and walked in, he saw the food in the glass cabinet.

"Can I have a ham and cheese panini, please? And some shoe-string fries."

The man behind the counter smiled and handed the docket to the woman next to the fat fryer. He picked up a glass and filled it from the water jug on the side counter and chose a seat in the far corner to sit down. The food arrived quickly, and he ate it fast, taking the odd sip of water between swallows. By the time he'd finished, not only did he feel better, but he'd decided to go into the Warkworth Library and sit there for the afternoon. At least the homework would distract him instead of worrying about what would happen tonight. All he knew was that he'd have to keep the phone on and wait for instructions sometime late afternoon.

71

When Annika returned home, Crystal was curled up on the couch with one of the quilts and was thumbing through the book on the coffee table.

"I hope you don't mind me reading this?"

"Don't be silly. I've just finished it. You can borrow it if you like."

"I think I've seen the cover in the village bookstore. It seems familiar."

"You probably have. Vivianne Harper is a local author and a good friend of mine.

We're in the same book club."

"Can anyone join?"

"Of course. We're a friendly bunch of ladies," Annika said, smiling. "It's my friend Deb's birthday, and we're all catching up for lunch today. You're welcome to come along. It will be great for you to meet them."

"I wouldn't want to intrude on your friend's birthday."

"Don't be silly. You're very welcome, and to be honest, we do a lot more than just read books," Annika said. "And there's generally some very tasty food and the odd glass of wine involved. Oh, and laughs are compulsory."

Crystal relaxed. Annika could see that her seemingly idyllic lifestyle might not be all it was cracked up to be. The poor woman was lonely and needed some friends.

"Erm, do you think we could swing by home so I could get out of these training clothes on the way?"

"Sure thing. I hear you. What about Andrei? Won't he be there?

"Not at this time of the day. He'll be at work."

IT WAS ALMOST LUNCH, and the book club members were meeting at The Farmers Daughter on Omaha Flats Road. Annika and Crystal drove to Point Wells, which was on the way. Even though she had more than enough work to do in the studio, Annika recognised her friend needed a friendly ear, and she was a good listener. It had always been one of her strong traits and why she'd loved teaching so much. She sensed Crystal tensing up as they drove through the new subdivision.

"It'll be all right. Don't worry. I'm sure Andrei feels like a fool for overreacting as he did."

"Hmm, I'm not too sure about that," Crystal said as they turned into the street and caught sight of the house. She picked at a hangnail, obviously bracing herself for the interaction.

They pulled up outside the garage, and Annika watched as Crystal took a deep breath to steady herself.

"Do you want me to come in with you?"

"No, it's all right." She could see that Andrei's car wasn't there. "He's usually well gone by this time of the day."

"Just text me if you need me to come in."

"Thanks. Give me five minutes to throw some decent clothes on."

"Sure, there's no rush."

Crystal got out of the car. Annika could see her pin in the security code on the keypad at the front door. Marvels never cease, but then again, this was a smart house, so why should she be surprised? Heck, they still had one of the old-fashioned large keys for their old front door. It wasn't the most secure lock, but she never felt unsafe.

The first time at Crystal and Andrei's house, she'd been a bit overwhelmed and had not really taken in the surroundings. The next time was the other night, but it had been dark. So, this time she could afford to take in the large compound. The house was beautiful, but she hadn't really noticed the secondary dwelling, which mirrored the main house on a smaller scale. Everything was well thought through, and the grounds would be stunning once finished. The lawn looked like it had been mowed recently; Zac must have just been.

She worried about him. He was still at university and there were so many distractions. For him to work was a good thing as it would teach him responsibilities. As far as she knew, no permanent girlfriend was on the scene, but she was sure there had been opportunities. Lately, he'd been a little quiet. She worried about his mental health because he often put too much pressure on himself, which wasn't good. Then again, becoming a vet was no walk in the park, either. Perhaps next year, he could get a part-time job at the vets in Warkworth and gain some real work experience in his chosen field.

A few minutes later, Crystal came out. Her long hair was tied up in a ponytail. The dark slim-fit jeans and pink jumper made her look like herself again.

Annika felt every bit her age as her merino wool top hugged across her slightly podgy tummy.

"Hope I didn't keep you waiting too long. I tried to hurry. I also wrote a note to say that I was with you and that I'd be home later."

"That's probably a good thing. I'm sure everything will be fine when you see him then."

"I hope so, too."

~

THE GRAVEL CAR park outside the café was full. They'd stopped at a road stall on the way, and Crystal had bought a beautiful bunch of flowers. She said she'd feel better if she brought something along.

The beautiful spot just before the causeway to Omaha was always popular, and Annika was glad they'd booked a table in advance.

"Are you sure it's okay if I come along?" Crystal said.

"Of course, they'll be thrilled to meet you." Annika had already put a message on their group chat telling the book club ladies that Crystal would be joining them. Everyone replied that it was absolutely fine.

Crystal gave Annika a worried smile as they entered the café. The five women were seated at the back by the window, with two tables pushed together, and were already engaged in a lively conversation cut through by laughter. The atmosphere in the small café was welcoming, with the unusual set-up of the kitchen being in the dining area, making it an intimate dining experience.

"Happy birthday, Deb!" Annika said, handing over her smartly wrapped gift. "Ladies, this is Crystal. She's a good friend of mine."

"Happy birthday, and thank you for letting me join you today," Crystal said, handing the flowers to Deb as she and Annika sat down.

"So lovely to meet you, and thank you all for the beautiful gifts," Deb said, smiling widely. The noise level in the room was already high, and the café's atmosphere enveloped them like a big hug. After the initial introductions, it wasn't long before Crystal was one of them.

"Let's get some food ordered. I'm starving," Vivianne said, grabbing one of the menus.

"I'll have the beef brisket with the gnocchi and the courgettes," Annika said.

"That's what I had last week. It was delicious!" Annie said. "I'll go for the salmon with whipped feta on sourdough today."

"The Abundance bowl with mushrooms and feta looks amazing," Crystal said, reaching for a refill of the bubbles that had been opened in celebration. Annika was pleased to see Crystal start to relax. She deserved to have a pleasant time.

"I'm so sorry I'm late, girls," Lexi said, rushing in the door and giving Deb a big hug. "Happy birthday. I couldn't leave until we'd finished pouring the cheese moulds. Anyway, what have I missed?" Lexi laughed, obviously pleased to be joining the ladies.

Annika introduced Crystal, and the conversation flowed along with the wine, especially for those who weren't driving. Annika had one glass, as did Deb since she had to drive home as well. Girlfriends are the best, Annika thought.

"I'm glad I walked here," Vivianne said, pouring her third glass of rosé. The table erupted in laughter.

As the food arrived, the door flung open, and Andrei strode in. When Crystal saw him, her smile vanished, and she crumpled in front of their eyes. He waved and made a beeline for their table; his charm switched on as he reached them.

"Ladies, sorry to intrude. I just need a word with Crystal for a moment, if that's okay."

Crystal followed him outside as the ladies watched them both silently.

"That guy gives me the creeps. Did you see the look in his eyes when he first walked in? And what was that plastered-on fake smile as he arrived?" Annie said, not pulling any punches.

Annika could see them through the café window. Andrei flung his arms around as he talked to Crystal, who took a step back. They were having words, but Annika was prepared to intervene should she have to. She could handle conflict.

"He seems a bit controlling to check up on her like this," Vivianne remarked.

"We really have no idea what's going on. Let's cut the guy some slack," Tyra said. She was the eternal peacemaker.

"Stop it, guys. Here she comes. Let's not make her feel any more awkward than she already does," Annika said.

Crystal tried her best to put on a brave face, but Annika could tell she was rattled and a little embarrassed. The conversation returned, and they enjoyed their food, but the atmosphere had taken a dent.

As they settled the account and said their goodbyes, Vivianne pulled Annika aside. "I'm sure it's nothing serious. I just wanted to let you know that I saw Zac with some mates in Omaha last night. It was late. I had Bramble out for a late-night toilet break. They were on the street where I live."

Annika's stomach knotted as the realisation of something she didn't want to know came to light.

"I don't know how to say this, but all of them were quite drunk, which on its own is not so bad when it comes to young people. However, they knocked a few letterboxes over and behaved, well, not with the best of manners. I could smell the smoke from a joint, and at least one of them urinated in the street."

Annika was speechless. She couldn't believe what she was being told.

"I think they were the same lads I saw on the weekend, the night of Jett Starr's party, but, of course, I didn't know Zac was one of them until I met him on Monday night at your place," Vivianne said.

"Erm, I don't know what to say. I'm deeply embarrassed. What on earth was he thinking? Are you sure it was Zac?"

"I am. One of the lads thought it was hilarious and even said something about Zac being the son of the local cop."

Annika felt like the ground was about to open up. "Thanks for letting me know. I really appreciate it. What the hell is he playing at, for goodness' sake? Bill will hit the roof, but we'll deal with it."

"I'm so sorry to have to tell you this, but I thought you needed to know," she said, her whispery voice competing with the jingling silver charm bracelet on her wrist.

Annika's shock turned to anger. That little shit. She knew something was awry with Zac, but never in her wildest dreams would she have thought he'd be involved in the destruction of property. What was he thinking? Just wait until she sees him later.

Annika was upset as she left the café with Crystal. "Do you want me to take you home, or how do you feel? By the way, how did Andrei know where to find us?"

"Oh, I think he checked 'Find My iPhone' and figured it out. He's done it before," she said, without a hint of it being anything out of the ordinary.

"Everything all right?" Annika couldn't believe he had checked up on Crystal. They certainly had an unconventional relationship. She'd be so angry if Bill spied on her and kept tabs on her exact movements.

"Everything is fine. He apologised to me, and yes, if you would please drop me at home, that would be awesome."

Annika was secretly relieved. She and Bill needed to have a serious talk with Zac tonight. They needed to find out what the hell was going on with him. One thing was for sure, this kind of destructive behaviour was more than just boys having fun. The last thing he needed was to throw away his education. It was hard enough to keep your place at university without this carry-on. She didn't mind if he had fun with his friends, but to smoke weed and vandalise property was beyond what was acceptable.

72

Finn and Maggie turned themselves inside out with joy as Annika walked through the front door.

"All right, you two. Settle down."

Maggie voiced her displeasure and grumbled at being left at home for the afternoon. Annika's mind was still on the fact that her son had turned into someone she did not recognise. Where had they gone wrong as parents? Had they been too strict on him, expected too much? Was he buckling under the pressure of university?

She sat on the kitchen chair, and Finn, who was always needy, decided to sit on her foot. Annika absentmindedly ran her fingers through his curly coat as her thoughts wandered. The rather strange encounter with Andrei at the café played on her mind as well.

Even though Crystal had said he was contrite, Annika was not convinced she'd been completely truthful. She'd seen this pattern before—a female partner making excuses and normalising this kind of behaviour. Her worst nightmare was for the girls to end up in a narcissistic and abusive situation as adults. Hopefully, she and Bill had done enough to model a positive relationship.

She glanced at the time. It was nearly three, and the twins would be finished for the day at school. The arrangement was that they would wait until Katie got there by bus. Zac had promised to pick them up today. There wasn't enough time to go out to the studio, as she needed a few hours to get a decent amount of painting done. The day was written off. On the other hand, she'd had a lovely time seeing the book club girls and celebrating Deb's birthday.

Her phone bleeped in her pocket; it was a text message from Zac.

Sorry, I'm stuck at uni. Are you or Dad able to pick the girls up?

Annika quickly replied.

No worries. I'll get them. Will you be home for dinner? Love, Mamma.

She felt an enormous amount of guilt as she and Bill had thought they'd been lucky not to have Zac rebel when he was younger. Rebelling? Was that what he was doing now?

She still had half an hour until Katie's bus would get in, which meant there was time to pop by the Four Square and pick up a couple of things for dinner.

"Sorry, guys. I have to go and pick up the girls," she said, grabbing her jacket and car keys. Finn was not bothered, but Maggie turned her back to Annika and got into her bed to sulk.

Annika's mind was all over the place. She worried about Crystal and wondered how everything had gone once she got back home. Her mind wandered to what Vivianne had said about Zac. If this was indeed true, what on earth was he thinking? She slammed the front door, stomped down the wooden steps, and got into her car. The guilt and sadness were turning to anger. He should know better for Christ's sake. It wasn't like he was still in his mid-teens; on top of that, he was the local policeman's son. How had she been so arrogant to think they'd had a lucky escape with Zac? Everyone she knew had issues with their teenagers. She remembered Lexi's son, Gabe, who got into trouble last year and was on the verge of suspension from high school. Raising teenagers was not easy; no wonder she felt anxious.

73

It was after five, and the temperature had started to drop. There was no cloud cover, and it would be a cold night. Bill looked forward to getting home and spending time with the family. The twins still liked their parents' company, but Katie and Zac generally hung out in their rooms. Nevertheless, he liked to have them under the one roof as long as it was possible. Zac had talked about a move to Auckland for university, as the commute was a bit of a drag. Bill had sent Niko home an hour ago and looked forward to following suit shortly.

Bill was in the back room when he heard the groan of the wooden steps and then the creak of the front door opening.

He thought Niko might have forgotten something and popped his head around the corner when he saw Henry Long from the Surf Club walk through the door.

"Hi, Bill. I just wondered if you had a minute?"

"Sure, mate. Come in." Bill gestured for Henry to take a seat by his desk.

"Still no leads in the vandalism of the clubrooms?"

"No, and to be honest, I don't think we'll ever find out who did it and why. The most likely scenario is still the bored teens one. There's not much we can do without cameras."

"I hear you," Henry said, "and to prevent this kind of thing from happening again, we've mounted cameras inside and out. Those and the alarm are linked and monitored by a local firm. Hopefully, the warning signs will be enough of a deterrent."

"It will certainly help," Bill said, impressed with the swift action.

"Well, I won't take up any more of your time," Henry said as he walked towards the door and opened it. "I suppose it's knock-off soon?"

"Yes, mate, it's that time of the day," Bill said and locked the door behind the man as he left.

Bill lingered, watching Henry walk away. Why did he feel that the man had come in to tell him something? Something that wasn't mere chit-chat about the clubrooms.

74

The tension in the room could be cut with a knife. Crystal had been unusually quiet since she'd arrived home. Perhaps she should have stayed at Annika's. She hated it when Andrei sulked. They'd ordered pizza from the quaint little place on Omaha Flats Road as Crystal hadn't been organised for dinner nor in the mood to cook, so takeaways it was.

Daria seemed preoccupied as she folded her slice of pizza in half and shoved it in her mouth, biting a large piece off.

Crystal cut her slices with a knife and fork and enjoyed the cooked-to-perfection base smothered in home-cooked tomato sauce, mushrooms, and just the right amount of basil and mozzarella.

"I need you to come with Daria and me tonight. I'm not leaving you here on your own after what happened to Mike," Andrei said between mouthfuls.

Crystal was about to protest but decided against it when she looked at Andrei. "Where are we going?"

"I have some business to conduct over at the house in Ti Point. It shouldn't take long. Perhaps bring a book to read or something while you wait for me," he said, this time with a bit more warmth.

She thought he was exaggerating—why on earth would she not

be safe here at home? They had a state-of-the-art alarm system, including panic buttons. Despite this, she thought it best to do what he wanted to keep the peace.

They still owned the house at Ti Point. That's where they lived while their current house was being built. The Ti Point house was a bit dated, but she loved the private beach access, and many times they'd launch their Sealegs boat from there. Because it was an amphibian boat, it could be driven from the boat-shed down the small farm track to the sandy beach at the bottom of the property. She'd loved that property; sure, it was much older than this house, but you couldn't beat the location.

"I don't mind, but if you think I should come along, I'll do that."

"Good, that's settled then," he said, looking at her for a second. Then, a quick smile flashed past his lips. "We'll leave at eight. Make sure you bring something warm to put on, as it will take a little while to heat the house."

Crystal remembered how draughty the old house had been last winter and the rattling heat pumps, which weren't the most efficient.

They finished dinner, and the siblings disappeared into Andrei's office, leaving Crystal to clear up. Not that she minded: there were no pots and pans, just plates and cutlery to go into the dishwasher.

Crystal checked her phone for the time—it was still early. She lingered in the lounge and perused the bookcase, finding a book she could bring along. Her to-be-read pile was impressive, and it would be lovely to have an evening with her nose in a book.

Slight apprehension set in. Why was Andrei so adamant she had to go with them? And why would she not be safe in their house? Surely she would be safe in her own home. And if not, what was the threat to Andrei and, ultimately, to her? Should she be worried?

Anxiety crept from the pit of her stomach and squeezed her chest. The acid richness of the pizza's tomato sauce rose in her mouth.

75

You'll be picked up at Leigh General Store at 6:00 p.m. Don't be late. The text message came through on the burner phone just before five—Zac had an hour to get there. The drive to Leigh was twenty-five minutes at the most.

The library was about to close for the day, and he packed up his laptop and books. Ideally, he'd have preferred to drop off his computer at home, but if he did, his parents would ask questions he didn't want to answer. Not that he could answer much. The whole burner phone seemed a bit much. He had no idea what he would be asked to do tonight, and his imagination was in overdrive. It sounded dodgy. Hopefully, though, it was manual labour and not anything illegal.

The librarians tidied up and said goodbye to the visitors while he hurried up to get out of the building. Perhaps he ought to eat something. It had been hours since he'd had the panini, and he was hungry. Who knew if he would get a chance to eat?

He turned left on Roberts Corner and headed up the hill past the supermarket and the town hall and continued until he reached the main road out of town. He turned right and headed for The Grange to pick up a burger from McDonald's. The drive-through wasn't busy;

it was well after the high school kids had finished and too early for dinner. He ordered a Big Mac, large fries and a strawberry thick shake. That would do him until he got home, at God knew what time. He ate as he drove back on the main road to the Hill Street intersection and turned right on the green arrow towards Leigh. The fast food, combined with his nerves, made him feel a bit sick, although, to be fair, he was probably apprehensive, driving into the unknown.

Who was he meeting at the pick-up in Leigh? Where would they take him, and what did Andrei want him to do? He finished the burger and wasn't sure if he felt better. The strawberry thick shake tasted great but made his stomach feel like a concrete mixer going round and round. Perhaps it hadn't been the wisest choice. He might have to use the bathroom when he got there. Surely there would be a bog there?

He drove through Matakana, past their house, and a feeling of dread set in. What had he gotten himself into?

Zac pulled up outside the Leigh General Store and parked a little further up between the shop and the Bar and Eatery. He was early, it wasn't quite six, and he waited in the car, where he observed a few of the locals heading to the pub for an after-work pint. The primary school was opposite, and he saw a couple of boys on the newly installed skatepark. Apart from that, it was quiet.

As the time drew closer to the pick-up, he became very nervous. He glanced at his phone for the hundredth time—seven minutes to go. Did he have enough time to go to the loo? His stomach cramped and did somersaults. Whoever was meeting him here hadn't turned up yet, so he decided there was enough time to sneak into the pub and use the bathroom. He got out of the car, locked it and sprinted into the pub. The friendly woman by the bar said hello, and he pointed to the bathroom door. To his relief, she smiled and nodded.

Another wave of panic washed over him as he sat on the cold toilet seat. Perhaps there was still time to ring his dad. Bill wouldn't be thrilled to hear about the damage to the car, but he'd understand. Zac knew that whatever he'd been roped into was not ideal. He washed his hands and splashed some cold water on his face—not that it really improved how he felt.

As he opened the bathroom door, the woman was nowhere to be seen, and he made a beeline for the main doors. The cold air on his face made him feel better. To the right, just behind his car, was an old light blue Ford Sedan. Two men sat in the front. Zac took a deep breath.

It was time.

76

"Are you Zac?" a middle-aged man said as he stepped out of the Ford. His hair was grey, and he reminded Zac of the American actor Sam Elliott, complete with the moustache.

"Um, yes, that's me," Zac answered, unsure of what to do next.

"Hop in. We need to get going."

Zac did as he was told, slid into the back seat, and rummaged for the seatbelt.

"It's broken, mate. Don't worry about it. We're not going far. No cops around here at this time of the day," the man said and chortled.

"I'm Mazza and this is Peter. You don't have any warmer clothes with you?

"Nah, sorry. I didn't know I needed to bring any," Zac said, looking down at his washed-out jeans, sweatshirt and thin parka. "What are we doing anyway? What kind of work is it?"

"You should be all right. There might be a waterproof jacket in the boot if you need it; up to you. Anyway, this is the easiest money you'll earn for a while, but of course, we have to do some graft first."

Zac didn't ask any more questions. It was obvious the information would be given on a need-to-know basis. At least he would be able to start paying off his debt.

"You'll be all right, mate," Mazza said, glancing in the rear-view mirror.

Did he look that worried? His face must have betrayed what he was thinking. The more he thought about it, the more he needed the toilet again. The younger man in the front passenger seat looked familiar. He'd said nothing and Zac glanced at his profile. They looked about the same age, and he couldn't help but stare at his large hook nose. Then it dawned on him; he remembered the guy from high school. They had called him Chook, and he was a few years younger than Zac. If Chook had recognised him, he certainly hadn't let on.

They turned into Ti Point. Zac hadn't been there for a long time. The winding road on the peninsula took them past The Reptile Park to a property on the southern side. As they came up the hill, Zac could see the lights of Omaha. It was a clear night. He didn't know if the star-filled sky was a blessing or would make the situation worse.

They drove by the main dwelling: a dated brick and tile house that looked glum. Either no one was home, or it was uninhabited. The headlights illuminated the overgrown gardens, and everything looked a bit sad. The driveway narrowed, and the lights on the old Ford weren't great. A shed appeared ahead of them. The wooden exterior was in desperate need of a lick of paint. The large double doors had dropped and sagged in the middle, which created a diagonal gap at the top and left whatever was inside open to the elements.

Mazza parked the car and left the headlights on. The large chain reflected, and he could see a padlock draped in front of the barn doors.

Chook got out and fumbled with a bunch of keys until he found the one he needed. The chain clanked to the ground, and he opened the creaking doors to switch the light on. In the dim light, Zac could just make out a hull of some sort. As the switch was flicked, the shed's interior was bathed in light from the old fluorescent bulbs.

Mazza got out of the driver's seat, which prompted Zac to follow suit. His thoughts were a mile a minute. What were they doing here?

"You, grab the life jackets out of the boot," Steve said as he turned around.

"Okay," Zac said and popped the boot.

The cramped boot was full of tools and equipment, and he had to move some of it to one side to find the orange life vest. If they were going out in a boat at this time of night, he felt better knowing he could wear one, but still, Zac's stomach was cramped.

"Sorry, is there a toilet I could use?"

"Nah, mate. You can go behind the shed, or you'll have to hold it," Chook said, grinning.

"Do you have any experience on boats?" "Not a lot," Zac said.

"You'll be right, mate. Just listen and do exactly what I tell you to do." Zac nodded.

"There's some loo paper in the boot if you need to go. Just make it quick."

He didn't need to be asked twice and ducked into the bushes using his phone flashlight to see where he was going. He found a spot, and for a moment, he thought he could make a run for it. He weighed up the pros and cons and the wrath he'd most likely suffer from Andrei if he took off. It wasn't worth it, so he finished up and returned to the barn. It wouldn't be worth the risk for him or the repercussion on his family.

"Okay, mate. We really need to make tracks," Mazza said as Zac came around the corner.

"Yeah, no worries."

They'd opened the shed's seaward doors and started up the engine of the Sealegs boat.

"I've seen them, but I've never been on an amphibian boat before," Zac said.

"Well, there's a first time for everything," the man said.

"You, shine the torch so I can see where we're going."

Zac scampered to the front and aimed the light ahead. The

narrow, steep path was uneven and jerked the boat to the right. Zac was relieved as they drove onto the small strip of sand.

"Right, put your life jackets on," Mazza said.

Zac felt the cold sea breeze on his face. The wind went straight through his parka, and he wished he'd grabbed the jacket on offer, but it was too late now. He made sure his phone, as well as the one Andrei had given him, was tucked into the pocket of his parka and zipped it up. Hopefully, they would both stay dry. The last thing he needed was to have to tell Andrei that the phone he'd been given had been water damaged.

Zac had a healthy respect for the ocean and was relieved it was a calm night. He would have to put up with the cold. All he'd have to do now was make sure he didn't lose his footing and fall overboard.

He wasn't sure if these guys would bother to look for him.

77

As Bill pulled into the driveway at home, he realised how shattered he was. He was hungry and looked forward to dinner and perhaps a glass of wine while they watched something on the telly.

Finn and Maggie bounded out of the house to say hello to him before he even got out of the car. The chaos of long legs and curly coats was on him in seconds, and his uniform trousers were covered in muddy paw prints as they excitedly jumped up to welcome him home.

"All right, guys. It's lovely to see you as well," he said, playing boisterously with the dogs before they were distracted by something moving along the fence line. "You'll never catch those bunnies."

Annika stood in the doorway with her arms crossed over her chest. Her deep frown and serious facial expression spoke volumes. He could tell she was upset—most of the time, she was like an open book.

"What's up, darling?"

"I don't quite know where to start, to be honest," she said.

"Let's take a seat, and you can tell me all about it."

Bill knew his wife tended to overreact when it came to the kids and was, at times, a little dramatic. More often than not, she'd stew on something and would work herself into a complete tizz. He knew from experience that if he just listened to her, she would come up with the solution on her own.

"It can't be that bad?" Bill said, sitting at the kitchen table and taking her hand.

"It's Zac," she started.

"What about Zac?"

"Apparently, he's been up to no good with some of his mates. Vivianne Harper saw him in Omaha last night, but also the night of Jett Starr's party."

"Okay, so? He was out with his friends. It's semester break, after all."

"He said he'd stay over at a mate's place. I think they had a party to go to. I didn't ask any more questions. You know what he's been like lately, a bit moody and quiet."

"Do we know that it was him for sure?" Bill's police brain kicked in, and scenarios played out in his head.

"Vivianne recognised him. The other boys laughed about how he was the son of the local cop, for crying out loud," she said, her voice higher than usual. Annika's eyes filled with tears. "Drunk and disorderly, damage to private property, they appeared to be smoking dope, and who knows what else went down."

"Hang on a minute. We don't know for sure that he did all those things."

Bill suddenly remembered the phone call from a concerned resident in Omaha who had his letterbox damaged.

"And why didn't Vivianne say anything earlier, for Christ's sake?"

"You mean when you spoke to her after she found that young girl on the beach? I don't think the incident the night before with the boys crossed her mind, as she'd just found a dead body. Besides, she only met Zac a couple of days ago when I had the book club girls here."

"What the heck was he thinking?" Bill said. "He's not a teenager anymore. This kind of thing is such juvenile behaviour. It's not bloody good enough." He was furious.

Their conversation was interrupted by the twins and Katie, who'd come down for dinner. Just wait until the little prick gets home, Bill thought.

BILL'S MIND WORKED OVERTIME, and when it did, he was quiet. Annika tried her best to put a cheery face on, but Bill caught glimpses of her pained expression. It was tough for her. Bill dealt with juvenile ratbags all the time, but when it was one of your own kids, suddenly, it was all brought close to home.

"Where is Zac?" Katie asked. "He's normally home for dinner."

"I'm not sure what time he'll be home. He didn't say," Annika said and smiled at her oldest daughter.

"Typical! He was supposed to help me with my maths homework," she said, rolling her eyes.

"If he's promised, I'm sure he'll be home soon to help."

The girls finished their dinner and went back upstairs to their rooms while Bill helped Annika clear the table.

"Did he say where he was going when he messaged you?" Bill said.

"No, he never answered my question if he would be home for dinner."

"That's unusual. He normally replies."

"Yes, that's what's so odd," Annika said. "His behaviour seems out of character."

The tension in the room was high. Annika was more apprehensive compared to how he felt. He remembered being young and silly himself, although his dad had not been the local cop—that was the difference.

"We'll have to sit down and have a talk to him as soon as he gets home. How about I make us a cup of tea in the meantime?"

"Sounds great, love."

They went into the lounge and sat down. It was a cold night, and Bill lit the open fire, the familiar smell of firewood and flames somehow comforting.

Bill channel-surfed, and they settled on the latest season of a Danish political drama, something they both enjoyed. It was a welcome distraction.

Annika yawned and Bill cast an eye on his watch. It was after nine o'clock, and he couldn't shake the niggling feeling in his gut that something wasn't right.

Where the heck could Zac be?

78

After dinner, Andrei and Daria spent most of the evening in his office with the door shut. Crystal heard them arguing, although she couldn't make out what it was about. Both siblings were passionate, and the heated voices were a sure sign of a massive difference in opinion. She wondered if it had something to do with Andrei's accusation that someone had been in his office.

After Mike's death, a strange energy took hold, and they were all on edge. Crystal couldn't put her finger on why they quarrelled and wondered what was really going on. She'd tidied the kitchen after dinner and had packed a tote with an extra jumper and thick socks, as she knew the house would take a while to heat up. She packed the book she wanted to read and a snack. God knows how long they were going to stay there.

Just before eight, the office door swung open, and Daria stomped out.

"I don't know how you put up with him. He's a bloody idiot."

Crystal had no time to respond before Daria marched into the guest room and slammed the door.

"We're leaving in five minutes," Andrei said as he came into the kitchen.

"All good. I'm ready when you are. We're not staying overnight, are we?" Crystal said, her body showing unwillingness to camp out in an unoccupied house that was cold and damp.

"No, we should be home well before midnight."

"Andrei, what's going on? What is it that you and Mike were involved in? I'm a bit scared."

"Don't worry. Everything is fine. We're simply being a bit careful, taking precautions, that's all," Andrei said, pulling her close. His stubbled chin rested on top of her head, and she disappeared into his embrace. In that moment, she felt protected and loved, just like it used to be. What had happened to them? Was this the natural progression of a relationship? Did the honeymoon period really end so quickly? She savoured the faint but familiar aftershave with its woody green scent and fresh lemony notes and turned her face into his chest—how she had longed for some closeness and comfort.

"It's time. Are you guys ready to go?" Daria said as she walked into the room. She glared at her brother, and it was obvious Daria wasn't pleased.

Andrei let go of Crystal, and the spell was broken.

"We're all set. Let's go," Andrei said, and in an instant, the gulf between them appeared again. "I'll just grab my bag."

"I'll take my car and follow you," Daria yelled from the entrance. "You and Crystal take yours."

She couldn't hear Andrei's answer but hurried down the hallway and into the garage with the bag slung over her shoulder.

"How long do you plan to stay away?" Andrei asked, laughing. The sizeable tote was jam-packed with warm clothes and things she might need.

"I just thought I'd bring a few things as I don't know how long we'll have to stay."

"I'm only kidding." The joke fell flat, and she tried to muster a weak smile. "Don't worry, darling. I just have to oversee a business transaction."

Crystal didn't know what to think. When Andrei met with a

potential investor or a buyer, he'd wine and dine them, and she'd been to plenty of those events as eye candy on his arm.

Crystal was worried about tonight. What was really going on? She'd ignored the feeling that something wasn't quite right for a while. The sketchy details of tonight certainly didn't sound like their usual kind of buyer. And should she still be with him if Andrei was involved in something dodgy?

79

He checked over his gear one final time. It was all there, including the Sig pistol he'd obtained months ago from a shady contact of a contact. Nothing could be traced back to him; he'd made sure of that.

He held it, and the weight felt thrilling in his hand. He knew how to use it and had belonged to the local gun club for years. He was a pretty skilled shooter if he said so himself.

Of course, when he'd bought it, the guy had shown him how to use it when he'd handed over the cash, and he'd played along. The serial number was filed off. God knew what it had been used for before—not that he cared. It didn't matter; the weapon would be disposed of as soon as it had served its purpose.

Finally, the last few months of work were coming to fruition. He'd dreamt of this day, and now that it was here, he wasn't sure how to feel about it. Everything had suffered—his work and his relationships—but he knew it would all be worth it. He would clean up what the cops had been unable to do. The police certainly had not done enough at the time.

The tiny dot blinked on his phone screen. It had been too easy. He'd ordered the tiny GPS tracker online—amazing what you could buy online these days. He'd carried it with him for the last few weeks, and it had been too easy to place it behind one of the back wheels. The opportunity had presented itself one day last week, and he'd attached it at the first opportunity. Luckily, the magnetic base stuck on at the first attempt.

Tonight was the night it was all going to end. He'd planned it all. Meticulously, of course, as with everything he did. The conversation he'd overheard from the young lad they called Chook the other night at the pub had been pure gold. Chook and his dad Mazza were part of the regular crew—that much he'd heard.

He knew the arrogant twit Andrei Bowen was crooked and that the local gang distributed the drugs. To find out how the goods got here was more than he could have hoped for. For months, he'd watched and had his ear to the ground. It had finally paid off.

80

There was still no sign of Zac.

"I just hope he's not had an accident on the way home. You know what country roads are like. People are tired and often drive too fast," Annika said, working herself into a state.

"I'm sure he's fine," Bill said, but the small niggle of doubt lingered.

"Can we do a Find My iPhone on Apple Support?" Annika said anxiously.

"I suppose so. Do we know his Apple ID?"

"Hang on, the kids all share the same password. Let me grab it," she said, fetching the notebook with all the information.

Bill logged in on his phone. The girls' devices showed their last location here at home in Leigh Road. Zac's phone showed it had pinged in Ti Point, and the current location was off Takatu Point.

"Hang on, this can't be right," he said, scratching his head.

"What can't be right?" Annika came to his side to look at the iPhone screen. "What does it show?"

"By the looks of it," Bill said, "Zac's right in the middle of the shipping channel in the water off Takatu Point." Bill looked at Annika in disbelief.

"What? You mean to say that Zac was on a boat last time this phone sent a signal to the closest tower?" Annika frowned, her confusion apparent. "But . . . what on earth would he be doing out at sea, especially at night?"

Bill had a fair idea, even though it wasn't something he really wanted to admit.

"Well, love, it could be one of two things," Bill said as his heart dropped. "There are rumours circulating of clandestine pick up of drugs at sea in Auckland. The water police have found the odd lost drug package floating in the gulf. I didn't think we'd see it up here. So, either our son is involved in a criminal operation, or he's got himself involved in something well over his head. I don't know how to explain it otherwise. Why would he be at sea at night?"

"You can't be serious. Why would he throw away his life like that!" Annika said, close to tears.

"I've got to call this in. If this is what I think it is, it's serious. Don't worry, love. I won't let anything happen to him," Bill said, rushing to the front door.

"Let me know as soon as you know more, Bill," Annika pleaded. He could see the intense worry in her eyes.

"Will do."

Bill ran to the car. He was straight into work mode and would have to try his utmost to push his personal feelings aside.

He glanced at the phone screen. The marker indicated where the phone was located, and it appeared it had moved closer to land.

Bill called Niko—they needed to get there as soon as possible.

"Niko, there's an unfolding situation in Ti Point. I'll explain when I see you. Can you be ready in two minutes? I'm already on my way in."

"No worries, Sarge. I'll be downstairs waiting."

For a second, Bill felt like he would be sick. He was sweating profusely, and his heart pounded out of his chest. He hoped he was wrong and that there would be a perfectly logical explanation for why Zac's phone was out there on the sea.

"Get a grip, man. You're not doing your son any favours if you lose the plot," he said to himself.

There was no time to think; he was trained for this.

The drive to Matakana was a haze. As he pulled up in the main street opposite the pub, Niko was already waiting outside the door and jumped in the car.

"What's happened, Sarge?

"Long story short. We've just tried to locate Zac through the Find My iPhone app, and his phone is showing off Takatu Point on a vessel of some sort. We're not exactly sure of Zac's involvement and whether he's there of his own free will, but that's beside the point. We can deal with whatever it is," Bill said, realising he probably sounded like he was babbling incoherently.

Niko stared at him for a moment. "You talking drugs, Sarge?"

"Not sure, but whatever it is, we can deal with it."

They pulled into the station and grabbed what they needed.

"Are you sure you're up for this, boss?" Niko said.

"I'll be fine. Wild horses couldn't stop me. You'll see when you have kids of your own, mate."

That was the end of that conversation.

"You drive. I'll have to call Orewa and get reinforcements sent." Bill phoned headquarters and was put on hold.

"For fuck's sake. Who's the amateur on the switchboard today!" Bill slammed his fist on the dash in frustration when the call went to voicemail. "Jesus, you wouldn't think it was that difficult, would you?"

He redialled the number, was put through to the duty sergeant, and explained the situation.

"I know we haven't had any complaints or tips from the public, and I realise it's sketchy intel, but I'm telling you, something isn't right," Bill said, trying to control his tone and his temper. The arrogant ass on the other end of the phone couldn't be less interested if he tried and instead started to talk over him.

"I'm sorry, Granger. We have a major drug bust that's about to be executed in multiple locations on the north shore. I can't send anyone up that far on a hunch. We're stretched as it is."

"We are headed north on Leigh Road to Ti Point. I guess we'll check it out and report back if there's some suspicious activity," Bill said through clenched teeth. "To be honest, we've got no idea what we're about to walk into, but if this is drug-related, you can bet your last dollar there is gang involvement, which means heavy weapons. To complicate matters, and I regret to have to tell you this, according to the phone data I'm looking at, my son may be on the vessel," Bill said, his voice breaking at the last statement.

"Your son? Well, it could all be a wild goose chase, Granger. When you have some actual facts, get back in touch." The line went dead.

"For fuck's sake!!" Bill had reached his limit. "What an arrogant prick! He told me that since we didn't have anything concrete, he couldn't spare any officers and to get back in touch if there was an incident to report. You wouldn't want to have something major going down rurally, as it would take Orewa fucking ages to pull their finger out," Bill said, spitting out the words.

"As far as they're concerned, Sarge, if it's not in the city, it's not happening, or at least it's not a huge priority," Niko said. "We've been there before, Sarge." "I know," Bill snapped.

"Take it easy, Sarge. I'm sure there's a perfectly good explanation, and we'll be back home again with Zac before we know it."

Bill wished that were the case. The reality was that if Zac was involved in something criminal, he was in grave danger. The thought of his son getting hurt or worse didn't even bear thinking about.

81

The drive to Ti Point took less than ten minutes. Andrei was quiet and concentrated on the twists and turns of the road ahead.

"Who are you meeting with tonight?" Daria said as she pulled up and parked next to them.

"Best if you don't know," he said, stepping out of the car.

What did that mean, for goodness' sake? She was about to ask again when her brother gave her a look.

Crystal looked towards the sandy beach at the bottom of the garden. It was dark, but she could see a hint of the water's edge where she'd spent many a lazy summer day. She and Andrei had often launched the boat from there and enjoyed swimming. Why hadn't they rented or sold the house? It was a shame for it to be unoccupied.

"Why don't you go inside and turn some heaters on? We'll be in shortly." Andrei handed Crystal the key. She felt like a petulant teenager who had been sent to their room and begrudgingly took it from him. What could be this important and secretive that she couldn't know anything about it? It was obvious he didn't trust her, she thought as she skulked towards the front door.

The house was dark and gloomy and felt like an icebox. She shivered as she switched the lights and heat pumps on to make it more habitable. A faint mildew smell hung in the air. The windows were covered with thick thermal drapes, and she parted one in the lounge, peeking out to see Daria and Andrei deep in conversation. She was glad she'd brought an extra sweater and bent down to pull on the warm socks she'd also packed.

As Andrei and Daria turned to walk up the path to the house, she quickly pulled the curtains and went into the kitchen. She peeked in the fridge. It amazed her that there was milk and a few other things there. Andrei must have dropped them off earlier. Crystal filled the jug with fresh water and waited for it to boil.

She had a feeling it was going to be a long night.

82

Annika was beside herself with worry. Every possible disaster she could think of played out in her mind. Bill had left in such a rush, and she knew he was concerned. What on earth had Zac gotten himself involved in?

She paced from the kitchen to the lounge and back again until Maggie and Finn started to whine—they could feel her worry and nervous energy. The only saving grace was that the girls were all in bed. She contemplated ringing Lexi, but it was late. Annika grabbed a small cup from the cupboard above the sink and put it on the little shelf of the coffee machine before sticking a capsule in the compartment on top of the Nespresso maker. She turned the dial to Lungo and pressed the button. The comforting splutter combined with the rich bittersweet aroma calmed her. As she took the first mouthful of the steaming liquid, she sunk onto one of the kitchen chairs.

There was nothing she could do from here. She wanted to be there to comfort Zac. Whatever he'd done, she was sure they could sort it out. Bill would never have let her go with him. He'd talked about drug shipments. She was well aware that drugs existed in the community to some extent. She wasn't naïve enough to think they didn't, even though it was well away from Auckland. She took another sip of coffee, holding the cup in her hands to steady them.

If there were gangs involved, there would be weapons and violence. Her heart sank as she worried about Bill's safety. He wasn't on his own; Niko would be there, too. And if they needed it, she was sure backup from Warkworth and Orewa would be there. She thought of Zac—he was her son, and there was nothing more powerful than a mother's love for her children. She could hardly sit there idly while all this went down. Who knew what kind of trouble he was in?

Bill had told her to wait at home and that he would call her. But she knew she had to do something. Should she grab her car keys and drive over? She had no idea where in Ti Point to go; it was a large peninsula. The rational part of her brain said to trust Bill, but the nervous tension was killing her.

83

It was time to leave.

They'd agreed to meet at eight-thirty at the address in Ti Point. Usually, Mike had dropped the shipment off at a predetermined location, but as he'd been taken care of, it had been decided they would meet there. Mike had been a good go-between until he'd got sloppy, and Fanta had died.

Big Ed had always had a soft spot for his nephew and still felt the anger, mitigated somewhat since Mike had been made to pay for his mistakes.

The facility in the barn at their headquarters was all set for the new shipment. They'd gone through the last lot quicker than anticipated—a lot of the meth had gone straight up north.

The bundles of cash were in the sports bag: meth and ecstasy were a lucrative business. A few more years like this, and he'd be set. Someone else would take over the reins, and he'd be rid of this shit. He was sick of the life he led and the people around him. Lately, he'd thought perhaps it wasn't too late to change his life. He'd toyed with the idea of changing his name and disappearing into a small community somewhere far away from here to lead a simple life. But for now, he was stuck. The cops had clamped down a lot already, and it would probably get worse, but the demand was great. And that's what kept him in business despite the sizeable risks. He would need the money for his retirement.

He packed his shotgun, and he wasn't afraid to use it. He'd done so before. He had no regrets. The people he'd killed had all deserved to die. As for Andrei Bowen, he didn't like the little prick. He was an arrogant property developer, and Big Ed certainly didn't trust him. Someone would have already stepped into Mike's shoes when it came to his little ecstasy business on the side. No doubt, he would have done the same. Despite their different circumstances, they were all cut from the same cloth when it came down to it. He knew the type well and could certainly handle them. Even though he was an old hand, intimidation was his bread and butter. Always had been. He'd be all right, he thought and tucked the Glock into his waistband.

"Come on, Gazza," he said to the scruffy guy with the long, curly hair sitting on the couch in the lounge.

"Go get that useless son of a bitch, Iggy. We're leaving."

84

Bill drove past the address the GPS had indicated earlier and parked around the corner. He wasn't familiar with the property, but according to Google Maps, he could see the main dwelling—an outbuilding and what appeared to be a track down to the beach. If this was a seaward drug-running operation, it all made sense. If so, he wondered how long it had been going on right under his nose.

He checked the Find My iPhone app, which indicated Zac's phone was just north of Omaha, and that meant they were on the way back.

"All right, okay, let's do a reconnaissance to see if we can spot something we can go back to Orewa with," Bill said, turning to Niko as he strapped his body armour on.

"But, Sarge, what about Zac? If we call it in, he'll be in hot water, and you know it would definitely go to court."

Bill pressed his lips together and looked down at his armour as he secured it. "I'm fully aware of what the implications are for my son. But I can't turn a blind eye to what is more than likely going on here and probably has been for a while. These fuckers need to be stopped."

The weight of what he had just said sank in. Zac would definitely get into trouble; the depth of his involvement was yet to be determined, though.

Bloody kid!

Niko popped the boot, and they slotted the handguns in the holsters. They grabbed the Bushman rifle as a backup and made their way along the edge of the bush, the track illuminated by a full moon.

"Stop, listen!" Niko whispered, lifting his right hand.

A car rumbled towards them, and they took cover behind a dense clump of flax as the headlights of the car swept above their heads. A beaten-up old Toyota turned left into the same property they were headed to.

"More people turning up to the party," Niko whispered.

"By the looks of it, we have three individuals on approach. One in the backseat. But how many people are there already at the house?" Bill said. "Fucking Orewa. Screw their drug bust. If my hunch is right, we're looking not only at the source but also most likely a much bigger operation."

"I know what you mean, Sarge, but we need to get eyes on these jokers and ascertain that this is indeed the drug ring we've been after for a while," Niko cautioned.

Bill knew it was true. They needed positive intel before Orewa would get on board and dispatch units.

'Let's go. We'll cut through the bush next to the driveway. Let's hope we don't fall down a gully on the way," Niko said.

"I'm too old for this kind of shit," Bill said, holding his ribs.

Close to the main house, they could see the light seeping through the gaps in the curtains. There were four cars parked up—one of them was a Maserati.

"What's Bowen doing here?" Bill said, looking at the car.

"At this stage, we have no idea how many individuals are here," Niko said. "Most likely, the associates are all inside the house."

Bill looked at the phone screen to check where Zac was

pinpointed. "It looks like the vessel is just about back where it started out, down that strip of beach."

His heart beat faster, and he hoped his son would be all right. He knew this kind of scum; they were ruthless and human life was cheap. They thought nothing of offing someone. These seasoned criminals didn't have the same moral compass as most of the general public.

"Let's take a peek through the gap in the blind to see if we can establish how many people are there, then I suggest we make our way down towards the beach," Bill said. "Remember, we're here to collect intel, and if there's a chance, we'll try to get Zac out before the cavalry arrives."

"Shall we call it in now? Just to be safe?" Niko said.

"Nah, that dumbass in Orewa won't let me live it down if it's a wild goose chase. We'll approach the water's edge with caution. If all the signs point to what we think it is, you call it in."

Niko did a crouching run up to the house and peeked through the narrow gap in the curtain.

"All I can see is a female, about thirty. She's sitting on the couch and appears to be reading a book," Niko said. "Can't see anyone else in there."

"All right, let's move down to the water. You cover me," Bill said, unclipping his gun.

The uneven ground made it precarious as they made their way down the slope, staying well to the left of the track as much as they could.

"Shhh," Bill said, raising a hand. "I hear an engine. Let's move but make sure we are undetected."

They scurried down the bank, and within moments, they were on a plateau above the sandy beach. A large Pōhutukawa provided excellent cover, its branches hanging over the small bay. The narrow strip of sand was just below them, and as it was high tide, the water was only twenty metres away.

"There's Zac, Sarge!"

The amphibian boat approached the beach with three individuals onboard. The silver moonlight turned the scene into a dark Gothic horror movie, and it was eerily still.

"I can see that," Bill said, motioning for Niko to be quiet. He could feel the stress, and his heart rate increased as he saw Zac in the boat.

They heard voices. Bill recognised Andrei's posh private school accent. He could also hear an unknown female; her voice was also polished and clear, and her tone assertive. It appeared they were in conversation with an older man.

The outboard engine changed gear as the crew of the boat came closer to land. Bill could smell the mix of salty air and engine oil as he strained to hear the conversation.

"Fucking hell, there's no way we can get Zac away from this group of people," Bill whispered to Niko.

As the Sealegs drove up on land, the engine cut off.

"Did you get it all?" Andrei called out to the skipper.

"Yes, mate, it's all here, and it's a full load."

Bill crouched below the Pōhutukawa branches, craning his neck through the foliage to make sure he wasn't seen from the beach below.

"Niko, you go up the hill out of earshot and call it in. I'll sit tight for a while and see what unfolds. We need a roadblock set up on the intersection of Leigh Road and Ti Point Road. Tell them to send units from Warkworth as well. They'll be here quicker," Bill whispered.

He didn't want to go in half-assed and potentially jeopardise his son's life. Ideally, the best thing would be to flush them out, to catch them red-handed with the shipment.

85

The night was still. He heard voices as he followed the track down along the water's edge to the beach.

He'd not thought until now that Andrei and his crew might be armed. It was too late for regrets, anyway. He'd come too far. The pain and suffering would have all been for nothing if he didn't get revenge. Drugs had taken her life. Now he was about to cut the head off the snake that not only supplied the evil drugs but also made his dirty money.

He never thought he had it in him to kill another human being. The old rocker Jett, had been the first one, his parties being where she'd been introduced to drugs. You couldn't stop young people who wanted to experiment with drugs, but this asshole had made her into a junkie.

Nothing had come out after the inquiry. The rich asshole had made sure his name stayed out of it, and his daughter's tragic death was just that—tragic. Much later, he'd found the text messages between them.

She'd been actively encouraged to take drugs, and God knew what else he'd used her for. As an aggrieved father, yes, he could have gone to the police with what he had found, but then, he wouldn't have got his payback. And by God, revenge was going to feel good.

Not that it would bring back his darling Bella, but at least he'd remove this one sick fuck from society and make sure he could no longer supply young girls with drugs and exploit them.

Now it was this prick's turn to suffer for his sins. And suffer, he would.

86

The winter moon hung low in the sky, its light caressing the water's surface. It would have been a beautiful night if it hadn't been for the pick-up.

She was a little apprehensive. Even though this was more low-key than the cartel rendezvous, Big Ed was a major figure in the underworld and not to be taken lightly. She didn't know his associates and could care less as she looked at the scruffy-looking gang members. No doubt they'd be armed, especially given that they carried large amounts of cash. Daria had her bag slung across her body and felt good knowing she still had the sawn-off shotgun within reach.

"Well, this worked out well, despite Mike not being here to sort it all out," Big Ed said.

Daria tensed. She didn't like his flippant tone.

"I hope your skipper didn't lose anyone overboard this time?" Big Ed continued, his tone laced with sarcasm and obviously referring to Mike for the loss of his nephew.

"Listen, mate. I told you. It was an accident. No one's to blame for Fanta's death, as tragic as it was. He was well aware of the risks," Andrei said. "I know it tore Mike up to lose a man overboard on his watch."

Big Ed harrumphed. Obviously, Andrei's answer did nothing to make him feel less animosity. "Mike was a cocky bastard. It was only a matter of time before someone would have knocked him off anyway."

"What are you saying?" Andrei said, locking eyes with Big Ed.

"Nothing, man. It's just that when someone is careless, and a senseless death occurs, there's generally retribution."

The veiled message was loud and clear, and Daria understood exactly what Big Ed meant. The anger boiled from her insides. "Did you have anything to do with Mike's death?" she asked through clenched teeth. She placed her hand over the bag; felt the sawn-off shotgun. Daria wanted to shoot the cocky bastard.

"Not personally," he said and smirked.

"What the fuck does that mean?" Andrei said, taking a step forwards on the compact sand. Gazza and Iggy—Big Ed's lieutenants—closed ranks on their boss, but Big Ed wasn't fazed and stood his ground.

"All I'm saying is that if one of the brothers took it into his own hands to deal with the situation, I wouldn't have stood in the way. Mike deserved everything he got."

The ground beneath Daria swayed; she couldn't believe what she'd heard. They'd killed Mike in a horrid manner. There was no remorse. She could no longer contain herself. The emotional roller-coaster between anger and despair had turned to uncontrolled rage, and the red mist consumed her. Tunnel vision set in, and everything moved in slow motion.

She didn't hear Andrei's barrage of profanities or notice as her brother completely lost it. He took a swing at Big Ed but was stopped by Gazza and his sidekick.

Daria's heart had already been ripped out when she'd found out that Mike was dead— to hear this animal talk about it pushed her over the edge. She swung her bag around to her front, lifted the flap, and pulled the weapon out.

It was all over in seconds.

87

Bill moved closer and crept along the flax bushes. It improved his vantage point. The moonlight illuminated the tense stand-off happening on the narrow strip of sand below. He could hear what they were saying. It was obvious the situation had escalated. Just as Andrei stepped forwards, Big Ed's men pushed in, and a scuffle was in full motion.

It was two against Andrei as Big Ed looked on in amusement, but he didn't seem intimidated. One of the skinny men pulled a gun out and pointed it at Andrei.

"Back the fuck off, dude."

"All right," Andrei said, taking a step back. "All right."

From the periphery, Bill saw the woman. No one seemed to take the slightest notice of her because all eyes were on Andrei.

Bill watched as she swung the tote bag across her body to the front and pulled out what looked like a sawn-off shotgun with one swift motion. He could see the stock was cut down as well, which left only a pistol grip.

In seconds, she raised it and fired two rounds, which hit Big Ed square in the chest, flinging him backwards. Bill reacted immediately and scrambled parallel to the beach as Niko emerged farther up the hill. Bill gestured for him to cover his flank.

The big man had a look of surprise on his face as crimson patches spread across his chest. He hit the sand with a thud.

Jesus Christ, Bill thought as he took cover behind the large tree, desperately trying to work out the next move.

"What the fuck, Daria?" Andrei shouted as he swung around to his sister. While one of the men tried to stop Big Ed's bleeding, the other pulled a gun out and pointed it at Daria and Andrei.

"Let's calm the fuck down," Andrei said as he backed up to protect his sister, at the same time pulling a gun from his waistband.

Bill rounded the tree next to the track, with Niko close behind, and approached cautiously with his gun drawn.

"Police! Drop your weapons!" Bill shouted.

"This is just great," Andrei said, dropping his gun on the ground. The skinny gang member reluctantly followed suit.

The woman froze, her aim still on the men and her finger poised on the trigger.

"YOU, DROP THE WEAPON," Bill boomed, aiming at her.

He could sense Niko to the side of him, the Bushmaster rifle in his peripheral vision aimed at the woman still holding the gun.

"I'M WARNING YOU. If you don't put the gun on the ground immediately, we'll shoot."

"Drop the fucking weapon, Daria," Andrei yelled at his sister.

The woman snapped out of her hypnotic state and placed the sawn-off shotgun on the sand. She swayed and looked like she was about to keel over. Her eyes were wide open, and her breathing was rapid. She looked like she was on the verge of collapse as she sunk to her knees. The adrenaline turned into shock—Bill had seen it before.

"EVERYONE BACK OFF. Don't move a fucking muscle," he shouted. "What's the status on the man who's been shot?"

"I think he's gone, man," the skinny guy said, his clothes and hands covered in blood.

Bill glanced over to the boat. He saw Zac and two other men on the vessel. Zac was pale and clung white-knuckled to the side of the boat. He looked like he was going to be sick. The three men were in shock and disbelief over what had just unfolded on the beach.

"You three. Drive the boat further up the beach and get off slowly and with your hands where I can see them," Bill barked at the skipper. Bill recognised him but didn't know his name. Zac hung his head in shame. Bill forced himself to put his personal feelings aside, but he was angry. And he was sure Zac felt it, too.

The skipper immediately turned the key and moved the craft further up the beach.

88

He waded in the shallows, the low-hanging branches giving him suitable cover as he neared the beach.

He arrived just as a heated exchange was going on between Andrei and the heavy-set asshole. As the first shot went off, he looked up and was surprised to see the woman next to Andrei standing there with a sawn-off shotgun. Then, he watched as the man she'd shot fell to the ground like a sack of potatoes. *Who was the bitch next to Andrei?* She had balls; he'd give her that. He hadn't expected them to turn on each other, but it worked well in his favour. Good riddance. At least that was one less fucker he'd need to deal with.

Then the cops turned up out of nowhere, and he was surprised to see them. He hadn't seen the police car as he came down the driveway. It was a minor irritant, though. He was a marksman in his youth. He was sure he could get a shot in before the country coppers raised their weapons. How often were they involved in something like this?

From what he could see, the property developer still looked smug despite Bill and the other cop crashing the party. Where was the reinforcement? Didn't the police generally have heavy artillery for this kind of bust? Since he could only see the two officers, it meant they were on their own and had no backup.

He could still get to Andrei.

The younger cop had rounded them up like cattle. They were outnumbered, which would play right into his hands. Backup was likely to be on its way, so he had to act quickly. He stepped over a couple of gnarly tree roots.

It was the point of no return, and he knew he had to go through with the plan. He'd come too far. Besides, he had nothing to lose since he had lost everything worth living for.

If he took a shot at Andrei, the cops would shoot. That's what they were trained for. Their aim was always for the largest part of the body, the torso. He understood he might not survive this, but he was okay with that and had made his peace. There were worse things than 'death by cop'.

All his affairs were in order, and he was ready, whatever the outcome might be. If he died tonight, it would be in a blaze of glory.

He would try to take as many of the bastards with him as he could. He hoped he wouldn't be forced to shoot at the cops—he'd always liked Bill Granger. But if he were forced to, he would.

89

They'd only carried one set of handcuffs each and had to improvise with the rest. Niko had found some thin nylon rope in the boat and got his pocket knife out to cut metre-long pieces, which he used to tie the suspects' wrists.

"Sorry, mate. I have to put this on," he said to Zac, who was teary-eyed and unable to speak.

Bill looked over. Zac didn't make eye contact with his dad. A range of emotions swirled in Bill's head. He was angry, but at the same time, it was a huge relief to know Zac was safe. All he wanted was to give his son a hug, but it would have to wait. The question remained: how the hell had Zac gotten mixed up with these people? Not to mention how on earth he'd explain to his superiors what had happened.

For now, all they could do was keep the situation under control until backup from Warkworth and Orewa arrived.

Niko had already checked over Big Ed—there was nothing anyone could do. Life had been blasted out of the big guy.

The initial rush of adrenaline had settled, and Niko worked his way through the detainees while Bill kept an eye on the situation. These people were ruthless. The last thing he wanted to do was to turn his back on any of them.

"Any news on the backup?" Bill asked quietly as Niko made his way over to him.

"Hang on, let me check," he said and pulled his phone out of his pocket. "The guys from Warkworth should be here any minute."

"Great. Let's hope we don't have any other surprises before then," he said and surveyed the scene. His eye was drawn to Zac.

The night time temperature had dropped considerably. It wouldn't take long before they would start to complain. The damp air made his breath white as he breathed out.

The moon illuminated the narrow strip of beach, framed by dense pockets of darkness from the surrounding bush.

Something moved near low-hanging branches, farther along the beach. Bill squinted, certain he'd seen a fleeting movement. Nothing. Was this his mind playing tricks?

It had been a stressful night, after all.

His senses heightened.

A scream.

He turned to Niko.

A shot rang out. A gun flash.

A woman's scream.

Bill swung around, desperately searching for a who and a what. He was in fight or flight mode. A lone figure emerged from the shadows and stood not far from one of the suspects. Andrei had been shot and thrown onto his back. He'd been a sitting duck with no chance to get away. He couldn't tell if Andrei was still alive. The woman's loud wails echoed in the still night. Bill had no idea what the shooter's agenda was, only that they had to stop him to prevent further victims.

"DROP YOUR WEAPON!" Bill shouted, running towards the lone figure. The man slowly lifted his firearm again. This time his aim was straight at Bill.

"DROP YOUR FUCKEN WEAPON, OR I'LL SHOOT!"

Bill sensed Niko to his right, the Bushman rifle aimed at the shooter.

"DROP IT, AND NO ONE WILL GET HURT," Bill continued. The

man said nothing. In the glum moonlight, he couldn't quite make out the camouflaged person's features; he was still too far away, but it looked like this person was an older man. His slightly generous girth did nothing for his agility. He looked a bit like Henry from the Surf Club from where Bill was standing, but he wasn't sure. And why would Henry be here, anyway?

"Hey, listen, mate. Drop the weapon now. You are outnumbered, and the place will be crawling with cops soon. Either way, better for you if you surrender yourself now," Bill said, changing tack and softening his approach.

"I can't do that," the man said, his black peaked obscuring most of his features.

Bill recognised the voice. As the realisation of who it was flashed through his head, the man squeezed the trigger. The first shot hit Bill's right shoulder, and he buckled. The second bullet glanced off his arm. He tried to return fire, but no matter how much he willed his right arm to lift, he couldn't take aim and squeeze the trigger. The signals from his brain would not go through.

"DAD!!" Zac yelled, and Bill saw his son trying to get up. But his wrists were tied, and he couldn't move. Niko opened up and let four rounds off.

"GET DOWN!" Bill shouted and crawled for cover behind an old tree stump, hoping Zac was safe. He counted the shots; it was an old habit. *Always count the rounds so you can estimate what's left in the magazine.* Blood dripped down his arm and onto the ground.

Bill switched the gun to the other hand while applying pressure to the wound. He couldn't see how bad it was through his jacket, but he felt the pulsating sensation and warm sticky blood soaking his sleeve. The taste of metal and bile filled his mouth, and he swallowed hard to avoid being sick.

The shooter was down, and Niko stood over him, saying, "It's Henry Long."

Bill couldn't understand why Henry was there. But emotions and flashbacks coursed through Bill, his vision narrowed, and he was brought back to the old warehouse—that fateful night ten years ago.

"You okay, Sarge?" Niko yelled, still bending over the shooter.

"I'm all right," Bill shouted, pulling himself up.

A wave of dizziness came over him, and he steadied himself for a few seconds before walking over. He had his torch in his left hand and shone the light across the eerie scene. The light swept across the detainees, their eyes wide with the shock at being caught in the crossfire.

"Dad, you've been shot!!" Zac yelled as he saw the blood.

"I'm okay, son," Bill said, mustering a weak smile.

Niko applied first aid to Henry while his blood seeped into the sand. The man was conscious, but his life would drain away if help didn't come soon. Bill crouched next to the shot man.

"Bloody hell, Henry. Do you realise what you've done? Why?"

"I had to do this," he said, blood slowly trickling from the side of his mouth. "I'm sorry . . . you got caught in the crossfire, Bill . . . but I had no choice. These assholes had to die, besides . . . I only aimed for your shooting arm," he said, struggling to speak. And then his head fell to the side.

"I've got no pulse. Damn it," Niko said as he straightened up. His hands and trousers were covered in Henry Long's blood.

"You did all you could, Niko."

Bill shone his light over Andrei Bowen's slumped body. He wasn't moving, and there was little doubt that he was gone. The woman on the ground screamed as she, too, could see he was dead.

"Calm down," Bill commanded, which shocked her into sliding down and sitting on the sand again. Her body shook as she sobbed loudly. A low primeval noise slowly built to a guttural wounded animal wail. Bill felt her pain.

The bullet appeared to have gone right through the middle of Andrei's forehead, a clean entry wound with a trail of blood oozing out of it. From where he stood, he could see that the back of the head where it had exited was another matter; half the skull was blown off. As he moved closer, the rank smell of blood mixed with faeces rose from the body.

Bill cast an eye on Zac and the boat crew, who had been placed between Andrei and the gang members to separate the two.

"Fucking hell," the skinny man with the dirty jeans said.

Zac had been closest to Andrei and was covered in brain matter and various fluids. As the reality sunk in, his son turned and vomited loudly.

The woman calmed and rocked back and forth on her heels.

Bill's mind furiously tried to work out the connection between these individuals. His mind whirred, and he felt increasingly light-headed as the pain increased.

He looked over at Henry, the well-respected community spokesman and Surf Club president.

Was there a connection between the daughter he lost some years ago and this vendetta? What did he know that the police didn't?

90

Crystal thought she'd heard a gunshot a little while ago. Farmers and vineyard owners shot possums and rabbits all the time—this was the country, after all. But something wasn't right. She put her book down and went outside into the night. She stood on the front steps and peered into the dense bush. She'd been tucked up on the couch reading her book while she waited for Andrei and Daria to finish the business deal.

It was strange, though: why would they meet at night and in a location like this? But what did she know?

She listened as she breathed in the cold air but heard nothing but the wind rustling in the dense bush nearby. An eerie feeling descended over the property, and she felt a little scared and lonely. She jumped when a lone Morepork hooted in the distance, and she pulled her jacket close across her chest.

Crystal decided it might be best to go back inside when another loud bang echoed across the treetops, followed by a series of shots and a woman's screams. This time she was convinced it was nearby. It sounded like it came from the beach. A cold fear filled her body, and she sprinted towards the boat-shed and the beach.

Where were Andrei and Daria, for God's sake? She stopped dead in her tracks when she saw the people sitting on the sand and the two police officers, one of whom was Bill, Annika's husband.

Her brain struggled to compute what she was seeing. Their boat was out. Had someone stolen it? Andrei would not be pleased when he found out.

As she walked towards Bill, he put his hand out and touched her arm. If he was surprised to see her, he was not showing it.

"Bill, what's going on?"

She looked down and noticed the blood on his sleeve and hands.

"You're bleeding!!"

Her mind was working overtime. Why was he bleeding, and where was Andrei? And had someone else got shot?

"It's for the best if you stay here, Crystal," Bill said, trying to lead her away.

"Tell me what's going on, for Christ's sake! Andrei will be ropable when he finds out someone tried to steal the boat," she said.

"I need you to go back up to the house immediately."

"But why?" she said. Then, she looked behind Bill and saw Daria and Andrei. She recognised his jeans and the jacket he'd worn. Why was Andrei lying on his back? What was going on? And who were the other men on the beach?

She tore away from Bill and ran towards Andrei. Daria sat close by, sobbing and shaking.

"Why is Andrei on the ground?" Crystal yelled.

Daria looked at her, unable to speak and with tears running down her face. Crystal reached Andrei and saw the emptiness in his eyes and a blood trail running down his temples and around his ears.

"NOOOO," she screamed, falling to her knees by his body. She buried her face in her hands and started crying. Damp seeped through her jeans and into her knees and lower legs, but she didn't care.

Strong hands gripped her shoulders, pulling her up and leading her away. She struggled to walk and stumbled, but someone caught her before she fell to the ground. Her feet barely moved one foot in front of the other, and she had no memory of the walk up the drive and being helped into the house.

A FEMALE CONSTABLE sat her down and made her a cup of tea, trying her best to coax her to drink it. Through the window, she could vaguely see the red and blue lights that flashed from the police and ambulance in the driveway. The strobe light captivated her in a strange way as she tried to process what was going on.

She saw Annika hurrying up the path. Her friend spoke to one of the constables outside before she was allowed to come through the door.

Crystal felt relief as Annika put her arms around her. Tears ran down Crystal's face, and she sniffed loudly.

"Andrei is dead," she sobbed. "I can't believe it. How did this even happen? Who would have wanted to hurt him so badly?"

"I'm so very sorry, Crystal," Annika said, gently stroking her back.

She wondered if she was trapped in a bad nightmare. She wanted to wake up, to shake the horrible feeling off. She willed Andrei to walk through the door and say that everything was okay.

But when she looked out the window again, the lights still flashed. Two ambulance officers carried what looked like a covered body on a gurney. Something in her heart had shattered into a thousand pieces. Was that Andrei on the stretcher? She pulled away from Annika's embrace and sat up. The reality of what had just happened dawned on her. It was real.

"Here, take a sip of your tea. You've had a terrible shock," Annika said.

Crystal obliged and swallowed hard as another sob emerged.

"How did you know?"

"Bill called me. I came over as quickly as I could," Annika said.

So many thoughts whirled around in Crystal's head. The world as she knew it had collapsed in the minute it took for her to run down to the beach.

91

The reinforcement had arrived, and Bill could finally check on Zac. His son's pale complexion worried him. He'd seen things a young person should not have to experience—atrocious, senseless violence and loss of lives. He'd taken Zac down to the water's edge to help him get cleaned up.

"What about you, Dad? Are you sure you're okay? You've been shot!"

"I'll be fine. But Zac, you need to tell me what you were doing out on the water with those drug dealers."

"I'm so sorry, Dad. I damaged Andrei's car, and he said I could work it off. I had no idea what tonight was about, honest. You've got to believe me."

"It's all right, son. I believe you," Bill said, putting his arm around Zac. His son breathed a loud sigh of relief and sniffed loudly, trying his best not to cry.

"Listen up. I'm sure everything will be straightened out. What will happen now is that you will be transferred to Auckland, where you'll be questioned. I can't get you out of this one, mate, but you will be all right. You just need to tell the truth. Promise me that."

"Of course, Dad. If I had known what was about to happen, I

would have called you for help," Zac said, looking down at his feet. "I can't believe three men died here tonight." Zac's voice cracked.

"Life is cheap in these circles, son. I'm just glad you are okay," Bill said, hugging him tightly.

"I've already called Mamma. She knows you're safe."

"Granger, bring the suspect over here. We're about to go," one of the detectives called out.

"Let's go, son." Bill led Zac over to the detective, and Bill sensed his son was resolved to go.

"Hey, this is my son. He was caught up in this mess without knowing what he was getting into," Bill said to the officer who took Zac by the arm. "Go easy on him."

"Sure thing, Granger. I'll pass that on."

As the suspects were taken away, one of the medics came over and checked on Bill, his sleeve and hands covered in blood.

"Are you able to walk up to the ambulance yourself?" the medic said.

"Yeah, that should be fine," Bill said, holding his shoulder to put pressure on the wound. He was exhausted, and his legs a little wobbly, not that he would let on.

He saw Rudd and Copeson coming down the hill.

"You do seem to attract trouble, Granger. Are you all right?" Rudd said with a touch of concern, looking at his bloodstained clothing.

"I'll be right, mate. I'm sure it's not too serious."

The walk up the hill took it out of him. The relief he felt about Zac being okay made him feel better, but the exhaustion set in as the adrenaline dissipated—and so did the pain in his arm.

The bullet had gone through his upper arm and just missed the bone, which was lucky, but it still hurt like a bitch. After Niko had done the tourniquet, the medic gave it a good clean and bandaged him up, wanting to transfer him to hospital immediately. Bill refused the offer and promised he'd make his way there later. Much later, he thought.

When he'd rung Annika, he may have omitted that he'd been shot. There was no point in worrying her about that now. All she needed to know was that Zac was safe and taken care of—albeit on his way to the Orewa police station.

Bill hoped they'd let him go when they realised he'd been drawn into this accidentally. He'd already put a call into his boss to let them know what had happened.

What was important now was that Crystal needed a familiar face and a friend to look after her. She'd suffered a terrible loss. The detective had spoken to her and agreed that she could make a statement later. It was for the best. The poor woman was in shock and was not making any sense.

With some pain relief on board, he walked back down to the beach to check on the progress.

What a bloody mess, he thought. Three men had been killed. Zac could have been one of them, but it didn't bear thinking about.

92

A dull ache throbbed in Bill's upper arm. He'd been prodded and poked and given a bag of pain medications to get him through the next week or so. Annika was pale and shaken. It was well after three in the morning when they were home again. Maggie and Finn were delighted to see them.

She'd held it together until now, but Bill could see she'd reached her limit. The dogs felt the tension and leaned against Annika to comfort her.

Zac had been quiet the whole drive back; there was a lot to process. Bill knew that the next little while would be hard on him, and they were all a bit worse for wear.

While Zac sloped off to the shower, Bill sat at the kitchen table with Annika. Maggie and Finn joined them, curling up by their feet.

"We could have lost our son tonight," Annika said as soon as Zac was out of earshot.

He could see she fought to hold back the tears.

"I know. I can't tell you how relieved I am," Bill said, squeezing her hand.

"You could have been killed as well, Bill." Annika's voice broke, and the words became stuck in her throat.

Bill winced as he leaned forward to hug her.

"How's the shoulder?"

"It's not too bad. I'm sure I'll be fine in a couple of days," he said, smiling at her.

"Fancy a cup of tea? I don't know about you, but I could certainly do with one," she said and walked over to the bench.

"That would be great."

He looked at Annika with immense pride; she'd been a rock for everyone involved. She'd cared for Crystal and had organised for Vivianne to come and pick her up. The last thing Crystal needed was to go home to an empty house.

Then, Annika had driven Bill to North Shore Hospital in Auckland to get the wound looked at. Thankfully, they were able to collect Zac from the police station on the way home, as he'd been let go without charges being laid. Bill assumed his boss might have had something to do with it and had straightened things out. No one was more relieved than Annika to have Zac home again.

She put the two cups of tea on the table and pulled the lid off the cake tin, which caused Maggie and Finn to stir. The two dogs stuck their noses in the air for a few seconds, then lay down again and went back to sleep. Since it wasn't cheese or anything savoury, they weren't really interested.

"I made these yesterday," Annika said, offering him the tin.

"Mazarin, my favourite!" Bill said as he reached for the delicate butter pastry topped with a thin layer of icing. These little morsels were the darlings of Swedish cafés, and when you took a bite of the luscious almond filling, you wondered where this cake had been all your life. Bill agreed with that sentiment and savoured the divine flavours.

"Do you think things will ever get back to normal? I can't imagine the carnage Zac had to witness."

"He'll be all right. We just have to encourage him to talk to us and not bottle things up. Seek help if he needs to."

The psychological scars for the young man would take time to heal. Bill knew this from experience, and they would both be there for him, no matter what.

EPILOGUE

Thursday the 13th of July

Niko was already at the office when Bill came through the door, his right arm in a sling. Niko was out of uniform and dressed in his civvies.

"Morning, Sarge. How's the shoulder?"

"It aches and throbs like nothing else, but I'll live. You're early. No gym today, and should you even be here, mate?"

"I'm not really sure what to do with myself. I rang the Independent Police Conduct Authority straight away after the shooting and spent a large part of last night giving my version of events at CIB in Orewa. The IPCA has put me on special leave until further notice, and I have to go back to Orewa this afternoon."

"Once they are involved, they leave no stone untouched, but it's a good thing, and we know everything was done by the book. It was either him or who knows how many casualties.

I know I owe you my life; thank you, mate. I really mean it." Bill was completely sincere.

"No worries, Sarge, you would have done the same for me." Niko seemed uncomfortable with the heart-to-heart and kept looking at his feet.

The normally youthful-looking man had dark circles under his eyes and looked absolutely exhausted.

Niko had delivered the shots that had killed Henry Long. It was obvious he felt the gravity of having taken someone's life.

"I didn't sleep a wink last night. It was weird. I was completely shattered physically, but no matter how much I wanted to sleep, my mind kept replaying the sequence of events."

"I know, mate. It's bloody rough. No one could have predicted any of what went down. Most importantly, you did what was required; there's no doubt about that at all."

Bill knew exactly how he felt. He'd gone through the same thing only a couple of months ago. He still felt the guilt from taking someone else's life and imagined Niko felt the same.

"Come on, let's have a coffee and a chat," Bill said as he went into the lunchroom and boiled the jug. Niko pulled up a chair and sat down. He absentmindedly picked at the marks on the worn table with his fingernails. Niko looked up as Bill handed him a steaming hot mug of coffee.

"You've got to take one day at a time, mate, and it won't help if you beat yourself up. Trust me."

"I'm all right, Sarge. I know it was him or us, and I'll have to live with the consequences until the end of my days," Niko said, bowing his head slightly. Bill was aware of his religious upbringing. As far as he knew, Niko wasn't a regular churchgoer, but still, this was something that wasn't easy to grapple with.

"There was no choice, mate. This is what we are trained to do, to protect the public and ourselves in every respect."

"I know. I just wish it didn't have to come to this. But it still feels a little like suicide by cop."

"I agree and was thinking the same. Henry knew exactly what he was doing and was prepared for all eventualities, including that he might lose his own life in the process." "By the way, how's Zac doing?" Niko said.

"He's doing okay. I'm sure it will take some time, but he's alive. That's all that matters."

"For sure. Did you find out how he became drawn into this whole mess?"

"Apparently, Andrei had sent him to do some extra work. I'm sure if he'd known it was drugs that they were picking up, I think he'd have bailed and called for help."

"By the way, they called from headquarters in Orewa while I was on my way into work," Bill said. "This meth bust is one of the largest that we've seen, and because of this, Andrei and Daria's drug distribution network has been obliterated."

"Well, that's great news, and lots of drugs off the street," Niko said. "I'm sure HQ feels a little sheepish after not responding when we requested the initial backup." Niko reached across the bench for the open packet of biscuits.

"Apparently, Daria spent a lot of time in South America and had links to one of the large cartels. She is what you'd call a real Queen of Meth. Despite her not cooperating yet, the evidence is mounting, and she will be charged. I'm sure the ripples will be felt all the way to Mexico," Bill said. "The other big piece of news is that one of Big Ed's lieutenants sang like a canary when they put a little pressure on him and confessed to the murder of Mike Fenton."

"You don't say?"

"On top of that, it transpires that Mike had his own little ecstasy empire going on the side. We know this because he supplied all that he could get his hands on to the gang for distribution locally and in the Far North, and Andrei was none the wiser."

"You're kidding? Well, that's an interesting spin on loyalty."

"Apparently, Crystal has stated that Mike wasn't always treated that well. Perhaps he'd had enough and wanted something of his own."

"Regardless, having the Molly removed from circulation will make a difference in the area. No more preying on high school kids," Niko said.

"The investigation has just started, but Orewa has gone scorched earth on the whole thing. By the time charges have been laid, there won't be many people standing. Deservedly so," Bill continued. "And interestingly, Henry Long left a letter on the seat of his car." "Oh? What did it say?" Niko said.

"It seems he was on a mission to eradicate the root of the drug problem in the area. In the letter, he confessed to killing Jett Starr, as he was the one who apparently supplied drugs to his daughter, Bella."

"That certainly explains the motive," Niko said.

"Henry had his personal reasons for feeling so strongly against drugs, as his daughter had been a user and had been recruited by the local gang to do their dirty work. Despite family and other support around her, she got deeper into a life of drugs and crime and sadly succumbed to it. It's a good few years since her body was found at the old cement works in Warkworth—another common place for drug deals to go down."

Even though the officers from Warkworth had attended the death. Bill remembered it well. The autopsy had been inconclusive. The body was covered with bruises and needle marks, and Bill felt for Henry. No amount of time would ever heal such wounds.

"We also know that April West died of a drug overdose. I guess we'll never know how it happened, but it might not be a long bow to draw to assume she got them from someone at Jett's party," Niko said as he thought out loud.

"It would be nice to be able to tell her parents exactly what happened, but I don't think we'll never know," Bill said.

"But what I don't get is how Henry had the intel to show up last night, and how did he know that Andrei was involved?" Niko said.

"Apparently, he explained things very well in his letter. It appears our man was quite resourceful. He'd overheard one of the suspects in the pub talking about the regular drug pick-ups. Andrei and Big Ed's names were mentioned. Henry did some digging and put two and two together. There was no way he could get to Big Ed; he knew that. Andrei was a lot easier, and to keep tabs on him, Henry put a small tracker on the developer's car. That's how he found them."

"You don't say?" Niko said. "What is it with these civilians who take the law into their own hands? You would have thought he would want to come to us with the intel."

"Well, I can't say for sure, but if someone hurt my kids this badly, and you felt no one was charged and punished for the crime, I think it would be difficult not to exact revenge on the guilty culprit," Bill continued.

"I thought you said this was a sleepy area," Niko said, laughing.

"There's generally much more than what meets the eye when you see rings on water appear."

ACKNOWLEDGMENTS

To all the wonderful readers who have encouraged me along the way, your support and positive comments mean so very much. I feel very lucky to have so many people cheering me on, and patiently waiting for the next book. Thank you from the bottom of my heart, writing a book is solitary, and this means so much.

I've been truly fortunate to have the best team around me, these wonderful people have helped in so many ways, my sincere gratitude and thanks to the following:

My first readers and of course my loving family, Adrian, Holly and Olivia, thank you for believing in my ability and the story. Your support encourages me to keep going. I couldn't have done this without you. You're my world.

My wonderful editor Kim, working with you have been an absolute dream and your advice and guidance have been more than I could ever wish for. Thank you for wrangling the manuscript into the best it could be. I'm truly very grateful.

Robyn, you've been amazing as always. Your attention on to detail and keen eyes reading over the manuscript multiple times has been invaluable. I'm so very thankful for your help.

Bede, as always thank you for letting me ask loads of questions and for reading through the manuscript early. Your expertise and willingness to share what you know is more helpful than you think, and I appreciate it very much.

Frances, your friendship means so much to me. Thank you for the wonderful support and for encouraging me. You're the best.

Jeroen, my wonderful designer. Thank you from the bottom of my heart, I really don't know how you manage to convert the images in my head to these fantastic covers. Your work is extraordinaire and I'm so very thrilled !

Westie Advice Group (UK)WAG

As Westies are very close to my heart, I'm thrilled to have been able to contribute in a small way to the yearly WAG's fundraiser by auctioning my "Pick a Westie Character" for this book.

The prize entailed naming rights for two Westies and for these to feature in Rings On Water. Huge congratulations and thank you to Sue Makepeace for organising this very worthy fundraiser, and to Jan Benson for choosing the name Bramble and Faye Andrews for choosing the name Duchess. I hope I made you both proud.

Lastly, my constant companions, The Three Musketeers-Harry, Archie and Jemma. These four legged family members have been the best. Sadly while writing this book, we lost both Jemma and Harry within six months of each other last year. They've both left rather huge holes in our hearts, and we continue to remember them fondly, with lots of love.

ABOUT THE AUTHOR

Madeleine Eskedahl was born in Sweden, living in New Zealand for the last thirty years. She's married and have two daughters as well as Archie, the family's West Highland Terrier, and a loves to live close to the beach, in a rural community.

Having been fortunate to grow up in a small village on the island of Gotland in the Baltic sea, this particularly resonates with her, and she very much remains an islander at heart.

As well as writing crime novels, Madeleine is passionate about conservation and enjoys being a "penguin ranger." This job includes regular monitoring of the Korora, The Little Blue Penguin and their nesting sites along the coast where she lives.

Her love of books and reading started from an early age, with especially fond memories of her maternal grandmother, Mormor, taking her to the local library, spending hours reading and getting lost in the fabulous world of make believe. This in turn inspired her creativity from an early age.

Madeleine's first thriller Blood On Vines was released in 2021 and is the first instalment in The Matakana Series. Blood On Vines was a huge success and made the Kete New Zealand Top 10 list, and remained there for eight weeks. This book was also voted onto the prestigious Whitcoulls Top 100 list for the year 2022/2023.

The third book in the Matakana Series, Angels Of Clay is underway.

As well as being a book worm and a polygot, Madeleine loves walking on the beach, spending time with family and friends, pottering in the garden and catching up on the latest Scandinavian crime dramas, while plotting the next book in the series.

Inspiration

"I feel incredibly fortunate to live in an environment so full of factors to draw inspiration from. The proximity to our largest city, the rich tapestry of artisans and creatives, the stunning scenery, the history, and of course everyday life.

Combined, this makes the perfect environment for a crime novel.

The feedback regularly received is that the strong cast of characters are not only very relatable, but the writing grabs the reader's attention and holds it in the manner of a Jane Harper or a Liane Moriarty novel."

ALSO BY MADELEINE ESKEDAHL

BLOOD ON VINES

Four friends, a shared past, a common enemy.

In New Zealand's Martinborough, an ex-wine maker is murdered. The precise planning and execution by the unknown assailant begin a series of vile attacks. Meanwhile north of Auckland, the long, hot summer is over and the tourists have left the Matakana wine country. A tranquil atmosphere descends and warm autumnal winds sweep across the grape-laden valleys. With the harvest due, grapes sit bursting upon the manicured vines awaiting the pick. Within this vista of peace, a rampage of death is about to rock the local community to its core. **Will it be their shared history that sees the four friends being picked off one-by- one?**

THE MATAKANA SERIES

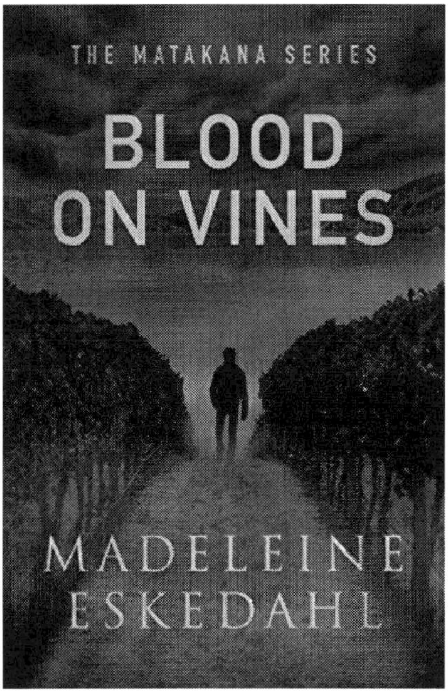

BLOOD ON VINES, the first book in THE MATAKANA SERES

BOOK CLUB QUESTIONS

1. What was your favourite part of Rings On Water?

2.Which scene stuck with you the most?

4.What surprised you the most about Rings On water ?

5.Are there lingering questions from the book that you're still thinking about ?

6. Who's your favourite character and why?

7.If you could ask Madeleine a question, what would it be?

Printed in Great Britain
by Amazon

32896826R00216